ACCLAIM FOR THE BOURNE THRILLERS

ROBERT LUDLUM'S™
THE BOURNE OBJECTIVE

"Thriller addicts who love an adrenaline rush of action and global adventure will snap this one up."

—*Library Journal*

"Fast-paced and exciting...and you cannot look away for a split second for fear of missing something important...It is reassuring to know that, in the able hands of Eric Van Lustbader, Jason Bourne is alive and well and continuing to search for the truth to his own existence and overall purpose. Here's hoping that Lustbader keeps this classic character going for more episodes of international intrigue and adventure."

—BookReporter.com

"The rogue spy is one of the best characters in the genre."

—US Metro Newspapers

"This novel rocks—it's filled with action, adventure, and has plenty of plot twists and turns...an entertaining, thrilling roller-coaster ride you won't want to end... a heart-pounding, adrenaline-inducing, action-packed novel that fans of the Jason Bourne franchise should eagerly embrace. It's a great novel, really, whether you are a longtime fan, or are relatively new to the series...an excellent novel."

—BestsellersWorld.com

ROBERT LUDLUM'S™
THE BOURNE DECEPTION

"Powerful and poignant development of characters old and new, as well as a hard-hitting plot, reinvent the series and ensure its place in contemporary political fiction...Once again, Van Lustbader has written a gripping novel that the reader can easily imagine being developed into another blockbuster film."

—*Fredericksburg Free Lance-Star*

"I plowed through [this book], my heart racing at every turn of the page."

—*Wichita Falls Times Record News* (TX)

"Fast-paced, intense action...a compelling read. The number of characters and their interconnections create a fascinating puzzle."

—*RT BookReviews Magazine*

ROBERT LUDLUM'S™
THE BOURNE SANCTION

"Twisted, dark, and exciting."

—*Oklahoman*

"A thrill-a-minute work...This is one novel that will keep you reading long into the night."

—BookReporter.com

"Another jet-speed, action-packed episode...jam-packed with explosive action, shocking violence, and breathtaking betrayals...Suspense builds to a crescendo of a conclusion."

—BookLoons.com

ROBERT LUDLUM'S™
THE BOURNE BETRAYAL

"Breathless writing that makes the pages fly."
—*Kirkus Reviews*

"A fun thriller."
—*Chicago Tribune*

"A cleverly plotted, incisive thriller with a hero I'm glad is on the good guys' side. In an amazing work of fiction, Lustbader takes us into the minds of terrorists."
—NightsandWeekends.com

"Lustbader is an excellent storyteller and is not afraid to keep the twists and turns coming in this sequel...This is an explosive addition to a series with an unrivaled heritage and storied pedigree."
—BookReporter.com

ROBERT LUDLUM'S

THE

BOURNE
OBJECTIVE

A NEW JASON BOURNE NOVEL BY
ERIC VAN LUSTBADER

VISION

NEW YORK   BOSTON

This book is a work of fiction. Names, characters, places, and incidents are the product of the author's imagination or are used fictitiously. Any resemblance to actual events, locales, or persons, living or dead, is coincidental.

Copyright © 2010 by Myn Pyn, LLC
Excerpt from *The Bourne Dominion* copyright © 2010 by Myn Pyn, LLC

Vision
Hachette Book Group
237 Park Avenue
New York, NY 10017
Visit our website at www.HachetteBookGroup.com

Vision is an imprint of Grand Central Publishing.
The Vision name and logo is a trademark of Hachette Book Group, Inc.

The publisher is not responsible for websites (or their content) that are not owned by the publisher.

Printed in the United States of America

Originally published in hardcover by Hachette Book Group, Inc.
First international mass market edition, December 2010
First United States oversize mass market edition, May 2011

10 9 8 7 6 5 4 3 2 1

For Jaime Levine,
whose editorial expertise and
unbounded enthusiasm
make this so much more fun

Prologue

NIGHT DESCENDED LIKE a curtain of scuttling insects, coming alive with the setting of the sun. The noise was atrocious, as was the stench of unwashed bodies, human excrement, rotting food, and decomposing bodies. The garbage of Bangalore shifted back and forth like a sludgy tide.

Leonid Danilovich Arkadin sat in a darkened room that smelled of hot electronics, stale smoke, and cooling dosas. Firing up a cigarette with his chrome lighter, he stared down at the ribbed skeleton of Phase Three, part of the ever-expanding Electronic City rising out of the slums clinging to Bangalore like a disease. Electronic City, built in the 1990s, was now the world capital of technology outsourcing; virtually every major high-tech company had IT offices here, making it the hub of the technical support industry spawned by technologies that morphed every six months.

Gold from concrete, Arkadin thought, dazzled. He'd read up on the history of alchemy, because of its transformative nature it had become a special interest of his. At this early hour of the evening—early, that is, for the outsourcing crowd whose offices by and large filled the buildings to capacity—the lobby and corridors were as quiet and still as they would be if they were in New York City at 3 AM. The outsourcing crowd was geared to the workday in the United States, which made them as virtual as ghosts when they were at their consoles, cordless earphones wrapped around their heads.

After the fiasco in Iran, when he had royally screwed Maslov, he had set up operations here, away from those he wished eventually to hunt, who were already hunting him: Dimitri Ilyinovich Maslov and Jason Bourne.

From his suite of offices he had a perfect view of the block-square work site, a pit excavated out of the earth where the footings for the foundations of another office tower were being laid. Usually the site was lit by glaring floodlights, so the crews could work through the night, but work had stopped unexpectedly two weeks ago and hadn't yet resumed. As a result the excavation had been invaded by the city's ragtag army of beggars, whores, and gangs of young kids trying to fleece everyone who passed by.

Now and again, as he let the smoke drift from his nostrils, he could hear the stealthy cat-like padding of his men strategically placed throughout the suite, but he was alone in this room with Hassan, a large, square software magician who smelled faintly of circuits and cumin. Arkadin had brought his men with him, loyal Muslims all, which presented a problem only insofar as the native Hindus hated Muslims. He'd looked into using a detail of Sikh mercenaries, but he couldn't find it in himself to trust them.

Hassan had proven invaluable. He had been the computer programmer for Nikolai Yevsen, the late and unlamented arms dealer whose business Arkadin had appropriated out from under Maslov. Hassan had made a copy of all the customer, supplier, and contact data on Yevsen's mainframe before wiping it clean. Now Arkadin was working Yevsen's list, raking in unimaginable mountains of money by supplying war matériel for virtually every local warlord, despot, and terrorist organization around the globe.

Hassan sat hunched over his computer, using encrypted software slaved to the remote servers Arkadin had set up in a secure location. He was a man who lived to work. In the weeks since Hassan's defection and Yevsen's death in Khartoum, Arkadin had never once seen him leave these offices. He slept after eating a light lunch, from one to three thirty precisely, then it was back to the computer.

Arkadin's attention was only partially on Hassan. On a sideboard nearby lay a laptop, with hot-swappable drive bays, into which he'd slid the hard drive from the laptop one of his men had stolen from Gustavo Moreno just before the Colombian drug lord was shot to death in his Mexico City compound. Turning to it, Arkadin felt his face bathed in the eerie blue electronic glow, hard as marble, hard as his father's callused fist.

Stubbing out his cigarette, he scrolled through the files, which he'd already pored through again and again; he had a number of computer hacks on his payroll, but he hadn't allowed any of them—even Hassan—to comb through this particular hard drive. He went back to the ghost file that had reluctantly shown its enigmatic face only under the duress of a powerful anti-virus program. He could see it now, but it was still locked away, encrypted with a logarithm his cryptographic software still hadn't been able to crack despite running for more than twenty-four hours.

Moreno's laptop, which was hidden in a safe place, was as mysterious as this ghost file. It had a slot in the side that lacked the receptor for a USB plug-in and was too big to accommodate an SD card, too small to be a fingerprint reader. Clearly, it was a custom retrofit, but for what?

What the hell was in that file, anyway? he wondered. And where would a drug lord get an unbreakable logarithm like this one—not at your local hacker's mart in Cali or Mexico City, that was for sure.

Lost in thought as he was, Arkadin's head nevertheless came up as if he scented the sound, rather than heard it. His ears practically twitched like a hunting dog's, and then, moving back into the shadows, he said, "Hassan, what's that light moving down in the construction site?"

Hassan glanced up. "Which one, sir? There are so many fires . . ."

"There." Arkadin pointed. "No, farther down, stand up and you'll see it clearly."

The moment Hassan rose, leaning forward, a spray of semi-automatic fire demolished the office windows, spraying Hassan, the desk, and the surrounding carpet with an ice storm of glass crystals. Hassan, slammed backward, lay on the carpet, gasping and drooling blood.

Arkadin ejected the hard drive just before a second hail of bullets flew through the shattered windows, gouging the wall opposite. Taking shelter within the desk's leg hole, he took up a Skorpion vz. 61 submachine gun and shot to ribbons the computer Hassan was working on. By this time staccato semi-automatic gunfire had begun to erupt from within the office suite itself. The overlapping noises resounded, peppered with shouted commands and the screams of the dying. No help from his men, that much was clear enough. But he did recognize the language in which the laconic orders were being delivered: Russian. And more specific than that, Moscow Russian.

Arkadin thought Hassan was speaking or at least making sounds, but whatever he was saying was lost within the explosions of gunfire. Since the attackers were Russian, Arkadin had no doubt they were after Yevsen's priceless information. He was now trapped inside a pincer assault both from within the suite and from the grounds outside the blown-out windows. He had only moments in which to act. Rising, he scuttled over to where Hassan lay, his hot, bloodshot eyes staring up at him.

"Help...help me." Hassan's voice was thick with blood and terror.

"Of course, my friend," Arkadin said kindly, "of course."

With luck, his enemies would have mistaken Hassan for him, which would buy him the precious time to escape. But not if Hassan began to scream. Jamming the hard drive deep into his pocket, he pressed his shoe onto Hassan's throat until Hassan arched back and his eyes nearly bugged out of his head. But with his windpipe crushed, he could make no sound. Behind him, Arkadin heard a confused swirl of sounds on the other side of the door. His men would defend him to the death, he knew, but in this case they seemed to have been caught off guard and might even be outnumbered. He had only seconds to act.

As in all modern office buildings, the large windows were sealed shut, possibly as a safeguard against suicide attempts, which now and then occurred in any event. Arkadin cranked open a side window and slipped out into the unquiet night. Six floors below him was the excavation pit from which the cavernous new building would rise. Enormous earthmoving machines reared up amid the makeshift cardboard hovels and cook fires like long-necked dragons slumbering in the semi-darkness.

The sleek, post-modern building had no horizontal sills outside the window, but between the windows were lengths of decorative outcroppings of concrete and steel running vertically. Arkadin swung onto one just as a fistful of bullets pinged through the door to his office—his men had lost their valiant battle with the intruders.

The smells of the Bangalore night, of ghee, frying dosas, betel juice, and human waste, rose up from the excavation pit six floors below like a noxious mist as he began to shinny down the concrete-and-steel column. At that moment he became aware of crisscrossing beams of light below him: Having determined that they hadn't shot him to death up in his office, they were beginning the search for him in earnest on the ground. Acutely conscious of how exposed and vulnerable he was clinging like a spider to the side of the building, he stopped at the fourth-floor level. The panes were smaller and more evenly spaced here because this floor was given over to the air-conditioning system, the water and electrical systems, and the like. He kicked at the windowpane on the floor below using the toe of his boot, but to no avail, the glass was impervious to the blows. Lowering himself farther, he swung his foot into a metal plate below the window. It dented, a corner twisted up but would not come off, so he scuttled down until, in this precarious position, he was able to insert his fingers into the space between the metal and the wall. Applying pressure, he levered the plate off. Now he was confronted with an oblong hole that appeared to be just large enough for his body. Grabbing onto the pillar with both hands, he swung his feet into the gap, pushed, inserting his legs, then his buttocks. Only then did he let go of the pillar.

For a moment his head and torso dangled in space, long enough for him to see, even upside down, the searchlights rising toward him, creeping up the facade of the building. An instant later he was dazzled, caught in their light. He heard raised voices, guttural shouts in Russian before he gathered himself and pushed himself fully into the gap. Followed closely by the explosive sounds of gunfire, he tunneled into utter darkness.

He lay still, regaining his breath and equilibrium. Then, using his feet and knees, he urged himself through the space, wriggling first one shoulder, then the other. This method served him well for three or four feet, until he came up against what seemed to be a barrier. Craning his neck, he could just make out a faint patch of gray floating somewhere in the blackness ahead of him, which meant he hadn't come up against a barrier at all—the space had narrowed unexpectedly. He pushed with his legs, but this only seemed to wedge his shoulders in more securely, so he stopped and did nothing at all, willing his body to relax while his mind ran through strategies to extricate himself.

He began a series of deep-breathing exercises, slowing with each exhale. He willed himself to think of his body as boneless, as infinitely malleable, until his mind was utterly convinced. Then he contracted his shoulders, bringing them in toward his chest as he'd once seen a contortionist do in the Moscow circus. Slowly, ever so gently, he pushed with the outer edges of his boot soles. At first nothing happened; then, contracting farther, he began to inch forward, coming through the narrow section and out the other side. Soon enough after that the top of his head butted against the inner grille. Drawing his legs up as far as the confined space allowed, he imagined them going through the grille. Then all at once he slammed his legs straight, battering the grille with such force it popped off, and he tumbled into what appeared to be a closet, stinking of hot metal and grease.

Closer inspection revealed that the cubicle was an electrical switch station for the elevator. Coming out the other side, he found himself in the elevator shaft. He could hear the shouts of the Russian assassins. The elevator car was moving downward toward the fourth floor; the men outside must have informed those inside of where he had reentered the building.

He looked around and saw a vertical ladder bolted to the wall directly across from where he stood. But before he could make a move the hatch on the roof of the elevator car swung up and one of the Russians poked his head and torso out. Seeing Arkadin, he brought up a submachine gun.

Arkadin ducked as a burst of gunfire sparked off the

wall at the spot his head had just been. In a crouch, he aimed from the hip and sent a hail of bullets into the Russian's face. The top of the car was almost level with him, and he vaulted upward, landing on it. The moment his boot touched the roof, a burst of bullets exploded upward through the open hatch almost knocking him off his feet, but he kept going. Taking another long stride to the far edge of the roof, he leapt across the gap to the vertical ladder, down which he immediately scrambled. Behind him, the elevator car began to descend. When it was a good six feet below him it stopped.

He braced himself, swung his upper torso around, and the moment he saw movement out of the open hatch, sent three quick bursts pinging against the roof. Then he continued down the ladder, dropping two and three rungs at a time in order to make himself a more difficult target to track.

Answering fire started up, sparking against the metal rungs as he spidered his way down. Then abruptly the firing stopped, and risking a glance upward, he saw at once that one of the surviving Russians had crawled out of the open hatch and swung down onto the vertical ladder, coming after him.

Arkadin paused long enough to raise his weapon, but before he could fire the Russian let go of his hold and, plummeting down, grabbed onto him, almost ripping his arms out of their sockets. He swung wildly with the added weight and the momentum from the falling body, and in that moment the Russian swatted the weapon out of his hand. It went banging down the shaft, clanging and caroming this way and that. At the same time, the elevator resumed its descent.

The Russian had one hand pressed against Arkadin's throat, while the other ripped a K-Bar knife out of its sheath. The Russian pushed Arkadin's chin up, exposing his throat. The thick, wicked blade arced through the air and Arkadin drove one knee upward. The Russian's body bent like a bow, intersecting with the bottom of the elevator as it came down.

Even braced as he was, Arkadin was almost dragged into the side of the elevator as the Russian's body was ripped from him. For a moment he dangled upside down, and only his ankles hooked through a rung of the ladder saved him. He let himself swing while he oriented himself, then he reached out, his powerful hands gripping the ladder as he unhooked his ankles and swung down until he was right-side up again. The strain on his shoulders was enormous, but this time he was prepared and did not falter. His feet found a rung below him and he resumed his downward climb.

Below him the elevator continued its descent to the ground floor, but no one poked their head out of the open hatch. Landing on the roof, he peered cautiously inside. He counted two bodies; neither one was left alive. He dropped down, stripped one of the corpses of its weapon, then hit the BASEMENT button.

The basement of the tower was a vast, fluorescent-lighted parking garage. It was not, however, well used, since most people who worked in the building couldn't afford cars. Instead they called taxi services to take them to and from work.

Apart from his own BMW, two gleaming Mercedeses,

a Toyota Qualis, and a Honda City, the garage was bereft of vehicles. Arkadin checked them; all were empty. Avoiding his car, he broke into the Toyota and after several moments of fiddling with the electronics managed to defeat the starter cutoff switch. Settling himself behind the wheel, he put the car in gear, drove across the bare concrete and onto the up-ramp to the street.

With a spray of sparks from the undercarriage Arkadin bounced out at the rear of the building onto the roughly paved street. Directly ahead of him lay the construction pit. So many fires flared among the rubble and the gigantic machines, the entire site seemed in danger of bursting into flame.

To either side of him he heard the throaty roar of powerful motorcycle engines as two Russians rode their mechanical beasts toward him in a pincer movement. It seemed clear that they had been waiting for him at either end of the street so that no matter which way he turned, left or right, they could head him off. Pressing the accelerator to the floor, he drove straight ahead, crossing the street, and crashed through the flimsy fence that encircled the building site.

Immediately the Toyota's nose dipped down as the car descended almost precipitously into the pit. The shocks took most of the force of its landing, but Arkadin still bounced in his seat as the car hit bottom and, tires squealing, leveled out. Behind him the two motorcycles lifted into the air as they followed him into the pit—landing, bouncing—and took off after him.

He headed directly toward one of the fires, scattering vagrants as he went. Passing through the flames, he veered hard to his left, threading the proverbial needle between two huge machines and—just managing to avoid one of the slicks of greasy garbage—turned hard right toward another fire and another group of lost souls.

Glancing in his side mirror, he saw one of the motorcycles still on his tail. Had he lost the other one? Approaching the flames, he waited until the last minute, when the glare was at its height, then jammed on the brakes. As people ran in every direction, the motorcycle, with its driver half blinded, plowed into the rear of the Toyota, launching the Russian off the seat. Tumbling head-over-heels, he smashed into the top of the Toyota, bounced, and slid off.

Arkadin was already out of the car. He heard the rider groaning, trying to get up off the dirt, and kicked him hard in the side of the head. He was on his way back to the car when the shots struck the fender near him. He ducked; the assault rifle he'd pulled off the dead man in the elevator lay on the passenger's seat out of reach. He tried to crab-walk to the driver's door, but each time he was driven back by shots that plunged into the Toyota's side.

He lay down, scrambled underneath the car as the syrupy, pungent air struck him another hammer blow. Emerging on the opposite side, he hauled open the rear door of the Toyota, and almost got his head shot off. He dived back under the car to regroup and within seconds realized that he had been given no choice but to abandon the car. Understanding that this was what his adversary wanted, he determined how to neutralize, or at the very least minimize, the mounted Russian's advantage.

For a moment he closed his eyes, picturing where the

Russian cyclist must be by the direction from which the bullets came. Then, turning ninety degrees, he pulled himself out from under the Toyota by hooking his fingers around the front bumper.

Bullets caused the windshield to shatter, but due to the safety glass it held together in a spiderweb so complex that it turned the windshield opaque, cutting off his pursuer's view of his escape. Down low was the dense, stinking mass of the homeless, downtrodden, disaffected. He saw their faces as he ran, zigzagging madly through the morass of skeletal humanity, pale as ash. Then he heard the guttural cough of the motorcycle engine through the chatter of Hindi and Urdu. These goddamn people were moving like a sea, parting as he scrambled through their midst, and it was this movement that the Russian was following like the ping on a sonar screen.

In the near distance he could make out a support structure of metal beams attached to the deep-set concrete footings, and he ran toward them. With a throaty roar, the motorcycle broke free of the surf of people, zooming after him, but by that time he had vanished into the jungle gym structure.

The Russian slowed as he approached the beams. To his left was a temporary fence of corrugated iron, already rusting in the gluey Indian air, so he turned to the right and began a tour around the side of the metal beams. He peered down into the darkness of the abyss into which the massive footings had been set like molars. His AK-47 was at the ready.

He was halfway along when Arkadin, lying along an upper beam like a leopard, leapt onto him. As the Russian's body twisted backward, his hand reflexively squeezed the throttle, and the motorcycle surged forward, its balance off as the momentum of Arkadin's leap tipped its front end up. The chassis accelerated as it spun out from under them, and they were both thrown against the metal beams. The Russian's head struck the middle of a beam, and the AK-47 flew out of his hand. Arkadin tried to lunge at him but discovered that a shard of metal had penetrated the flesh at the back of his thigh all the way to the bone. He was impaled. With a violent wrench that momentarily took his breath away, he pulled the shard out of his leg. The Russian rushed him while he was still seeing sparks in front of his eyes and his breath felt like steam in his lungs. He was pounded by a flurry of blows to the side of the head, his ribs, his sternum before he swung the metal shard around, driving it into the Russian's heart.

The Russian's mouth opened in surprise, his eyes looked at Arkadin with incomprehension, just before they rolled up in his head and he sank to the blood-soaked ground. Arkadin turned and walked toward the ramp to the street, but he felt as if he had been injected with a paralytic. His legs were stiff, barely responding to commands from a brain that seemed increasingly encased in sludge. He felt cold and unfocused. He tried to catch his breath, couldn't, and fell over.

All around him, it seemed, fires burned, the city was on fire, the night sky was the color of blood, pulsing to the beat of his laboring heart. He saw the eyes of those he'd killed, red as the eyes of rats, crowding in on him. *I don't want to share the darkness with you,* he thought as he felt himself about to plunge into unconsciousness.

* * *

And perhaps it was this thought alone that caused him to pause, to take deep breaths, and then, in that moment of repose or weakness, to improbably accept water from those crowding around him, who, he saw now, weren't the familiar dead, but the unfamiliar living. Filthy, ragged, and without hope they might be, but they recognized an underdog when they saw one, and this brought out their innate altruism. Instead of picking him clean like a flock of vultures, they had taken him into their hearts. Isn't it the downtrodden, the ones who can least afford to give up anything, who are more willing to share what they have than the millionaires inhabiting the gated towers on the other side of the city? This was Arkadin's thought as he took their gift of water, in return giving them a wad of rupees from his pocket. Not long after, he felt strong enough to call the local hospital. Then he ripped off an arm of his shirt and wrapped it around his leg to stanch the bleeding in his thigh. There was a pack of boys, runaways or children whose parents had been killed in one of the many sectarian skirmishes that from time to time swept through the neighborhoods, a whirlwind of hate and blood. They watched him as if he were the hero of a video game, as if he were not quite real. They were afraid of him, but they were also drawn like moths to a flame. He motioned to them and they surged forward as if each one were a leg of some giant insect. They had the Russian's motorcycle in their midst, and he saw that they had it surrounded, that they were protecting it.

"I won't take the bike away from you, it's yours," he said in Hindi. "Help me out to the street."

By then the sound of a siren had become a wail, and with the lost boys supporting him he limped out of the pit into the arms of the medical team, who bundled him into the back of the ambulance, where they laid him down, one of them taking his pulse, checking his heart, while the other began to assess the wound.

Ten minutes later he was being wheeled into the emergency room on a collapsible gurney, then transferred facedown to one of the ER's beds. The arctic air woke him as if from a high fever. He watched the comings and goings in the ER as he was given an injection of local anesthetic, then a surgeon washed his hands in the disinfectant gel from a dispenser affixed to a column, snapped on gloves, and began the process of cleaning, disinfecting, and suturing the wound.

The procedure allowed Arkadin time to reflect on the raid. He knew that it was Dimitri Ilyinovich Maslov who had ordered the assault. Maslov was the head of the Kazanskaya, the Moscow mafia, known colloquially as the *grupperovka*. Maslov was his onetime employer, from whom Arkadin had taken the illegal arms business. This business was critical to Maslov because the Kremlin was coming down hard on the *grupperovka*, slowly yet inexorably stripping the families of the power base they had built up since glasnost. But over the years Dimitri Maslov had proved himself different from the heads of the other *grupperovka*, who were all either losing power or already in prison. Maslov prospered, even in these difficult times, because he still had the political muscle to defy the authorities or at least keep them at bay. He was a dangerous man and an even more dangerous enemy.

Yes, Arkadin thought now, as the surgeon cut the suture cords, *Maslov surely ordered the raid, but he didn't plan it.* Maslov had his hands full with political enemies closing in on all sides; besides, it was a long time since he'd been on the streets and he'd lost that keen edge only the streets can provide. Who, Arkadin asked himself, had he given this job to?

At that moment, as if by divine intervention, he received his answer because, there, standing in the shadows of the ER, unseen or ignored by the hurrying staff and groaning patients, was Vylacheslav Germanovich Oserov, Maslov's new underboss. He and Oserov had a long, vengeful history reaching back to Arkadin's home city of Nizhny Tagil; nothing but hatred and venom lay between them. Still vivid in his memory was their most recent encounter—a nasty incident in the highlands of northern Azerbaijan where he was training a raiding party for Maslov while scheming to double-cross him. He'd called Oserov out, almost beaten him to a pulp—the latest in a long line of violent responses to the atrocities Oserov had perpetrated many years ago in Arkadin's hometown. Of course Oserov was the perfect man to plan the raid, which, he was certain, included his own death whether or not Maslov had ordered it.

Oserov, who stood in the shadows, arms crossed over his chest, appeared to be looking at nothing, but in fact he was observing Arkadin with the single-minded concentration of a hawk tracking its prey. The face was pocked and scarred, the knotty evidence of murders, street brawls, and near-death encounters, and the corners of his wide, thin-lipped mouth turned up in the familiar hateful smile that seemed both condescending and obscene.

Arkadin was shackled by his trousers. They were rucked around his ankles because it had been too awkward to get them off him completely. He felt no pain in his thigh, of course, but he didn't know how the shot he'd received would affect his ability to sprint or run.

"That's it," he heard the surgeon say. "Keep the wound well dry for at least a week. I'm prescribing an antibiotic and a painkiller. You can pick them up from the pharmacy on your way out. You're lucky, the wound was clean-edged and you got here before any infection could set in." Then the surgeon laughed. "No marathons for a while, though."

A nurse applied a surgical pad, which she set in place with surgical tape.

"You shouldn't feel a thing for another hour or so," she said. "Be sure to start both your prescriptions before then."

Oserov unwound his arms and came off the wall. He was still not looking directly at Arkadin, but his right hand was in the pocket of his trousers. Arkadin had no idea what sort of weapon he carried, but he wasn't about to wait around to find out.

He asked the nurse to help him on with his trousers. When he'd buckled his belt and sat up, she turned to leave. A certain tension came into Oserov's body. As Arkadin slid off the bed onto his feet he whispered in the nurse's ear, "I'm an undercover cop. That man over there has been sent by criminals to kill me." When the nurse's eyes opened wide, he added, "Just do what I tell you and everything will be fine."

Keeping her between him and Oserov, Arkadin moved to his right. Oserov matched him step for step.

"You're heading away from the exit," the nurse whispered to him.

Arkadin kept going, nearing the column where the surgeon had disinfected his hands from the dispenser. He could tell the nurse was becoming more and more agitated.

"Please," she whispered, "let me call security."

They were standing beside the column. "All right," he said and pushed her so hard she stumbled into a crash cart, sending another nurse and a doctor tumbling. In the confusion he saw a security guard appear from the hallway and Oserov coming toward him, a wicked-looking stiletto in his hand.

Arkadin grabbed the disinfectant dispenser and ripped it free of its brackets. He swung it hard, slamming it into the head of the security guard, who skidded on the linoleum floor as he went down. Tucking the dispenser under one arm, Arkadin vaulted over the guard's prone body and took off for the hallway.

Oserov was right behind him, gaining with every step. Arkadin realized that he had unconsciously slowed his pace, worried that he would rip out the stitches. Disgusted with himself, he shouldered past a pair of startled interns and put on a burst of speed. The hallway in front of him was clear, he dug in his pocket for his lighter, flicked on the flame. Then he pumped disinfectant out of the dispenser's nozzle. He could hear the pounding of Oserov's shoes, almost imagine the quickening of his breath.

All at once he turned and, in one motion, lit the highly flammable sanitizer, thrust out the dispenser, and threw it at his oncoming pursuer. He turned and ran, but the explosion caught him anyway, hurling him halfway down the corridor.

A fire alarm sounded, blasting through the cacophony of shouts, screams, running feet, flailing bodies, and flickering flames. He took off, but slowed to a walk as he rounded a corner. Two security guards and a pack of older doctors pushed by him, nearly knocking him off his feet. Blood started to trickle down his leg, hot and vital. Everything he saw was crystal clear, hard-edged, iridescent, pulsing with life. He held the door open for a woman in a wheelchair who held her baby in her arms. She thanked him and he laughed with such intensity that she laughed, too. At that moment a squad of grim-faced police came off the street through the door he was holding open, rushing right by him.

Book One

Book One

1

Y ES," SUPARWITA SAID, "that is the ring Holly Marie Moreau's father gave her."

"This ring." Jason Bourne held up the object in question, a simple gold band with engraving around the inside. "I have no memory of it."

"You have no memory of many things in your past," Suparwita said, "including Holly Marie Moreau."

Bourne and Suparwita were sitting cross-legged on the floor of the Balinese shaman's house deep in the jungle of Karangasem, in southeast Bali. Bourne had returned to the island to trap Noah Perlis, the spy who had murdered Holly years ago. He had pried the ring out of Perlis's grasp after he had killed him not five miles from this spot.

"Holly Marie's mother and father arrived here from Morocco when she was five," Suparwita said. "They had the look of refugees."

"What were they fleeing from?"

"Difficult to say for certain. If the stories about them are true, they chose an excellent place to hide from religious persecution." Suparwita was known formally as a *Mangku,* both a high priest and a shaman, but also something more, impossible to express in Western terms. "They wanted protection."

"Protection?" Bourne frowned. "From what?"

Suparwita was a handsome man of indeterminate age. His skin was a deep nut brown, his smile wide and devastating, revealing two rows of white, even teeth. He was large for a Balinese, and exuded a kind of otherworldly power that fascinated Bourne. His house, an inner sanctum surrounded by a lush, sun-dappled garden and high stucco walls, lay in deepest shadow so that the interior was cool even at noontime. The floor was packed dirt covered by a sisal rug. Here and there odd items of indeterminate nature—pots of herbs, clusters of roots, bouquets of dried flowers pressed into the shape of a fan—sprouted from floor or walls as if alive. The shadows, which filled the corners to overflowing, seemed constantly in motion as if formed from liquid rather than air.

"From Holly's uncle," Suparwita said. "It was from him they took the ring in the first place."

"He knew they stole it?"

"He thought it was lost." Suparwita cocked his head. "There are men outside."

Bourne nodded. "We'll deal with them in a minute."

"Aren't you concerned they'll burst in here, guns drawn?"

"They won't show themselves until I've left here; they

want me, not you." Bourne touched the ring with his forefinger. "Go on."

Suparwita inclined his head. "They were hiding from Holly's uncle. He had vowed to bring her back to the family compound in the High Atlas Mountains."

"They're Berbers. Of course, *Moreau* means 'Moor,'" Bourne mused. "Why did Holly's uncle want to bring her back to Morocco?"

Suparwita looked at Bourne for a long time. "I imagine you knew, once."

"Noah Perlis had the ring last, so he must have murdered Holly to get it." Bourne took the ring in his hand. "Why did he want it? What's so important about a wedding ring?"

"That," Suparwita said, "is a part of the story you were trying to discover."

"That was some time ago. Now I wouldn't know where to start."

"Perlis had flats in many cities," Suparwita said, "but he was based in London, which was where Holly went when she traveled abroad during the eighteen months before she returned to Bali. Perlis must have followed her back here to kill her and obtain the ring for himself."

"How do you know all this?" Bourne asked.

Suparwita's face broke into one of his thousand-watt smiles. All at once he looked like the genie conjured up by Aladdin. "I know," he said, "because you told me."

Soraya Moore noticed the differences between the old Central Intelligence under the late Veronica Hart and the new CI under M. Errol Danziger the moment she walked into CI headquarters in Washington, DC. For one thing, security had been beefed up to the point that getting through the various checkpoints felt like infiltrating a medieval fortress. For another, she didn't recognize a single member of the security personnel on duty. Every face had that hard, beady look only the US military can instill in a human being. She wasn't surprised by this. After all, before being appointed as DCI by the president, M. Errol Danziger had been the NSA's deputy director of Signals Intelligence, with a long and distinguished career in the armed forces and then in the DoD. He also had a long and distinguished career as a brass-balled sonovabitch. No, what startled her was simply the speed with which the new DCI had installed his own people inside CI's formerly sacrosanct walls.

From the time that it had been the Office of Strategic Services during World War II, the agency had been its own domain, entirely free of interference from either the Pentagon or its intelligence arm, the NSA. Now, because of the growing power of Secretary of Defense Bud Halliday, CI was being merged with NSA, its unique DNA being diluted. M. Errol Danziger was now its director, and Danziger was Secretary Halliday's creature.

Soraya, the director of Typhon, a Muslim-staffed anti-terrorist agency operating under the aegis of CI, considered the changes Danziger had instigated during the several weeks she had been away in Cairo. She felt lucky that Typhon was semi-independent. She reported directly to the DCI, bypassing the various directorate heads. She was half Arab and she knew all her people, had in most instances handpicked them. They would follow her through the gates of hell, if she asked it of them. But what about her friends and colleagues inside CI itself? Would they stay or would they go?

She got off at the DCI's floor, drenched in the eerie green light filtered through bullet- and bombproof glass, and came up against a young man, reed-thin, steely-eyed, with a high-and-tight marine haircut. He was sitting behind a desk, riffling through a stack of papers. The nameplate on his desk read: LT. R. SIMMONS READE.

"Good afternoon, I'm Soraya Moore," she said. "I have an appointment with the DCI."

Lt. R. Simmons Reade glanced up and gave her a neutral look that nevertheless seemed to hold the hint of a sneer. He wore a blue suit, a starched white shirt, and a red-and-blue regimental striped tie. Without glancing at his computer terminal he said, "You *had* an appointment with Director Danziger. That was fifteen days ago."

"Yes, I know," she said. "I was in the field, cleaning up the loose ends of the mission in northern Iran that had to be—"

The light's greenish tint made Reade's face seem longer, sharper, dangerous, almost like a weapon. "You disobeyed a direct order from Director Danziger."

"The new DCI had just been installed," she said. "He had no way of knowing—"

"And yet Director Danziger knows all he needs to know about you, Ms. Moore."

Soraya bristled. "What the hell does that mean? And it's *Director* Moore."

"Not surprisingly, you're out of date, Ms. Moore," Reade said blandly. "You've been terminated."

"What? You've got to be joking. I can't—" Soraya felt as if she were being sucked down a sinkhole that had just appeared beneath her feet. "I demand to see the DCI!"

Reade's face got even harder, like a pitchman for the "Be All You Can Be" slogan. "As of this moment, your clearance has been revoked. Please surrender your ID, company credit cards, and cell phone."

Soraya leaned forward, her fists on the sleek desktop. "Who the hell are you to tell me anything?"

"I'm the voice of Director Danziger."

"I don't believe a word you say."

"Your cards won't work. There's nowhere to go but out."

She stood back up. "Tell the DCI I'll be in my office when he decides he has time to debrief me."

R. Simmons Reade reached down beside his desk and lifted a small, topless cardboard box, which he slid across to her. Soraya looked down and almost choked on her tongue. There, neatly stacked, was every personal item she'd had in her office.

I can only repeat what you yourself told me." Suparwita stood up and, with him, Bourne.

"So even then I was concerned with Noah Perlis." It wasn't a question and the Balinese shaman didn't treat it as such. "But why? And what was his connection to Holly Marie Moreau?"

"Whatever the truth of it," Suparwita said, "it seems likely they met in London."

"And what of the odd lettering that runs around the inside of the ring?"

"You showed it to me once, hoping I could help. I have no idea what it means."

"It isn't any modern language," Bourne said, still racking his damaged memory for details.

Suparwita took a step toward him and lowered his voice until it was just above a whisper. Nevertheless, it penetrated into Bourne's mind like the sting of a wasp.

"As I said, you were born in December, Siwa's month." He pronounced the god Shiva's name as all Balinese did. "Further, you were born on Siwa's day: the last day of the month, which is both the ending and the beginning. Do you understand? You are destined to die and be born again."

"I already did that eight months ago when Arkadin shot me."

Suparwita nodded gravely. "Had I not given you a draft of the resurrection lily beforehand, it's very likely you would have died from that wound."

"You saved me," Bourne said. "Why?"

Suparwita gave him another of his thousand-watt grins. "We are linked, you and I." He shrugged. "Who can say how or why?"

Bourne, needing to turn to practical matters, said, "There are two of them outside, I checked before I came in."

"And yet you led them here."

Now it was Bourne's turn to grin. He lowered his voice even further. "All part of the plan, my friend."

Suparwita raised a hand. "Before you carry out your plan, there is something you must know and something I must teach you."

He paused long enough for Bourne to wonder what

was on his mind. He knew the shaman well enough to understand when something grave was about to be discussed. He'd seen that expression just before Suparwita had fed him the resurrection lily concoction in this very room some months ago.

"Listen to me." There was no smile on the shaman's face now. "Within the year you will die, you will need to die in order to save those around you, everyone you love or care about."

Despite all his training, all his mental discipline, Bourne felt a wave of coldness sweep through him. It was one thing to put yourself in harm's way, to cheat death over and over, often by a hairbreadth, but it was quite another to be told in unequivocal terms that you had less than a year to live. On the other hand, he had the choice to laugh it off—he was a Westerner, after all, and there were so many belief systems in the world that it was easy enough to dismiss 99 percent of them. And yet, looking into Suparwita's eyes, he could see the truth. As before, the shaman's extraordinary powers had allowed him to see the future, or at least Bourne's future. *"We are linked, you and I."* He had saved Bourne's life before, it would be foolish to doubt him now.

"Do you know how, or when?"

Suparwita shook his head. "It doesn't work like that. My flashes of the future are like waking dreams, filled with color and portent, but there are no images, no details, no clarity."

"You once told me that Siwa would look after me."

"Indeed." The smile returned to Suparwita's face as he led Bourne into another room, filled with shadows and the scent of frangipani incense. "And the next several hours will be an example of his help."

* * *

Valerie Zapolsky, Rory Doll's personal assistant, brought the message to DCI M. Errol Danziger herself, because, as she said, her boss did not want to entrust the news to the computer system, even one as hackproof as CI's.

"Why didn't Doll bring this himself?" Danziger frowned without looking up.

"The director of operations is otherwise engaged," Valerie said. "Temporarily."

She was a small dark woman with hooded eyes. Danziger didn't like that Doll had sent her.

"Jason Bourne is alive? What the fuck—!" He leapt off his chair as if he'd been electrocuted. As his eyes scanned the report, which was brief and lacking actionable detail, his face grew red with blood. His head fairly trembled.

Then Valerie made the fatal mistake of trying to be solicitous. "Director, is there anything I can do?"

"Do, do?" He looked up as if coming out of a stupor. "Sure, here's what, tell me this is a joke, a sick, black joke on Rory Doll's part. Because if not, I sure as hell am going to fire your ass."

"That will be all, Val," Rory Doll said, appearing in the doorway behind her. "Go on back to the office." Her expression of deliverance only partially assuaged his guilt at thrusting her into the line of fire.

"Goddammit," Danziger said. "I swear I *will* fire her."

Doll strolled into the office and stood in front of

Danziger's desk. "If you do, Stu Gold will be on you like flies on shit."

"Gold? Who the fuck is Stu Gold and why should I give a shit about him?"

"He's CI's lawyer."

"I'll fire his ass, too."

"Impossible, sir. His firm has an ironclad contract with CI, and he's the only one with clearance all the way up—"

The DCI's hand cut across the air in a vicious gesture. "You think I can't find just cause to can her?" He snapped his fingers. "What's her name?"

"Zapolsky. Valerie A. Zapolsky."

"Right, what is that, Russian? I want her re-vetted down to the brand of toenail polish she uses, understood?"

Doll nodded diplomatically. He was slender and fair-haired, which only caused his electric-blue eyes to blaze like flares. "Absolutely, sir."

"And God help you if there's a spot, however small, or even a question, on that report."

Ever since Peter Marks's recent defection the DCI had been in a foul mood. Another director of ops had not yet been named. Marks had been Doll's boss and Doll knew that if he could prove his loyalty to Danziger, he'd have a good shot at Marks's position. Grinding his teeth in silent fury, he changed the subject. "We need to talk about this new bit of intel."

"This isn't a file photo, is it? This isn't a joke?"

"I wish it were." Doll shook his head. "But, no, sir. Jason Bourne was photographed applying for a temporary visa at Denpasar Airport in Bali, Indonesia—"

"I know where the hell Bali is, Doll."

"Just being complete, sir, as per your instructions to us on first-day orientation."

The DCI, though still fuming, said nothing. He held the report, and its attendant grainy black-and-white photo of Bourne, in his fist—his mailed fist, as he liked to call it.

"Continuing, as you can see by the electronic legend in the lower right-hand corner, the photo was taken three days ago, at two twenty-nine PM local time. It took our signals department this long to ensure there was no transmission error or interception."

Danziger took a breath. "He was dead, Bourne was supposed to be dead. I was sure we'd shut him down forever." He crushed the photo, threw it in the hopper attached to the paper shredder. "He's still there, I assume you know that much."

"Yes, sir." Doll nodded. "At this moment he's on Bali."

"You have him under surveillance?"

"Twenty-four hours a day. He can't make a move without us knowing about it."

Danziger considered for a moment, then said, "Who's our wet-work man in Indonesia?"

Doll was ready for this question. "Coven. But, sir, if I may point out, in her last written report filed from Cairo, Soraya Moore claimed that Bourne had a major hand in preventing the disaster in northern Iran that brought down Black River."

"Almost as dangerous as his rogue status is Bourne's ability to—how shall I put it?—influence women unduly. Moore is certainly one of them, which is why she was fired." The DCI nodded. "Activate Coven, Mr. Doll."

"Can do, sir, but it will take him some time to—"

"Who's closer?" Danziger said impatiently.

Doll checked his notes. "We have an extraction team in Jakarta. I can get them on a military copter within the hour."

"Do it, and use Coven as backup," the DCI ordered. "Their orders are to bring Bourne in. I want to subject him to extensive, ah, questioning. I want to pick his brains, I want to know his secrets, how he manages to keep evading us, how at every turn he cheats death." Danziger's eyes glittered with malice. "When we're done with him we'll put a bullet through his head and claim the Russians killed him."

2

THE LONG BANGALORE night was nearly at an end. Thick with the stench of raw sewage, disease, and human sweat, dense with terror, displaced rage, thwarted desire, and despair, the ashen dawn did nothing to return color to the city.

Finding a physician's surgery, Arkadin broke in and took what he needed: sutures, iodine, sterile cotton, bandages, and antibiotics to take the place of the ones he hadn't been able to pick up at the hospital. Loping through the wheezing streets, he knew he needed to stop the bleeding of the wound at the back of his thigh. It wasn't life threatening, but it was deep, and he didn't want to lose any more blood. Even more, though, he needed a place to hide, where he could stop the clock that Oserov had set ticking, a place of respite where he could assess his situation. He cursed himself for having been caught flat-footed by the enemy. But he was also acutely aware that his next step was a crucial one, disaster could so quickly compound itself into a catastrophe of deathly proportions.

With his local security penetrated, he could no longer trust any of his usual contacts in Bangalore, which left only one option: the place where he maintained absolute leverage. On the way, entering an encrypted number that gave him access to a relay of secure signal routers, he called Stepan, Luka, Pavel, Alik, as well as Ismael Bey, the figurehead leader of the Eastern Brotherhood, which he controlled.

"We're under attack from Maslov, Oserov, the entire Kazanskaya," he told each one brusquely and without preamble. "As of this moment we're in a state of war."

He had trained them well, none of them asked superfluous questions, merely acknowledged the order with curt replies. Then they rang off in order to commence the preparations Arkadin had blueprinted for them months ago. Each captain had his specific role to play, each was activating his piece of a plan that literally stretched across the globe. Maslov wanted war, that's precisely what he was going to get, and not merely on a single front.

Arkadin shook his head and barked a laugh. This moment was always in the wind, as inevitable as their next breath. Now that it was upon him there was a palpable sense of relief. No more grinning through gritted teeth, no more pretending a friendship where only bitter enmity existed.

You're a dead man, Dimitri Ilyinovich, Arkadin thought. *You just don't know it yet.*

A touch of watery pink had tinged the sky, and he was almost at Chaaya's. Time to make the difficult call. He punched in an eleven-digit number. A male drone at the other end said "Federal Anti-Narcotics Agency" in Russian. The now infamous FSB-2 that, under its leader, a man named Viktor Cherkesov, had become the most powerful and feared agency within the Russian government, surpassing even the FSB, the KGB's successor.

"Colonel Karpov, if you please," Arkadin said.

"It's four AM. Colonel Karpov is unavailable," the drone said in a voice not unlike one of the undead from a George Romero film.

"So am I," Arkadin said, honing his sardonic edge, "but I'm making the time to talk to him."

"And who might you be?" the emotionless voice said in his ear.

"My name is Arkadin, Leonid Danilovich Arkadin. Go find your boss."

There was a quick catch of the drone's breath, then, "Hold the line."

"Sixty seconds," Arkadin said, looking at his watch and starting the countdown, "no more."

Fifty-eight seconds later a series of clicks was followed by a deep, gruff voice that said, "This is Colonel Karpov."

"Boris Illyich, we've almost met so many times over the years."

"Would that I could cross out the *almost*. How do I know I'm speaking to Leonid Danilovich Arkadin?"

"Dimitri Maslov is still giving you fits, isn't he?"

When Karpov gave no response, Arkadin continued. "Colonel, who else could give you the Kazanskaya on a silver platter?"

Karpov laughed harshly. "The real Arkadin would never turn on his mentor. Whoever you are, you're wasting my time. Good-bye."

Arkadin gave him an address hidden in the industrial outskirts of Moscow.

Karpov was silent for a moment, but Arkadin, listening carefully, could hear the harsh soughing of his breathing. Everything depended on this conversation, on Karpov believing that he was, in fact, Leonid Danilovich Arkadin and that he was telling the truth.

"What am I to make of this address?" the colonel said after a time.

"It's a warehouse. From the outside it looks exactly like the hundred or so on either side of it. Inside, as well."

"You're boring me, *gospadin* Whoever-You-Are."

"The third door on the left near the back will take you into the men's room. Go past the urinal trough to the last stall on the right, which has no toilet, only a door in the rear wall."

There was only a moment's hesitation before Karpov said, "And then?"

"Go in heavy," Arkadin said. "Armed to the teeth."

"You're saying that I should take a squad with—"

"No! You go alone. Furthermore, you don't sign out, you don't tell a soul where you're going. Tell them you're going to the dentist or for an afternoon fuck, whatever your comrades will believe."

Another pause, this one dark with menace. "Who's the mole inside my office?"

"Ah, now, Boris Illyich, don't be so ungrateful. You don't want to spoil my fun, not after the gift I've just given you." Arkadin took a breath. Having witnessed the colonel take the bait, he judged the moment right to sink the hook all the way in. "But were I you, I wouldn't use the singular—*moles* is more like it."

"What—? Now, listen to me—!"

"You'd best get rolling, Colonel, or your targets will have packed up for the day." He chuckled. "Here's my number, I know it didn't come up on your phones. Call me when you return and we'll talk names and, quite possibly, much, much more."

He cut the connection before Karpov could say another word.

Near the end of the workday Delia Trane was sitting at her desk looking over a three-dimensionally rendered computer model of a diabolically clever explosive device, trying to find a way to disarm it before the timer went off. A buzzer deep inside the bomb would sound the instant she failed—if she cut the wrong wire with her virtual cutter or moved it inordinately. She herself had created the software program that had rendered the virtual bomb, but that didn't mean that she wasn't having the devil's own time figuring out a way to disarm it.

Delia was a plain-looking woman in her midthirties with pale eyes, short-cropped hair, and skin deeply burnished by the genes from her Colombian mother. Despite her relative youth and her often ferocious temper, she was one of the ATF's most coveted explosives experts. She was also Soraya Moore's best friend, and when one of the guards from reception called to say Soraya was in the lobby she asked him to send her right up.

The two women had met through work, had sparked off each other's feistiness and independence, recognizing and appreciating kindred spirits, so difficult to find in the hermetically sealed public sector inside the Beltway. Because they had met on one of Soraya's clandestine assignments they had no need to conceal from each other their life's work and what it meant to them, the number one relationship killer in DC. Further, both of them realized that, for better or for worse, their entire lives were bound up in their respective services, that they were unsuited for anything but work they couldn't talk about with civilians, which in a way validated their existence, their independence as women, and their importance irrespective of the gender bias that existed here as virtually everywhere else in Washington. Together they daily took on the DC establishment like a pair of Amazons.

Delia returned to the contemplation of her model, which to her was like an entire world in miniature. Within seconds she was completely immersed in her problem, so she didn't give a second thought to what her friend was doing here at this time of day. When a shadow fell over her work she looked up into Soraya's face and knew something was terribly wrong.

"For God's sake, sit down," she said, pulling over a spare chair, "before you fall down. What the hell happened, did someone die?"

"Only my job."

Delia looked at her quizzically. "I don't understand."

"I've been canned, fired, sent to the showers," Soraya said. "Terminated without extreme prejudice—but certainly with prejudice," she added with grim humor.

"What the hell happened?"

"I'm Egyptian, Muslim, a woman. Our new DCI doesn't need any other reasons."

"Not to worry, I know a good lawyer who—"

"Forget it."

Delia frowned. "You're not going to let them get away with this. I mean, it's discrimination, Raya."

Soraya waved a hand. "I'm not spending the next two years of my life going up against CI and Secretary Halliday."

Delia leaned back. "It goes that high up, huh?"

"How could they do this to me?" Soraya said.

Delia rose and went around her desk to hug her friend. "I know, it's like being jilted by a lover, someone you thought you knew but who turned out to be using you and, worse, was betraying you all the while."

"Now I know how Jason felt," Soraya said morosely. "All the times he's pulled CI's hand out of the fire and what did he get for it? He was hunted down like a dog."

"Good riddance to CI, I say!" Delia kissed the top of her friend's head. "Time to start over."

Soraya looked up at her. "Really? Doing what, exactly? This shadow world is all I know, all I want to do. And Danziger's so pissed off I didn't come back to CI when he ordered me to that he's put me on a clandestine service blacklist, making it impossible for me to work in the governmental intelligence community."

Delia looked thoughtful for a moment. "Tell you what, I need to do some things down the hall, make a call, and we'll go for some drinks and dinner. Then I have someplace special to take you. How's that sound?"

"Better than going home, stuffing my face with ice cream, and staring at TV."

Delia laughed. "That's my girl." She waved a finger in the air. "Don't you worry, we'll have so much fun tonight you won't remember to be sad."

Soraya gave her a rueful smile. "What about bitter?"

"Yeah, we can take care of that, too."

Bourne sprinted out of Suparwita's house without looking to either the left or the right. To the people watching he would appear to be a man on an urgent mission. He suspected that they would want to follow him to his next destination.

He could hear them trailing him through the forest, drawn in closer by his focused behavior. He hurried through the underbrush, wanting them close to him so that his agitation would become their agitation. His life wasn't in danger, he knew, until they had interrogated him. They wanted to know what he knew about the ring. No doubt they felt they were being discreet, but nothing was a secret in Bali. Bourne had heard that they had been asking about it in Manggis, the local village. Once he'd learned they were Russians, he had little doubt that they worked for Leonid Arkadin. He had last seen his enemy, the first graduate of Treadstone's ultimate soldier program, in the battle-torn area of northern Iran.

Now, in the midst of the emerald-and-umber Balinese jungle, Bourne made a hard right, heading for an enormous *berigin*—what Westerners called a banyan—the Balinese symbol of immortality. He leapt into the *berigin*'s many arms, working his way up through the labyrinth of branches until he was high enough to get a panoramic view of the area. Birds called to one another and insects droned. Here and there spears of sunlight pierced the many-layered canopy, turning the soft ground the color of chocolate.

A moment later he spied one of the Russians, stalking cautiously through the dense undergrowth, making his way around stands of thickly foliaged trees. He cradled the barrel of an AK-47 in the crook of his left arm, the forefinger of his right hand lay against the trigger, ready to spray bullets at the slightest noise or disturbance. He advanced slowly toward Bourne's *berigin*. Every so often he glanced up into the trees, his scowling eyes dark and searching.

Bourne moved silently through the branches, positioning himself. He waited until the Russian was directly beneath him before he fell like one of the spears of sunlight. His heels struck the Russian's shoulders, dislocating one, throwing him off his feet. Rolling himself into a ball, Bourne took the brunt of the fall on one shoulder blade, tumbling harmlessly head-over-heels. He was up and at the Russian before the stalker could regain his breath. Nevertheless the Russian's training asserted itself, his leg flicking out and catching Bourne in the sternum.

Bourne grunted. The Russian, teeth gritted against the pain, sought to gain his feet, and time seemed to stand still, as if the primordial forest around them were holding its breath. Bourne's right arm lashed out, the edge of his hand breaking the bones in the Russian's dislocated shoulder. The Russian moaned, but at the same time he drove the butt of the assault rifle into Bourne's side.

Leaning heavily on the AK-47, the Russian rose to

his feet, stumbled over to where Bourne lay tangled in vines. He pointed the muzzle of the rifle but, as he did so, Bourne aimed a scissors kick at his adversary's knee, bringing the Russian down to his level. A short burst from the rifle scythed upward, raining bits of leaves, bark, and branches onto both of them. The Russian swung the AK-47, trying to use it as a battering ram, but Bourne was already inside the arc of his swing. A swift strike with the edge of his hand broke the Russian's collarbone, and the heel of Bourne's other hand slammed into his nose with such force, it drove cartilage and bone into the Russian's brain. As he keeled over, dead, Bourne snatched the assault rifle out of his bloody grip. He could see the crude tattoo of a serpent wrapped around a dagger that the Russian had gotten in prison, proof positive that he was a member of the *grupperovka*.

Bourne was unwrapping the vines around him when he heard a guttural voice from behind.

"Drop your weapon," it said in Moscow-accented Russian.

Bourne turned slowly and saw the second Russian stalker. He must have followed the sound of the gunfire.

"I said drop it," the Russian growled. He, too, held an AK-47, which was aimed at Bourne's midsection.

"What do you want?" Bourne said.

"You know very well what I want," the Russian said. "Now drop your weapon and hand it over."

"Hand what over? Just tell me what you want and I'll give it to you."

"I'll take the ring now. Right after you drop my partner's rifle." He made a beckoning motion. "Come on, fucker. Otherwise I'm going to shoot one leg off, then the other, and if that fails—well, you know how painful a gut wound can be, how long you'll linger in agony before you bleed to death."

"Your partner. Too bad about him," Bourne said, at the same time letting the AK-47 slip out of his grip.

It was pure instinct, the Russian couldn't help glancing over at his fallen companion. As he did so the motion of the AK-47 made him look down. That was when Bourne whipped the vine up and out. It caught the Russian around the neck, and with a powerful pull Bourne jerked him forward, right into his fist. The Russian doubled over. Bourne, dropping the vine, drove both fists down on the back of his neck.

The Russian crumpled, and Bourne, crouched over him, rolled him onto his back. The man was still dazed, gasping and flopping like a fish on the bottom of a boat. Bourne slapped him into full consciousness, then pressed a knee into his sternum, using his full weight.

The man stared up at him out of blue eyes. His face was unnaturally ruddy, and he could not hold back a dribble of blood from the corner of his mouth.

"Why did Leonid send you?" Bourne said in Russian.

The man blinked. "Who?"

"Don't do that." Bourne pressed down and the man groaned. "You know perfectly well who I mean. Leonid Arkadin."

For a moment the Russian stared up at him, mute. Then, despite his dire circumstances, he laughed. "Is that what you think?" Tears rolled from the corners of his eyes. "That I work for that shitbag?"

The Russian's response was too spontaneous, too unexpected to be false. Besides, why would he lie? Bourne paused for a moment, reassessing the situation. "If not Arkadin," he said slowly and carefully, "then who?"

"I'm a member of the Kazanskaya." There was no mistaking the pride in his voice; this, too, was genuine.

"So Dimitri Maslov sent you." Not long ago Bourne had met the head of the Kazanskaya in Moscow under unpleasant circumstances.

"In a manner of speaking," the Russian said. "I report to Vylacheslav Germanovich Oserov."

"Oserov?" Bourne had never heard of him. "Who is he?"

"Director of operations. Vylacheslav Germanovich plans every phase of the Kazanskaya action while Maslov handles the increasingly annoying government."

Bourne considered for a moment. "Okay, so you report to this Oserov. Why was it funny that I thought Arkadin had sent you?"

The Russian's eyes blazed. "You're as ignorant as a head of cabbage. Oserov and Arkadin hate each other's guts."

"Why?"

"Their feud goes back a long way." He spat out some blood. "Interrogation finished?"

"What's the nature of their enmity?"

The Russian grinned up at him through bloody teeth. "Get the fuck off my chest."

"Sure thing." Bourne stood up, grabbed the Russian's AK-47, and slammed the butt into the side of his head.

3

I SHOULD HAVE KNOWN," Soraya said.

Delia turned to her, a twinkle in her eye. "Known what?"

"That an inveterate player like you would take me to the best private poker game in the district."

Delia laughed as Reese Williams led them down a wallpapered hallway peppered with paintings and photos of African wildlife, predominantly elephants.

"I've heard about this place," Soraya said to Williams, "but this is the first time Delia's seen fit to bring me here."

"You won't be sorry," Williams said over her shoulder, "that I promise you."

They were in her Federalist brownstone off Dupont Circle. Reese Williams was the strong right arm of Police Commissioner Lester Burrows, indispensable to him in many ways, not the least through her extensive contacts within the upper echelons of DC's politicos.

Williams threw open the double pocket doors, revealing a library that had been converted into a gambling den, complete with a green baize table, comfortable chairs for six, and clouds of aromatic cigar smoke. As they entered the only sounds in the room were the click of chips and the barely audible flutter of a deck of cards being expertly shuffled, then dealt to the four men sitting around the table.

Besides Burrows, Soraya recognized two senators, one junior, one senior, a high-powered lobbyist, and, her eyes opened wide, was that—?

"Peter?" she said incredulously.

Peter Marks looked up from counting his chips. "Good God. Soraya." At once he stood up, said, "Deal me out," and came around the green baize table to embrace her. "Delia, how about taking my place?"

"With pleasure." She turned to her friend. "Peter's a regular here and I called him from the office. I thought you could use seeing an old compatriot."

Soraya grinned and kissed Delia on the cheek. "Thanks."

Delia nodded and left them, sitting down at the table. She took her usual stacks of chips from the bank, signing an IOU for the amount.

"How are you?" Marks said, holding Soraya at arm's length.

Soraya surveyed him critically. "How do you think I am?"

"I heard through my pals in CI what Danziger did to you." He shook his head. "I can't say that I'm surprised."

"What d'you mean?"

Marks led her across the hall to a quiet corner in the

deserted sitting room, where they were ensured complete privacy. French windows looked out on a shadowy alley of greenery. The room was wallpapered a warm persimmon color, the walls covered with photos of Reese Williams in Africa amid crowds of tribesmen. In some of them she was also with an older man, possibly her father. Plush sofas and several deep-cushioned armchairs of striped fabric were arrayed before a fireplace with a marble mantelpiece. A low polished wooden table and a sideboard with two trays of liquor bottles and cut-crystal glasses completed the picture. No amount of municipal salary or rake-offs could account for this magnificent house. Soraya thought Reese must come from enormous wealth.

They sat side by side on a deep-cushioned sofa, turned partly toward each other.

"Danziger's just looking for excuses to get rid of CI's top management," Marks said. "He wants his people—and by that I mean Secretary Halliday's people—in positions of power, but he knows he has to tread carefully to avoid it looking like a wholesale slaughter of the old guard, even though that's been the plan all along. It's why I bailed when I knew he was coming in."

"I've been in Cairo, I didn't know you'd left CI. Where did you land?"

"Private sector." Marks paused for a moment. "Listen, Soraya, I know you can keep a secret, so I'm willing to go out on a limb here and tell you." He paused, his eyes flicking toward the door, which he'd carefully closed behind them.

"So?"

Marks leaned in farther, so their faces were close together. "I've joined Treadstone."

For a moment, there was nothing but shocked silence and the *tick-tock* of the brass ship's clock on the marble mantel. Then Soraya tried a laugh. "Come on, Treadstone is dead and buried."

"The old Treadstone, yes," he said. "But there's a new Treadstone, resurrected by Frederick Willard."

Willard's name wiped the smile from Soraya's face. She knew of Willard's reputation as the Old Man's Treadstone sleeper agent inside the NSA, who had been instrumental in exposing the former director's criminal interrogation techniques. But since then he'd seemed to vanish off everyone's radar. So Peter's information was all too credible.

She shook her head, her expression troubled. "I don't understand. Treadstone was an illicit operation, even by CI's covert standards. It was shut down for very good reasons. Why on earth would you sign up for it now?"

"Simple. Willard hates Halliday as much as I do—as much as you do. He's promised me that he's going to use Treadstone's resources to destroy Halliday's credibility and his power base. That's why I want you to join us."

She was taken aback. "What? Join Treadstone?" As he nodded, her eyes narrowed in suspicion. "Wait a minute. You knew I was going to get canned the minute I walked through the doors to HQ."

"Everyone knew, Soraya, except you."

"Good Lord." She jumped up and began to stalk around the room, running her fingertips over the tops of the books on the shelves, the contours of bronze elephants, the textures of the heavy drapes without even being aware of it. Peter had the good sense to say nothing. Finally, she turned to him from across the room and said, "Give me one good reason why I should join you—and please don't state the obvious."

"Okay, putting aside the fact that you need a job, step back and think for a minute. When Willard makes good on his promise, when Halliday is gone, how long d'you think Danziger will last at CI?" He stood up. "I don't know about you, but I want the old CI back, the one the Old Man ran for decades, the one I can be proud of."

"You mean the one that used Jason over and over again whenever it suited its purpose."

He laughed, deflecting her blade of cynicism. "Isn't that one of the things intelligence organizations do best?" He came toward her. "Come on, tell me that you don't want the old CI back."

"I want to be running Typhon again."

"Yeah, well, you don't want to know how Danziger's going to fuck up the Typhon networks you built up."

"To tell you the truth, Typhon's future is all I've been thinking about since I walked out of HQ this afternoon."

"Then join me."

"What if Willard fails?"

"He won't," Marks said.

"Nothing in life is assured, Peter, you of all people should know that."

"Okay, fair enough. If he fails, then we all fail. But at least we'll feel that we've done whatever we could to bring back CI, that we haven't simply knuckled under to Halliday and an NSA run rampant."

Soraya sighed, picked her way across the carpet to join Marks. "Where the hell did Willard get the funding to resurrect Treadstone?"

Just by asking the question she saw she had agreed to

his offer. She knew she was hooked. But while weighing this understanding, she almost missed the pained look on Peter's face. "I'm not going to like it, am I?"

"I didn't like it, either, but..." He shrugged. "Does the name *Oliver Liss* mean anything to you?"

"One of the principals of Black River?" She goggled at him. Then she burst out laughing. "You're kidding, right? Jason and I were instrumental in discrediting Black River. I thought the three of them were all indicted."

"Liss's partners were, but he severed all ties to Black River months before the shit you and Bourne threw hit the fan. No one could find a trace of his participation in the illegal activity."

"He knew?"

Peter shrugged. "Possibly he was simply lucky."

She gave him a penetrating look. "I don't believe that and neither do you."

Marks nodded.

"You're damn right I don't like it. What does that say about Willard's sense of ethics?"

Marks took a deep breath and let it out slowly. "Halliday plays as dirty as anyone I've ever known. Whatever it takes to defeat him, bring it on, I say."

"Even making a deal with the devil."

"Perhaps it takes one devil to destroy another devil."

"Whatever the truth of what you say, this is a treacherous slope, Peter."

Marks grinned. "Why d'you think I want you on board? At some point I'm going to need someone to pull me out of the shit before it closes over my head. And I can't think of a better person to do that than you."

* * *

Moira Trevor, Lady Hawk pistol strapped into her thigh holster, stood looking at the empty offices of her new but compromised company, Heartland Risk Management, LLC. The space had so quickly become toxic that she wasn't sad to leave it, only dismayed because she had been in business for less than a year. There was nothing here now but dust, not even memories she could take with her.

She turned to leave and saw a man filling the open doorway to the outside hall. He was dressed in an expensively cut three-piece suit, spit-shined English brogues, and despite the clear weather he carried a neatly rolled umbrella with a hardwood handle.

"Ms. Trevor, I presume?"

She stared hard at him. He had hair like steel bristles, black eyes, and an accent she couldn't quite place. He was holding a plain brown paper bag, which she eyed with suspicion. "And you are?"

"Binns." He offered his hand. "Lionel Binns."

"Lionel? You must be joking, no one's named Lionel these days."

He looked at her unblinkingly. "May I come in, Ms. Trevor?"

"Why would you want to do that?"

"I'm here to make you an offer."

She hesitated for a moment, then nodded. He crossed the threshold without seeming to have moved.

Peering around, he said, "Oh, dear. What have we here?"

"Desolation Row."

Binns gave her a quick smile. "I'm an early Dylan fan myself."

"What can I do for you, Mr. Binns?"

She tensed as he lifted the brown paper bag and opened it.

Taking out two paper cups, he said, "I brought us some cardamom tea."

The first clue. "How nice," Moira said, accepting the tea. She took off the plastic top to peer inside. It was pale with milk. She took a sip. And very sweet. "Thank you."

"Ms. Trevor, I am an attorney. My client would like to hire you."

"Lovely." She looked around Desolation Row. "I could use some work."

"My client wants you to find a notebook computer that was stolen from him."

Moira paused with the cup halfway to her lips. Her coffee-colored eyes watched Binns with uncommon scrutiny. She had a strong face with a personality to match.

"You must have me confused with a private detective. There's no shortage of those in the district, any one of them—"

"My client wants you, Ms. Trevor. Only you."

She shrugged. "He's barking up the wrong tree. Sorry. Not my line of work."

"Oh, but it is." There was nothing sinister or even discomforting in Binns's face. "Let me see if I have this right. You were a highly successful field operative for Black River. Eight months ago you left and started Heartland by poaching the best and the brightest from your former employer. You didn't back down when Black River tried to intimidate you, in fact you fought back and were instrumental in bringing to light the company's criminal dealings. Now, for his trouble, your old boss Noah Perlis is dead, Black River has been disbanded, and two of its founding principals are under indictment. Stop me if I've gotten anything wrong so far."

Moira, astonished, said nothing.

"From where my client sits," he continued, "you're the perfect candidate to find and retrieve his stolen laptop."

"And where, exactly, does your client sit?"

Binns grinned at her. "Interested? There's quite a handsome remuneration for you."

"I'm not interested in money."

"Despite needing the work?" Binns cocked his head. "But never mind, I wasn't speaking of money, though your entire usual fee will be paid in advance. No, Ms. Trevor, I'm talking about something more valuable to you." He looked around the empty room. "I'm talking about the reason you've moved out of here."

Moira froze, her heartbeat accelerating. "I don't know what you mean."

"You have a traitor in your organization," Binns said without inflection. "Someone on the NSA's payroll."

Moira frowned. "Just who is your client, Mr. Binns?"

"I'm not authorized to reveal his identity."

"And I suppose you're also not authorized to tell me how he knows so much about me?"

Binns spread his hands.

She nodded. "Fine. I'll find my goddamn traitor myself."

Oddly, this response brought a cat-like smile to Binns's face. "My client said that would be your answer. I didn't believe him, so now I'm out a thousand dollars."

"I'm sure you'll find a way to make it up in fees."

"Once you get to know me, you'll realize I'm not that sort of man."

"You're being overly optimistic," Moira said.

He nodded. "Possibly." Retreating to the doorway, he lifted a hand. "If you'll accompany me..." When she made no move to follow him, he added, "Just this once, I beg you to indulge me. It will only take fifteen minutes of your time, what do you have to lose?"

Moira couldn't think of a damn thing, so she allowed him to usher her out.

Chaaya lived in the penthouse of one of Bangalore's glittering high-rise mini-cities, a gated residential community guarded day and night against the city's multitude of ravages. But whether the precautions kept the city out or imprisoned the denizens in its citadel, Arkadin thought, was only a matter of perspective.

Chaaya opened the door to his knock, as she always did no matter what time he appeared. She had no choice, really. She came from a wealthy family and lived in the lap of luxury, but all of that would evaporate if they knew her secret. She was Hindu and the man she was in love with was Muslim, a mortal sin in the eyes of her father and three brothers should they become aware of her transgression. Though Arkadin had never met her lover, he had arranged that her secret be kept safe; Chaaya owed him everything, and acted accordingly.

Lush-figured, dusky-hued, in a gauzy dressing gown, her eyes still heavy with sleep, she moved through her skylit apartment with the sensual grace of a Bollywood actress. She was not particularly tall, but her bearing gave that illusion; when she walked into a room heads turned, both male and female. Whether she liked Arkadin, what she thought of him altogether, was of absolutely no interest to him. She feared him, which was all that was required.

It was brighter up here above the rooftops, giving the false impression that the day had already started. But then this apartment, mirroring both their lives, was full of fake impressions.

She saw his bloody leg at once and took him into her spacious bathroom, all mirrors and pink-and-gold veined marble. While he stripped off his trousers, she ran hot water. She had a deft touch with the sutures, and he asked her if she'd done this before.

"Once, long ago," she said enigmatically.

That was why he had come here now, at this moment, when trust was at a premium. He and Chaaya recognized something in each other, something of themselves, dark and broken. They were both outsiders, uncomfortable in the world most people inhabited, they'd rather skim along the margins, half hidden by the flickering shadows that terrified everyone else. They were apart, strangers perhaps even to themselves, but companionable with each other because of that very fact.

While she washed him and worked on closing his wound, he considered his next move. He needed to get out of India, of that there was no doubt. Where would that shithead Oserov guess he might go? Campione d'Italia in Switzerland, where the Eastern Brotherhood maintained a villa, or perhaps its headquarters in Munich. By necessity Oserov's list of options would be short; even Maslov had his limits as far as sending hit squads around the world on what might be a wild goose chase. He'd never been one to squander manpower or resources, which was why he still headed the single most powerful *grupperovka* family in an era when the Kremlin was aggressively dismantling the mob.

Arkadin knew he had to remove himself to a location that was absolutely secure. He had to choose a place neither Oserov nor Maslov would ever consider. And he would tell no one in his organization—at least, not until he could figure out how Oserov had been tipped to his temporary HQ here in Bangalore.

So he had to arrange for travel out of the city, and the country. But first he had to retrieve Gustavo Moreno's laptop from its hiding place.

When Chaaya was finished and they had moved into the living room, he said, "Please fetch the present I gave you."

Chaaya cocked her head, a small smile playing around the corners of her mouth. "Are you saying that I can finally open it? I've been dying of curiosity."

"Bring it here."

She rushed out of the room and a moment later returned with a rather large silver-colored box tied with a purple ribbon. She sat across from him, tense and expectant, the box lying across her thighs. "Can I open it now?"

Arkadin was eyeing the package. "You've already opened it."

A look of fear crossed her face as swiftly as a gull scuds across a dock. Then she forced a smile onto her beautiful face. "Oh, Leonid, I couldn't help myself, and it's such a beautiful robe, I've never felt silk like it, it must have cost you a fortune."

Arkadin held out his hands. "The box."

"Leonid..." But she did as he bade. "I never took it out, I just touched it."

He untied the ribbon, which he saw she'd retied with great care, then set the top aside.

"I love it so, I'd have killed anyone who came near it."

Actually, he'd counted on that. When he'd given it to her with the instructions not to open it he'd seen the covetousness in her eyes and knew then that she'd never have the fortitude to comply. But he also knew that she'd guard it with her life. That was Chaaya through and through.

The robe, which was in fact exceptionally expensive, was folded meticulously into thirds. He removed the laptop, which he'd carefully hidden within its luxurious folds, then handed her the robe.

Busy unscrewing the underside of the laptop so he could insert the hard drive into its original home, he hardly heard her squeals of delight or the thank-yous she showered on him.

DCI M. Errol Danziger most often ate lunch at his desk while poring over intelligence reports from his directorate chiefs, comparing them with their counterparts he had sent over daily from the NSA. However, twice a week he ate his midday meal outside CI headquarters. He always went to the same restaurant—the Occidental on Pennsylvania Avenue—and dined with the same person, Secretary of Defense Bud Halliday. Danziger—all too aware of how his predecessor had been killed—traveled the sixteen blocks to these meetings in an armored GMC Yukon Denali accompanied by Lieutenant R. Simmons Reade, two bodyguards, and a secretary. He was never alone; it disturbed him to be alone, a condition he had brought with him from a childhood filled with the shadows of parental strife and abandonment.

Soraya Moore was waiting for his arrival. She had obtained the DCI's schedule from her former director of ops, who was running Typhon on a temporary basis. Seated at a table at the Willard Hotel's Café du Parc, which abutted the Occidental's outdoor section, she noted the arrival of the Denali on the dot of 1 PM. As the rear door opened, she rose, and by the time the entourage was grouped on the sidewalk she was as close to the DCI as the bodyguards would allow. In fact, one of them, with a chest as broad as the table where she'd been seated, had already stepped in front of her, facing her down.

"Director Danziger," she said loudly over his shoulder, "my name is Soraya Moore."

The second bodyguard had a hand on his firearm when Danziger ordered them both to stand down. He was a short, square man with sloping shoulders. He'd made it his business to study Islamic culture, which only increased his unwavering antipathy for a religion—more, a way of life—he found backward, even medieval in its conventions and customs. It was his firm belief that Islamics, as he privately called them, could never reconcile their religious beliefs with the pace and progress of the modern world, no matter what they claimed. Behind his back, but not without some admiration, he was known as the Arab because of his avowed desire to rid the world of Islamic terrorists and any other Islamics foolish enough to get in his way.

Stepping between his bodyguards, Danziger said, "You're the Egyptian who felt it necessary to stay in Cairo despite being recalled."

"I had a job to do, on the ground, in the field, where the bullets and bombs are real, not computer-generated simulations," Soraya said. "And for the record I'm American, same as you."

"You're nothing like me, Ms. Moore. I give orders. Those who refuse to take them can't be trusted. They don't work for me."

"You never even debriefed me. If you knew—"

"Get it through your head, Ms. Moore, you no longer work for CI." Danziger, leaning forward, had taken on the pugnacious stance of a boxer in the ring. "I have no interest in debriefing you. An Egyptian? God alone knows where your loyalty lies." He leered. "Well, maybe I do. With Amun Chalthoum, perhaps?"

Amun Chalthoum was the head of al Mokhabarat, the Egyptian secret service in Cairo, with whom Soraya had recently worked and with whom she had stayed in Cairo when Danziger had summarily ordered her home prematurely, in contradiction of CI's mission guidelines. In the performance of her mission, she and Amun had fallen in love. She was shocked, or perhaps *stunned* was a better word for it, that Danziger was in possession of such personal information. How in the hell had he found out about her and Amun?

"Birds of a feather," he said. "Far from the professional behavior I expect from my people, fraternizing—is that the right word for it?—with the enemy."

"Amun Chalthoum isn't the enemy."

"Clearly he isn't *your* enemy." He stepped back, a clear sign for his bodyguards to close ranks, blocking whatever limited access she'd had to him. "Good luck getting another government position, Ms. Moore."

R. Simmons Reade smirked in the background before turning away, following in the DCI's wake as, surrounded by his entourage, Danziger strode into the Occidental. The bystanders closest to them were staring at her. Putting a hand to her face, she discovered that her cheeks were burning. She had wanted her day in court; however, this was his court and she had seriously misjudged both his intelligence and the scope of his knowledge. She had mistakenly assumed that Secretary Halliday had inveigled the president to install nothing more than a cat's-paw, a dimwit whom Halliday would have no trouble controlling. More fool her.

As she walked slowly away from the scene of the disaster, she vowed she'd never make that mistake again.

The man on the phone, whoever he was, was right about one thing: The warehouse on the outskirts of Moscow was indistinguishable from those around it, marching away in neat rows. Boris Karpov, hidden in the shadows across from the front door, checked the address he had written down during his phone conversation with the man who called himself Leonid Arkadin. Yes, he had the right location. Turning, he signaled to his men, all of whom were heavily armed, armored in bulletproof vests and riot helmets. Karpov had a nose for traps and this one stank of it. There was no way he would have come alone, no matter how well armed, no way he was going to stick his neck into a noose devised for him by Dimitri Maslov.

Why was he here then? he asked himself for the hundredth time since the call. Because if there was a chance the man actually was Leonid Danilovich Arkadin and he was telling the truth, then it would be a criminal mistake not to follow up on the lead. The FSB-2 and Karpov in particular had been after Maslov, after the Kazanskaya as a whole, for years now, with little success.

He had been given a mandate—to bring Dimitri Maslov and the Kazanskaya to justice—by his immediate superior, Melor Bukin, the man who had lured him away from FSB with a promotion to full colonel and a command of his own. Karpov had watched the meteoric rise of Viktor Cherkesov and was determined to get on board. Cherkesov morphed the FSB-2 from an anti-drug directorate into a national security force that rivaled the vaunted FSB itself. Bukin was a childhood friend of Cherkesov's—which more often than not was how these things worked in Russia—and now he had Cherkesov's ear. Bukin, being Karpov's mentor, had brought Karpov that much closer to the top of FSB-2's pyramid of power and influence.

Bukin was on the phone when Karpov had told him where he was going and why. He'd listened briefly, then waved a cursory benediction.

Now, having silently deployed his squad in a close perimeter around the target, Karpov led his men in a frontal assault on the warehouse. He directed one of his men to shoot out the lock on the front door, then he took them inside. He signaled to his men to take each aisle between the stacked crates. It was hours after the end of the normal workday, so they didn't expect workers, and they weren't disappointed.

When all of his men inside had appeared and checked in, Karpov led them through the door into the bathroom, which was where the voice had said it would be. The urinal trough was on the left, while opposite was the line of stalls. His men banged open the doors as they proceeded down the line, but all were empty.

Karpov paused before the last stall, then charged through. Just as the voice had described, there was no toilet, only another door set flush with the rear wall. Karpov, a cold ball of dread beginning to form in his stomach, disintegrated the lock with a furious burst from his AK-47 assault rifle. At once he shouldered his way through to find an interior set up with an office against the rear wall, raised off the floor and accessed by a metal ladder.

No one was in the office. The phones had been pulled from the wall outlets, the upended file cases and desks, their drawers open, mocked him with their complete barrenness, the obvious haste with which they had been denuded. He turned slowly in a circle, his practiced eye running over everything. Nothing, there was nothing.

Contacting his men at the perimeter, he confirmed what the ice ball growing in his stomach already told him: No one had entered or left the warehouse from the time they had arrived in the area.

"Fuck!" Karpov set one ample buttock on the corner of a desk. The man on the phone had been right all the way down the line. He had warned Karpov not to tell anyone, warned him that Maslov's people might be warned. He had to have been Leonid Danilovich Arkadin.

The Rolls-Royce was gargantuan, something out of the automotive Jurassic age. It stood gleaming like a silver train at the curb outside the office building. Stepping ahead of her, Lionel Binns opened the curbside rear door. As Moira bent and stepped inside, a wash of incense rolled over her. She sat down on the leather seat as the attorney closed the door after her.

As she settled herself, her eyes slowly adjusting to the murky gloom, she found herself sitting beside a rather large, blocky man with walnut-colored skin and windswept eyes, dark as the inside of a well. He had a great shock of dark hair, almost ringlets, and a beard long, thick, and as curly as Nebuchadnezzar's. Now the cardamom tea made sense to her. He was some sort of Arab. Inspecting further, she noticed that his suit, though clearly Western, draped his shoulders and chest like a Berber robe.

"Thank you for coming," he said in a great, booming voice that echoed off the finely polished walnut surfaces of the spacious interior, "for taking a small leap of faith." He spoke with a heavy, almost guttural accent, but his English was impeccable.

A moment later the driver, unseen behind a walnut panel, pulled the Rolls out into traffic, heading south.

"You are Mr. Binns's client, correct?"

"Indeed. My name is Jalal Essai, my home is in Morocco."

Yes, indeed. Berber. "And you had a laptop that was stolen."

"That's right."

Moira was sitting with her right shoulder against the door. She felt abruptly chilled; the interior now seemed suffocatingly small, as if the man's presence had spilled out of his body, invading and darkening the backseat, stealing over her, worming its way inside. She tried to catch her breath and managed only to shiver. The air seemed to fizz or shimmer, as if she were seeing a desert mirage. "Why me? I still don't get it."

"Ms. Trevor, you have certain, shall we say, unique abilities that I believe will be invaluable in finding my laptop and returning it to me."

"And those abilities would be..."

"You have successfully taken on both Black River and the NSA. Do you think that I could find a single private detective who has also done so?" He turned and smiled at her with a set of large, brilliant white teeth shining out of a dusky cardamom face defined by flat planes, high cheekbones, and deep-set eyes, hooded as a hawk's. "No need to answer, that wasn't a question."

"Okay, I'll ask you a question: Do you believe that clandestine agencies were involved in the theft?"

Essai appeared to consider this for some time, though Moira had the distinct impression that he knew for certain.

"It's possible," he said at length. "Even likely."

Moira crossed her arms over her breasts as if to protect herself from the way his logic was chipping away at her resolve, the waves of dark energy emanating from him like nothing she had felt before, as if she were sitting too near a particle collider. She shook her head emphatically. "Sorry."

Essai nodded. It seemed as if nothing she said or did surprised him.

"In any event, this is for you."

He handed over a manila folder, which Moira eyed with mounting suspicion and an eerie dread. Why did she feel like Eve taking the apple of knowledge? Nevertheless, as if her hands were obeying someone else's command, she took possession of the folder.

"Please. There are no strings," Essai said. "Rest assured."

She hesitated a moment, then opened it. Inside was a surveillance photo of one of the top operatives she'd poached from Black River meeting with the director of field operations for the NSA.

"Tim Upton? He's the NSA mole? This wasn't Photoshopped, was it?"

Essai said nothing, so she dropped her gaze to read the accompanying sheet of observed times and places when Upton met clandestinely with various members of the NSA. She sighed deeply, sitting back against the cushion, and slowly closed the file.

"This is extremely generous of you."

Essai shrugged as if it were nothing. And as if on cue the Rolls slowed and pulled to the curb.

"Good-bye, Ms. Trevor."

Moira actually got as far as grabbing the door handle before she turned back to the bearded man and said, "So what is it that makes this laptop of yours so valuable?"

Essai's smile shone like a beacon.

4

BOURNE ARRIVED IN London on a depressingly murky, windblown morning. A misty rain swirled along the Thames, obscuring Big Ben, and the low sky, heavy as lead, pressed down against the modern rise of the city. The air stank of petrol and coal dust, but possibly it was just the industrial grit whipped up by the wind.

Suparwita had told him the address of Noah Perlis's flat. It was the only specific clue he had left himself from that now forgotten time in his life. Sitting in the back of a taxi on the way in from Heathrow, he stared out at the passing scenery without seeing anything. There seemed whole stretches now when he forgot that he'd had a life before his amnesia, but then, like a slap in the face, a shard of it would unexpectedly surface to remind him of what he was missing, what he could never retrieve. In that first instant he felt diminished, a man living half a life, living with a shadow he could never see or even barely feel. Yet it was there, a part of him he could touch only briefly and in frustratingly limited fashion—flashes in the farthest periphery of his vision.

This was what had happened to him in Bali when, trying to find Suparwita several weeks ago, he had ascended to the first temple at the Pura Lempuyang complex. He stood on the very spot he had been dreaming about and discovered that in the time before his amnesia he had been supposed to meet Holly Marie Moreau there. A memory had surfaced. He recalled watching from too great a distance to help her as she fell down the steep flight of stone steps to her death. In fact, as he had subsequently discovered, Noah Perlis, hidden in the shadows of the high carved stone gates, had pushed her.

Perlis's flat was in Belgravia, an area of West London between Mayfair and Knightsbridge, in what had once been a merchant's Georgian mansion but which, in modern times, had been carved into individual living quarters. The shining white building featured a deep terrace that overlooked a tree-lined square. Belgravia was filled with glowing white Georgian row houses, embassies, and posh hotels, a lovely walking neighborhood.

The front-door lock posed no problem, neither did the one on Perlis's second-floor flat. Bourne walked into a generously proportioned sitting room, neatly and fashionably furnished, probably not by Perlis himself who surely hadn't the time for such domestic matters. Despite the sunlight, the air was cold, somber, thick and sluggish with abandonment, the vague sorrow of the forgotten or the disappeared. A small vibration hovered at the edge of Bourne's senses as if left over from the last time Perlis had been here. There was nothing now but a whisper of wind through the old window sashes and the somnolent stirring of dust motes in the diagonal ribs of light.

Though there was a distinctly masculine feel to the place—whiskey-colored leather sofa, burly woods, deep hues on the walls—Bourne couldn't help but suspect a female touch in the accessories, the pewter candelabra with ivory-colored candles half burned down, the delicate swirl of Moroccan lamps, Mexican kitchen tiles bright as a tropical bird's plumage. But it was the bathroom, with its retro pink-and-black glass tiles, and neat as a pin, that clearly revealed the flourishes of the woman's hand. While he was there, he checked behind the toilet tank and, lifting the lid, inside it to see if Perlis had taped anything in those favorite hiding places.

Finding nothing, he moved on to Perlis's bedroom, which interested him the most. Bedrooms were where people—even ones as professional and security-minded as Perlis—tended to hide their intimate possessions, the items that if discovered might give themselves away as clues to the inner self.

He started with the closet, with its rows of black or dark blue trousers and jackets—but no suits—all this year's fashions. Someone had been shopping for Perlis, as well. Pushing aside the rack of clothes, Bourne tapped on the back wall, checking for hollow areas, finding none. He did the same with the side walls, then lifted the shoes pair by pair to check the floor for a hidey-hole. Next, he went through the chest of drawers, feeling under each for anything Perlis might have taped there. At the rear of the bottom drawer he found a Glock. Checking it, he discovered that it was well oiled and loaded. He pocketed it.

Finally, he came to the bed, swinging aside the mattress to check the box spring for papers, photos, thumb drives, or a hidden compartment that might contain them. Under the mattress was a childish place to hide anything of value, but that was precisely why most people did it. Old habits died hard. He moved the box spring off the metal frame so he could flip it over, but found nothing out of the ordinary. Putting the bed back together, he sat on the edge and contemplated the seven framed photos on the top of the dresser. They were lined up in such a way that they were likely the last things Perlis saw before he went to sleep and the first things he saw when he woke up in the morning.

Perlis himself appeared in all but one. He had been walking in Hyde Park with Holly Marie Moreau. They had stopped in front of one of the soapbox ministers, and obviously Noah had grabbed someone from the crowd to take the shot. In another—clearly self-timed—they were boating, perhaps upriver on the Thames. Holly was laughing, possibly at something Noah had said. She seemed at ease, which Bourne, knowing Perlis and the end of their tragic history, found deeply unsettling.

The third photo showed Noah shoulder-to-shoulder with a handsome young man in a fashionable three-piece suit. His skin was dark, with exotic features. Something in his face spoke to Bourne, as if he'd seen him in his un-remembered life, or at least someone like him. Another shot of the two of them with arm candy, in a swank London nightclub. There was some kind of a gaming table in the background, where bettors hovered tensely, bent at the waist like the elderly. Bourne looked more closely at the arm candy. The two women were half hidden behind the men, slightly out of focus, but as he scrutinized the photo more closely he recognized Holly...and Tracy. Which came as a shock to him. He'd met Tracy a month ago on a plane to Seville and they had become allies as they traveled together to Khartoum, where she had died in his arms. It was only later that he had discovered she was taking orders from Arkadin.

So Tracy, Perlis, Holly, and the unknown young man had been a foursome. What strange stroke of fate had brought them together, had caused them to be friends?

Next came a portrait of the young man, watching the camera with a mixture of suspicion and sardonic amusement, a mocking smile that only scions of wealthy families are rich enough to use as either weapon or lure. The seventh and last photo was of the three of them, Perlis, the young man, Holly Marie Moreau. Where was Tracy? Taking the photo, no doubt, or maybe she was away on one of her innumerable trips. Their faces were lit up from below by the candles of an ornate cake. It was Holly's birthday. She was between the two men, slightly bent, one hand pushing back her long hair, her cheeks billowed out while she prepared to blow out the candles. She had a faraway look as she considered what to wish for. She looked very young and totally innocent.

Bourne considered the lineup once again, then he rose and in random order took them apart. Taped to the back of the birthday photo was a passport in Perlis's name, a spare. Pocketing it, Bourne reassembled the elements and replaced the framed photo, staring intently at it. What was Holly Marie Moreau like? How had Perlis met her? Had they been lovers, friends, or had he used her? Had she used him? He ran his hand through his hair, rubbing at his scalp as if he could stimulate his brain into remembering what it clearly couldn't. He had a moment of pure panic, as if he were in a tiny boat set adrift on a fogbound sea, his sight obscured in every direction. Try as he might he could not recall his time with her. In fact, if it hadn't been for the persistent dream of her death he'd had in Bali, he wouldn't have remembered her at all. Was there no end to the nightmare of not remembering, of people appearing out of the dense fog of his past, hovering like ghosts caught in the corners of his vision? Usually he had his emotions under control, but he knew why this time was different: He could still feel the life draining out of Tracy Atherton as he held her in his arms. Had he held Holly the same way as she lay broken at the foot of the Balinese temple's steep staircase?

He sat on the bed, hunched over, staring into a well of memories, of people close to him who were now dead—because of him? Because they had loved him? He'd loved Marie, of that there was no question. But what about Tracy? Could you love someone after only days, a week? Even a month seemed too short a time to know. And yet Tracy remained in his mind, vibrant and infinitely sad, someone he wanted to touch, to talk with, and couldn't. He rubbed the heels of his hands into his eyes. And then there was the agony of knowing that Holly had meant something to him, that she had walked beside him, possibly laughing as she had with Noah Perlis, but he would never know. His only memory was of her falling down the temple steps, falling, falling...And now he was alone again, because he didn't want Moira to suffer the fate of all the others who had tried to get close to him. Alone, always and forever...

Tracy had shivered against him, as if she had been exhaling for the last time. *"Jason, I don't want to be alone."*

"You're not alone, Tracy." He remembered his lips pressing against her forehead. *"I'm here with you."*

"Yes, I know, it's good, I feel you around me." Just before she died she had given a sigh, akin to a cat's purr of contentment.

The curtains in Noah Perlis's flat twitched and shivered as if alive, and a harsh, flat laugh escaped his pulled-back lips. Had Holly whispered to him as Tracy had: *"It's in our darkest hour that our secrets eat us alive."* Little did Tracy know that every hour of his amnesiac life was his darkest hour, that the secrets eating him alive were secrets even from him. He missed Tracy, missed her with the sharpness of a stiletto slipped between his ribs so that he gasped out loud. The curtains shivered in the wind through the sash and it was as if Tracy were here with him again, looking at him with her huge blue eyes, her wide megawatt smile so like Suparwita's. In the wind he heard her laugh, felt the back of her hand brush against his cheek, cooling his flesh.

He had only known her a very short time, but those days had consisted of the compressed time in battle, when staying alive became the be-all and end-all of existence, when every moment contained the taint of death, when company mates become lifelong friends.

Tracy had touched him in a place both heavily defended and starkly tender. She had wormed her way inside him and now remained there, coiled and breathing, even after death.

And then, so close to her, hearing her voice in his mind, he remembered something she had said the night before she'd been killed: *"I live in London, Belgravia. If you saw my flat—it's a tiny thing, but it's mine and I love it. There's a mews out back with a flowering pear tree that a pair of house martins nest in come spring. And a nightjar serenades me most evenings."*

He caught his breath. Was it really a coincidence that both Tracy and Perlis lived in Belgravia? Bourne didn't believe in coincidences, especially not with this group of people: Tracy, Holly, Perlis, the Hererras, Nikolai Yevsen, Leonid Arkadin. Perlis and Yevsen were dead, as were Tracy and Holly, and Arkadin was God only knew where. That left the Hererras as the living tendons that held this constellation together.

Only the photo of the handsome young man with the mocking half smile was left unexplored. Where had he seen that face before? It was maddeningly familiar and yet subtly changed, as if he'd seen the man when he was younger... *or older!* In a sudden frenzy he slid out the cardboard backing and discovered a small key taped to the back of the photo. He peeled it off. The size indicated that it was from either a public locker at one of the airports or the train station or... There was a paper tag attached by a small piece of thin wire that had a series of numbers handwritten on it in ink. Safe-deposit box. He turned the key over. Imprinted on its obverse was a logo consisting of two tiny interlinked letters: AB.

Everything clicked into place. This man was Diego Hererra, son and heir of Don Fernando Hererra, who had dealt in illicit gun trafficking with the late great Nikolai Yevsen, the legendary arms dealer whom Bourne had killed last month. Don Hererra's legitimate business was the Aguardiente Bancorp: AB. He had given Diego the job of running Aguardiente's London office.

Noah Perlis was friends with Diego Hererra, and they both knew Holly. Picking up the photo of the three of them at Holly's birthday, he looked from one face to another and saw the identical complicit look in their eyes. Perlis had been friends with Holly and he had killed her. That complicit look of friendship . . . and then murder.

And then it hit him with the force of an express train. He was part of this constellation. According to Suparwita, Holly had been given the ring by her father, Perlis had killed her to get it, and now he had it. Slowly, he took out the ring and rolled it between his fingers. What did the engraving mean?

The photo of the three of them—Perlis, Diego, and Holly—mocked him. What had been the basis of their friendship? Was it a sexual three-way, a physical attraction that in the end had meant nothing to Perlis, or had he become Holly's friend for a specific reason? And how did these three relate with Tracy? Something was going on here that Bourne didn't understand, something intimate and at the same time repellent. One thing he knew for certain, however: Understanding their connection to one another was vitally important to discovering the secret of the ring.

The man known to CI Ops Directorate as Coven had arrived in Bali just in time to turn around and follow Bourne to London. Now he sat in his rental car, binoculars to his eyes, watching the second-floor window of the late Noah Perlis's Belgravia flat. The curtains moved again, and he tried to make out who was in the apartment. On his lap was a PDF of the Perlis file he had requested. He now knew everything CI knew about Perlis—which admittedly wasn't much, but it was enough to make Coven wonder why Perlis had come to Jason Bourne's attention. Though his original mission had been to incapacitate Bourne and bring him back to CI in cuffs, this was changed after he'd asked for the file on Perlis. Directly following his request, DCI Danziger had come on the line and quizzed him mercilessly about why he was interested in Perlis. Normally Coven didn't stick his nose into executive matters, preferring to infiltrate, accomplish his wet work as quickly, cleanly, and efficiently as possible, and get out, no questions asked. But in a way he couldn't define, this situation was different. The moment DCI Danziger himself seized control of the operation, his hackles rose. Then DCI Danziger confirmed his suspicion and fueled his curiosity by changing the mission midstream: His orders were now to find out the connection between Bourne and Perlis before Coven brought the rogue agent in.

Darkness at noon. The lowering clouds let go the first stuttering spurt, then the rain started in earnest, pocking the sidewalks, running in the gutters, hurling itself onto the car's roof, against the windshield, turning the world smeary, draining it of color.

Coven had been an agnostic when it came to the changing of the guard at DCI level. Wet work was wet work; he didn't think that his job, a universe away from the district, would be jeopardized no matter who was running the show. But that was before DCI Danziger had issued new orders, which he considered unprofessional at best, a potential disaster at worst.

Now, squinting through the rain as Bourne emerged from the building, Coven found himself wondering at DCI Danziger's hidden agenda. It wouldn't be the first time a DCI had one, but this man was new, hadn't come up through the ranks, had hardly earned loyalty from people like Coven who risked their lives in the field every hour of every day and night. The thought that this interloper might be running him as part of his own designs pissed Coven off royally. So the moment he spied Bourne exiting the building, he decided to handle the assignment his way and screw DCI Danziger and his secret agenda. If Bourne had something he wanted that badly, Coven would do well to take it for himself.

My family's entire history is on that laptop," Jalal Essai said.

"That would hardly be a reason for Black River and the NSA to be after it," Moira countered.

"No, of course not."

Essai sighed as he sat back against his chair. They were seated at a corner table in the heart of the terrace restaurant at Caravanserai, a small, exclusive boutique hotel in Virginia, which Essai owned. Ivy-covered brick walls rose on three sides, the fourth being taken up by a row of enormous French doors that led to the restaurant's interior section.

Mint tea had been set before them, along with an elegant menu of the day's fresh offerings, but Moira was far more interested in her host. He was more relaxed now, either because she was on the verge of agreeing to his proposal or because they were in surroundings he could control. While the restaurant's interior was a bit more than half filled, theirs was the only occupied table on the flagstone terrace. A veritable fleet of servers stood by, waiting to be summoned by their master. There was something distinctly Eastern in the tone of the service that made it easy to imagine they were outside the borders of the United States. Far outside.

"I could lie but I have too much respect for you." Essai moistened his lips with the tea. "The history of my family is of interest—quite possibly great interest—to elements of your government, as well as to a number of individuals and organizations in the private sector."

"Why would that be?" Moira asked. "And please be specific."

Essai smiled. "I knew the moment we met that I would like you, and I was right."

"Did you make a bet with Mr. Binns?"

Essai laughed, a dark, bronze-edged sound that sounded uncannily like a gong being struck. "He told you about our bet, did he?" He shook his head. "Our Mr. Binns is a conservative sort, one wager is all he would accede to."

Moira noted the *our* but decided to ignore it for the moment. "Let's get back to basics."

Essai took more of his tea. As with most Arabs, direct conversations were not a part of his repertoire; he preferred a circuitous route that would allow both parties time to gain valuable knowledge before closing a business deal. Moira knew this, of course, but Binns and Essai had blindsided her and she didn't like it. She needed to regain the ground she had lost during the string of surprises Essai had sprung on her in the Rolls, and she calculated that the best way do this was to dictate the pace and flow of the conversation.

"This has something to do with Noah, doesn't it?" she said suddenly. "I worked for him at Black River and he was involved with the laptop, which is why you chose me, correct?"

Essai looked at her directly. "You are the right person for this job for many reasons, as I told you. One of them is, yes, your relationship with Noah Perlis."

"What did Noah do? Was he the one who stole the laptop?"

Essai had picked up his menu and perused it. "Ah, the Dover sole is a special today. I highly recommend it." He looked up, his dark eyes serious. "It's plated with authentic Moroccan couscous."

"Then how could I refuse?"

"Splendid!" He looked genuinely delighted and, when he turned, a server was at his right elbow. He ordered for them, then handed the server their menus. When they were alone again he steepled his fingers and said, in much the same tone of voice, "Your late, and I gather unlamented, boss Mr. Perlis was very much involved."

Moira found herself leaning forward in anticipation. "And?"

He shrugged. "We cannot go forward, you and I, until our deal is ratified. Will you or won't you agree to find my laptop?"

Moira felt herself breathe, but it was as if she were detached from her body, as if she were looking down at this scene from a height. This was it: She could say no, even now. But she found that she didn't want to walk away from this assignment. She needed work, needed a new door opened for her, and since this man had given her information that could save her new company from ruin she thought she might as well say yes.

"All right," she heard herself say. "But I want double my usual fee."

"Done." Essai nodded, as if he was expecting this answer all along. "Most gratifying, Ms. Trevor. I thank you from the bottom of my heart."

"Thank me when I've returned your laptop," she said. "Now about Noah."

"Your Mr. Perlis was something of a pilot fish. That is to say, he thrived on going after other people's initiatives." He spread his hands. "But I'm not telling you anything you don't already know, am I?"

Moira shook her head.

"This was no exception. Mr. Perlis came to the game a bit on the late side."

A warning bell went off in Moira's head. "How late?"

"The mission to find and obtain my notebook by illegal means was the brainchild of CI. More accurately, the small DoN—"

"DoN?"

"Dead of Night," Essai explained. "This term isn't known to you?" He waved a hand: It was of no matter. "The DoN arm known as Treadstone."

Moira felt stunned. "Alex Conklin wanted your laptop?"

"That's right." Essai sat back as the appetizers of prawn salad, the heads still on, were placed in front of them. The server vanished without a word.

"And he engineered the raid?"

"Oh, no, not Conklin."

Essai took up his fork with his right hand and for a moment concentrated on deftly separating the heads from the bodies of his prawns. With one head still impaled on the tines of his fork, his gaze met hers again in such a shocking manner that she instinctively moved back, as if scrambling out of the line of fire.

"It was your friend Jason Bourne who came into my house, where my family eats and sleeps and laughs."

In that frozen moment, while her heart seemed to cease beating, she knew the dislocated feeling for what it really was: the terrifying moment when your car's brakes fail and, accelerating beyond your control, you see another vehicle about to slam into you head-on.

"Where my wife sews my clothes, where my daughter rests her head on my lap, where my son is day by day learning to be a man." A dark vibration, as of a vengeance-filled scream, turned his voice ragged. "Jason Bourne violated every sacred tenet of my life when he stole my laptop." He lifted the shrimp head as if it were a banner on the field of war. "And now, Ms. Trevor, by all that's holy you're going to get it back."

5

THE CITY OF London, just over a mile square, is the historic core of what is now London proper. In medieval times it encompassed London, Westminster, and Southwark, guarded by a defensive wall built by the Romans in the second century, around which the modern metropolis threw its many arms like a spider extending its web. These days the City, slightly expanded, was the financial hub of London. Aguardiente Bancorp, being largely a commercial rather than a retail bank, had its one and only branch on Chancery Lane, just north of Fleet Street. From its large, stately windows, which faced southwest, Bourne could imagine rising the Temple Bar, the historic gate that a century ago linked the City, the financial center, to the road to Westminster, London's political seat. The Temple Bar, named after the Temple Church, once home of the Knights Templar, was soberly presided over by statues of a griffin and a pair of dragons. Bourne did not, of course, look like Bourne, but rather Noah Perlis, the result of having made a number of purchases at a theatrical makeup shop in Covent Garden.

The gray stone and black marble interior of the bank was equally sober, as befitted an institution that counted as its clients a majority of the international companies doing business in the City. The ecclesiastical vaulted ceiling was so high, it seemed hazed like the sky outside—which, having delivered its burden, hovered now like the ravens in the Tower of London. Bourne crossed the softly echoing floor to the Safe Deposit desk, where a gentleman straight out of a Charles Dickens novel stood with shoulders as thin as a coat hanger, a sallow complexion, and a pair of beady eyes that looked like they had seen everything life had to offer pass them by.

Bourne introduced himself using Perlis's passport as proof of identity. The Dickens cartoon pursed his lips as he squinted at the fine print, his liver-colored hands tilting the open passport into the light. Then abruptly he closed it, said, "One moment please, sir," and vanished into the mysterious interior of the bank.

In the low glass barrier guarding each side of the sallow clerk's window Bourne watched the dim reflections of the people—both customers and bank personnel—behind his back, moving about their business. As he did so, his gaze fell upon a face he had seen before. He'd glimpsed it once inside the shop on Tavistock Street earlier this morning. There was absolutely nothing unusual about it, in fact it was ordinary in every way imaginable. Only Bourne, and perhaps a handful of others with similar experiences and skills, would detect the intentness of the gaze, the way the eyes sliced and diced the vast lobby of the bank into a neat mathematical grid. Bourne watched the eyes moving back and forth in a familiar pattern. The man was figuring possible pathways to him, distances of escape routes to the exits, the placements of the bank guards, and so on.

A moment later the Dickens cartoon returned with no discernible change in his face, which remained as closed as the bank's vault.

"This way, sir," he said in a watery voice that reminded Bourne of a man gargling. He opened a panel in the marble half wall, and Bourne stepped through. He shut it with a soft click of a locking mechanism before leading Bourne between rows of polished wooden desks at which sat a platoon of men and women in dark, conservatively cut suits. Some were talking on phones, others addressing customers who sat on the other side of their desks. None of them looked up as the sallow clerk and Bourne passed them by.

At the end of the regiment of desks, the Dickens cartoon pressed a buzzer beside a door with a pebbled-glass panel that revealed the light from within but nothing else. The buzzer was answered, the door swung open, and the clerk stood aside.

"Straight ahead, then left. The corner office." And then with a vicious little smile: "Mr. Hererra will receive your request." He even talked like a Dickens character.

With a quick nod, Bourne took his left and proceeded to the corner office, whose door was closed. He rapped on it, heard the one word, "Come," and entered.

On the other side of the door he found himself in

a large, expensively furnished office with a stupendous view of the bustling City, both its historic spires and its odd post-modern skyscrapers, the past and future commingling, it seemed to Bourne, uneasily.

In addition to the usual practical office ensemble of desk, chairs, credenzas, cabinets, and the like was a clubby section off to the right dominated by a leather sofa and matching chairs, a glass-and-steel coffee table, lamps, and a sideboard set up as a bar.

As Bourne walked in Diego Hererra, looking even more like his father than he did in the photos, rose, came out from behind his desk, and with a big smile extended his hand for Bourne to shake.

"Noah," he said with a deep hearty voice. "Welcome home!"

The moment Bourne took his hand the tip of a switchblade was pressed against his jacket in the spot over his right kidney.

"Who the hell are you," Diego Hererra said.

Bourne's face held no emotion. "Is this any way for a banker to act?"

"Fuck that."

"I'm Noah Perlis, just like my passport—"

"The hell you are," Diego Hererra said flatly. "Noah was killed in Bali by person or persons unknown less than a week ago. Did you kill him?" He dug the point of the switchblade through Bourne's jacket. "Tell me who you are or I'll bleed you like a pig at slaughter."

"Lovely," Bourne said as he wrapped an arm around Diego Hererra's knife arm, locking it in place. When the banker tensed, he said, "Make a move and I'll fracture your arm so badly it will never work right."

Diego Hererra's dark eyes blazed with barely suppressed fury. "You fucker!"

"Calm down, Señor Hererra, I'm a friend of your father's."

"I don't believe you."

Bourne shrugged. "Call him, then. Tell him Adam Stone is in your office." Bourne had little doubt that Hererra's father would recognize the alias Bourne had used when he met him in Seville several weeks ago. When Diego Hererra made no sign of acquiescence, Bourne switched tactics. His tone was now distinctly conciliatory. "I was a friend of Noah's. Some time ago he'd delivered a set of instructions to me. In the event of his death I was to go to his apartment in Belgravia, where I would find in specific places a duplicate of his passport and the key to a safe-deposit box that resides here. He wanted me to take possession of whatever was in the box. That's all I know."

Diego Hererra remained unconvinced. "If you were a friend of his, how is it he never spoke of you?"

"I imagine it was to protect you, Señor Hererra. You know as well as I do what a secretive life Noah led. Everything was neatly compartmentalized, friends and associates included."

"What about acquaintances?"

"Noah had no acquaintances." This Bourne had intuited from his brief but intense encounters with Perlis in Munich and Bali. "You know that as well as I do."

Diego Hererra grunted. Bourne was about to add that he'd been a friend of Holly's, but some sixth sense born of years of experience warned him against it. Instead he added, "Besides, I was a good friend of Tracy Atherton's."

This seemed to affect Diego Hererra. "Is that so?"

Bourne nodded. "I was with her when she died."

The banker's eyes narrowed. "And where was that?"

"The headquarters of Air Afrika," Bourne said without a moment's hesitation. "Seven seventy-nine El Gamhuria Avenue, Khartoum, to be exact."

"Christ." At last Diego Hererra relaxed. "That was a tragedy, a first-class tragedy."

Bourne let go of his arm, and Hererra closed the switchblade, then gestured for them to cross to the clubby nook. As Bourne sat, he stood in front of the bar.

"Even though it's early, I think we could use a drink." He poured three fingers of Herradura Seleccion Suprema añejo sipping tequila into two thick old-fashioned glasses, handed one to Bourne, then sat down himself. After they'd both savored the first sip, he said, "What happened at the end, can you tell me?"

"She was delivering a painting," Bourne said slowly. "She got caught in a crossfire when the offices were raided by Russian security forces who were after Nikolai Yevsen."

Diego Hererra's head came up. "The arms smuggler?"

Bourne nodded. "He was using his company, Air Afrika, to pick up and deliver the contraband."

The banker's eyes clouded over. "Who was she working for?"

Bourne lifted his glass to his lips, watching Diego's face carefully without seeming to do so. "A man by the name of Leonid Danilovich Arkadin." He took another sip of the aged tequila. "Do you know him?"

Diego Hererra frowned. "Why do you ask?"

"Because," Bourne said slowly and distinctly, "I want to kill him."

He's alive, Leonid Arkadin thought. *Vylacheslav Germanovich Oserov didn't burn to death in that Bangalore hospital corridor. Fuck me, he's still alive.*

He was staring down at a surveillance photo of a man the right side of whose face was horribly disfigured. *But I did him some serious hurt,* he thought, touching his own leg wound, which was healing nicely, *that's for certain.*

He had installed himself in an old convent, dusty and dry as an outdated philosophical text, risen on the outskirts of Puerto Peñasco, a coastal town in the northwest of the Mexican state of Sonora. But then virtually everything in Puerto Peñasco was outdated. An unlovely industrial sprawl, it was redeemed by its broad white beach and warm water.

Puerto Peñasco was off the edge of most people's maps, but that was only one of the reasons he had chosen it. For another, at this time of the year college students poured across the border from Arizona to take advantage of the surf, the high-rise hotels, and a police force that looked the other way as long as sufficient numbers of American dollars changed hands. With so many young people around, Arkadin felt relatively safe; even if by some means Oserov and his hit squad managed to find him, as they had in Bangalore, they'd stick out like monks on spring break.

How Oserov had tracked him down in India was still a vexing mystery. Yes, Gustavo Moreno's laptop was safe and he'd been able to reconnect with the remote server that contained the contracts with his arms clients, but half a dozen of his men were gone and, worse, his vaunted security clearly had a hole. Someone within his organization was funneling information to Maslov.

He was about to go down to the beach when his cell phone rang, and because reception was spotty in this odd backwater, he stayed where he was, staring out at tiers of clouds in the west lit like neon signs.

"Arkadin."

It was Boris Karpov; he felt a certain satisfaction. "Did you keep your destination to yourself?" The pregnant pause was all he needed. "Don't tell me, no one was there, everything was cleaned out."

"Who are they, Arkadin? Who are Maslov's moles inside my organization?"

Arkadin mused for a moment, letting the colonel feel the sharpness of the hook. "I'm afraid it's not as simple as that, Boris Illyich."

"What do you mean?"

"You should have gone alone, you should have believed what I told you," Arkadin said. "Now your end of the bargain has become so much more complicated."

"What bargain?" Karpov asked.

"Take the next international flight you can get on." Arkadin watched the sunset splash the clouds with more and more color until they became so supersaturated, they made his eyes throb. Still, he refused to look away, the beauty was overwhelming. "When you arrive at LAX—I assume you know what that is."

"Of course. It's the international airport in Los Angeles."

"When you get to LAX call the number I'm about to give you."

"But—"

"You want the moles, Boris Illyich, so let's not equivocate. Just do it."

Arkadin closed the connection and walked across the sand. Bending over, he rolled up his trousers. He could already feel the wavelets break over his bare feet.

Arkadin may not have killed Tracy himself," Bourne said, "but he's the one responsible for her death."

Diego Hererra sat back for a moment, his glass balanced on one knee as he held it reflectively. "You fell in love with her, didn't you?" He held up a hand, palm outward. "Don't even bother answering, everyone fell in love with Tracy, without even trying she had that effect." He nodded as if to himself. "Speaking for myself, I think that was the part that made it the most devastating. Some women, you know, they're trying so hard you can practically taste the desperation, and what a turnoff that is. But with Tracy it was another matter entirely. She had..." He snapped his fingers several times. "...what do you call it?"

"Confidence."

"Yes, but more than that."

"Self-possession."

Diego Hererra considered this for a moment, then nodded vigorously. "Yes, that's it, she was almost preternaturally self-possessed."

"Except when she got airsick," Bourne said, thinking of how she had vomited on the horrendous flight from Madrid to Seville.

This caused Diego to throw his head back and laugh.

"She hated planes, all right—pity she was on them so often." He took some more tequila into his mouth, savoring the taste before swallowing. Then he put aside his glass. "I imagine you want to get on with the posthumous assignment our mutual friend charged you with."

"The sooner the better, I suppose." Bourne rose and, together with Diego Hererra, went out of his office, along several corridors, hushed and shadowed, down a long ramp that ended in the open vault. Bourne took out his key, but he saw that he had no need of telling Diego the box number because the banker went right to it. Bourne inserted the key into one of the locks and Diego put his master key into the other.

"Together on the count of three."

They both turned their keys in concert, and the small metal door opened. Diego removed the long box and took it over to a row of small curtained alcoves that ran along one side of the wall. Setting the box down on a ledge inside one of the alcoves, he said, "It's all yours, Señor Stone." He gestured. "Please ring this bell when you're finished and I'll personally fetch you."

"Thank you, Señor Hererra." Bourne entered the alcove, closed the curtain, and sat in the wooden armchair. For a moment, while he listened for Diego Hererra's soft footfalls receding into the distance, he did nothing. Then, leaning forward, he opened the safe-deposit box. Inside was a small book and nothing more. Lifting it out, Bourne opened it to the first page. It seemed to be a kind of diary or, reading a bit farther, a history of sorts, accumulated one incident at a time, from various sources, it appeared. Bourne came to the first of the names and the hairs on his arms stirred. Involuntarily, he glanced around the cubicle, though there was no one around but him. And yet there was a distinct stirring, a restless energy as the ghosts and perhaps goblins emerged from Perlis's very private notes, accumulating around his feet like starving dogs.

Leonid Arkadin, Vylacheslav Germanovich Oserov—or Slava, as Perlis called him—and Tracy Atherton. With a line of sweat appearing at his hairline, Bourne began to read.

Damp sand and salt water squooshed between Arkadin's toes, girls in tiny bikinis and thin dudes in surfer shorts down to their bony knees played volleyball or jogged up and down the beach, just above the high-tide line, beer cans clutched in their hands.

Arkadin was brimming with rage at the corner Maslov and, especially, Oserov had backed him into. He had no doubt that Oserov had convinced Maslov to go after him directly. A frontal assault wasn't Maslov's style; he was more cautious than that, especially in times so fraught with danger for him and the Kazanskaya. The government was gunning for him, just waiting for him to make a mistake. So far, with a combination of indebted friends and Teflon guile, he had managed to stay one step ahead of the Kremlin—neither its inquisitors nor its prosecutors had been able to manufacture charges against him that would stick. Maslov still had too much dirt on enough key federal judges to stave off those forays.

Without having thought about it consciously, Arkadin had waded out into the ocean, so that the water rose above his knees, soaking his trousers. He didn't care;

Mexico afforded a breadth of freedom he'd never before tasted. Maybe it was the slower pace or a lifestyle where pleasure came from fishing or watching the sunrise or drinking tequila long into the night while you danced with a dark-eyed young woman whose multicolored skirts lifted with each twirl she made around you. Money—at least the amounts of money he was used to—was irrelevant here. People made a modest living and were content.

It was at that moment that he saw her, or thought he saw her, emerging from the surf like Venus lifted on her gleaming pink shell. The red sun was in his eyes and he was obliged to squint, to shade his eyes with one hand, but the woman he saw emerging was Tracy Atherton: long and sleek, blond and blue-eyed with the widest smile he'd ever seen. And yet it couldn't be Tracy, because she was dead.

He watched her coming toward him. At one point she turned and looked directly at him and the resemblance fell apart. He turned away into the last of the canted sunlight.

Arkadin had met Tracy in St. Petersburg, at the Hermitage Museum. He had been in Moscow two years, working for Maslov. She was there to view the czarist treasures, while he was there for an onerous rendezvous with Oserov. But then all his meetings with Oserov were onerous, often ending in violence. Maslov's chief assassin at the time had killed a child—a little boy no more than six years old—in cold blood. For this obscenity, Arkadin had beaten his face to a pulp and dislocated his shoulder. He would have killed him outright if his friend Tarkanian hadn't intervened. Ever since that incident the resentment between the two men continued to build until most recently igniting in Bangalore. But Oserov, like a vampire, could not be easily killed. With an ironic laugh, Arkadin decided that next time he'd pound a wooden stake through Oserov's heart. That Dimitri Maslov had continually forced them to work together, Arkadin was convinced, was a deliberate act of sadism for which Maslov would one day pay.

That icy winter's morning in St. Petersburg he had arrived early to ensure that Oserov hadn't set up some arcane form of trap. Instead he found a tall slim blonde with huge cornflower-blue eyes and an even wider smile contemplating a portrait of Empress Elizabeth Petrovna. The blonde wore an ankle-length deerskin coat with a high collar dyed an improbable sky blue, beneath which, just peeking out, was a blood-red silk shirt. Without preamble she asked him what he thought of the portrait.

Arkadin, who had taken absolutely no notice of the painting or of anything else of a decorative nature in the vast rooms, peered at the portrait and said, "That was painted in 1758. What possible meaning could it have for me?"

The blonde turned, contemplating him with the same disarming intensity she had given to the painting. "This is the history of your country." She pointed with a slim, long-fingered hand. "Louis Tocque, the man who painted this, was one of the leading artists of the day. He traveled all the way from Paris to Russia at the behest of Elizabeth Petrovna to paint her."

Arkadin, ignoramus that he was, shrugged. "So?"

The blonde's smile widened even more. "It's a measure of Russia's world status and power that he came. In those days France was quite enamored with Russia and vice versa. This painting should make all Russians proud."

Arkadin, about to make an acerbic retort, instead bit his tongue and returned his gaze to the regal woman in the painting.

"She's beautiful, isn't she?" the blonde said.

"Well, I've never met anyone remotely like her. She doesn't seem real."

"And yet she was." The blonde made a gesture as if to guide his eyes back to the empress. "Imagine yourself in the past, imagine yourself in the painting standing next to her."

And now, as if looking at the empress for the first time, or through the blonde's eyes, Arkadin heard himself agree. "Yes," he said. "Yes, I suppose she is beautiful."

"Ah, then my time here has been a success." The blonde's smile hadn't faded one iota. She extended her hand toward him. "I'm Tracy Atherton, by the way."

For a moment Arkadin considered giving a false name, which he did almost by rote. Instead he'd said, "Leonid Danilovich Arkadin."

The air had suddenly been perfumed with the tincture of history, a spicy, mysterious scent of rose and cedar. Much later he'd worked out what it was that drew him as well as shamed him. He felt like a student, too ignorant or truant to have learned his lessons. Around her he'd always felt his lack of formal education, like a nakedness. And yet, even from that first meeting, he sensed a use for her, that he could absorb what she had learned. He learned from her the value of knowledge, but part of him never forgave her for the way she made him feel, and he used her mercilessly, treated her cruelly, as he bound her ever closer to him.

This clarity came later, of course. At the moment all he felt was an onrush of anger and, without a word, he whirled away from her, stalking off to find Oserov, whose company, for the moment, seemed preferable to this creature's.

But finding Oserov did nothing to allay his sudden discomfort, so he insisted on changing protocol, removing them from the Hermitage altogether. They walked out onto Millionnaya Street, where he found a café before their lips and cheeks grew too chapped from the icy wind.

Snow had begun to fall with an odd dry rustle like predators snuffling in the underbrush, and Arkadin would never forget how Tracy Atherton had materialized out of it. Her deerskin coat swayed about her ankles like icy surf.

In those days, directly after Dimitri Maslov had sent Oserov and Mischa Tarkanian to liberate him from the prison of his hometown of Nizhny Tagil, Oserov was his superior, a fact that Oserov lorded over him. Oserov was in the middle of lecturing him on how to properly kill a politician, the reason for their trip to St. Petersburg. This particular politician had stupidly aligned himself against Maslov, and so had to be eliminated as quickly and efficiently as possible. Arkadin knew this, and Oserov knew he knew it. Nevertheless, the shit gleefully drove home his points with mind-numbing repetitiveness, as if Arkadin were a backward and insolent five-year-old.

Not many people would have dared interrupt Oserov, but Tracy did. Entering the café, she spotted Arkadin, strode confidently up to their table, and said, "Why, hello, fancy meeting you here," in her soft British accent.

Oserov, pausing in mid-rant, looked up at her with a glare that would turn most people to stone. Tracy merely widened her smile and, pulling up a chair from a nearby table, said, "You don't mind if I join you, do you?" She sat down and ordered a coffee before either of them uttered a word.

The moment the waiter left, Oserov's face darkened ominously. "Listen, I don't know who you are or why you're here, but we're in the middle of important business."

"I saw that," Tracy said blandly, waving a hand. "Go ahead, don't mind me."

Oserov pushed his chair back with a teeth-grinding scrape. "Hey, fuck off, lady."

"Calm down," Arkadin began.

"And you, shut the fuck up." Oserov stood, leaning over the table. "If you don't leave now—right this fucking second—I'm going to throw you out on your pretty little ass."

Tracy stared up at him without blinking. "There's no need for that kind of language."

"She's right, Oserov. I'll escort her—"

But just at that moment Tracy took hold of the end of Oserov's tie, which was threatening to dip into her coffee, and Oserov lunged at her, grabbing at the collar of her coat and hauling her to her feet. Her silk shirt ripped, the violent action bringing them unwanted attention from the café's patrons and staff. Their mission was supposed to be under the radar, and Oserov was ruining that.

Arkadin, on his feet, said softly, "Let her go." When Oserov maintained his grip, he added, even more quietly, "Let her go, or I'll knife you right here."

Oserov looked down at the point of a switchblade that Arkadin had aimed at his liver. His face darkened further, and something malefic bloomed in his hard, glinting eyes.

"I won't forget this," he said in an eerie tone as he released her.

Since he was still staring into Tracy's face it was unclear to whom Oserov was speaking, but Arkadin suspected he was addressing both of them. Before anything worse happened Arkadin came around the table and, taking Tracy by the elbow, walked her out of the café.

The snow was swirling down with singular intent, and almost immediately their hair and shoulders were coated with it.

"Well, that was interesting," she said.

Arkadin, searching her face, could find no fear in it. "You've made a very bad enemy, I'm afraid."

"Go back inside," Tracy said, as if she hadn't heard him. "Without your coat you're liable to freeze to death."

"I don't think you understand—"

"Do you know Doma?"

He blinked. Did she never listen to what anyone said to her? But the tide she rode was taking him farther and farther from the known shore. "The restaurant on the Hermitage embankment? Everyone knows Doma."

"Eight o'clock tonight." She gave him one of her

patented smiles and left him there in the snow, observed by the glowering Oserov.

The girl whom he'd mistaken for Tracy was long gone, but Arkadin could still make out the damp traces of her narrow footprints in the sand beyond the high-tide line. There were jellyfish in the water now, opalescent and glowing. In the distance a Mexican woman sang a sad ranchera from the speakers of a radio. The jellyfish seemed to be swaying to the music. Night was falling, a black sky studded with stars heading his way. Arkadin returned to the convent to light candles instead of switching on the electric lights, listen to sad rancheras instead of turning on the TV. Seemingly overnight Mexico had seeped into his blood.

I'm beginning to understand why Arkadin and Oserov are mortal enemies, Bourne thought as he looked up from Perlis's notebook. Hate is a powerful emotion, hate makes normally smart people stupid, or at least makes them less vigilant. Perhaps I've finally found Arkadin's Achilles' heel.

He'd read enough for the moment. Closing the lid on the safe-deposit box, he pocketed the book and rang the bell to indicate that he was finished. While on the surface it seemed odd that Perlis would use such an old-fashioned method to record what he obviously considered vital intelligence, on further consideration it made perfect sense. Electronic media were all too prone to hacking in so many forms that a handwritten copy was the answer. Kept in a vault, it was perfectly secure, and if the need arose it could be irrevocably destroyed with nothing but a match. These days going low-tech was often the best defense against computer hackers, who could infiltrate the most sophisticated electronic networks and retrieve even supposedly deleted files.

Diego Hererra pulled aside the curtain, took the metal box, returned it to its numbered niche, closed the door behind it, and the two men secured the box with their respective keys.

As they walked out of the vault Bourne said, "I need a favor."

Diego glanced at him expectantly, but noncommittally.

"There is a man who has been following me. He's in the bank, waiting for me to return."

Now Diego smiled. "But of course. I can show you to the door used by customers who require, shall we say, a higher degree of discretion than is the norm." They were almost at his office when a ripple of concern crossed his face. "Why is this man following you, may I ask?"

"I don't know," Bourne said, "though I seem to collect people like him like flies."

Diego gave a low laugh. "Noah often said more or less the same thing."

Bourne realized that this was as close as Diego Hererra was going to get to asking him if he worked for Perlis's outfit. He was beginning to like Diego as much as he liked his father, however, that was no reason to tell him the truth. He nodded as if in tacit answer to Diego's unspoken question.

"I don't know who he is, either, but it's important I find out," Bourne said.

Diego spread his hands. "I am at your service, Señor Stone," he said in true Catalan style.

Diego may be living in London, Bourne thought, *but his heart is still in Seville.*

"I need to get this man out of your bank and onto the street before I leave. A fire alarm would do nicely."

Diego nodded. "Consider it done." He lifted a finger. "On the condition that you come to my house tomorrow evening." He gave Bourne an address in Belgravia. "We have friends in common, it would be rude of me not to offer my hospitality." Then he grinned, showing even, white teeth. "We'll have a bite to eat, then, if you fancy a flutter, we'll go out to the Vesper Club on the Fulham Road."

Diego had a take-charge attitude that was more no-nonsense than egotistical, again very much like his father. This was in line with the profile he'd gleaned from his Web search some weeks ago, but the Vesper Club, a members-only casino strictly for high-rollers, was not. Bourne stuck the anomaly in the back of his mind and prepared to go into action.

The fire alarm went off in Aguardiente Bancorp. Bourne and Diego Hererra watched as the guards swiftly and methodically herded everyone out the front door, Bourne's tracker among them.

Bourne emerged from the side entrance of the bank, and as the clients milled around the sidewalk, unsure what to do next, he located his tail, keeping the crowd between them. The man was watching the front entrance for Bourne, all the while in a position to check out the bank's side entrance.

Slipping through the crowd, which had now doubled in size due to curious pedestrians and drivers gawking from their stopped cars, Bourne came up behind the tracker and said: "Walk straight ahead, up the road toward Fleet Street." He dug his knuckle into the small of the man's back. "Everyone will think a silenced pistol shot is a lorry backfiring." He slammed the heel of his hand against the back of the man's head. "Did I tell you to turn around? Now start walking."

The man did as Bourne ordered him, snaking into the fringes of the crowd and picking his way, more quickly now, up Middle Temple Lane. He was broad-shouldered with a dirty-blond crew cut, a face empty as an abandoned lot, with rough skin as if he had an allergy or had been in the wind for too many years. Bourne knew he'd try something, and sooner rather than later. A businessman, lost on his cell phone, hurried toward them, and Bourne felt Crew-Cut leaning toward him. Crew-Cut deliberately bumped against the businessman, allowed himself to be jostled sideways by the collision, and was in the process of turning back on Bourne, his right arm bent, his fingers coming together to form a cement block, when Bourne slammed him behind the knee with the sole of his shoe. At almost the same instant Bourne caught his right arm in a vise created by his elbow and forearm, and cracked the bone.

The man buckled over, groaning. When Bourne bent to lift him to his feet, he would have driven his knee into Bourne's groin, but Bourne sidestepped and the knee struck him painfully, if harmlessly, on the thigh instead.

At that point Bourne became aware of a car racing the wrong way down the street, too fast in fact to slow down, let alone stop before it hit them. He threw the man's body into the path of the oncoming vehicle and, using the man's shoulders as a base, vaulted over the hood. With a screech of brakes, the car tried valiantly to decelerate. The moment his shoes hit the top of the car bullets pierced it from the interior, trying to find him, but he was already sliding down the trunk.

Behind him he heard the liquid *thunk!* as the car slammed into the body, then the stink of burning rubber flayed off the tires. Risking a glance over his shoulder he saw two men emerge, armed with Glocks—the driver and the shooter. As they turned toward him, the huge knot of patrons and staff that had been standing outside Aguardiente Bancorp came streaming up the street, voices raised, cell phone cameras clicking like a forest of cicadas, trapping the two men, pinning them in place. Now curious pedestrians appeared from Fleet Street. Within moments the familiar high–low clamor of police klaxons filled the air, and Bourne, worming into the midst of the throng, slipped quietly away, turned the corner onto Fleet Street, and melted into the city.

6

'VE LOST TOUCH with him," Frederick Willard said.

"You've lost touch with him before," Peter Marks pointed out, he thought helpfully.

"This is different," Willard snapped. He was wearing a conservatively cut chalk-striped suit, a starched blue shirt with white collar and cuffs, and a navy-blue bow tie with white polka dots. "Unless we're both careful and clever, this is liable to become permanent."

Since coming aboard the resurrected Treadstone, Marks had learned quickly that it was a mortal sin to mistake Willard's age for a loss of vigor. The man might be in his sixties but he could still outrun half the field agents at CI, and as for critical brain function—the ability to think through a problem to its best solution—Marks thought him as good as Alex Conklin, Treadstone's founder. On top of all that, he possessed the uncanny ability to ferret out his adversary's weak spots, finding the most novel ways of exploiting them. That Willard was something of a sadist, Marks had no doubt, but that was nothing new in their line of shadow work where sadists, masochists, and every other psychological variant congregated like flies on a rotting corpse. The trick, Marks had found, was discovering the quirk of each person's personality before he used it to bury you.

They had arranged themselves on a sofa in the foyer of a members-only—and from the looks of things men-only—organization to which Oliver Liss belonged.

"The Monition Club," Marks said during his hundredth glance around. "What the hell kind of place is this?"

"I don't know," Willard said waspishly. "I've been trying to find out all day without discovering a scrap of information about it."

"There must be something. Who owns this building, for instance?"

"A holding company in Grenada." Willard grunted. "Clearly a shell corporation, and the trail gets more convoluted after that. Whoever these people are they definitely don't want to be known."

"No law against that," Marks said.

"Perhaps not, but it strikes me as both strange and suspect."

"Maybe I should look into it further."

The interior was as echoey as a cathedral and, with its stone-block walls, Gothic arches, and gilded crosses, resembled an ecclesiastical institution. Thick carpets and oversize furniture abetted the oppressive hush. Now and again someone strode by, spoke briefly to the uniformed woman behind the high desk in the lobby's center, then passed into the shadows.

The atmosphere reminded Marks of the prevailing mood of the new CI. From what he'd gleaned from his former colleagues, a new set of unsmiling faces in the support staff and an almost bitter level of gloom infected the hallways. This toxic tone somewhat assuaged the guilt he'd been feeling about bailing on CI, especially because he hadn't been there for Soraya when she'd returned from Cairo. On the other hand, Willard had assured him that he'd be of more help to her now that he'd moved on. *"This way your wisdom and advice will seem more objective and therefore have more weight,"* Willard had said. As it turned out, he'd been right. Marks was quite sure that he was the only one who could have persuaded her to join Treadstone.

"What are you thinking?" Willard said unexpectedly.

"Nothing."

"Wrong answer. Our number one priority is to figure out a way to reestablish clandestine contact with Leonid Arkadin."

"What makes Arkadin so important? Besides, of course, the fact that he's Treadstone's first graduate and the only one that got away."

Willard glared. He didn't care for his own words being thrown back in his face, especially by an inferior. That was the problem with Willard—one of his many quirks—as Marks, as quick a study as had ever entered CI's ranks, had come to understand: Willard was convinced of his superiority, and he treated everyone accordingly. That there might be a grain or two of truth to his belief only solidified his fierce control. In fact, Marks guessed that this arrogance was what had allowed Willard to infiltrate and maintain his position as steward inside the NSA for so many years. It had to be so much easier to take orders from your masters when you knew you were in the process of fucking them over.

"It pains me to have to spell this out for you, Marks, but inside Arkadin's mind lie the last secrets of Treadstone. Conklin submitted him to a raft of psychological techniques that are now lost."

"What about Jason Bourne?"

"Because of how Arkadin turned out, Conklin didn't use that technique set on Bourne, so in that sense the two of them are different."

"How so?"

Willard, whose attention to detail was legendary, shot his cuffs so that they were of precisely equal lengths. "Arkadin has no soul."

"What?" Marks shook his head as if he hadn't heard correctly. "Unless I miss my guess, there's no known technique scientific or otherwise for destroying a soul."

Willard rolled his eyes. "For God's sake, Peter, I'm not talking about a machine out of a science-fiction novel." He rose to his feet. "But ask your parish priest the next time you see him. You'll be surprised at his answer." He beckoned for Marks to do the same. "Here comes our new lord and master, Oliver Liss."

Marks glanced at his watch. "Forty minutes late. Right on time."

Oliver Liss lived on the wrong coast. He looked, acted, and possibly even thought of himself as if he were a movie star. He was handsome in that way the Hollywood elite cultivated, except that he didn't seem to work at it. Maybe it was simply superb genes. In any event, when he entered a room he required no other entourage than his own personal sun burning at his back. He was tall, lean, and athletic, engendering bitter envy in those men he met. He liked his drinks strong, his meat red, and his women young, blond, and buxom. He was, in short, precisely the sort of man Hugh Hefner had envisioned when he created *Playboy*.

Cranking up a mechanical smile without breaking stride, Liss gestured for them to follow him past Cerberus's gates and into the Monition Club proper. It was breakfast time. Apparently, following Monition Club tradition, that meal was taken on an enclosed brick terrace, which overlooked a cloistered atrium whose center was as neatly laid out as an herb garden, though this time of the year there was scarcely anything to see but fallow ground and a geometry of low cast-iron fences, presumably to keep the mint out of the sage.

Liss led them to a spacious table of inlaid stone. He exuded the scents of beeswax and expensive cologne. Today he was dressed like a country gentleman in flannel trousers, tweed jacket, and a tie with a print of hungry-looking foxes. His expensive ox-blood loafers shone like mirrors.

After they ordered, drank their fresh-squeezed juice, and sipped their bracing French-press coffee, he came right to the point. "I know you have been busy moving into our new offices, taking possession of the electronics and so forth, but I want you to set all that aside. I'm hiring an office manager for that, anyway, you're both far too valuable to waste." His voice was as rich and lustrous as his shoes. He rubbed his hands together, a beloved uncle delighted at the latest family reunion. "I want you both concentrated on one matter and one matter only. It seems that with his untimely demise Noah Perlis left some loose ends."

Willard was taken slightly aback. "You're not asking us to swim in Black River's toxic waste, are you?"

"Not in the least. I spent six months untangling myself from the organization I helped found because I could see the train wreck coming. Imagine how that feels, gentlemen." He raised a finger. "Oh, yes, Frederick, in your case you have a glimmering of what I've been going through." He shook his head. "No, Noah was handling this particular bit of business for me personally, no one else in Black River had a clue." He sat back as their breakfasts were served, then, over his perfectly cooked eggs Benedict, he continued. "Noah had a ring. He obtained this ring at great cost and, I believe, personal tragedy. It is, not to put too fine a point on it, a singular ring. Though on the outside it looks like a simple gold wedding band, it is something far different. Here, take a look at these." He passed around several color photos of the item in question.

"As you can see, there are a series of symbols—graphemes, if you want to be technical—engraved around the inside."

"What is a grapheme?" Marks asked.

"The basic unit of language, any language, really."

Willard squinted. "Yes, but what the devil language is it?"

"Its own, manufactured out of ancient Sumerian,

Latin, and God alone knows what other dead language, possibly one that's been lost to the modern world."

"You want us to drop everything for this?" Marks looked incredulous. "Who do you think we are, Indiana Jones?"

Liss, who had been in the process of chewing a bite of food, smirked. "This is not so old as that, my smart-aleck friend. In fact, it probably hasn't been in existence more than a decade or two."

"A ring?" Willard shook his head. "What do you want with it?"

"Eyes Only." Liss winked and tapped the side of his nose. "In any event, Noah had the ring when he was killed by Jason Bourne. It's clear that Bourne killed him in order to get the ring."

Marks shook his head. His lack of antipathy toward Bourne was well known. "Why would he do that? He must have had a good reason."

"What you need to keep in mind is that Bourne has murdered again, without provocation." Liss looked hard at him. "Find Bourne and you'll find the ring." He carefully broke a yolk and dipped a triangle of toast into it. "I got a tip that Bourne was seen in the Heathrow arrivals terminal, so it's a good bet he's gone to Noah's apartment in Belgravia. Start there. I've sent all the particulars to your cells and booked you on an evening flight to Heathrow so you'll be bright-eyed, bushy-tailed, and ready to hit the tarmac at a full sprint when you arrive tomorrow morning."

Willard put aside the photos and made a face that sent warning bells ringing in Marks's head.

"When you agreed to fund Treadstone," Willard said

in a quietly ominous voice, "you agreed that I would be in charge of operations."

"Did I?" Liss rolled his eyes as if trying to recall. Then he shook his head. "No. No, I didn't."

"Is this . . . What is this, some kind of joke?"

"I don't think so, no." Liss popped the toast triangle into his mouth and chewed luxuriously.

"I have a very specific agenda." Willard carefully enunciated each word with a cutting edge. "A particular reason for jump-starting Treadstone."

"I'm well aware of your obsession with this Russian Leonid Arkadin, but the fact is, Frederick, you didn't jump-start Treadstone. I did. Treadstone is mine, I fund it lock, stock, and ammunition. You work for me, to think otherwise is to gravely misjudge the parameters of your singular employment."

Marks suspected that it had dawned on Willard that by switching from CI to Oliver Liss, he'd merely exchanged one hated taskmaster for another. And as he himself had said when he'd recruited Marks, there was no turning back from a deal with the devil. They were both in this to the bitter end, into whatever circle of hell that might lead them.

Liss was also watching Willard. He smiled benignly and pointed with the eggy tines of his fork. "You'd better eat up, your breakfast is getting cold."

After catching a bite to eat, during which time he read more of Perlis's account of the blood feud between Arkadin and Oserov, Bourne returned to Belgravia, this time to the street where Tracy Atherton had lived. It was green and cool through the mist that swirled in the gutters and entwined around the chimneys of the row houses. Her house was neat and trim, identical to its neighbors. A steep flight of steps ran up to the front door where, he observed, there was a brass plate with the names of the people inhabiting the six flats.

He pressed the bell for T. ATHERTON, as if she were still alive and he was arriving to spend the afternoon with her in cozy repose, drinking, eating, making love, and talking about art and its long, complex history. He was surprised, then, when the buzzer sounded, unlatching the front door. Pushing his way inside, he found himself in a narrow vestibule, dim and damply chilly in the way only London indoor spaces can be in winter or spring.

Tracy's flat was on the third floor, up flights of narrow, very steep stairs, the treads of which creaked beneath his weight now and again. He found it all the way in the rear and he recalled her saying, *"There's a mews out back with a flowering pear tree that a pair of house martins nest in come spring."* He imagined the house martins would be nesting there right about now. It was a bittersweet thought.

The door opened a crack as he was warily approaching. The figure that revealed itself was backlit and for a moment he stood stock-still, his heart racing, because he was quite certain he was looking at Tracy. Tall, willowy, blond hair.

"Yes? May I help you?"

Her eyes broke the spell; they were brown, not blue, and they weren't as large as Tracy's. He felt himself breathe again. "My name is Adam Stone. I was a friend of Tracy's."

"Oh, yes, Trace told me about you." She did not offer her hand. Her expression was carefully neutral. "I'm Chrissie Lincoln, Tracy's sister."

Still, she did not move out of the doorway. "She met you on a flight to Madrid."

"Actually, the flight was from Madrid to Seville."

"That's right." Chrissie watched him warily. "Trace traveled so much, it was a good thing she liked flying."

Bourne could see that he was being tested. "She hated flying. She got sick on the flight five minutes after she introduced herself." He waited for her to say something, then: "May I come in? I'd like to speak to you about Tracy."

"I suppose." She stood back, almost reluctantly.

He walked in and she closed the door behind him. Tracy had been right, the flat was tiny, but as beautiful as she had been. Furniture in butter yellows and deep oranges, crisp cream curtains framed each window, throw pillows here and there in polka dots, animal prints, and stripes added bright bits of color. He walked across the living room and into her bedroom.

"Are you looking for something in particular, Mr. Stone?"

"Call me Adam." Somehow he knew there would be French doors out onto the back, and there was the pear tree in the mews. "I'm looking for the house martins."

"I beg your pardon?" Her voice was pitched a bit higher, thinner, and her speech was more rapid than her sister's had been.

"Tracy said that come spring a pair of house martins nested in that pear tree."

She was at his shoulder. Her hair smelled of lemon.

She wore an inexpensive cotton man's shirt with the sleeves rolled up, revealing sun-browned arms, jeans, not the fashionable low-riding ones, but sturdy Levi's with the cuffs rolled up, cheap flats, scuffed and worn at the heels, and was in a light sweat as if she had been cleaning or rooting around for some time. She wore no jewelry, not even a wedding band. And yet her last name was Lincoln, not Atherton.

"Do you see a sign of them?" she asked in a brittle voice.

"No," he said, turning away.

She frowned momentarily and remained silent for a long time.

"Chrissie?"

When she didn't answer he went and got her a glass of cold water from the kitchen. She took it without comment and drank it slowly and methodically, as if it were medicine.

When she put the glass down, she said to him, "I'm afraid this was a mistake letting you in. I'd prefer if you left."

Bourne nodded. He'd seen the flat; he didn't know what he'd expected to find, maybe it was nothing at all, save the scent of her, lingering long after she had left. The night they had shared in Khartoum was far more intimate than if they had made love, an act that despite its name could seem impersonal, even detached. The revelation that came later, that Tracy had been working for Leonid Arkadin, had come like a cold slap across the face. But in the weeks after her death he'd been haunted by the notion that something was wrong with that equation. Not that he doubted she'd been in Arkadin's em-

ploy, but deep down he couldn't escape the notion that
the story wasn't that simple. It was altogether possible
that he'd come here looking for some form of proof, a
confirmation of his suspicion.

They had moved back to the front door now, and
now Chrissie opened it for him. As he was about to step
out, she said, "Mr. Stone—"

"Adam."

She tried to smile and failed, her face seemed tight
and pained. "Do you know what happened in Khartoum?"

Bourne hesitated. He stared out into the hallway,
but what he was seeing was Tracy's face, spattered with
blood, as he cradled it in his lap.

"Please. I know I've been less than hospitable. I—I'm
not thinking straight, you see." She stood back for him
to reenter.

Bourne turned back one hand on the partially open
door. "Her death was an accident."

Chrissie looked at him fearfully, expectantly. "You
know this?"

"I was there."

He saw the blood leave her face. She was staring at
him fixedly, as if she couldn't look away, as if with a terrible clarity she saw an accident about to happen.

"Will you tell me how she died?"

"I don't think you want to hear the details."

"Yes," she said. "I do. I—I need to know. She was my
only sibling." She shut the door and locked it and went
over to an armchair, but she did not sit down. Rather,
she stood behind it, staring into the middle distance.
"I've been in a kind of personal hell since I got the news.

A sister's death, it's—well, it's not like any other death. I—I can't explain it."

Bourne watched her as she stood, her fingers dug into the high, arched back of the chair.

"She was struck by shards of glass, one went through her. She bled out in minutes; there was nothing anyone could do."

"Poor Trace." She was gripping the chair back so hard, her knuckles had turned white. "I begged her not to go, just as I begged her not to take that cursed assignment."

"What assignment?"

"That bloody Goya."

"Why did she tell you about the Goya?"

"It wasn't the painting, but the assignment. She said it was going to be her last. She wanted me to know that. Because she knew I disapproved of what she did, I suppose."

She shuddered. "Evil thing, that Black Painting."

"You say that as if it were alive."

She turned back to him. "In a sense it was, because it was connected with that man."

"Arkadin."

"She never told me his name. From what I could gather he gave her extremely dangerous assignments, but he paid her so well she accepted them all, at least that's what she told me."

"You didn't believe her?"

"Oh, I believed her, all right, when we were young we made a pact never to lie to each other." Her hair was a shade darker than her sister's, and thicker, lush even, and her face was a bit less angular, softer, more open. It was also more careworn. She moved more quickly than Tracy, or perhaps it was that she moved in nervous bursts as if set off by a series of tiny interior explosions. "The problem arose when we grew up. I'm positive there were a great many things about her private life she refused to share."

"You didn't push it."

"Secrecy was her choice," she said defensively. "I honored her wishes."

He followed her back into the bedroom. She stood looking around as if dazed, as if she'd lost her sister and now inexplicably couldn't find her. Light slanting in through the window was splintered in lozenges and rectangles by the pear tree. It was mellow, toned, like the surface of a sepia print. She moved into one of those luminous geometric shapes now.

Her arms wound around her waist as if she were trying to hold in her emotions. "But of one thing I'm quite certain. That man's a monster, she'd never have worked for him voluntarily. I'm sure he must have had something on her."

An echo of his own suspicions. Maybe she had something to tell him after all. "Can you think of what it might be?"

"I already told you, Trace was the most secretive person on earth."

"So there was nothing, no odd response to your questions, nothing of that nature."

"No." Chrissie drew the word out into two syllables. "I mean there was one thing, but, well, it's kind of ridiculous."

"Ridiculous? How so?"

"I remember one time we were together and, for once, there didn't seem to be anything to talk about after I'd exhausted the news about me. I was bored with all that, anyway, it was old news to me. I guess I got a bit frustrated, because I said, laughing, you know, something about was she hiding someone up her sleeve."

Bourne cocked his head. "And?"

"Well, I mean she didn't think it was funny, did she? She didn't laugh, that's for sure. I'd meant a boyfriend or a husband but she said, quite fiercely, that I was the only family she had."

"You don't think—"

"No, I don't," Chrissie said emphatically. "That wouldn't be like her at all. She didn't get on well with Mum and Dad, she was offended by everything about them. And they were deeply offended by her rebelliousness. I was the good daughter. I became a professor at Oxford, following in my father's footsteps. But Trace . . . God only knows what they thought she was up to. Anyway, from the time she was thirteen or so they would fight like cats and dogs, until one day she stormed out of the house and never went back. No, I can tell you that she didn't want a family of her own."

"And you find that sad."

"No," Chrissie said, rather defiant. "I find it admirable."

Well, at least we get to go after Bourne," Marks said. "That's some consolation, he's one half of the Treadstone equation, isn't he?"

"Don't be dense," Willard snapped. "Liss didn't even

bother to mention it as a peace offering because he knew I'd laugh in his face. He knows I'm the only person on earth—at least one under his control—who can get to Bourne without having his neck or back broken. No, he planned this out from the beginning, it was his whole reason for agreeing to back Treadstone in the first place, and I played right into his hand."

"That's a pretty damn high price to pay for a ring," Marks said. "It must be very rare, costly, or important."

"I'd like to have another look at that photo of the engraving," Willard mused. "That's our best chance of finding out something about the ring, since Liss won't tell us."

They had been walking across the Mall, from the Washington Monument toward the Lincoln Memorial, hands in overcoat pockets, backs bowed against the wind, but at the last instant they had decided to make a detour to the Vietnam Veterans Memorial. Along the way they had, each in his own way, checked for tags and tails. They didn't trust anyone, least of all Oliver Liss.

They stopped, and Willard stared at the wall, somber in its eternal shadows, sighed deeply, and closed his eyes. A small, secret smile crept across his lips with the stealth of a cat. "He thinks he's checkmated me, but I've got a queen he can't control."

Marks shook his head. "I have no idea what you're talking about."

Willard's eyes popped open. "Soraya Moore."

Marks looked at him, alarmed. "Oh, no."

"I told you to try to recruit her and you did."

A pair of vets in uniform, one pushing the other, who was in a wheelchair, came down the long, graceful ramp into the full majesty of the wall and stopped in front of the names. The vet in the wheelchair was without legs. He handed his friend a small bouquet and a miniature American flag on a wooden stand. His friend laid them at the foot of the wall where their compatriots' names were engraved for all time.

There was a glitter in Willard's eyes as he turned away from the scene. "I have her first assignment: Find Leonid Arkadin."

"You said you'd lost him," Marks pointed out. "Where is she going to start looking?"

"That's her problem," Willard said. "She's a smart girl, I've been following her career since she came to prominence at Typhon." He smiled. "Have a little faith, Peter. She's first-rate material, plus, she's got a built-in advantage over you or me. She's a very good-looking female—highly desirable—which means Arkadin will have her scent before she comes within a block of him."

His brain was traveling at speed in its own peculiar orbit. "I want her with him, Peter. I want her attached to Arkadin, she's going to tell me what he's doing and why he's doing it."

The two vets' heads were bowed, locked within their private memories as tourists and relatives of other fallen filed by, some touching names here and there. A Japanese tour leader, yellow pennant held high, gathered her photo-clicking flock to her.

Marks ran a hand through his hair. "You can't expect me—What? Jesus, you want me to pimp her out?"

Willard looked like he was sucking on a lemon. "Since when did you become a Boy Scout? Not in CI, surely. The Old Man would've had your heart for lunch."

"She's a friend of mine, Fred. Longtime."

"There are no friends in this business, Peter, just the bitterly oppressed. I am Liss's slave and you are mine and she is yours. That's how it works."

Marks looked as glum as Willard had at the end of their breakfast with Liss.

"You will give her her assignment before we leave for the airport—" Willard glanced at his watch. "—which gives you less than six hours to prep for London and do the deed." His smile was all teeth. "More than enough time for a clever fellow like you, wouldn't you say?"

7

"TIME FOR ME to go," Bourne said. "We should both get some sleep."

"I don't want to go to sleep," Chrissie said and, with a bleak smile, sang, *"Bad dreams in the night."* She cocked her head inquiringly. "Kate Bush. Do you know her songs?"

"That's from 'Wuthering Heights,' isn't it?"

"Yes, my daughter, Scarlett, is a big fan. Not much Kate Bush up at Oxford, I can tell you."

It was after midnight. He had ventured out to an Indian restaurant, bought their dinner, and had taken it back to Tracy's flat, where, after swallowing a couple of desultory bites, Chrissie watched him eat. Considering the violent events earlier, outside the bank, it was best if he didn't venture too far afield, even back to his hotel.

Watching her sitting across from him on the sofa, he

recalled another fragment of the conversation he'd had with Tracy in Khartoum the night before she died:

"In your mind you can be anyone, do anything. Everything is malleable, whereas in the real world, effecting change—any change—is so bloody difficult, the effort is wearying."

"You could adopt an entirely new identity," he had replied, *"one where effecting change is less difficult because now you re-create your own history."*

She had nodded. *"Yes, but that has its own pitfalls. No family, no friends—unless, of course, you don't mind being absolutely isolated."*

"The night before she died," he said now, "she told me something that led me to believe that in another time, another place she would have enjoyed having her own family."

For a moment it seemed as if all the air had gone out of her. "Well, that's bloody irony for you." Then, recovering somewhat, she went on, "You know, the funny thing is—well, it's bloody tragic, when I think about it now—I sometimes envied *her.* She wasn't tied down, had never married, she could go where she pleased, when she pleased, and she did. She was like a skyrocket, in that way, because of how she loved to walk on the wild side. It was as if danger was—I don't know—an aphrodisiac, or maybe it was more like the feeling people get when they ride a roller coaster, that sense of going so fast they're almost, but not quite, out of control." She gave a bitter little laugh. "The last time I rode a roller coaster I got sick to my stomach."

Part of him genuinely felt for her, but another part, the professional part, the Bourne identity, in other words, was seeking a way to worm his way farther in, a probe to see if there was anything else Chrissie could tell him about Tracy and her mysterious relationship with Leonid Arkadin. He saw her only as a means to an end, a stepping-stone, not a human being. He hated himself for feeling that way, and yet his dispassion was part of what made him successful. This was who he was, or at least what Treadstone had made of him. In any event, for good or for ill, he was damaged, trained, highly skilled. Just like Arkadin. And yet there was a gulf between them—an abyss so vast, Bourne could not see its bottom or even guess at its depth. He and Arkadin faced each other across this divide, invisible perhaps to anyone but themselves, searching for ways to destroy each other without destroying themselves in the process. There were times when he wondered whether that would be possible, whether to rid the world of one, both had to go.

"You know what I wish?" She turned to him. "Remember that film *Superman,* not a great film, admittedly, but anyway, Lois Lane dies and Superman is so grief-stricken that he launches himself into the air. He flies around the earth, faster and faster, faster than the speed of sound, faster than the speed of light, so fast that he reverses time to the moment just before Lois will be killed, and he saves her." Her eyes had settled on his face, but it was something else she was seeing. "I wish I were Superman."

"You'd turn back time and save Tracy."

"If I could. But unlike what the screenwriters allowed Superman to do in the film, if I couldn't, well, at least...at least I'd understand what the bloody hell to do with this grief." She tried to take a deep breath but succeeded only in choking on her tears. "I feel weighed down, as if I have an anchor tied to my back, or Tracy's body, cold and stiff and . . . never moving ever again."

"That feeling will pass," Bourne said.

"Yes, I suppose it will, but what if I don't want it to?"

"Do you want to follow her down into darkness? What about Scarlett, what will happen to her then?"

Chrissie got red in the face and jumped up. Bourne followed her as she stalked into the bedroom, where he found her staring out the French doors at the pear tree, flooded now in silvery moonlight. "Bloody hell, Trace, why are you gone? If she were here now I swear I'd wring her neck."

"Or at least make her promise to have nothing more to do with Arkadin."

Bourne hoped injecting Arkadin's name back into the conversation would lead her back to a memory she might have overlooked. He sensed they might be at a crucial juncture. He had no intention of leaving, as long as she didn't throw him out. He didn't think she would, he was her only link with her sister now, he'd been there when Tracy had died. That meant the world to her, he sensed that it brought the two of them closer, made Tracy's sudden death a bit more bearable.

"Chrissie," he said gently, "did she ever tell you how she met him?"

She shook her head, then said, "Maybe in Russia. Saint Petersburg? She'd gone there to have a look at the Hermitage. I remember because I was all set to go with her when Scarlett came down with an ear infection, high fever, disorientation, the works." She shook her head.

"God, what different lives the two of us have led! And now...now it's come to this. Scarlett will be devastated."

Then she frowned. "Why did you come here, Adam?"

"Because I wanted something to remind me of her, because I had nowhere else to go." He realized, a bit belatedly, that it was the truth, or at least as much of it as he was prepared to share with her.

"I didn't, either," she said with a sigh. "Scarlett was visiting my folks when the call came. She was having a grand time, still is, judging by our last texts." Her eyes were on him, but again her attention was fixed somewhere else. "Of course you can have a look around, take whatever keepsake you want."

"I appreciate that."

She nodded absently, then turned back to her contemplation of the mews and its budding pear tree. A moment later she gave a tiny gasp. "There they are!"

Bourne rose and joined her at the window.

"They've returned," he said. "The house martins."

Arkadin woke at dawn, climbed into swim shorts, and went out for a run in the surf. The sky was filled with cormorants and pelicans. Greedy gulls walked along the sand, plucking at the remnants of last night's drunken parties. He ran south until he reached the outskirts of one of the big resort clubs, then turned around. After that he plunged into the water and swam for forty minutes. When he returned to the convent there were more than twenty messages waiting for him on his cell phone. One was from Boris Karpov. He showered and dressed, then chopped up fresh fruit. Pineapple, papaya, bananas, oranges. He ate the sweet chunks with a large dollop of yogurt. Ironically, he was learning to eat healthily in Mexico.

Wiping his mouth with the back of his hand, he took up his phone and made his first call. He was informed that the most recent shipment from Gustavo Moreno's pipeline had not reached the client. It had been delayed, or possibly it had gone missing. At the moment, he was told, it was impossible to say. He ordered his man to keep him informed, then disconnected.

Reflecting that he'd have to deal with the missing shipment himself and, if warranted, dole out harsh punishments, he punched in Karpov's number.

"I'm in LAX," Boris Karpov said in his ear. "Now what?"

"Now we meet face-to-face," Arkadin said. "There's a late-morning flight to Tucson. Call ahead, order a rental car—a two-seater convertible, the older and more battered the better." He gave Karpov instructions and driving directions. "Approach with the top down. Be prepared to wait at the rendezvous point for an hour, maybe more, until I determine that you have fulfilled all the terms of our meet. Is that clear?"

"I'll be there," Karpov said, "before sundown."

Bourne was still up, listening to the sounds of the flat, the building, the neighborhood, listening to London itself inhale and exhale as if it were a great beast. He turned his head when Chrissie appeared in the living room. An hour before, close to four, she had gone into the bedroom, but by the bedside lamp and the dry rustle of pages turning, he'd known she hadn't fallen asleep. Possibly she hadn't even tried.

"Haven't you gone to sleep yet?" Her voice was soft, almost burred, as if, in fact, she had just woken up.

"No." He was sitting back on the sofa, his mind still and dark as the bottom of the sea. But sleep hadn't come. Once, he thought he'd heard her sigh, but it was only the city breathing.

She came and sat down at the other corner of the sofa, tucked her legs under her. "I'd like to be in here, if it's all right."

He nodded.

"You haven't told me anything about yourself."

Bourne said nothing; he didn't feel inclined to lie to her.

Outside a car passed, then another. A dog barked in the silence. The city seemed stilled, as if frozen in ice, not even its heart beating.

The ghost of a smile played across her wide lips. "Just like Trace."

After a time, her eyelids grew heavy. She curled up like a cat with her head on her arms. Now she did sigh and, within moments, was fast asleep. A short time later, so was he.

Y ou must be insane," Soraya Moore said. "I'm not going to seduce Arkadin for you, Willard, or anyone else."

"I understand your concern," Marks said. "But—"

"No, Peter, I don't think you do. I really and truly don't. Otherwise there would be no *but*."

She got up and walked to the railing. They had been

sitting on a bench down by the canal in Georgetown. Lights glittered and boats lay still and sleeping in their berths. Behind them, young people strolled by, drinking and nuzzling. Occasional bursts of laughter erupted from a scrum of teenagers some distance away who appeared to be texting one another. The night was blessedly mild with just a hint of clouds scudding across the filthy-looking sky.

Marks rose and followed her. He sighed, as if he were the aggrieved party, which further antagonized her.

"Why is it," she said hotly, "that women are so devalued, men only use them for their bodies."

It wasn't a question and Marks knew it. He suspected that a good deal of her anger stemmed from the fact that it was him—a good and trusted friend—asking this of her. And of course that had been Willard's scheme. He knew this assignment would be offensive to Soraya, more so than, perhaps, to other women who had a less positive self-image; he knew that Marks was the only person who would be able to sell it to her. Indeed, Marks was quite certain that if Willard had given her this assignment directly she would have told him to go fuck himself and left without a backward glance. And yet, as Willard must have foreseen, here she was. Though visibly fuming, she hadn't told him to fuck off.

"For centuries, as women were systematically held down by men, they devised their own unique ways to get what they wanted: money, power, a decision-making position in a male-dominated society."

"I don't need a lecture on women's role in history," she snapped.

Marks decided to ignore her comment. "Whatever

else you might think, the indisputable fact is that women possess a unique ability."

"Would you please stop saying *unique*?"

"An ability to attract men, to seduce them, to find the chinks in their armor, and to use that weakness against them. You know better than I what a potent weapon sex can be when applied judiciously. This is especially true in the clandestine services." He turned to her. "In *our* world."

"Jesus Christ, you are the little fucker, aren't you?" She leaned on the railing, fingers enlaced, as a man might, with a man's confidence that was typical of her.

Marks pulled out his cell, brought up a head shot of Arkadin, handed it to her. "Handsome sonovabitch, isn't he? Magnetic, too, so I'm told."

"You disgust me."

"That sort of outrage doesn't become you."

"But screwing Arkadin does?" She thrust the cell back at him, but he didn't reach for it.

"Fight against it all you want, the fact remains that espionage work is what you do, this is what you are. More to the point, this is the life you *chose*. No one ever twisted your arm."

"No? What are you doing now?"

He took a calculated risk. "I haven't given you an ultimatum. You can get up and walk away anytime."

"And then what? I'll have nothing, I'll be nothing."

"You can return to Cairo, marry Amun Chalthoum, have babies."

He said this not unkindly, but the concept itself was unkind, or rather despicable. In any event, this was how it struck her. And all at once the full realization of how thoroughly M. Errol Danziger had fucked her dealt her its last, worst body blow. She was done at CI, which was bad enough, but he had made sure that she couldn't get a position at a competing government agency. One of the private risk management firms was also out of the question; she wasn't about to get involved with an organization of mercenaries like Black River. She turned away and bit her lip in order to hold back her tears of frustration. She felt the way she imagined women had felt down through the ages when they had ventured into a man's world, taking orders, biting back their opinions, hoarding secrets revealed in the whispered aftermath of sex, until the day came . . .

"This guy isn't unknown to you," Marks said, careful to keep the urgency he felt out of his voice. "He's as bad as they get, Raya. This playing up to him, it's a good thing you'll be doing."

"That's what you all say."

"No, we all do what needs to be done. That's the beginning and the end of it."

"Easy for you to say, you're not being asked to—"

"You don't know what I've been asked to do."

She turned away again. He watched her staring out at the canal, at the smears of lights on the water. Off to their left, the kids burst out into a rolling wave of laughter that seemed to gain in intensity as it circled the group.

"What I wouldn't give to be one of them now," Soraya said softly. "Not a care in the fucking world."

And Marks breathed a silent sigh of relief, knowing now that she would swallow the bitter pill he offered. She would take the assignment.

* * *

Curious. Very curious, indeed." In the warm light of the morning sun Chrissie was studying the engraving on the inside of the gold band Bourne had taken from Noah Perlis.

"I know linguistics," Bourne said, "but this isn't a known language, is it?"

"Well, it's hard to say. There are some characteristics of Sumerian, possibly Latin as well, though it's really neither." She looked up at him. "Where did you get this?"

"It makes no sense, does it?"

She shook her head. "No, it doesn't."

She had made coffee while Bourne rooted around in the freezer. He came up with a pair of crumpets, though judging by the ice crystals clinging to the bag they had been in there for some time. They found some jam and ate standing up, both of them filled with nervous energy. Neither of them mentioned last night. Then Bourne had showed her the ring.

"But that's only my opinion and I'm far from an expert." She handed the ring back to Bourne. "The only way to find out for sure is to take it up to Oxford. I have a friend who's a professor at the Centre for the Study of Ancient Documents. If it can be deciphered, he's sure to know."

It was after midnight when Lieutenant R. Simmons Reade tracked his boss down at an all-night squash court in Virginia, where the DCI worked out for two strenuous hours with one of the resident instructors three times a week. Reade was the only one inside CI who could deliver bad news to DCI Danziger without a qualm. He had been Danziger's prize pupil when Danziger was briefly teaching at the NSA's clandestine Academy for Special Operations, which the Old Man, who had contempt for everything the NSA stood for, used to call the Academy for Special Services, so he could jokingly refer to it as ASS.

Reade sat through the end of the last game, then made his presence known to the DCI by walking out onto the court, which was hot and smelled of sweat despite the fierce air-conditioning.

Danziger tossed his racquet at the instructor, wrapped a towel around his neck, and walked over to his adjutant.

"How bad?" No preliminaries were needed; the fact that Reade had sought him out at this hour, that he had chosen to come in person rather than through a phone call, was enough to clue him in.

"Bourne has neutralized the extraction team. They're either dead or in police custody."

"Jesus Christ," Danziger said, "how does Bourne do it? No wonder Bud needed me to take over."

They walked over to a bench and sat. No one else was on the court, the only sound came from the hum of the air-conditioning vents.

"Is Bourne still in London?"

Reade nodded. "As of this moment, yes, sir, he is."

"And Coven is there, Lieutenant?"

Danziger only called him by his rank when he was truly pissed off. "Yes, sir."

"Why didn't he intervene?"

"The site was too public, there were too many witnesses for him to try to snatch Bourne off the street."

"Other options?"

"Woefully lacking," Reade said. "Shall I do something about that? I can reach out to our people at NSA for—"

"In time, Randy, but for now I can't shake the tree and bring in my men wholesale, not politic, as Bud is quick to remind me. No, we have to make the best of the hand we've been dealt."

"Judging by his kill record, sir, Coven is damn good."

"Fine." The DCI slapped his thighs and stood up. "Set him loose on Bourne. Tell him he has a free hand, whatever it takes to bring Bourne in."

8

AFTER PETER MARKS had given her the assignment to find and attach herself to Arkadin, Soraya Moore had returned to Delia Trane's apartment where she had been holed up. For the last two hours she had been on her plugged-in cell phone with a number of her field agents at Typhon. Though Typhon was no longer hers, the same could not be said for the people she had hired, trained, and mentored for the highly specialized jobs monitoring and infiltrating the various Sunni and Shi'a cadres, insurgent groups, jihadists, and extreme splinter politicos in virtually every country in the Middle and Far East. No matter what their current orders were or who was now in charge of Typhon, their loyalty was to her.

Currently she was talking to Yusef, her contact in Khartoum. Arkadin was well known in that part of the world now that he supplied the majority of the armament.

"Arkadin isn't anywhere in the Middle East," Yusef said, "or holed up in the mountains of Azerbaijan, for that matter."

"And he's not anywhere in Europe, Russia, or Ukraine, I've already made certain of that," Soraya said. "Do you know why he's gone to ground?"

"Dimitri Maslov, his old mentor, has taken out a fatwa, or whatever the Russians call it, on him."

"I can understand why," Soraya said. "Maslov hired him to get the arms business from Nikolai Yevsen, which is what he was doing in Khartoum several weeks ago. Instead he made off with Yevsen's entire client list, which was stored on a computer server."

"Well, the word is that Maslov caught up with Arkadin in Bangalore, but was unable to either kill or capture him, so now he's vanished."

"In this day and age," Soraya said, "no one can vanish, at least for long."

"Well, at least now you know where he *isn't*."

"True enough." Soraya thought a moment. "I'll get someone to run through immigration security tapes in the Americas, maybe Australia, too, and see what they come up with."

David Webb had been to Oxford University, the oldest institution of higher learning in the English-speaking world, twice that Bourne could recall, though, of course, there could have been more visits. In those days the Centre for the Study of Ancient Documents had been located in the university's Classics Centre at the Old Boys' School in George Street. Now it was housed in a new home, the ultramodern Stelios Ioannou School for Research in Classical and Byzantine Studies at 66 St Giles', as incongruous to the study of ancient languages as it was to Oxford's stately eighteenth- and nineteenth-century buildings. This part of St Giles' was in the center of Oxford, an ancient city whose charter had been enacted in 1191. The center was known as Carfax, a word derived from the French *carrefour,* meaning "crossroads." And indeed, the four great thoroughfares of Oxford, including High Street, met at this juncture, as famous in its own way as Hollywood and Vine, and with a whole lot more history.

Chrissie had phoned her friend, a professor by the name of Liam Giles, before they started out from London. Oxford was only fifty-five miles away, and it took them just over an hour to get there using her old Range Rover. Tracy had given it to her when she started traveling so much.

The city was precisely as he remembered it, transporting all who arrived there back in time to an age of top hats, robes, horse-drawn carriages, and communications by post. It was as if it and all its inhabitants had been preserved in amber. Everything about Oxford belonged to another, simpler age.

By the time Chrissie found a parking spot the sun had begun to peer out from behind voluminous clouds, and the day had begun to warm, as if it might really be spring. They found Professor Liam Giles ensconced in his office, a large space set up as a workroom-cum-laboratory. Shelves were filled with manuscripts and thick hand-bound books. He was bent over one of them, scrutinizing a copy of a papyrus with a magnifying glass.

According to Chrissie, Professor Giles was the Richards-Bancroft Chair of the department, but as he glanced up Bourne was surprised to see a man of barely forty. He sported a prominent nose and chin and was balding, small round glasses pushed up onto his ever-expanding forehead. He had fur on his forearms, which were also short, like a kangaroo's.

Bourne's one concern about returning to Oxford had been that someone would recognize him as David Webb. But even though faculty members hung on decade after decade the university was huge, encompassing many colleges, and they were far from All Souls, the college where he had made several guest lectures.

In any event, Giles accepted him as Adam Stone. He seemed genuinely happy to see Chrissie, asking after her solicitously, and after Scarlett, whom he clearly knew personally.

"Tell her to stop by sometime," he said. "I have a little surprise for her that I think she'll like. I know she's eleven, but she's got the mind of a fifteen-year-old, so this ought to tickle her pink."

Chrissie thanked him, then introduced the enigma of the ring's curious engraving. Bourne handed the ring over and Giles, switching on a special lamp, studied the engraving on the inside first with the naked eye, then through a jeweler's loupe. He went to a shelf, took down textbooks, leafed through them, his forefinger moving down the large pages of dense paragraphs and small, hand-drawn illustrations. He went back and forth between the texts and the ring for some time. At last he looked up at Bourne and said, "I think it will help if I can take some pictures of the item in question. Do you mind?"

Bourne told him to go ahead.

Giles took the ring to a curious mechanism, which looked like the end of a fiber-optic cable. He carefully clamped the ring so that the filament was in its center. Then he handed them goggles with treated dark lenses, slipped on a pair himself. When he was sure they were protected, he typed two commands on a computer keyboard. A series of mini-flashes of blinding blue light ensued, and Bourne knew that he had activated a blue laser.

The silent outburst was over almost as soon as it had begun. Giles removed his goggles, and they did the same.

"Brilliant," the professor said as his fingers flew over his keyboard. "Let's have a look, shall we?"

He turned on a plasma screen inset into the wall, and a series of high-definition photographs—close-ups of the engraving—appeared. "This is how the writing appears to the naked eye, being engraved on a three-hundred-and-sixty-degree surface. But what," he said, "if it was meant to be read—or seen—on a flat surface, like most writing?" Here he manipulated the digital images until they merged into one long strip. "What we're left with is what appears to be one long word, which seems improbable." He zoomed in. "At least, that's how it appears on the circular surface of the ring. However, now, in its flat form, we can see two breaks, so that what we're actually looking at are three distinct groups of letters."

"Words," Bourne said.

"It would seem so," Giles said with a mysterious lilt in his voice.

"But I see some cuneiforms," Chrissie said. "I reckon they're Sumerian."

"Well, they certainly *look* Sumerian," Giles said, "but in fact they're Old Persian." He slid one of the open texts toward her. "Here, take a look." As she was doing that he addressed Bourne. "Old Persian is derived from Sumero-Akkadian, so our dear Christina can be forgiven her error." The affection with which he said this punctured the pompousness of the statement. "However, there's a crucial difference between the two without which decipherment is impossible. Akkadian cuneiforms represent entire syllables, whereas the cuneiforms of Old Persian are semi-alphabetic, which means each one represents a letter."

"What are the Latin letters doing mixed in?" Chrissie said. "And those unknown symbols, are they a language?"

Giles smiled. "You, Mr. Stone, have presented me with a most curious—and I must say damn exciting—mystery." He pointed to the screen. "What you see here is a composite of Old Persian, Latin, and—well, for lack of a better term, something else. I reckon I'm familiar with every ancient language mankind has discovered and cataloged, and this one is a definite outlier." He waved a hand. "But I'll get back to that presently."

He moved his mouse pointer horizontally just below the engraving. "The first thing I can tell you is that there is no such thing as a composite language—cuneiform and letters just don't mix. So if this isn't a *language*, per se, exactly what is it?"

Bourne, who had been studying the line of the engraving, said, "It's a cipher."

Giles's eyes widened behind the lenses of his glasses. "Very good, Mr. Stone. I applaud you." He nodded. "Indeed, this seems to be a cipher, but like everything else about this engraving, it's of a curious sort." Here he once again manipulated the image, literally rearranging the blocks, separating the Old Persian cuneiforms and Latin letters into two distinct groups, the third group being the "letters" of the outlier language.

"*Severus,*" Bourne said, reading the Latin word from the scramble.

"Which could mean any number of things," Chrissie said, "or nothing."

"True enough," Giles said. "*But* now we come to the Old Persian." He manipulated the cuneiforms. "See here, now we have a second word: *Domna.*"

"Wait a minute." Chrissie thought for a moment. "Septimius Severus was made a Roman senator by Marcus Aurelius in about 187. Subsequently he rose to become emperor in 193, and he ruled until his death eighteen years later. His reign was a strict military dictatorship, a response to the horrific corruption of his predecessor, Commodus. On his deathbed he famously advised his sons to 'Enrich the soldiers and scorn all other men.'"

"Lovely," Giles said.

"Some interesting things about him. He was born in what is now Libya, and when he increased the size of the Roman army he added auxiliary corps, soldiers from the far eastern borders of Rome's empire, which must have included many from North Africa and beyond."

"How is that relevant?" Giles said.

Now it was Chrissie's turn to have a mysterious lilt to her voice. "Septimius Severus was married to Julia Domna."

"Severus Domna," Bourne said. Something went off in the back of his head, deep down, beyond the veils his memory could not penetrate. Maybe it was a flash of déjà vu, or maybe a warning. Whatever it was, like all the free-floating bits of his previous life that suddenly, mysteriously surfaced, it would become an itch he couldn't scratch. He'd have no choice but to run it to ground until he unearthed its link to him.

"Adam, are you all right?" Chrissie was looking at him with a puzzled, almost alarmed expression.

"I'm fine," he said. He'd have to watch himself with her; she was as perceptive as her sister. "Is there more?"

She nodded. "And it gets more interesting. Julia Domna was Syrian. Her family came from the ancient city of Emesa. Her ancestors were king-priests of the powerful temple of Baal, and so very influential throughout Syria."

"So," Bourne said, "here we have an engraving—both a cipher and an anagram—made up of an ancient Western and Eastern language, merged."

"Just the way Septimius Severus and Julia Domna merged West and East."

"But what does it mean?" Bourne mused. "It seems that we're still lacking the key." He looked at Giles expectantly.

The professor nodded. "The third language. I reckon you're right, Mr. Stone. The key to the meaning of Severus Domna must lie in the third word." He handed the ring back to Bourne.

"So the language is still a mystery," Chrissie said.

"Oh, no. I know exactly what it is. It's Ugaritic, an extinct written proto-language that arose in a small but important section of Syria." He looked at Chrissie. "Just like your Julia Domna." He pointed. "You can see here—and here—and again here—that Ugaritic is an important link between the earliest proto-languages and the written word as we know it today because it's the first known evidence of the Levantine and South Semetic alphabets. In other words the Greek, Hebrew, and Latin alphabets find their sources in Ugaritic."

"So you know that this word is Ugaritic," Bourne said, "but you don't know what the word is."

"Again, yes and no." Giles walked up to the screen, and as he pointed to each Ugaritic character he pronounced the letter. "So I know all the letters, you see, but like the two others, this word is an anagram. Though Ugaritic appears briefly in the study of Middle Eastern languages, the study of Ugaritic on its own is quite a specialized field, and rather a small one, I'm afraid, because of the prevailing belief that it is a dead end—a *facilitation* language, rather than an *active* one. There are only two or three Ugaritic scholars in the world and I'm not one of them, so for me to decipher the anagram would take an inordinate amount of time—which, frankly, I don't have."

"I'm surprised there's anyone studying it," Chrissie said.

"Actually, there's only one reason there are any scholars at all." Giles walked back to his computer keyboard. "There is a small group that believes Ugaritic has, uh, shall we say magic powers."

"What," Bourne said, "like black magic?"

Giles laughed. "Oh my, no, Mr. Stone, nothing so fantastic. No, these people believe that Ugaritic is a key part to the workings of alchemy, that Ugaritic was created for priests, chants to make manifest the divine. They believe, further, that alchemy itself is a blending of Ugaritic—articulating the right sounds in the proper order—and the specific scientific protocols."

"Lead into gold," Chrissie said.

The professor nodded. "Among others things, that's right."

"Once again, the blending of East and West," Bourne said, "like *Severus* and *Domna,* like Old Persian and Latin."

"Intriguing. I hadn't thought of it in that light, but yes. It sounds far-fetched, I know, and you have to take an enormous leap of faith, but, well, now that you've brought up Julia Domna and her origins, look here." Giles worked the keyboard. The screen changed to a map of the Middle East that quickly zoomed in on modern-day Syria, and then, zooming in farther, a specific section of the country. "The epicenter of the Ugaritic language was the part of Syria that includes the Great Temple of Baal, considered by some to be the most powerful of the old pagan gods."

"Do you know any of these Ugaritic experts, Professor?" Bourne asked.

"One," Giles said. "He's, how shall I say, eccentric, as they all are in this arcane and rather outré field. As it happens, he and I play chess online. Well, it's a form of proto-chess, actually, enjoyed by the ancient Egyptians." He chuckled. "With your permission, Mr. Stone, I'll e-mail him the inscription right now."

"You have my blessing," Bourne said.

Giles composed the e-mail, attached a copy of the inscription, and sent it off. "He loves puzzles, the more obscure the better, as you can imagine. If he can't translate it, no one can."

Soraya, propped up on the bed in the guest room at Delia's apartment, was dreaming of Amun Chalthoum, the lover she had left behind in Cairo, when her cell phone began to throb on her lap. Hours ago she had switched it to vibrate mode so as not to disturb her friend, fast asleep in her bedroom.

Her eyes snapped open, the veils of her dream parted, and, putting the cell to her ear, she said, "Yes," very softly.

"We've got a hit," the voice said in her ear. It was Safa, one of the women in Typhon's network, whose family had been killed by terrorists in Lebanon. "At least it's a possible. I'm uploading several images to your laptop now."

"Hold on," she said.

Soraya had a phone company Internet card plugged into her laptop, and she switched it on. A moment later she was connected. She saw that the file was delivered and opened it. There were three photos. The first was a file shot, head and shoulders, of Arkadin, the same one Peter had showed her, so it must be the only decent shot they had of him. This version was larger and clearer, however. Marks was right, he was a handsome specimen: hooded eyes, aggressive features. And blond. Positive or negative? She wasn't sure. The other two were obvious CCTV photos, the images flat, the colors poorly rendered, of a man, large and muscular, wearing one of those inexpensive sports hats with a Dallas Cowboys logo, which he probably bought at the airport. She couldn't see enough of his face to make a positive ID. But in the second CCTV image, he'd tipped his hat back on his head to scratch his scalp. His hair was very black, very shiny, as if it had just been dyed. He must have thought he was out of camera range, she thought as she studied the face. She compared it with the file shot.

"I think it's him," she said.

"So do I. The images are from the Immigration cameras at the Dallas/Fort Worth airport eight days ago."

Why would he fly into Texas, Soraya wondered, *rather than New York or LA?*

"He came in on a flight from Charles de Gaulle Airport in Paris under the name Stanley Kowalski."

"You're joking," Soraya said.

"I kid you not."

The man definitely had a sense of humor.

9

LEONID ARKADIN WATCHED with slitted eyes as the battered dirt-brown convertible came bouncing along the road that led to the wharf. The sun was a bloody flag on the horizon; it had been another scorching day.

Fitting the binoculars to his eyes, he watched Boris Karpov park the car, get out, and stretch his legs. With the top down and no trunk to speak of, the colonel had no choice but to come alone. Karpov looked around, for a moment looked right where Arkadin lay stretched out, before his eyes moved on without seeing him. Arkadin was perfectly camouflaged on the corrugated tin roof of a fish shed, peering out from the space below the hand-painted sign that said, BODEGA—PESCADO FRESCO A DIARIO.

Flies buzzed busily, the stink of fish enveloped him

like a noxious cloud, and the heat of the day, stored up by the tin, burned into his belly, knees, and elbows like a furnace floor, but none of these distractions interfered with his surveillance.

He watched as Karpov lined up for the sunset cruise, paid his fare, and climbed on board the schooner that daily took to the Sea of Cortés. Aside from the crew of grizzled Mexicans and sailors, Karpov was the oldest man on board by a good thirty years. *A fish out of water* was the only way to describe him, standing on the deck amid the partying bikini-clad girls and their drunken, hormonal escorts. The more uncomfortable the colonel was, the better Arkadin liked it.

Ten minutes after the schooner cast off and set sail, he climbed off the fish shack and strolled down to the wharf, where the cigarette—a long, sleek, fiberglass boat that was, basically, all engine—was docked. El Heraldo—God knew where the Sonoran man got that name—was waiting to help him cast off.

"Everything's all set, boss, just like you wanted."

Arkadin smiled at the Mexican and clamped a powerful hand on his shoulder. "What would I do without you, my friend?" He slipped El Heraldo twenty American dollars.

El Heraldo, a small, barrel-chested man with an old salt's wide, bandy-legged stance, grinned hugely as Arkadin climbed into the cigarette. Finding the prestocked ice chest, he opened it, dug down deep, and stowed an item he'd packed inside a waterproof ziplock bag. Then he went to the wheel. A long, deep, phlegmy growl rolled up through the water at the stern, along with a blue drift of smoke from the marine fuel as he started the engines. El Heraldo cast off the lines fore and aft, and waved to Arkadin who steered the boat clear of the docks, threading through the buoys that marked the brief channel. Ahead lay the deep water, where the warm colors of the setting sun stippled the cobalt-blue waves.

The waves were so small, they could have been in a river. Like the Neva, Arkadin thought. His mind returned to the past, to St. Petersburg at sunset, a velvet sky overhead, ice in the river, when he and Tracy sat facing each other at a window table at the Doma, overlooking the water. Apart from the Hermitage, the embankment was dominated by buildings with ornate facades that reminded him of Venetian palazzos, untouched by Stalin or his communist successors. Even the Admiralty was beautiful, with none of the brutalist military architecture found in similar buildings festering in other large Russian cities.

Over blini and caviar she talked about the exhibits at the Hermitage, whose history he absorbed completely. He found it amusing that not far away on the bottom of the Neva lay the corpse of the politician, wrapped and tied like a sack of rotten potatoes, weighed down with bars of lead. The river was as peaceful as ever, lights from the monuments dancing on its surface, hiding the murky darkness beneath. He wondered briefly if there were fish in the river and, if so, what they'd make of the grisly package he'd delivered into their world earlier that day.

Over dessert she said, "I have something to ask you."

He had looked at her expectantly.

She hesitated, as if unsure how to proceed or whether to go on at all. At length, she took a sip of water and said, "This isn't easy for me, though, oddly, the fact that we hardly know each other makes it a bit easier."

"It's often easier to talk to people we've just met."

She nodded, but she was pale and the words seemed to have gotten stuck in her throat. "It's a favor, really."

Arkadin had been waiting for this. "If I can help you, I will. What sort of favor?"

Out on the Neva a long sightseeing boat plowed slowly by, its spotlights illuminating great swaths of the river and the buildings on either embankment. They might have been in Paris, a city in which Arkadin had managed to lose himself many times, if only for a short time.

"I need help," she said in a lost little voice that caused him to put his elbows on the table and lean toward her. "The kind of help your friend—what did you say his name was?"

"Oserov."

"That's right. I've always been good at summing people up very quickly. Your friend Oserov strikes me as the kind of man I need, am I right?"

"What kind of man is that?" Arkadin said, wondering what she was getting at and why this normally articulate woman was now having such a hard time finding the words she needed.

"Disposable."

Arkadin laughed. She was a woman after his own mind. "What do you need him for, exactly."

"I'd rather tell him personally."

"The man hates your guts, so you're better off telling me first."

She looked out at the river and the opposite bank

for a moment, then turned back to him. "All right." She took a deep breath. "My brother's in trouble—serious trouble. I need to find some way—some permanent way—of extricating him."

Was her brother some sort of criminal? "So the police won't find out, I'm guessing."

She laughed without any humor. "I wish I could go to the police with this. Unfortunately, I can't."

Arkadin hunched his shoulders. "What's he gotten into?"

"He's in over his head with a loan shark—he's got a gambling problem. I gave him some money to help him out but he just blew through that and when he came up short yet again, he stole a piece of artwork I was delivering to one of my clients. I've mollified the client, thank God, but if it ever came out I'd be finished."

"I imagine it gets worse from here."

She nodded woefully. "He went to the wrong people to fence it, got a third of what he should have gotten, an amount that wasn't nearly enough. Now, unless something drastic is done, the lender will have him killed."

"This lender, he's powerful enough to make that happen?"

"Oh, yes."

"All the better." Arkadin smiled. He thought helping her would be fun, but also, like a chess player, he could already see how he could bring her into checkmate. "I'll take care of it."

"All I want you to do," she said, "is introduce me to Oserov."

"I've just told you, you don't need him. I'll do this favor for you."

No," she said firmly. "I don't want you involved."

He spread his hands. "I already am involved."

"I don't want you involved any deeper than you are." The low lamplight fell across her as if they were in an intimate scene in a play, as if she were about to say the things that would make the audience gasp after holding its collective breath. "And as for Oserov, unless I've mistaken him, he likes money more than he hates me."

Arkadin laughed again, despite himself. He was going to tell her she was forbidden to talk with Oserov, but something in her eyes stopped him. He suspected that she would get up, walk away, and he'd never see her again. And he very much did not want that to happen, because this opportunity to hold something vital over her, to use her, would be lost.

The increased jouncing of the cigarette boat returned Arkadin's attention to the present. He had crossed the wake of the schooner and was now bearing down across its port flank. He got on the two-way radio and spoke to the schooner's captain, with whom he had made prior arrangements.

Five minutes later he was bobbing alongside the schooner, a rope ladder had been lowered, and Boris Karpov's rather corpulent body was climbing down.

"A fine place for two Russians to meet, eh, Colonel?" he said with a grin and a wink.

"I admit I was looking forward to meeting you," Karpov said, "under vastly different circumstances."

"Me in manacles or dead in a pool of blood, I can only imagine."

Karpov seemed to be having trouble breathing. "You've amassed quite the reputation for mayhem and murder."

"It's difficult for any one person to live up to those rumors." Arkadin was amused to see that Karpov, rather green around the gills, seemed in no mood for banter. "Don't worry, seasickness lasts only as long as we're on the water."

He chuckled as the ladder was hoisted up. He pulled away from the schooner, cutting a pale wake through the water. The bow lifted as the cigarette began to slice through the waves, and Karpov sat down with an audible thump, head between his legs.

"Stand up," Arkadin suggested, "and keep your eye on a fixed spot on the horizon—that freighter, for instance. That'll minimize the nausea."

After a moment, Karpov did just that.

"Don't forget to breathe."

Arkadin steered them south by southeast and when he judged he'd put enough distance between the cigarette and the schooner, he cut the engines to just above an idle, turned, and regarded his passenger.

"One thing I have to say about our government," he said, "it trains its employees to follow orders to the letter." He made a little mock-bow. "Congratulations."

"Fuck you," Karpov said before he turned toward the water and vomited copiously over the side.

Arkadin dragged out the ice chest that El Heraldo had stocked, and drew out a bottle of chilled vodka. "We don't stand on ceremony at sea. Here's a little bit of home, it'll help settle your stomach." He handed the bottle to Karpov. "But do me a favor and rinse your mouth before you take a swig."

Karpov scooped a handful of seawater into his mouth, swished it around, and spat it out. Then he unscrewed the cap and took a long swig. His eyes closed as he swallowed.

"That's better." He returned the bottle to Arkadin. "Now to business, the sooner I get back on dry land the better." But before Arkadin could reply, he turned and vomited again, hanging over the side of the cigarette, sweaty and limp. He moaned. And then again when Arkadin patted him down, looking for a weapon or an electronic recording device.

Finding none, Arkadin stepped away and waited until Karpov had rinsed his mouth out again, then said, "It seems we'd better get you to land sooner rather than later."

Returning the bottle to the ice chest, he offered a handful of cubes to the colonel, then got back to driving the boat. He headed due south now, following a line of white-and-gray pelicans, flying in perfect formation, low to the inky water, at length turning in at the estuary of Estero Morua where he moored in shallow water. By that time darkness had engulfed the eastern sky. In the west it looked like a banked fire, all smoldering embers, glimmering dimly in a vain attempt to keep back the fall of night.

They waded ashore with Arkadin carrying the ice chest on one brawny shoulder. The moment he hit the beach Karpov sat down in the sand, or perhaps *collapsed* might have been a better word for it. He appeared bedraggled and still slightly ill as he clumsily pulled off his sopping shoes and socks. Arkadin, who wore rubber sandals, had no such problem.

Arkadin went about gathering a pile of driftwood and setting it alight. He had finished one Dos Equis and had popped the cap on another when the colonel asked, rather weakly, for a bottle.

"Better to have a bite to eat first."

Arkadin proffered a small wrapped parcel, but Karpov just shook his head.

"As you wish." Arkadin stuck his nose into a burrito of carne asada wrapped in a freshly baked tortilla and inhaled deeply.

"Good God," Karpov said, averting his face.

"Ah, Mexico!" Arkadin dug into the burrito with gusto. "Pity you didn't listen to me when you raided Maslov's warehouse," he said between enormous chews.

"Don't even start on that." Karpov bit off his words as if each one were Arkadin's head. "The most likely scenario was that you were setting a trap for me on Maslov's orders. What did you expect me to do?"

Arkadin shrugged. "Still, opportunity wasted."

"What did I just say?"

"What I mean is with a man like Maslov you're not going to get more than two."

"I know what the fuck you meant," the colonel said hotly.

Arkadin took this with admirable equanimity. "Water under the bridge." He popped the top on another Dos Equis and handed it over.

Karpov closed his eyes for a moment; it looked like he was mentally counting to ten. When he opened his eyes, he said in as even a tone of voice as he could muster, "I've come all this way to listen, so you'd damn well better have something of value to tell me."

Having wolfed down his burrito, Arkadin brushed off his hands and took another beer to wash down the food. "You want the names of the moles—I don't blame you, I'd want them if I were in your shoes—and I'll give them to you, but first I want some assurances."

"Here it comes," Karpov said wearily. He rolled the bottle across his sweating forehead. "All right, what's the price?"

"Permanent immunity for me."

"Done."

"And I want Dimitri Maslov's head on a platter."

Karpov gave him a curious look. "What is it between the two of you?"

"I want an answer."

"Done."

"I need a guarantee," Arkadin insisted. "Despite all your efforts, he's still got a fucking platoon of people—from FSB apparatchiks to regional politicos to federal judges—in his pocket. I don't want him squirming off the chopping block."

"Well, that depends on the quality, detail, and amount of intel you provide me, doesn't it?"

"Don't worry about that, Colonel. Everything I have is rock-solid and as damaging to him as it gets."

"Then, as I said, it's done." Karpov swigged down some beer. "Anything else?"

"Yes."

Karpov, who had taken up one of his sea-soaked shoes, nodded sadly. "There always is, isn't there?"

"I want Oserov to myself."

Karpov frowned as he extracted a bit of seaweed from inside the ruined shoe. "Oserov is Maslov's second in command, keeping him out of the bull's-eye is going to be a bit tricky."

"I could give a shit."

"Please try to surprise me," Karpov said drily. He considered a moment, then, making up his mind, nodded decisively. "All right, then." He raised a finger. "But I need to warn you that when I make my move you'll have twelve hours maximum to take care of him. After that, he's mine along with the rest of them."

Arkadin extended his hand and took Karpov's, whose grip was strong and callused, a workingman's grip. He liked that. A government employee he might be, but he was no drone: This was a man who would not fuck him, of that Arkadin was certain.

In that precise moment Karpov sprang at Arkadin, one hand around his neck, gripping his chin and lifting it while the other hand held a razor blade to his exposed throat.

"Inside your shoe." Arkadin sat perfectly still. "Very low-tech, very good."

"Listen, you fucking goon, I don't take kindly to being fucked over—you set me up to fail at the warehouse. Now Maslov has been warned, he's going to be on his guard, which is going to make bringing him down all the more difficult. You've done nothing but treat me with disrespect. You're a fucking murderer, the lowest form of what passes for life in a whole stinking pile of shit. You intimidate people, torture them, torment them, then kill them as if human life has no meaning. I feel unclean just being near you, but I want Dimitri Maslov more than I want to kill you, so I'll just have to live with the decision. Life is full of compromises and with each one your hands dip deeper into blood, I've come to terms with that. But if you and I are going to work together, you're going to give me the respect I deserve or I swear on my father's grave I'll slit your throat right here, right now, turn my back and forget I ever met you." He put his face next to Arkadin's. "Are we clear, Leonid Danilovich?"

"You're not going to be able to make a move against Maslov with the moles in place." Arkadin was looking straight ahead, which meant up at the night sky, where stars glittered like faraway eyes, watching the foibles of humankind with contempt or at least indifference.

Karpov jerked his head. *"Are we clear?"*

"Crystal." He relaxed somewhat as the colonel put away the blade. He had been correct about Karpov's essential nature: This was no man to be bullied, not even by the fearsome Russian bureaucracy. Arkadin silently saluted him. "Your first problem is to poison the moles in the FSB-2's kitchen."

"You mean the baseboards."

Arkadin shook his head. "If that were the case, my dear Colonel, your problems would all be simple ones. However, I do mean the kitchen, because Maslov owns one of the chefs."

There was silence for a time, just the soft lapping of the water, the last of the gulls' cries as they bedded down for the night. The moon emerged from behind a low bank of clouds, casting a bluish mantle over them even as it chipped away at the black sea, strewing pinpoints of light across its choppy surface.

"Which one?" Karpov said after a long time.

"I'm not sure you want to hear this."

"I'm not sure, either, but what the fuck, it's too late to stop now."

"It is, isn't it?" Arkadin took out a pack of Turkish cigarettes and offered one to the colonel.

"I'm trying to cut down on my bad habits."

"A futile preoccupation."

"Say that when you have high blood pressure."

Arkadin lit up, put the pack away, and took a deep drag. As the smoke drifted out of his nostrils, he said, "Melor Bukin, your boss, reports to Maslov."

Karpov's eyes blazed. "You shit, are you fucking with me again?"

Without a word Arkadin dug out the plastic bag he'd stowed in the bottom of the ice chest, zipped it open, and handed over the contents. Then he added several pieces of driftwood to the fire, which was waning.

Karpov moved a bit nearer to the fire in order to have a better look. Arkadin had handed him one of those cheap cell phones bought in any convenience store, a burner, which meant its calls couldn't be traced. He thumbed it on.

"Audio and video," Arkadin said as he used a stick to better arrange the wood. Planning for this day or one like it, he had used this cell to clandestinely record certain meetings between Maslov and Bukin that he'd attended. He knew there would be no doubt in the colonel's mind when he finished viewing the evidence.

At length, Karpov looked bleakly up from the tiny screen. "I'll need to keep this."

Arkadin waved a hand. "All part of the service."

Somewhere far off, the drone of a small plane came to them, a sound no more significant than a mosquito's whine.

"How many more?" Karpov asked.

"I know of two—their names are in the phone's directory—but there may be more. I'm afraid you're going to have to ask your boss."

Karpov's brow furrowed. "That won't be easy."

"Even with this evidence?"

Karpov sighed. "I'm going to have to take him by surprise, cut him off completely before he has a chance to contact anyone."

"Chancy," Arkadin said. "On the other hand, if you go to President Imov with the evidence he'll be so outraged he's sure to let you do whatever you want with Bukin."

Karpov appeared to be considering this approach. Good. Arkadin smiled inwardly. Melor Bukin had risen up through the apparatchik ranks mainly because of the president, before he'd been chosen by Viktor Cherkesov, the head of FSB-2. Inside the Kremlin a war was being waged between Cherkesov and the FSB's Nikolai Patrushev, a well-known disciple of Imov's. Cherkesov had built a formidable power base without the president's patronage. Arkadin had his own reason for wanting Bukin disgraced. When Karpov threw Bukin in prison, his mentor, Cherkesov, would not be far behind. Cherkesov was the one thorn in his side he hadn't been able to extricate, but now Karpov would take care of that for him.

Yet he had no time to gloat. His restless mind had already turned to more personal matters. Namely, the various routes he might take to avenge himself on Karpov for holding a knife to his throat. His mind was already afire with visions of slitting the colonel's throat with his own razor blade.

10

MOIRA AND JALAL Essai sat together in the temporary quarters of his DC hotel suite. Between them were Essai's netbook and the netbook that Moira had bought the day before, one she knew was absolutely clean. She had already souped it up far beyond its original specs.

She was going to ask him how to get started, because she had to assume that all her systems had been compromised, but she needn't have bothered. As it turned out he had a lot of information about the laptop, all of which he shared with her. Latterly it had fallen into the hands of Gustavo Moreno, a Colombian drug lord living in the outskirts of Mexico City. Moreno had been killed some months ago when his compound had been raided by a party of officers disguised as Russian oilmen.

"The raiding party was headed by Colonel Boris Karpov," Essai said.

Curious, Moira thought. But then she knew how small and insular this world was. She knew about the colonel from Bourne; they were friends, as much as two people like that could be friends.

"So Karpov has the laptop."

"Unfortunately, no," Essai said. "The laptop was taken from Moreno's compound, by one of his own people, sometime before the raid."

"One of his own people who was obviously working for who—a rival?"

"Possibly," Essai said. "I don't know."

"What's the thief's name?"

"Name, photo, everything." Essai turned the laptop's screen toward her and brought up the image. "But it's a dead end, literally. His body was found a week after the raid."

"Where?" Moira said.

"Outside of Amatitán." Essai pulled up Google Earth and punched in a set of coordinates. The globe of the planet revolved until the northwest coast of Mexico came into view. He pointed. Amatitán was in Jalisco, in the heart of tequila country. "Right here. As it happens on the estancia of Moreno's sister, Berengária, although now that she's married Narsico Skydel, the tequila magnate, she goes by the name of Barbara Skydel."

"I seem to recall a memo at Black River about Narsico. He's the cousin of Roberto Corellos, the jailed Colombian drug lord, isn't that right?"

Essai nodded. "Narsico has been trying to distance himself from his infamous cousin for some time. He hasn't been back in Colombia in ten years. Five years ago, apparently finding it too difficult to outrun his family's reputation, he changed his name and bought into the largest tequila distillery in Mexico. Now he owns it outright and over the past two years has been expanding its reach."

"Marrying Berengária couldn't have helped him," Moira pointed out.

"I don't know. She's proved herself to be a shrewd businesswoman. Most people's best guess is that she's the one behind the expansion. I think she's more willing to take calculated risks than he is, and so far she hasn't made a single misstep."

"How was her relationship with Gustavo?"

"By all reports the two siblings were close. They bonded early, after their mother died."

"Do you think she was involved in his business?"

Essai folded his arms over his chest. "Difficult to say. Whatever involvement she might have had was certainly not evident, there's nothing whatsoever to link her with Gustavo's drug trafficking."

"But you did say that she was a canny businesswoman."

He frowned. "You think she had the mole inside her own brother's shop?"

Moira shrugged. "Who can say?"

"Neither of them would be that stupid."

Moira nodded. "I agree, though if someone wants us to think one of them had the mole murdered, it seems talking to them would be useful. But first I want to pay a visit to Roberto Corellos."

Essai smiled the dark smile that chilled Moira's soul. "I think, Ms. Trevor, that you've already begun to earn your fee."

* * *

Bourne and Chrissie were on their way back in a driving rainstorm that had come upon them virtually without warning when Bourne's cell rang.

"Mr. Stone."

"Hello, Professor," Bourne said.

"I have some news," Giles said. "I've received an e-mail back from my chess partner. It seems that he has solved the riddle of the third word."

"What is it?" Bourne asked.

"Dominion."

"Dominion," Bourne repeated. "So the three words engraved on the inside of the ring are: *Severus Domna Dominion*. What does it mean?"

"Well, it could be an incantation," Giles said, "or an epithet, a warning. Even—and I'm being deliberately fanciful here—the instructions for turning lead into gold. Without additional information I'm afraid there's no way of knowing."

The road ahead was smeared with rain, the wipers slapped back and forth on their prescribed arc. Bourne checked the side mirror, as he did automatically every thirty seconds or so.

"There is an interesting tidbit about Ugaritic my friend provided, though I can't see how it's relevant. The basis of its interest for him and his colleagues is that there are documents—or fragments thereof—they claim come from the court of King Solomon. It seems that Solomon's astrologers spoke Ugaritic amongst themselves, that they believed in its alchemical powers."

Bourne laughed. "With all the legends of King

Solomon's gold, I can see where the scientists of an early age believed alchemy was the key to turning lead into gold."

"Frankly, Mr. Stone, I told him the same thing."

"Thank you, Professor. You've been most helpful."

"Anytime, Mr. Stone. A friend of Christina's is a friend of mine."

As Bourne put away his cell, he saw that the black-and-gold truck that had pulled into their lane three vehicles back some minutes ago was now right behind them.

"Chrissie, I'd like you to get off the motorway," he said quietly. "When you do, pull over."

"Are you feeling all right?"

He said nothing, his eyes flicking to the side mirror. Then he reached out and stopped her from using the turn signal. "Don't do that."

Her eyes opened wide and she gave a little gasp. "What's going on?"

"Just do what I tell you and everything will be all right."

"Not reassuring." She moved into the left-hand lane as the next exit sign became visible through the rain. "Adam, you're scaring me."

"That wasn't my intention."

She took the ramp, which immediately curved around to the left, and pulled onto the shoulder. "Then what is your intention?"

"To drive," he said. "Move over."

She got out of the Range Rover, covered her head, which was tucked down between her hunched shoulders, and went around, jumping into the passenger's side. Her door was not even fully closed when Bourne saw the truck making its way around the curve of the off-ramp. Immediately he put the vehicle in gear and pulled out.

The truck was directly behind him as if tethered to the Range Rover with a grappling hook. Bourne put on a burst of speed, went through a light on the red, then onto the motorway's entrance ramp. Traffic was moderate and he was able to weave in and out of the lanes. He was just thinking that a truck was an impractical vehicle to pursue them when a gray BMW pulled up abreast of them.

As the window slid down, Bourne yelled for Chrissie to get down. He pushed her, then bent low over the wheel as gunshots shattered his side window, showering him with glass pellets and fistfuls of rain. At that moment he saw the black-and-gold truck coming up fast behind him; they meant to box him in.

Both vehicles rocked back and forth, their sides scraping together dangerously. Bourne risked a glance in the rearview mirror. The black-and-gold truck was right on their tail.

"Brace yourself," he said to Chrissie, who was bent over as far as her seat belt would allow, her arms over her head.

He angled the car, then slammed on the brakes. For a split second the Range Rover skidded on the wet tarmac, then he had compensated. The offside rear bumper crumpled on impact with the truck, the Range Rover swerved at a sharp angle so that, as he had calculated, the driver's-side rear bumper plowed into the BMW with tremendous force, as if it had been shot out of a cannon. Impelled by the crash, the BMW veered hard right and, out of control, slammed into the guardrail with such force that the entire driver's side was staved in. A fireworks of sparks, a shrieking of tortured metal as the BMW bounced off the guardrail and spun. The front end was heading directly for the Range Rover and Bourne turned the wheel hard to the right, cutting off a yellow Mini. There was a horrific screech of tires, horns blared, fenders were dented or flattened in a chain reaction. Bourne accelerated into the gap, switched lanes again, then as he cleared more of the traffic moved back across to the fast lane.

"Jesus," Chrissie whispered. "Jesus Christ."

The Range Rover was still rocking on its shocks. Bourne could no longer see the smashed-up BMW or the black-and-gold truck in the rearview mirror.

After a crash or an accident, even a near miss, everything goes quiet, or possibly the human ear, traumatized like the rest of the organism, goes temporarily deaf. In any event, it was dead silent in the SUV as Bourne exited the motorway, turned off the access road as soon as he could, and rolled along streets lined with wholesalers and warehouses, where no one shouted in fear, no horns blared angrily or brakes screeched, where order still reigned and the chaos of the motorway seemed to belong to another universe. He didn't stop until he found a deserted block and pulled over.

Chrissie was silent, her face dead white. Her hands trembled in her lap. She was near to weeping with both terror and relief.

"Who are you?" she said after a time. "Why is someone trying to kill you?"

"They want the ring," Bourne said simply. After what had just happened she deserved at least a modicum of the truth. "I don't know why yet, I'm trying to figure that out."

She turned to him. Her eyes had paled, too, or perhaps that was simply a trick of the light. Bourne didn't think so.

"Was Trace involved with this ring?"

"Maybe, I don't know." Bourne started the car and pulled out into the street. "But her friends were."

She shook her head. "This is all going much too fast for me. Everything's turned upside down, I can't seem to get my bearings."

She ran her hands through her hair, then noticed something odd. "Why are we heading back toward Oxford?"

He gave her a wry look as he headed toward the on-ramp of the motorway. "Like you, I don't like people shooting at me.

"I need to get a better look at the BMW and our friend inside." Noting her terrified expression, he added, "Don't worry. I'll get out near the crash site. Are you okay to drive?"

"Of course."

He turned left and rolled onto the motorway, in the direction of Oxford. The worst of the rain had drifted away; only a light drizzle remained. He slowed the wipers down. "I'm sorry for the damage."

She shuddered and gave him a grim smile. "It couldn't be helped, could it?"

"When is Scarlett due back from your parents' house?"

"Not until next week, but I can pick her up anytime," she said.

"Fine." Bourne nodded. "I don't want you to go to your house in Oxford. Is there someplace else you can stay?"

"I'll go back to Tracy's flat."

"That's out, as well. These people must have picked me up there."

"What about my parents' house?"

"That's no good, either, but I want you to pick Scarlett up from them and go somewhere else, somewhere you haven't been before."

"You don't think—?"

Very deliberately, he produced the Glock he'd found in Perlis's flat and placed it in the glove compartment.

"What are you doing?"

"We were being followed, possibly all the way from Tracy's flat. There's no point in taking a chance these people know about Scarlett—and where your parents live, for that matter."

"But who are they?"

He shook his head.

"This is a nightmare, Adam." Her voice was brittle, as if her words were made of glass. "What on earth was Trace mixed up in?"

"I wish I had an answer for you."

Traffic on the opposite side of the motorway was at a standstill, which told him that they were nearing the crash site. Directly ahead the vehicles on their side were all but inching along, which would make it less difficult for him to get out and for Chrissie to take the wheel.

"What about you?" she asked as he put the Range Rover in neutral.

"Don't worry about me," he said. "I'll make my way back to London." Her worried expression revealed that she didn't believe him. He gave her his cell number. But when he saw her dig a pen out of her handbag he added, "Memorize it, I don't want you writing it down."

They got out of the Range Rover and she slid behind the wheel. "Adam." She reached out and grabbed his arm. "For God's sake, take care of yourself."

He smiled. "I'll be fine."

But she wouldn't let him go. "Why are you pursuing this?"

He thought about Tracy dying in his arms. He carried her blood on his hands.

Ducking his head through the window, he said, "I owe her a debt I can never repay."

Bourne vaulted over the median onto the other side of the rain-slick motorway. As he approached the crash site his mind was racing, taking in the welter of ambulances, emergency vehicles, and police cars. The personnel had come from all over the surrounding area, which was a stroke of luck for what he had in mind. The crash site had not yet been cordoned off. He saw a body laid out on the ground, covered by a tarp. A squad of forensics personnel patrolled the area adjacent to the corpse, taking notes or digital photos, marking out small bits of forensic evidence with numbered plastic cones, and conferring among themselves. Each fragment of evidence—drops of blood, shards of a broken taillight, bits of shredded fabric, the litter of a shattered car window, an oil slick—was being photographed from several angles.

Bourne moved to the side of one of the emergency vehicles and unobtrusively slipped into the cab, rooting through the glove compartment for a form of ID. Finding nothing there, he moved on to the sun visors. One of them had a rubber band around it. Pulling it down, he found several cards, one of which was an expired ID. It always amazed him that people grew so attached to their own history, they were reluctant to part with any tangible evidence of it. Hearing someone approaching, he grabbed a pair of latex gloves, slid over and out the other side. As he did so, he clipped the ID to his coat and walked purposefully into the melee of official personnel trying to make sense of the mess left on the smeared tarmac of the motorway.

He squinted at the BMW; the guardrail had finally impaled it like a harpoon, wrecking it entirely. Bourne saw where he'd driven Chrissie's car into the corner of the rear bumper. Squatting down next to it, he vigorously scrubbed off the few flecks of paint from her vehicle. He had just finished memorizing the plate number when a local police inspector crouched down beside him.

"What d'you reckon?" He was a whey-faced man with bad teeth and breath to match. He looked as if he had been raised on tepid beer, bangers and mash, and treacle.

"The speed must have been fantastic in order to do this damage." Bourne spoke in a hoarse voice, using his best South London accent.

"Cold or allergies?" the local inspector said. "Either way, you should take care of yourself in the bloody-minded weather."

"I'll need to see the victims."

"Righto." The inspector rose on creaky knees. The backs of his hands were chapped and reddened, the result of a long, hard winter stuck in an underheated office. "This way."

He led Bourne through the knots of people to where the corpse was still laid out. He lifted the tarp for Bourne to have a look. The body was broken up. Bourne was surprised to see that the man was older, he guessed in his late forties or early fifties—extremely odd for an executioner.

The inspector's wrists rested on his bony knees. "With no ID, it'll be a bitch trying to notify his wife."

The corpse wore what appeared to be a gold wedding band on the third finger of his left hand. Bourne thought that interesting, but he wasn't about to share his opinion, or anything else for that matter, with the inspector. He had to get a look at the inside of the ring.

"I'm going in," Bourne said.

The inspector guffawed.

Bourne slipped off the ring. This ring was far older than the one he already had. He held it up to see more clearly. It was scratched and worn, thinned out over time. It took gold maybe a hundred years or more to get this thin. He tipped the ring. It was engraved on the inside. He could make out the Old Persian and Latin, yes. He peered more closely, rotating the ring between his fingers. There were only two words, *Severus Domna*. The third one, *Dominion,* was missing.

"Find anything?"

Bourne shook his head. "I thought maybe there'd be some sort of engraving—'To Bertie, from Matilda,' something of that sort."

"Another dead end," the inspector said sourly. "Christ on a crutch, my knees are killing me." He stood up with a little groan.

Now Bourne knew what *Severus Domna* must stand for: a group or a society. Whatever you wanted to call them, one thing was clear—they had gone to great lengths to keep themselves secret from the world at large. And now, for whatever reason, they had surfaced, risking their secretive status—all for the ring engraved with their name and the word *Dominion*.

11

OLIVER LISS, STRIDING down North Union Street in Alexandria's Old Town, checked the time and, a moment later, stepped into one of those large chain drugstores that carried most everything. He went past the dental hygiene and foot care sections, picked out a cheap cell phone with thirty prepaid minutes, and took it up to the checkout counter where an Indian woman rang it up, along with a copy of *The Washington Post*. He paid cash.

Back out on the street, the paper tucked under one arm, he pulled apart the plastic blister pack and walked back beneath a dull and starless sky to where he'd parked his car. He got in and attached the phone to his portable charger, which would give it a full charge in less than five minutes. While he waited, he put his head back against the seat and closed his eyes. He hadn't had much sleep last night or, for that matter, any night since he'd agreed to fund the resurrected Treadstone.

Not for the first time he wondered whether he had done the right thing, and then he tried to recall the last time he'd made a business decision of his own free will. More than a decade ago he'd been approached by a man who called himself Jonathan, though Liss soon enough surmised that wasn't his name at all. Jonathan said that he was part of a large multinational group. If Liss played his cards right, if he pleased Jonathan and, therefore, the group, Jonathan would ensure that the group became Liss's permanent client. Jonathan had then suggested to him that he found a private risk management firm under cover of which the business could become a private contractor for the US armed forces in overseas hot spots. That was how Black River had been formed. Jonathan's group had provided the seed money, just as Jonathan had promised, and brought in the two partners. It was this same group that, through Jonathan, had given him advance warning of events taking place that would blow Black River out of the water sooner rather than later. The group had extricated him without him being implicated in any future investigation, congressional hearings, the filing of criminal charges, trials, and the inevitable incarcerations.

Then, only weeks after his parachute to safety, Jonathan had presented another suggestion, which wasn't a suggestion at all, but an order: provide seed money for Treadstone. He hadn't even heard of Treadstone, but then he'd been given an enciphered file detailing its creation and workings. That was when he'd learned that only one member of Treadstone remained alive: Frederick Willard. He contacted Willard and the rest had unfolded just as predicted.

Every once in a while he allowed himself the luxury of wondering how this group possessed such a staggering wealth of classified information. What were its sources? It seemed irrelevant whether the information was about American, Russian, Chinese, or Egyptian secret service agencies, to name just a few. The intelligence was always of the highest caliber and always correct.

The most mysterious aspect of this entire chapter of his life was that he'd never met any of these people face-to-face. Jonathan made suggestions, via the phone, to which he acceded without the faintest hint of a protest. He was not a man who enjoyed being enslaved—but he did savor every moment of being alive, and without these people he long ago would have been a dead man. He owed everything to Jonathan's group.

Jonathan and his colleagues were hard taskmasters—utterly serious, intent on their goals—but they were generous with their rewards. Over the years the group had recompensed Liss beyond his wildest dreams—and that was another aspect of its existence that only added to the mystery: the group's seemingly limitless wealth. Just as importantly, the group protected him, a promise Jonathan had made to him, a promise borne out when he had been extracted from the disaster that landed his two former Black River partners in federal penitentiaries for the rest of their lives.

A low beep alerted him that the cell phone was fully charged. Disconnecting it from the charger, he turned it on and punched in a local number. After two rings, the line connected and he said: "Delivery." There was a short pause, then an automated female voice said, "Ecclesiastes three: six-two."

It was always a book of the Bible, he had no idea why. He disconnected, picked up the paper. "Ecclesiastes" referred to the sports section. "Three: six-two" meant third column, sixth paragraph, second word.

Running his forefinger down the specified column he discovered today's code word: *steal.*

He picked up his cell and punched in a ten-digit number. "Steal," he said when the line engaged after one ring. Instead of a voice he heard a series of electronic clicks and pops as the complex network of servos and switchers rerouted his call again and again to a remote location that was God alone knew where. Then the icy sound of encrypting devices being engaged and, at last, a voice said:

"Hello, Oliver."

"Good afternoon, Jonathan."

The enciphering slowed the speech down, stripping it of emotion and tone, rendering it unrecognizable, closer to the voice of an automaton.

"Have you sent them on their way?"

"They took off an hour ago, they'll be in London early tomorrow morning." It was the voice that had sent him the dossier on the ring in the first place. "They have their orders, but..."

"Yes?"

"All Willard talks about is Arkadin and Bourne and the Treadstone program that created them. According to him, he's discovered a method to make them even more... *useful,* I think was the term he used."

Jonathan chuckled. At least Liss assumed it was a

chuckle, though it came across to him as a dry rustle, as of a swarm of insects infesting high grass.

"I want you to stay out of his way, Oliver, is that clear?"

"Sure it's clear." Liss rubbed his forehead with his knuckles. What the hell was Jonathan's purpose here? "But I've told him to put his plans on hold until the ring is found."

"Just as you should have done."

"Willard wasn't happy."

"You don't say."

"I have a feeling that he's already plotting to bolt the farm."

"And when he does," Jonathan said, "you will do nothing to stop him."

"What?" Liss was stunned. "But I don't understand."

"Everything is as it should be," Jonathan said just before he disconnected.

Soraya, in the Dallas/Fort Worth airport, approached every rental-car agency with a photo of Arkadin. No one recognized him. She had something to eat, bought a paperback novel and a Snickers bar. While she ate the bar slowly, she strolled over to the desk of the airline Arkadin had flown in on and asked for the supervisor on duty.

This turned out to be a large man named Ted, who appeared to be an ex-football-lineman going to fat, as they all did sooner or later. He appraised her through the dusty lenses of his glasses and, after asking her name, suggested they go back into his office.

"I'm with Continental Insurance," she said, snapping off a chunk of her Snickers. "I'm trying to locate a man named Stanley Kowalski."

Ted sat back for a moment, laced his thick hands over his stomach, and said, "You're kidding me, right?"

"No," Soraya said, "I'm not." She gave him the flight info on Kowalski.

Ted sighed and shrugged. Swiveling around, he checked his computer terminal. "Well, how about that," he said, "there he is, just like you said." He turned back to her. "Now, how can I help you?"

"I'd like to find out where he went from here."

Ted laughed. "Now I know this is some kind of joke. This airport is one of the largest and busiest in the world. Your Mr. Kowalski could have gone anywhere, or nowhere at all."

"He didn't rent a car," Soraya said. "And he didn't make a connection to a national carrier because he went through Immigration right here in Dallas. Just to make sure, though, I checked the CCTV logs for that day."

Ted frowned. "You sure are thorough, give you that." He thought a moment. "But now I'm going to tell you something I bet you didn't know. We have a number of regional carriers flying out of here."

"I checked their CCTV logs as well."

Ted smiled. "Well, I know you didn't check the CCTV for our charter flights, 'cause they don't have 'em." He began to write on a slip of paper he tore off a pad. Then he handed it over. "These are their names." He winked at her. "Good huntin'."

She hit the jackpot at the fifth name Ted had given her. A pilot there remembered Arkadin's face, though he didn't give his name as Stanley Kowalski.

"Said his name was Slim Pickens." The pilot screwed up his face. "Weren't there an actor by that name?"

"Coincidence," Soraya said. "Where did you take Mr. Pickens?"

"Tucson International Airport, ma'am."

"Tucson, huh?"

Soraya thought, *Why in hell would Arkadin want to go to Tucson?* And then, as if a switch had been thrown in her head, she knew.

Mexico.

Having checked into a small hotel in Chelsea, Bourne stood under a hot shower, sluicing away the sweat and grime of his ordeal. The muscles in his neck, shoulders, and back throbbed with a deep-seated ache in the aftermath of the collision and his long run off the motorway.

Just thinking the words *Severus Domna* sent echoes through his mind. It was maddening not being able to pluck the memories out of his fogbound past. He was certain that he had once known about it. Why? Had the group been the target of a Treadstone mission Conklin had sent him on? He had obtained the Dominion ring somewhere, from someone, for some specific reason, but beyond those three vague facts was only an impenetrable mist. Why had Holly's father stolen the ring from his brother? Why had he given it to Holly? Who was her uncle, what was the ring to him? Bourne couldn't ask Holly. That left her uncle, whoever he was.

He turned off the water, stepped out of the stall, and vigorously rubbed himself down with a towel. Perhaps he should return to Bali. Were either of Holly's parents still alive, still living there? Suparwita might know, but he had no phone, there was no way to contact him save to return to Bali and ask him in person. Then it came to him. There was a better way to get the information he needed, and the plan he was formulating would serve two purposes because it would trap Leonid Arkadin.

His mind still working at a fever clip, he put on clothes he had bought at Marks & Spencer in Oxford Street on his way to the hotel. These included a dark-colored suit and black turtleneck. He polished his shoes with the kit provided in the room, then took a taxi to Diego Hererra's house in Sloane Square.

This proved to be a redbrick Victorian affair with a steeply pitched slate roof and a pair of conical turrets, sticking up into the night sky like horns. A brass door-knocker in the shape of a stag's head looked stoically out on all visitors. Diego himself opened the door to Bourne's knock.

He smiled thinly. "No worse for the wear and tear of yesterday's adventure, I see." He waved a hand. "Come in, come in."

Diego wore dark trousers and an elegant evening jacket probably more appropriate to the Vesper Club. Bourne, however, still held the clothing instincts of an academic professor and was as uncomfortable in formal dress wear as he would have been in a medieval suit of armor.

He led Bourne through an old-fashioned parlor, lit by antique lamps with frosted-glass shades, into a dining room dominated by a polished mahogany table over which hung a crystal chandelier, now dimly lit, casting the light of a thousand stars across jewel-toned wallpaper and oak wainscoting. Two place settings beckoned. While Bourne sat, Diego poured them glasses of an excellent sherry to go with the small plates of grilled fresh sardines, *papas fritas,* paper-thin slices of rosy Serrano ham, small disks of fat-speckled chorizo, and a platter of three Spanish cheeses.

"Please help yourself," Diego said when he joined Bourne at the table. "This is the custom in Spain."

As they ate Bourne was aware of Diego watching him. At length, Diego said, "My father was very pleased that you came to see me."

Pleased or interested? Bourne wondered. "How is Don Fernando?"

"As always." Diego was eating like a bird, picking at his food. He either had no appetite or had something important on his mind. "He's quite fond of you, you know."

"I lied to him about who I was."

Diego laughed. "You do not know my father. I'm quite sure he was interested only in whether you were friend or enemy."

"I am Leonid Arkadin's enemy, as he well knows."

"Precisely." Diego spread his hands. "Well, we all have that in common. This is the tie that binds."

Bourne pushed away his plate. "Actually, I was wondering about that."

"In what way, may I ask?"

"We're all bound by our acquaintance with Noah Perlis. Your father knew Perlis, didn't he?"

Diego didn't miss a beat. "As a matter of fact he didn't. Noah was my friend. We'd go to the casino—the Vesper Club—and gamble the night away. This is what

Noah liked to do best when he was in London. The moment I knew he was coming I'd set it all up—his credit line, the chips."

"And, of course, the girls."

Diego grinned. "Of course the girls."

"Didn't he want to see Tracy—and Holly?"

"When they were here, but most times they weren't."

"You were a foursome."

Diego frowned. "Why would you think that?"

"Judging by the photos in Noah's flat."

"What are you implying?"

Something almost imperceptible had crept into Diego's demeanor. A tension akin to a subtle ripple emanating from the core of him. Bourne was pleased that his probing had struck a nerve.

Bourne shrugged. "Nothing, really, other than in those photos you all looked very close."

"As I said, we were friends."

"Closer than friends, I would think."

At that moment Diego glanced down at his watch. "If you fancy a bit of a flutter, now's the time to take ourselves to Knightsbridge."

The Vesper Club was a very posh casino in London's very posh West End. It was one of those discreet affairs, hardly noticeable from the street, the polar opposite of the exclusive velvet-rope nightclubs in New York and Miami Beach that revel in their crassness.

Inside it was all butter-soft leather banquettes at the restaurant, a long, snaking brass-and-glass, neon-lit bar, and a number of gaming rooms clad in marble, mirrors, and stone columns with Doric capitals. They passed among the slots. Off to one side was the electronic gaming room whose high-decibel rock music and neon lights seemed to blink *Go!* Bourne peered in, saw that it was patrolled by a guard. He guessed the club figured the younger clients were more apt to get rowdy than the older, more established ones.

They went down several steps into the more sedate but no less opulent main gaming area, featuring all the usual suspects: baccarat, roulette, poker, blackjack. The oval room was filled with the low buzz of bets being made, roulette wheels spinning, the calls of the croupiers, and the ubiquitous clink of glassware. They wound their way through this expanse to a green baize door guarded by a large man in a tuxedo. The moment he caught sight of Diego, he smiled and gave a small deferential nod.

"How are you this evening, Mr. Hererra?"

"Quite all right, Donald." He gestured. "This is my friend Adam Stone."

"Good evening, sir." Donald opened the door, which swung inward. "Welcome to the Vesper Club's Empire Suite."

"This was where Noah liked to play poker," Diego said over his shoulder. "Only high stakes, only expert players."

Bourne looked around at the dark walls, the solid-marble floor, three kidney-shaped tables; the hunched shoulders and concentrated expressions of the men and women who sat around the green baize analyzing the cards, sizing up their opponents and placing their bets accordingly. "I wasn't aware that Noah had the kind of money to be a high-roller."

"He didn't. I staked him to it."

"Wasn't that risky?"

"Not with Noah." Diego grinned. "When it came to poker he was an expert's expert. Before an hour went by I'd get my money back and then some. I'd go and play with the profit. It was a good deal for both of us."

"Did the girls come here?"

"What girls?"

"Tracy and Holly," Bourne said patiently.

Diego looked thoughtful. "Once or twice, I suppose."

"You don't remember."

"Tracy liked to gamble, Holly didn't." Diego's shrug was an attempt to conceal his growing discomfort. "But surely you know this already."

"Tracy didn't like to gamble." Bourne kept any hint of accusation out of his voice. "She hated her job, which caused her to gamble almost every day."

Diego turned back to him, a look of consternation on his face, or was it fear?

"She worked for Leonid Arkadin," Bourne continued. "But surely you knew this already."

Diego licked his lips. "Actually, I had no idea." He looked as if he wanted to sit down. "But how . . . how is this possible?"

"Arkadin was blackmailing her," Bourne said. "He had something on her, what was it?"

"I . . . I don't know," Diego said in a shaky voice.

"You need to tell me, Diego. It's vitally important."

"Why? Why is it vitally important? Tracy is dead—she and Holly are both dead. And now Noah, too. Shouldn't they all be left in peace?"

Bourne took a step toward him. Though he lowered

his voice, it was full of menace. "But Arkadin is still alive. He was responsible for Holly's death. And it was your friend Noah who murdered Holly."

"No!" Diego stiffened. "You're wrong, he couldn't possibly—"

"I was there when it happened, Diego. Noah pushed her off a flight of steps at the top of a temple in East Bali. That, my friend, is fact, not the fiction you've been feeding me."

"Drink," Diego said in a voice made thin and hoarse by his consternation.

Bourne took him by the elbow and walked him over to the small bar at the rear of the Empire Suite. Diego lurched on stiff legs as if he were already drunk. As soon as he collapsed on a stool he ordered a double whiskey—no refined sherry for him now. He drank the whiskey off in three long gulps, then asked for another. He would have downed all of that, as well, if Bourne hadn't pulled the glass out of his unsteady hand and set it down on the black granite bartop.

"Noah killed Holly." Diego was slumped over, staring into the depths of the whiskey, into a past that he'd thought he knew. "What a fucking nightmare."

Diego did not seem to be a man prone to foul language. He was clearly out of his element, which indicated that he wasn't privy to his father's illicit arms trafficking. Neither, apparently, did he know what Noah had done for a living.

Suddenly his head swung around and he looked at Bourne. "Why? Why would he do that?"

"He wanted something she had. Apparently she wouldn't give it to him voluntarily."

"So he *killed* her?" Diego looked incredulous. "What kind of man would do something like that?" He shook his head slowly and sadly. "I can't conceive of anyone wanting to harm her."

Bourne noticed that Diego hadn't said, *I can't conceive of Noah wanting to harm her.* "Clearly," he said, "Noah was not who you thought he was." He refrained from adding, *Neither was Tracy.*

Diego grabbed the glass and finished off the second double. "Good God," he whispered.

Very gently Bourne said, "Tell me about the four of you, Diego."

"I need another drink."

Bourne ordered him a single this time. Diego lunged for the glass like a life jacket thrown to a drowning man. At one of the tables a woman in a glittery gown cashed in, rose, and walked out. Her place was taken by a man with the shoulders of a football player. A heavyish older woman with frosted hair, who had apparently just come in, sat down at the middle table. All three tables were full up.

Diego took two convulsive swallows of whiskey, then said in a voice bled dry, "Tracy and I had a thing, nothing serious, we saw other people—at least she did. It was very off-and-on, very casual. We had a few giggles, nothing more. We didn't want it to disturb our friendship."

Something in his voice alerted Bourne. "That's not all of it, is it?"

Diego's mournful expression deepened, and he looked away. "No," he said. "I fell in love with her. I didn't mean to, I didn't even want to," he added, as if it had been within his power to choose. "She was so nice about it, so kind. But still..." His voice drifted away on a tide of sad memories.

Bourne thought it time to move on. "And Holly?"

Diego seemed to snap out of his daze. "Noah seduced her. I saw it happening, I thought it was amusing, in a way, that no harm would come of it. Please don't ask me why."

"What happened?"

Diego sighed. "As it turned out Noah had a thing for Tracy, a very bad thing. For her part she wanted nothing to do with him, she told him flat-out." He took another gulp of his whiskey. He was drinking it as if it were water. "The thing she wouldn't say, even to me, was that she didn't really like Noah, or at least she didn't trust him."

"Which meant?"

"Tracy was very protective of Holly, she saw Noah moving in on Holly because he couldn't have her. She felt Noah was just being cynical and self-destructive while Holly was taking the liaison far more seriously. She believed it would end in tears—Holly's tears."

"Why didn't she step in, tell Noah to back off?"

"She did. He told her—far too bluntly, if you ask me—to stay out of it."

"Did you talk to him?"

Diego looked even more miserable than before. "I should have, I know, but I didn't believe Tracy, or maybe I chose not to believe her because if I did, then the situation had already gotten so messy and I didn't..."

"What, you didn't want to get your hands dirty?"

Diego nodded, but he wouldn't meet Bourne's eyes.

"You must have had your own suspicions about Noah."

"I don't know, perhaps I did. But the fact is I wanted to believe in us, I wanted to believe that everything would work out all right, that we would make it all right because we cared about one another."

"You cared about one another all right, but not in the right way."

"Looking back now everything seems twisted, no one was who they said they were, or liked what they said they liked. I don't even understand what drew us together."

"That's the point, isn't it?" Bourne said, not unkindly. "Each one of you wanted something from someone else in the group; in one way or another all of you used your friendships as leverage."

"Everything we did together, everything we said or confided to one another was a lie."

"Not necessarily," Bourne said. "You knew Tracy was working for Arkadin, didn't you?"

"I told you I didn't."

"When I asked you what Arkadin had on her, do you remember what you said?"

Diego bit his lip, but said nothing.

"You said that Tracy was dead—that she and Holly were both dead, and shouldn't they be left in peace?" He peered into Diego's face. "That's a response of a man who knows exactly what he's been asked."

Diego slapped the flat of his hand onto the bartop. "I promised her I wouldn't tell anyone."

"I understand," Bourne said gently, "but keeping it a secret now doesn't help her."

Diego passed a hand across his face, as if trying to wipe away a memory. At the second table from them a man said, "I'm out," pushed his chair back, rose, and stretched.

"All right." Diego's eyes met Bourne's. "She said that Arkadin had helped get her brother out of terrible trouble and now he was using that against her."

Bourne almost said, *But Tracy didn't have a brother.* He caught himself and said, "What else?"

"Nothing. It was after...before we went to sleep. It was very late, she'd had too much to drink, she'd been depressed all evening and then as soon as we finished she couldn't stop crying. I asked her if I'd done anything wrong, which only made her cry harder. I held her for a long time. When she calmed down she told me."

Something was very wrong. Chrissie said they had no brother, Tracy told Diego they did. One of the two sisters was lying, but which one? What possible reason could Tracy have for lying to Diego, and what reason would Chrissie have to lie to him?

At that moment Bourne saw movement out of the corner of his eye. The man who had cashed in was making his way toward the bar, and within another two steps Bourne knew that he was heading straight for them.

Though the man wasn't large he gave a formidable appearance. His black eyes seemed to smolder out of a face the color of tanned leather. His thick hair and close-cropped beard matched the color of his eyes. He had a hawk-like nose, a wide thick-lipped mouth, and cheeks like slabs of concrete. A small diagonal scar bisected one furry eyebrow. He moved with a low center of gravity, his arms loose and relaxed, though not swinging or even moving at all.

And it was this gait, this way of holding himself that marked him as a man of professional intent, a man with whom death walked from dusk until dawn. It was also these things that triggered a memory, causing it to pierce the maddening veils of Bourne's amnesia.

A shiver of recognition passed down Bourne's spine: This was the man who had helped him obtain the Dominion ring.

Bourne moved away from Diego. This man, whoever he was, didn't know him as Adam Stone. As Bourne approached him, he extended his hand and a smile creased his face.

"Jason, at last I've caught up with you."

"Who are you? How do you know me?"

The smile lost its luster. "It's Ottavio. Jason, don't you remember me?"

"Not at all."

Ottavio shook his head. "I don't understand. We worked together in Morocco, an assignment from Alex Conklin—"

"Not now," Bourne said. "The man I'm with—"

"Diego Hererra, I recognize him."

"Hererra knows me as Adam Stone."

Ottavio nodded, at once focused. "I understand." He glanced over Bourne's shoulder. "Why don't you introduce us?"

"I don't think that would be wise."

"Judging by Hererra's expression, it will look odd if you don't."

Bourne saw that he had no choice. Turning on his heel, he led Ottavio back to the bar.

Bourne introduced them, "Diego Hererra, this is Ottavio—"

"Moreno," Ottavio said, extending his hand for Diego to take.

As Diego did so his eyes opened wide in shock and his body slumped down onto the stool. That was when Bourne saw the scarred man pull out the slender, ceramic blade of the knife, which through sleight of hand he had palmed and slipped through Diego's chest. Its tip was curved slightly upward, mimicking his smile, which now seemed ghastly.

Bourne grabbed him by the shirtfront and hauled him off his feet, but the scarred man would not let go of Diego's hand. He was immensely powerful, his grip was like a vise. Bourne turned to Diego but saw that the life was already fleeing his body, the knife tip had probably pierced his heart.

"I'll kill you for this," Bourne whispered.

"No you won't, Jason. I'm one of the good guys, remember?"

"I don't remember a thing, not even your name."

"Then you'll just have to trust me. We've got to get out—"

"I'm not letting you go anywhere," Bourne said.

"You have no choice but to trust me." The scarred man glanced toward the door, which had just opened. "Regard the alternative."

Bourne saw Donald the bouncer come into the Empire Suite. He was accompanied by two other brawny men in tuxedos. All of them, Bourne noted with an electric shock that passed clear through him, were wearing gold rings on the forefingers of their right hands.

"They're Severus Domna," the scarred man said.

Book Two

Book Two

12

I N THE ABSOLUTE stillness of inaction, the only sound was the whisper of gamblers losing money. Ottavio handed Bourne a pair of specially baffled earplugs, along with the whispered word: "Now."

Bourne fitted the plugs into his ear canals. He saw what looked like a ball bearing palmed out of Ottavio's pocket, held between the forefinger and middle finger of his left hand. Only its rough surface and the earplugs gave clues to what it might be: a USW, an ultrasonic weapon.

At that moment Ottavio let the USW drop to the floor, where it rolled across the slick marble squares toward the three Severus Domna agents standing between them and the green baize door. The USW activated as soon as it hit the floor, sending out an AFS, an area field of sound, that affected the inner ears of everyone in the room, causing them to collapse in waves of dizziness.

Bourne followed Ottavio past the tables, leaping over prone bodies. Donald and the other two bouncers were on the floor with the gamblers and the dealers, but as the scarred man stepped over a bouncer the man reached up and, pulling hard on the back of his jacket, toppled him backward, then struck him hard just above the right ear. Bourne sidestepped Ottavio's falling body. As the bouncer rose, Bourne recognized him as the man patrolling the electronic gaming room; he wore earplugs to mute the rock music. They weren't the kind Bourne and the scarred man were using, but they had dampened the field enough for him to overcome his disorientation.

Bourne slammed his fist into the bouncer's side. The bouncer grunted, and when he turned, he held a Walther P99 in his hand. Bourne drove the edge of his hand down onto the bouncer's wrist. He wrested the Walther away from him and swung its butt into the bouncer's face, but he ducked away out of reach. Bourne drove him against the wall; the bouncer hit him hard on the right biceps and Bourne's arm went numb. The bouncer, seeking to build on his advantage, drove his fist toward Bourne's solar plexus, but Bourne deflected the blow, buying himself time to regain feeling in his right arm.

They fought savagely and silently in a room bizarrely filled with people slumped over the gaming tables or puddled on the floor like spilled Jell-O. Their soundless fury was a blur of intense motion in a room otherwise devoid of it, lending the vicious give-and-take of hand-to-hand combat an eerie quality, as if they were battling underwater.

Oxygenated blood was rushing back into Bourne's right arm when the bouncer got himself inside Bourne's defense and landed a powerful blow in the same spot. Bourne's arm dropped as if it were made of stone, and he could see the grin of triumph informing the bouncer's face. He feinted right, which didn't fool the man, whose grin widened. Bourne's left elbow connected with his throat, breaking the hyoid bone. The bouncer made an odd, clicking sound as he went down and stayed down.

By this time Ottavio had regained his feet and was shaking off the effects of the blow to his head. Bourne pulled open the door and, together, they went out into the casino's main room, walking quickly but not fast enough to draw attention to themselves. The sonic field hadn't penetrated here. Everything was moving at a normal pace, no one yet suspected what had happened in the Empire Suite, but Bourne knew it was just a matter of time before the head of security or one of the managers went looking for Donald or one of the other two bouncers.

Bourne tried to hurry them along, but the scarred man hung back.

"Wait," he said, "wait."

They had removed their earplugs and the scrapes and rustlings of the rarefied world around them plunged in on them like the roar of angry surf.

"We can't afford to wait," Bourne said. "We need to get out of here before—"

But it was already too late. A man with a ramrod-straight back and the clear no-nonsense air of authority was striding across the main room toward them. There were too many people around for a confrontation, nevertheless Bourne saw Ottavio heading toward the manager.

Bourne cut him off and, smiling broadly, said, "Are you the floor manager?"

"Yes. Andrew Steptoe." He made an attempt to look over Bourne's shoulder at the green baize door outside of which Donald should have been stationed. "I'm afraid I'm rather busy at the moment. I—"

"Donald said someone would call you over." He took Steptoe's elbow and, inclining his head toward him, said in a confidential whisper, "I'm in the middle of one of those high-stakes battles that come along once in a great while, if you understand me."

"I'm afraid I don't—"

Bourne turned him away from the door to the Empire Suite. "But of course you do, a mano-a-mano duel over the poker table, I know you do. It's a matter of money, you see."

Money was the magic word. He had Steptoe's full attention now. Behind the manager's back he could see the scarred man break out into a sly smile. He walked Steptoe closer and closer to the cashier, which was on the right side of the slots room, conveniently located near the entryway so that the clientele could buy chips on their way in and the occasional winners could cash out as they left—if they made it past all the other glittering lures the gambling profession threw at them.

"How much money?" Steptoe could not keep a note of greed out of his voice.

"Half a million," Bourne said without hesitation.

Steptoe didn't know whether to frown or lick his chops. "I'm afraid I don't know you..."

"James. Robert James." They were nearing the cashier's cage and, by proximity, the front door. "I'm an associate of Diego Hererra's."

"Ah. I see." Steptoe pursed his lips. "Even so, Mr. James, this establishment does not know you personally. You understand, we cannot put up such a large amount—"

"Oh, no, that's not what I meant to imply." Bourne feigned shock. "Rather I need your permission to leave the premises during the game in order to obtain the amount in question, so that I can remain in the game."

Now the manager did frown. "At this time of night?"

Bourne radiated confidence. "A wire transfer can be effected. It will only take twenty minutes—thirty, at most."

"Well, it's highly irregular, don't you know."

"Half a million pounds, Mr. Steptoe, is a large amount of money, as you yourself pointed out."

Steptoe nodded. "Quite so." He sighed. "I suppose that under the circumstances it can be allowed." He waggled a forefinger in Bourne's face. "But be quick about it, sir. I can give you no more than half an hour."

"Understood." Bourne shook the manager's hand. "Thank you."

Then he and the scarred man turned, went up the steps, across the entryway, through the glass doors, and into the windswept London night.

Several blocks away, as they turned a corner, Bourne rammed the scarred man hard against the side of a parked car and said, "Now tell me who you are and why you killed Diego."

As the scarred man reached for his knife Bourne

gripped his wrist. "Let's have none of that," he said. "Give me answers."

"I would never harm you, Jason, you know that."

"Why did you kill Diego?"

"He'd been told to bring you to the club at a certain time tonight."

Bourne remembered Diego looking down at his watch and saying, *"Now's the time to take ourselves to Knightsbridge."* An odd way to put it, except if this man was telling the truth.

"Who told Diego to bring me there?" But Bourne already knew.

"The Severus Domna got to him—I don't know how—but they gave him precise instructions on how to betray you."

Bourne remembered Diego picking at his food as if he had something important on his mind. Had he been anticipating the betrayal? Was Ottavio right?

The scarred man stared into Bourne's face. "You really don't know me, do you?"

"I told you I didn't."

"My name is Ottavio Moreno." He waited a beat. "Gustavo Moreno's brother."

A tiny tremor of recognition raced through Bourne as the veils of his amnesia stirred and tried to part.

"We met in Morocco." Bourne's voice was barely a whisper.

"Yes." A smile creased Ottavio Moreno's face. "In Marrakech, we traveled into the High Atlas Mountains together, didn't we?"

"I don't know."

"Good God!" Ottavio Moreno's face registered surprise, perhaps even shock. "And the laptop? What about the laptop?"

"What laptop?"

"You don't remember the laptop?" He grabbed Bourne by the arms. "Jason, come on. We met in Marrakech in order to get the laptop."

"Why?"

Ottavio Moreno frowned. "You told me it was a key."

"Key to what?"

"To the Severus Domna."

At that moment they heard the familiar high–low wail of police sirens.

"The mess we left behind in the Empire Suite," Moreno said. "Come on, let's go."

"I'm not going anywhere with you," Bourne said.

"But you must, you owe me," Ottavio Moreno said. "You killed Noah Perlis."

In other words," Secretary of Defense Bud Halliday said as he scanned the report in front of him, "between retirements, normal attrition, and requests for transfer—all of which, I see, have been not only granted but expedited—a quarter of the Old Man's CI has moved on."

"And our own personnel have moved in." DCI Danziger did not bother to keep the satisfaction out of his voice. The secretary appreciated confidence as much as he disliked indecision. Danziger took back the report and carefully folded it away. "It will be only a matter of months, I believe, before that number will increase to fully a third of the old guard."

"Good, good."

Halliday rubbed his large, square hands over the remnants of his Spartan lunch. The Occidental was abuzz with the jawing of politicos, reporters, flacks, power brokers, and industry influence peddlers. All of them had paid their respects to him in one circumspect manner or another, whether it was with a slightly terrified smile, an obeisant nod of the head, or, as in the case of the elderly and influential Senator Daughtry, a quick handshake and a down-home how-dee-do. Swing-state senators accumulated power even during non-election years, both parties seeking to curry favor. It was simply standard operating procedure inside the Beltway.

For some time, then, the two men sat in silence. The restaurant began to thin out as the denizens of the DC political pits straggled back to work. But soon enough their place was taken by tourists in striped shirts and baseball caps they'd bought from the vendors down by the Mall imprinted with CIA or FBI. Danziger returned to his lunch, which, as usual, was more substantial than Halliday's unadorned strip steak. All that was left on the secretary's plate were several pools of blood, clotted with congealed fat.

Across the table Halliday's mind had drifted to the dream he couldn't remember. He had read articles that dreams were a necessary part of sleep—REM sleep, the eggheads called it—without which a man would, eventually, go insane. On the other hand, it was certainly true that he couldn't recall a single dream. His entire sleeping existence was a perfect blank wall on which nothing was ever scrawled.

He shook himself like a dog coming out of the rain. Why did he care? Well, he knew why. The Old Man had once confided in him that he suffered from the same strange illness—that's what the Old Man called it, an illness. Strange to think that the two of them had once been friends, more than friends, come to think of it—what had they called it then? Blood brothers. As young men they had confided all their little tics and habits, the secrets that inhabited the dark corners of their souls. Where had it all gone wrong? How had they become the bitterest of enemies? It might have been the gradual divergence of their political views, but friends often dealt with disagreement. No, their separation had to do with a sense of betrayal, and in men such as they were, loyalty was the ultimate—the only—test of friendship.

The truth was they had betrayed what they had built as young men, as their idealism was burned away in the crucible of the nation's capital, where they had both chosen to serve lifetime sentences. The Old Man had been an acolyte of John Foster Dulles while he had attached himself to Richard Helms—men with wildly divergent backgrounds, methodologies, and, most importantly, ideologies. And since they were in the business of ideology and that business was their life there was no recourse but to turn on each other, to try with every fiber of their being to prove the other wrong, to bring him down, to destroy him.

For decades the Old Man had outwitted him at every turn, but now the tables were turned, the Old Man was dead, and he had the prize he'd set his gaze on so long ago: control of CI.

Danziger clearing his throat brought Halliday back from the chasm of the past.

"Is there anything we've failed to cover?"

The secretary regarded him as a child studies an ant or a beetle, with the curiosity reserved for a species so far below him that it seemed inconceivably distant. Danziger was far from a stupid man, which was why Halliday had chosen him as his knight to move back and forth across the chessboard of the American clandestine services. But apart from his usefulness on the board, he viewed Danziger as entirely expendable. Halliday had closed himself off the moment he felt the Old Man's betrayal. He had a wife and two children, of course, but he scarcely thought of them. His son was a poet—good Christ, a poet, of all things! And his daughter, well, the less said about her and her female partner the better. As for his wife, she had betrayed him as well, giving birth to two disappointments. These days, apart from formal functions where the strict code of Washington family values required her to be on his arm, they lived entirely separate lives. It had been years since they had slept in the same room, let alone the same bed. Occasionally they found themselves having breakfast together, a minor torture Halliday escaped as quickly as he could.

Danziger was leaning forward confidentially across the table. "If there's anything I can help you with, you only have to—"

"I think you've confused me with a friend," Halliday snapped. "The day I ask for your help is the day I put a gun in my mouth and pull the trigger."

He slid out of the booth and walked away without a backward glance, leaving Danziger to pay the check.

* * *

Alone for the moment while Boris Karpov slept inside the convent, Arkadin poured himself a mescal and took the drink out into the steamy Sonora night. Dawn would soon be scything through the stars, extinguishing them as it went. The shorebirds were already awake, flocking out of their nests to sweep along the beachfront.

Arkadin, breathing deeply of the salt and the phosphorus, punched in a number on his cell. The phone rang for a very long time. Knowing there would be no voice mail, he was about to hang up when a raspy voice sounded in his ear.

"Who in the unholy name of Saint Stephen is this?"

Arkadin laughed. "It's me, Ivan."

"Why, hello, Leonid Danilovich," Ivan Volkin said.

Volkin had once been the most powerful man in the *grupperovka*. Unaffiliated with any family, he had for many years been a negotiator, both between families and between the bosses of certain families and the most corrupt businessmen and politicians. He was a man, in sum, to whom practically anyone in power owed favors. And though long retired, he had defied convention by becoming even more powerful as his age advanced. He was also particularly fond of Arkadin, whose strange ascent in the underworld he'd followed since the day Maslov had him brought to Moscow from his hometown of Nizhny Tagil.

"I thought you might be the president," Ivan Volkin said. "I told him I couldn't help him this time."

The thought of the president of the Russian Federation calling Ivan Volkin for a favor caused Arkadin to chuckle all the more. "Pity for him," he said.

"I did some digging regarding your problem as you

outlined it to me. You do indeed have a mole, my friend. I was able to narrow the candidates down to two, but that's as far as I was able to get."

"That's more than enough, Ivan Ivanovich. You have my undying gratitude."

Volkin laughed. "You know, my friend, you're just about the only person on earth I don't want anything from."

"I could give you virtually anything you want."

"As I well know, but to tell you the truth it's a relief to have someone in my life who owes me nothing and to whom I owe the same. Nothing changes between us, eh, Leonid Danilovich."

"No, Ivan Ivanovich, it doesn't."

After Volkin had given Arkadin the names of the two suspects, he said, "I have one more bit of information that will be of interest to you. I find it curious that I cannot tie either of these suspects to the FSB or, for that matter, any Russian secret service whatsoever."

"Then who is running the spy in my organization?"

"Your mole has been extremely careful to keep his identity a secret—he wears dark glasses and a sweatshirt with a hood over his head, so there's no good photo of him. However, the man he's been meeting has been identified as Marlon Etana."

"Odd name." It rang a bell deep inside Arkadin's mind, but he was unable to access it.

"Odder still is that I cannot find a single scrap of information on Marlon Etana."

"Ah, a pseudonym, surely."

"One would have expected that, yes," Volkin said. "However, that would mean a legend to give the pseudonym reality. I have found nothing, except that Marlon Etana is a founding member of the Monition Club, which has many branches throughout the world, but whose headquarters seems to be in Washington, DC."

"A deep-cover arm of CI or one of the many Hydra heads of the American Department of Defense."

Ivan Volkin made an animal sound deep in his throat. "When you find out, Leonid Danilovich, be sure to let me know."

Be sure to let me know," Arkadin had said to Tracy some months ago. "Anything and everything you find out about Don Fernando Hererra, even the most minute, seemingly irrelevant bit of information."

"Including the regularity of his bowel movements?"

He sat watching her, his feral eyes glittering, not moving, not blinking. They were seated at a café in Campione d'Italia, the picturesque Italian tax haven tucked away in the Swiss Alps. The tiny municipality rose steeply off the glassy ultramarine-blue surface of a clear mountain lake, studded with vessels of all sizes from rowboats to multimillion-dollar yachts, complete with the helipads, the copters, and, on the largest of these, the females to go with them.

For the five minutes before she had arrived, Arkadin had been watching an obscenely large yacht on which two long-stemmed models preened as if for paparazzi. They had the kind of perfectly bronzed skin only the kept woman knows how to acquire. As he sipped a small cup of espresso, which was all but lost in his large, square hand, he thought, *It's good to be the king*. Then he saw the naked hairy back of this particular king and turned away in disgust. You can take the man out of hell but you can't take hell out of the man. This was the operative phrase for Arkadin.

Then Tracy had shown up and he forgot the hell of Nizhny Tagil that plagued him like a recurring nightmare. Nizhny Tagil was where he had been born and raised, where he'd lost three toes to rats when his mother had locked him in a closet, where he had killed and was almost killed so many times he'd lost count. Nizhny Tagil was where he had lost everything, where, one could say, he had died.

He had ordered Tracy an espresso with sambuca, which was what she liked. As he stared into her beautiful face, he continued to be confounded by his conflicting feelings. He was drawn to her, intensely, but he also hated her. He hated her erudition, her vast knowledge. Every time she opened her mouth she reminded him of how little formal education he'd had. And to make matters much worse, he learned something valuable every time he was with her. How often do we despise our teachers, who lord it over us with their superior knowledge, who throw that knowledge and their experience in our faces. Every time he learned something, he was reminded of how inexorably tied to her he was, how much he needed her. Which was why he treated her as a bipolar might. He loved her, rewarded her with more and more money at the completion of each assignment, showered her with gifts between assignments.

She had never slept with him. He hadn't tried to seduce her, fearing that in the throes of passion his iron control might weaken, that he would grab her by the throat and throttle her until her tongue poked out and her eyes rolled up in her head. He would regret her death. Over the years she had proved indispensable. With the inside knowledge she had given him, he'd been able to blackmail her wealthy art clients, and those he chose not to suborn he used as patsies, delivering drugs all over the world secreted in the crates that held their precious artwork.

Tracy ran the crescent of lemon rind around the rim of her cup. "What's so special about Don Fernando?"

"Drink your espresso."

She stared down at her cup but didn't touch it.

"What's the matter?" he said at last.

"Let's skip him, shall we?"

He waited a moment, quietly. Then, suddenly leaning forward, he grasped her knee beneath the table in an agonizing grip. Her head snapped up, her eyes engaged with his.

"You know the rules," he said with soft menace. "You don't question assignments, you take them."

"Not this one."

"All of them."

"I like this man."

"All. Of. Them."

She stared at him, unblinking.

He despised most of all when she got like this, that enigmatic mask that came down over her face, making him feel like a dim-witted child who had failed to learn how to read properly. "Have you forgotten the damaging evidence I have on you? Do you want me to go to your client and tell him how you accommodated your brother when he stole your client's painting to cover his debts? Do you really want to spend the next twenty years of your life in prison? It's more terrible than you can imagine, believe me."

"I want out," she said in a strangled voice.

He had laughed. "God, you're a stupid cow." *Once, just once,* he thought, *I'd like to make you cry.* "There is no out. You signed on, a contract in blood, metaphorically speaking."

"I want out."

He sat back, releasing her knee. "Besides, Don Fernando Hererra is only a secondary target—at least, for now."

She had begun to shake, very slightly, and there was a tic under her left eye. She took up her espresso and drained the cup. There was a slight clatter when she set it down.

"Who are you after?"

Close, this time, he thought. *Very close.* "Someone special," he had said. "A man who calls himself Adam Stone. And this assignment is a bit different." His hands had spread wide apart. "Adam Stone is not his real name, of course."

"What is it?"

Arkadin's smile held real malice. He turned his head and ordered them two more espressos.

Dawn was spreading its wings over Puerto Peñasco as Arkadin's brief flare of memory subsided into darkness. A freshening breeze off the water brought the scent of a new day. There had been women in his life—Yelena, Marlene, Devra, others, surely, though their names now escaped him—but no one like Tracy. Those three—Yelena, Marlene, and Devra—had meant something to him, though he'd be hard put to say precisely what. Each in her own way had changed the course of his life. Yet none had enriched it. Only Tracy, his Tracy. He clenched his fist. But she hadn't been his Tracy, had she? No, no, no. Good Christ, no.

Rain drummed against the roof of the cottage, fat drops sliding down the windows. A rumble of approaching thunder. The lace curtains stirred. In the dead of night Chrissie lay fully dressed on one of the twin beds, staring at the window, speckled as a robin's egg. Scarlett lay curled on the other bed, breathing evenly in her sleep. Chrissie knew she should be sleeping, that she needed her rest, but after the incident on the motorway her nerves would not stop singing. Several hours ago she had contemplated taking half a lorazepam to calm herself into sleep, but the thought of drifting off made her more anxious.

The singing of her nerves had only increased when she'd picked Scarlett up from her parents. Her father, always well attuned to her moods, had suspected something was up with her the moment he opened the door to her knock, and he was not convinced when she tried to reassure him that everything was fine. She could still see his thin, oblong face as he stood looking after her while she bundled Scarlett into the Range Rover. It was the same stricken look he'd had standing over Tracy's coffin as it was lowered into the ground. As she got in behind the wheel, Chrissie breathed a sigh of relief that she'd had the foresight to park the SUV so that he couldn't see the scrapes along one side. She waved cheerfully to him as she drove away. He was still standing in the doorway when she went around a curve and disappeared from his view.

Now, hours later and miles away, she lay on the bed in a house owned by a girlfriend who was away in Brussels on business. She'd been able to pick up the keys from the woman's brother. In the dark she lay listening to all the tiny creaking and moaning, whispers and hissing of a strange house. The wind clawed at the window sashes, trying to find a way in. She shivered and pulled a blanket tighter around her, but the blanket didn't warm her. Neither did the central heating. There was a chill in her bones, caused by her vibrating nerves, and the dread that stalked her thoughts.

"We were being followed, possibly all the way from Tracy's flat," Adam had said. *"There's no point in taking a chance these people know about Scarlett—and where your parents live, for that matter."*

The thought that these people who had wanted to shoot Adam might know about her daughter gave her a sick feeling in the pit of her stomach. She wanted to feel safe here, wanted to believe that there was no danger now that she had separated herself from him, but the doubts continued to prey on her. Another roll of thunder, closer this time, and then another burst of rain rattled the windowpane. She sat up, gasping. Her heart was pounding, and she reached for the Glock that Adam had given her for protection. She had some experience with guns, though mostly rifles and shotguns. Against her mother's objections, her father had taken her hunting on winter Sundays, when the frost was brittle and the sun was weak and drained of color. She remembered the quivering flank of a deer, and how she had flinched when her father had fired a shot into its heart. She remembered the look in its eye as her father had taken his skinning knife to its belly. Its mouth was half open as if it had been about to ask for mercy before it was shot.

Scarlett whimpered in her sleep, and Chrissie rose and, leaning over, stroked her hair as she always did when her daughter was having a bad dream. Why were children burdened with nightmares, she wondered, when there was so much time for nightmares in adult life? Where was the carefree childhood she'd had? Was it a mirage? Had she also had nightmares, night terrors, anxieties? She could not now remember, which was a blessing.

She knew one thing, though, Tracy would have laughed at her for even having such thoughts. *"Life isn't carefree,"* she could hear her sister saying. *"What are you thinking? Life is difficult, at best. At its worst, it's a bloody nightmare."*

What would have led her to say such a thing? Chrissie asked herself. *What misfortunes had befallen her while I had my head stuck in my Oxford texts?* All at once she was overcome with the conviction that she had failed Tracy, that she should have seen the signs of her stress, her difficult life. But, really, how could she have helped her? Tracy had been lost in a world so distant, so alien, Chrissie was sure she would have found it incomprehensible. Just as she could make no sense of what had happened today. Who was Adam Stone? She had no doubt that he'd been friends with Tracy, but she suspected now that he was more—a compatriot, business partner, maybe even her boss. Something he hadn't told her, hadn't wanted to tell her. All she knew for certain was that her sister's life had been a secret, and so was Adam's. They had been part of the same alien world, and now all unknowing she had been dragged into it. She gave a shiver again and, seeing that Scarlett had quieted, lay beside her so that they were back-to-back. Her daughter's warmth seeped slowly into her, her eyelids grew heavy, and she began to drowse, sinking slowly, inexorably into the delicious cushion of sleep.

A sharp noise startled her awake. For a moment she lay completely still, listening to the rain, the wind, Scarlett breathing along with the cottage. She listened for the noise. Had she dreamed it or had she been asleep at all? After what seemed a long time, she got out of Scarlett's bed, reached over, and slid her hand under the pillow for the Glock. Padding silently toward the half-open bedroom door, she peered out at the wedge of pale light from the lamp she'd kept on in the bedroom across the hall so she and Scarlett could find the bathroom without barking their shins.

She moved into the hallway, listened fiercely. She became aware of sweat snaking down her sides from underneath her arms. Her breath felt hot in her throat. Every second that ticked by ratcheted up her anxiety, but also the hope that she had dreamed the noise. Gliding along the hallway, she peered down the stairs at the darkened living room. Standing at the head of the stairs, undecided, she had just about convinced herself that she'd been dreaming when she heard the small noise again.

Slowly she put one bare foot after the other as she descended from semi-darkness into blackness. She needed to get all the way down the stairs before she could reach the switch that turned on the living room lights. The staircase loomed before her, seeming steeper, more treacherous in the dark. Briefly she thought about going back upstairs to look for a flashlight, but felt that she might lose her nerve if she turned around now. She kept descending, tread by tread. They were of wood, polished to a high gloss, without the benefit of a runner. Once, she slipped and, pitching forward, almost lost her balance. Grabbing for the railing, she held on while her pulse beat wildly in her ears.

Calm down, she told herself. *Just bloody well calm those nerves, Chrissie. There's no one there.*

The noise came again, louder this time because she was closer to it, and she knew: Someone was inside the house.

Just after sunset, on the day Karpov had begun his long trek back to Moscow, Arkadin and El Heraldo set off in the cigarette. Arkadin maneuvered the slender powerboat beyond the slips without running lights, which was illegal, but necessary. Besides, as he had quickly learned, in Mexico the line between legal and illegal moved more times than the front lines of a war. Not to mention the fact that what was illegal and what was enforceable were often at odds.

The cigarette's powerful GPS system was deeply hooded, so that no illumination leaked out into the blue velvet of dusk. Stars had gathered in the eastern sky, eager to display their splendor.

"Time," Arkadin said.

"Eight minutes," El Heraldo replied, consulting his watch.

Arkadin altered their course by a couple of degrees. They were already past the perimeter of the *policía* patrols, but still he did not turn on any lights. The GPS screen told him everything he needed to know. The multi-baffled mufflers El Heraldo had installed on the exhaust were working to perfection; the cigarette made scarcely any noise as it skimmed over the water at high speed.

"Five minutes," El Heraldo intoned.

"We'll be in visual range in a moment."

That was El Heraldo's cue to take the wheel while Arkadin peered through a pair of military high-power night-vision binoculars toward the south.

"Got 'em," he said, after a moment.

At once El Heraldo cut their speed by half.

Arkadin, peering through the binoculars at the on-coming boat—a yacht that must have cost upward of fifty million dollars—saw the infrared flashes, two long, two short, visible only to him.

"All's well," he said. "Full stop."

El Heraldo cut the engines, and the cigarette cut through the swells on its own momentum. Dead ahead the yacht loomed up out of the darkness. It, too, had all its lights extinguished. As Arkadin prepared himself, El Heraldo put on the night goggles and manned the infrared beacon. The yacht was equipped with an identical beacon, which was how the two boats drew alongside each other without lights and without incident.

A rope ladder was unfurled over the yacht's port side, and El Heraldo made it fast to the cigarette. A man, dressed in black, handed down a small carton. El Heraldo received it on his shoulder, then placed it on the cigarette's deck.

Using a pocketknife, Arkadin slit the carton open. Inside were cans of prepackaged organic corn tortillas. Arkadin opened one, pulled out the roll of tortillas. Inside the roll were stacked four plastic-wrapped packages of a white powder. He stuck the blade of his knife into a packet and tasted its contents. Satisfied, he waved a prearranged signal to the crew member on the yacht. Inserting the bag of cocaine back into the can, he returned it to the carton, and El Heraldo lifted it up to the crewman.

A short whistle came from the yacht as the crewman vanished up the ladder, and Arkadin waited. Moments later two rather large bundles were lowered via a portable winch. The bundles, lying horizontal, were each perhaps six feet in length. They were cradled in a net as if they were a pair of tuna.

When the bundles reached the cigarette's deck, El Heraldo rolled them off the net, which was immediately winched back up to the yacht. Then El Heraldo detached the rope ladder, which was also withdrawn.

Another whistle, longer this time, came from the yacht. Behind the wheel, El Heraldo started the engines, put the cigarette into reverse, and began to back away from the yacht. When they had reached an adequate distance, the yacht began to move forward, continuing its journey northward, up the coast of Sonora.

As El Heraldo turned the cigarette around, heading them east, back toward shore, Arkadin took up a flashlight and, squatting down, slashed the coverings at one end of the bundles. Then he shone the flashlight on what was inside.

The faces of the two men appeared pale in the light,

except where their beards had started to grow. They were still groggy with the anesthetic they had been given when they had been abducted in Moscow. Nevertheless their eyes, which hadn't seen light for some days, screwed up, watering unstoppably.

"Good evening, gentlemen," Arkadin said, invisible behind the dazzle of the beam of light. "At last you have reached the end of your journey. For one of you, at least. Stepan, Pavel, you were two of my captains, two of my most trusted men. And yet one of you has betrayed me."

He showed them how the light turned the blade of his knife into a white streak. "In the next hour or so one of you will confess and will tell me everything he knows about his betrayal. A quick, painless death will be his reward. If not . . . has either of you ever known anyone who has died of thirst? No? God help you, that's not the way any human being should die."

For an instant Chrissie froze, unsure what to do as her fight and flight responses warred with each other. Then she took a deep breath and thought about the situation rationally. Retreating wouldn't help; she'd be trapped on the second floor, and whoever had invaded the cottage would be that much closer to Scarlett. Her only thought now was for her daughter. Whatever happened, she knew she had to keep her safe.

She took a tentative step down, then another. Five treads to go before she could flick the lights on. With her back to the wall, she slowly descended. The noise came again and she froze. It sounded as if someone had come in through the kitchen door and now moved into the living room. She raised the Glock, swinging it in a slow arc as she squinted into the gloom. But apart from the partial outline of the sofa and one wing of an armchair opposite the fireplace, she could make out nothing, certainly no movement, no matter how furtive.

Another step down, another step closer to the light switch. She was only one tread away from it now, her torso leaning forward, free hand outstretched when, with an indrawn gasp, she started back. Someone was close to her, at the bottom of the stairs. In a confused swirl she felt movement on the other side of the newel post, and she raised the Glock, aiming it.

"Who's there?" Her voice startled her, as if it belonged to a dream or to someone else. "Stay where you are, I've got a gun."

"Cookie, where in the bloody hell did you get a handgun?" her father said from out of the darkness. "I knew something was wrong. What's going on?"

She flipped on the light and saw him standing there, his face pale and pinched with concern.

"Dad?" She blinked, as if she couldn't believe it was really him. "What are you doing here?"

"Cookie, where's Scarlett?"

"Upstairs. She's sleeping."

He nodded. "Good, let's keep it that way."

He gripped the barrel of the Glock and pushed it down to her side. "Now come on over here. I'll light a fire, and you'll tell me what sort of trouble you're in."

"I'm not in any trouble, Dad. Does Mum know you're here?"

"Your mum is as worried about you as I am. Her way of dealing with things is to cook, which she's doing right now. I'm meant to bring you and Scarlett back home with me."

Like a sleepwalker, she came down off the stairs and into the living room. Her father was turning on lamps. "I can't do that, Dad."

"Why not?" He waved a hand. "Never mind, I didn't think you would." He stooped, putting some logs into the grate. Then he checked around. "Where are the matches?"

He padded into the kitchen. She could hear him pulling out drawers and rummaging through them.

"It's not that I'm not grateful, Dad. But really, you're an idiot for coming out here in the middle of the night. What did you do, follow me? And how did you get in here?" She followed him into the kitchen.

A callused hand came over her mouth and, at the same time, the Glock was wrenched out of her grip. A deep swirl of masculine scent. Then she saw her father lying unconscious on the floor and she began to struggle.

"Stay still," a voice whispered in her ear. "If you don't, I'll take you upstairs and blow your daughter's face off while you watch."

13

WHEN SORAYA ARRIVED at the Tucson airport, she went straight to the line of rental-car booths and showed the photo of "Stanley Kowalski" around to all the personnel without getting a hit. That name was not on their books—not that she had expected it to come up. A professional of Arkadin's skill level wouldn't be careless enough to rent a car under the same false name he'd used at Immigration. Undaunted, she sought out the managers of each company. Because she had the date and the time that Arkadin passed through the airport, she had arranged to arrive at more or less the same hour. She asked the managers who had been on duty nine days ago. The same personnel were on duty save one, a woman with the unlikely name of Biffy Flisser, who had quit to take a hospitality position at the Best Western airport hotel. None of the salespeople recognized Arkadin.

The manager was gracious enough to call the Best Western, and Biffy Flisser was waiting for Soraya when she walked into the cool, airy lobby. They sat in the lounge and had drinks while they spoke. Biffy had a pleasant nature and readily agreed to help Soraya with her search.

"Yeah, I know him," she said, tapping the surveillance photo on Soraya's phone. "I mean, I don't really know him, but yeah, he rented a car on that date."

"You're sure."

"Positive." Biffy nodded. "He wanted a long-term lease. A month or six weeks, he said. I told him in that case we could give him a special rate and he seemed pleased."

Soraya waited a moment. "Do you recall his name?" she asked casually.

"This is important, isn't it?"

"It would certainly help me out."

"Let me see." She drummed her lacquered fingernails against the tabletop. "Frank, I think, Frank something…" She concentrated all the harder, then brightened. "That's it! Frank Stein. Frank Norman Stein, actually."

Frank N. Stein. Soraya burst out into laughter.

"What?" Biffy seemed confused. "What's so funny?"

This Arkadin was a real card, Soraya thought on her way back to the airport. Then she was brought up short. Or was he? Why would he deliberately use a name that might stick out? Possibly he planned to ditch the car somewhere across the border.

She felt suddenly deflated. Even so, she continued her investigation. Seeking out the rental-car manager, she gave him the fake name Arkadin had used. "What car did he rent?"

"Just a moment." The manager turned to his computer terminal, input the name and the date. "A black Chevy, an old one, an '87. A heap, really, but apparently that satisfied him."

"You keep cars that long?"

The manager nodded. "For one thing, here in the desert they don't rust. For another, since so many of our cars are stolen, it pays to rent out the old ones. Besides, customers like the gentle prices."

Soraya copied down the information, including the license plate tag, but without much hope that if she even found the car it would lead to Arkadin. Then she rented a car of her own, thanked the manager, and walked into a café, where she sat down and ordered an iced coffee. She'd learned the hard way not to order iced tea outside New York, Washington, or LA. Americans liked their iced tea achingly sweet.

While she waited, she opened a detailed map of Arizona and northern Mexico. Mexico was a big country, but she guessed Arkadin might be somewhere within a hundred-mile radius of the airport. Otherwise, why specifically choose Tucson when he could have flown into Mexico City or Acapulco? No, she decided, his destination had to be northwestern Mexico, possibly even just across the border.

Her iced coffee came, and she drank it black and unsugared, savoring the acidic bite that chased its way down her throat and into her stomach. She drew a circle around the airport that encompassed one hundred miles. That was her search area.

* * *

The moment Soraya left his office, the manager took out a small key from his trouser pocket and unlocked the lowest drawer on the right side of his desk. Inside were files, a handgun registered in his name, and a head shot photo. He brought the photo into the light, staring at it for several moments. Then, pursing his lips, he turned the photo over, read the local number off to himself, and dialed it on his office phone.

When the male voice answered, he said, "Someone came looking for your man—the man in the photo you gave me...She said her name was Soraya Moore, she gave me no reason to disbelieve her...No official ID, no...I did just as you said...No sweat on that score...No, of course you don't understand. What I mean is that it'll be easy, I rented her a car..."

"...a Toyota Corolla, silver-blue, license tag...D as in David, V as in Victor, N as in Nancy, three-three-seven-eight."

There was a bit more, but it was of no interest to Soraya. The tiny electronic bug she had affixed to the underside of the manager's desk was working perfectly, the manager's voice came through with crystal clarity. Pity she couldn't hear the voice on the other end of the line. However, she now knew that someone had staked out the Tucson airport, possibly others near the border with Mexico. She also knew that whoever these people were they were going to follow her into Mexico. One thing stood out: The person the manager had called didn't understand American jargon. That left out Mexicans, who this close to the border made an almost fetishistic habit of learning every possible English colloquialism and street phrasing. The person had to be a foreigner, possibly Russian. And if, as she suspected, he was one of Arkadin's people put in place to look out for Dimitri Maslov's hit squad, this just might be her lucky day.

The first thing Peter Marks did on disembarking at London's Heathrow Airport was call Willard.

"Where are you?" Marks said.

"The less you know the better."

Marks bridled at that. "The last thing anyone needs in the field is to fly blind," he snapped.

"I'm trying to protect you from Liss. When he calls you—and believe me he will—you'll tell him truthfully that you don't know where I am, and for you that will be the end of it."

Peter showed his official government ID to Immigration, and they stamped his passport and waved him through. "But not for you."

"Let me worry about that, Peter. You have enough on your plate getting the ring from Bourne."

"I have to find him first," Marks said, approaching the baggage carousel.

"You've had dealings with Bourne," Willard said. "I trust you'll find him."

Marks was outside now, in a typically dreary London morning. He glanced at his watch. It was appallingly early and already the sky was spitting rain in fitful bursts.

"No one really knows Bourne," he said, "not even Soraya."

"That's because nothing about him makes sense," Willard pointed out. "He's completely unpredictable."

"Well, you can hardly complain. I mean Treadstone made him this way."

"It absolutely did not," Willard said hotly. "Whatever happened to him, the form of amnesia he's suffered has changed him irrevocably. Speaking of which, I want you to see a Chief Inspector Lloyd-Philips. Bourne may have been involved in a murder at the Vesper Club in the West End last night. Start looking for him there."

Marks made several quick notes on the palm of his hand. "You're the one who isn't understandable." He was standing in line for a taxi, periodically shuffling forward. Speaking in a low voice, he covered his mouth with his hand. "You went out of your way to help him in Bali, now you seem to want to examine him like a circus freak."

"He *is* a freak, Peter. A very dangerous freak—he's already murdered Noah Perlis and now he may be implicated in another death. How much more proof do you need that he's out of control? I don't want you to forget that fact or lose sight of our goal. The Treadstone training made him into an ultimate warrior, but then something unforeseen—a freak of fate or nature, whatever you choose to call it—altered him further. He became something unknown, something more. Which is why I've pitted him against Arkadin. As I've already explained to you, Arkadin, being the first of Treadstone's graduates, was subjected to a form of extreme training that—well, after he escaped and disappeared, Conklin decided to modify the training, to scale it back, make it less . . . extreme."

Having reached the head of the line, Marks slid into the backseat of the taxi and gave the address of a small hotel he liked in the West End.

"If Treadstone is to go forward, if it's to be successful, if it's to fulfill its promise, we must find out who will prevail." Willard's voice buzzed in Marks's ear like a wasp beating against a windowpane. "Depending on who is left alive, we'll know how to proceed."

Marks stared out the window, seeing nothing. "I want to get this straight. If Arkadin prevails, you'll go back to the initial training methodology."

"With several minor tweaks I've got in mind."

"But what if Bourne kills Arkadin? You don't know—"

"That's right, Peter, we'll be faced with an X-factor. The process will, therefore, take longer. We'll have to study Bourne in a controlled environment. We'll—"

"Wait a minute. Are you talking about imprisoning him?"

"Subjecting him to repeated batteries of psychological tests, yes, yes." Willard sounded impatient, as if he'd made his point but Marks was too stupid to get it. "This is the essence of Treadstone, Peter. This is what Alex Conklin devoted his life to."

"But why? I just don't get it."

"The Old Man didn't either, not really." Willard sighed. "Sometimes I think Alex was the only American to learn from the tragic mistakes of the war in Vietnam. It was his special genius, you see, to anticipate Iraq and Afghanistan. He saw the new world coming. He knew that the old methods of waging war were as antiquated, as certain to fail as the Napoleonic code.

"While the Pentagon was spending billions on stock-piling smart bombs, nuclear submarines, stealth bombers, supersonic jet fighters, Alex was concentrated on building the one weapon of war he knew would be effective: human beings. Treadstone's mission from the very first day of its inception was to build the perfect human weapon: fearless, merciless, skilled at infiltration, subterfuge, misdirection, mimicry. A weapon of a thousand faces who could be anyone, go anywhere, kill any target without remorse, and return to take on the next mission.

"And now you see what a visionary Alex was. What he saw has, indeed, come to pass. What we create in the Treadstone program will become America's most potent weapon against its enemies, no matter how clever they are, no matter how remote their location. Do you think I'm going to bury something invaluable? I made a deal with the devil so that Treadstone would be resurrected."

"And what," Marks said, "if the devil has other ideas for Treadstone?"

"Then," Willard replied, "the devil will have to be dealt with in some manner." There was a slight pause. "Arkadin or Bourne, it makes no difference to me. Only the outcome of their struggle for survival interests me. And either way, I will have them—one or the other—as the prototype for the graduates Treadstone will produce."

Start at the beginning," Bourne said. "This has all the earmarks of a nightmare."

"The long and the short of it," Ottavio Moreno said

with a sigh, "is that you had no right to kill Noah Perlis."

The two men were in a safe house in Thamesmead, a small developed area directly across the river from the London City Airport. It was one of those modern crack-erjack boxes being thrown up all over the sprawling suburbs that were as flimsy as they looked. They had driven there in Moreno's gray Opel, as anonymous a car as you were likely to find in London. They'd eaten some cold chicken and pasta out of the fridge, washed it down with a bottle of decent South African wine, and then had retired to the living room where they literally threw themselves onto the sofas.

"Perlis killed Holly Moreau."

"Perlis was business," Ottavio Moreno pointed out.

"So, I think, was Holly."

Ottavio Moreno nodded. "But then it became personal, didn't it?"

Bourne had no good reply to that, since the answer was obvious to both of them.

"Water under the bridge," Moreno said, taking Bourne's silence as acquiescence. "The point that you've forgotten is that I hired Perlis to find the laptop."

"He had no laptop; he had the ring."

Moreno shook his head. "Forget the ring and try to remember the laptop."

Bourne felt as if he were sinking deeper and deeper into quicksand. "You mentioned the laptop before, but I have no memory of it."

"In that event I imagine you have no memory of how you stole it from Jalal Essai's home."

Bourne shook his head helplessly.

Moreno dug his thumbs into his eyes for a moment.

"I see what you meant when you said start at the beginning."

Bourne, saying nothing, watched him carefully. The constant problem with people arising out of his past was this: Who were they really and were they telling him the truth? A man with no memory isn't difficult to lie to. In fact, Bourne reflected, it was probably fun to lie to an amnesiac and watch his reactions.

"You were given an assignment to get the laptop computer."

"By whom?"

Moreno shrugged. "Alex Conklin, I imagine. Anyway, we made contact in Marrakech."

Morocco again. Bourne sat forward. "Why would I contact you?"

"I was Alex Conklin's contact there." When Bourne gave him a skeptical look, he added, "I'm a half brother. My mother is a Berber, from the High Atlas Mountains."

"Your father got around."

"Make a joke, okay, it's all right, I won't gut you." Ottavio Moreno laughed. "Christ, this is a fucked-up world." He shook his head in disbelief. "Okay, look, my friend. My father had his thumb in a shitload of pies, most of them illegal, yes, I freely admit it. So what? So his business ventures took him to many places around the world, some of them strange."

"Business wasn't the only thing he had a healthy appetite for," Bourne said.

Ottavio Moreno nodded. "Too true. He had an eye for exotic women."

"Are there any other little half Morenos running around?"

Moreno laughed. "There very well might be, knowing my father. But if there are, I don't know about them."

Bourne decided there was nothing more to be gained by taking the subject of the elder Moreno's love life any farther. "Okay, you say that you were Conklin's contact in Marrakech."

"I don't *say* it," Ottavio Moreno said with a slight frown, "I *was* that man."

"I suppose you can't produce any canceled checks from the Treadstone account."

"Ha, ha," Moreno said, but it wasn't a laugh. He took out a pack of Gauloises Blondes, shook one out, and lit up. He stared at Bourne while he blew smoke at the ceiling. At length, he said, "Am I wrong in thinking we're on the same page?"

"I don't know. Are we?"

Bourne got up and went into the kitchen to get himself a glass of cold water. He was angry at himself, not Moreno. He knew he was at his most vulnerable at this juncture. He didn't like being vulnerable. More to the point, in his line of work he couldn't afford to be.

Returning to the living room, he sat down on an armchair facing the sofa where Ottavio Moreno still sat smoking slowly, as if in meditation. In Bourne's absence he'd turned on the TV to the BBC news. The sound was off, but the images of the Vesper Club were all too familiar. Lights were flashing off the tops of emergency vehicles and police cars. Personnel emerged from the club's front door carrying a stretcher. The body on it was draped in a cloth that covered its face. Then the scene switched to a newsreader in the BBC studios, mouthing whatever had been written for him moments before.

Bourne gestured and Moreno turned up the volume, but there was nothing for them in the story, and Moreno muted the sound again.

"It will be harder than ever to get out of London now," Bourne said shortly.

"I know more ways to get out of London than they do." He gestured at the cop being interviewed on the screen.

"So do I," Bourne said. "That isn't the issue."

Moreno leaned forward, stubbed out the butt in an ugly free-form ashtray, and lit another. "If you're waiting for me to apologize, you're going to be disappointed."

"Too late for apologies," Bourne said. "What's so important about the laptop?"

Moreno shrugged.

"Perlis had the ring," Bourne said. "He killed Holly to get it."

"The ring is a symbol of the Severus Domna, all members wear it or carry it unobtrusively."

"That's it? If there's nothing else important about it, why did Perlis murder Holly for it?"

"I don't know. Maybe he thought it would somehow lead him to the laptop." Again Moreno stubbed out his cigarette. "Look, is all this distrust because Gustavo was my half brother?"

"I wouldn't rule it out," Bourne said.

"Yeah, well, my big brother was a fucking thorn in my side ever since I can remember."

"Then it's a good thing for you he's dead," Bourne said drily.

Moreno eyed Bourne for a moment. "Jesus Christ, you think I've taken over his drug business."

"I'd be a fool if the thought hadn't crossed my mind."

Moreno nodded morosely. "Fair enough." He sat back and spread his hands wide. "Okay, then, how can I prove myself?"

"Up to you."

Moreno crossed his arms over his chest and thought a moment. "What do you remember about the four of them: Perlis, Holly, Tracy, and Diego Hererra?"

"Virtually nothing," Bourne said.

"I imagine you asked Diego about them. What did he tell you?"

"I know about their friendship, their romantic entanglements."

Moreno frowned. "What romantic entanglements?"

When Bourne told him, he laughed. "*Mano,* your boy Diego dropped one steaming pile of shit on your doorstep. There was no romance among the four of them. There was only friendship—until, that is, Holly started wearing the ring. One of them, maybe Tracy, I don't know, became interested in the engraving on the inside. The more interested she became in it, the more Perlis's curiosity was piqued. He took a photo of the engraving and brought it to Oliver Liss, his boss at the time. This led directly to the tragedy of Holly's death."

"How do you know all this?"

"I worked for Black River until Alex Conklin recruited me as a Treadstone agent in place. That gave the old boy a good deal of satisfaction—he despised Liss, as corrupt and exploitative an individual as you're likely to meet in this business. He feasted off other people's misery, hosed the government mercilessly, and directed his operatives to commit crimes and atrocities the government dared not do itself. Until you helped sink Black River, Liss was about the most successful modern-day agent of chaos, and believe me that's saying a lot."

"That still doesn't explain how—"

"Back in the day, Perlis reported to me, before Liss took charge of him directly and used him to carry out private missions."

Bourne nodded. "The ring was one of those private missions."

"It became one. Perlis needed help, so he came to me. I was the only one he trusted. He told me that the moment Liss saw the ring he flipped out. That was when he ordered Perlis to find the laptop."

"The one you helped me steal from Jalal Essai."

"That's right."

Bourne frowned. "But what happened to it?"

"You were supposed to deliver it to Conklin personally, but you didn't."

"Why not?"

"You discovered something about the laptop— something, you told me, that it was probable Conklin didn't want you to know. You took it upon yourself to change the mission on the fly."

"What did I discover?"

Moreno shrugged. "You never told me, and I was too well trained to ask."

Bourne was sunk deep in thought. The enigma of the ring was growing with every moment. Considering Liss's reaction when he saw the ring, it seemed likely that it was in some way connected to the laptop. That was if Moreno was telling him the truth. He felt as if he were in a hall of mirrors, each reflection distorted in a different way so that it was no longer possible to discern reality from carefully constructed fantasy, truth from cleverly worded fiction.

On the TV screen the newsreader had gone on to other stories, in other lands, but the images of Diego Hererra's corpse being taken out of the Vesper Club continued to flicker through Bourne's mind. Had it been necessary to kill him, as Moreno had said, or did Moreno have another, darker motive he was keeping from Bourne? The only way to find out the truth was to keep Moreno close to him, and to continue questioning him as subtly as possible until a chink in his armor appeared—or until he proved himself truthful.

"What do you know about Essai?" Bourne asked.

"Besides being a member of the Severus Domna ruling council, not much. He comes from an illustrious family, which dates back all the way to the eleven hundreds, if I'm not mistaken. His ancestors took part in the Moorish invasion of Andalusia. One of them ruled there for a number of years."

"What about in more modern times?"

"These days no one's interested in the Berbers or the Amazigh, which we call ourselves."

"And what of Severus Domna itself?"

"Ah, well, there I can be of some help. First off, I should point out that very little is known about the group. They fly so far below the radar that whatever footprints they leave are all but invisible or easily wiped away. No one knows how large the group is, but members are scattered in virtually every corner of the globe, all in positions of power in governments, businesses, media, and criminal activities. Any industry you care to name they're in."

"What's their aim?" Bourne was thinking of the word *Dominion* inscribed on the inside of his ring. "What do they want?"

"Power, money, control of world events. Who knows, but that's a better guess than any other. It's what everyone wants, isn't it?"

"If you're a student of history," Bourne conceded.

Ottavio Moreno laughed. "So many aren't."

Bourne took a breath and let it out slowly. He wondered what it was he'd found out about the laptop that had led him to change the mission. He wasn't aware of changing any of the Treadstone missions he'd been sent on, if only because he remembered that up until Conklin's murder he and the Treadstone boss had been on good terms, even friendly ones.

When he mentioned this, Moreno said, "You told me to tell Conklin that Essai didn't have the laptop, that you didn't know what had happened to it."

"And did you?"

"Yes."

"Why would you do that? Treadstone was paying your salary, Conklin was your boss."

"I'm not altogether certain," Ottavio Moreno confessed. "Other than there's a fundamental difference between field and office personnel. The one doesn't necessarily understand the motives of the other, and vice versa. Out here, if we don't have each other's backs, we're dead meat." He put the pack of Gauloises away. "When you told me you'd found something fundamental enough to change the mission I believed you."

* * *

So you have come to see the famous Corellos."

Roberto Corellos, Narsico Skydel's cousin, smirked at Moira. He sat in a comfortable armchair. The room, spacious, filled with light, with its deep-pile rug, porcelain lamps, paintings on the walls, looked like someone's living room. But as Moira was about to discover, Bogotá's prisons weren't like any others in the world.

"The American press wants to speak with the famous Corellos, now that he's in La Modelo, now that it's safe." He drew a cigar from the breast pocket of his guayabera shirt and with great fanfare bit off the end and lit up, using an old Zippo lighter. With another smirk, he said, "A present from one of my many admirers." It wasn't immediately clear whether he meant the robusto or the Zippo.

He blew a cloud of aromatic smoke toward the ceiling and crossed one linen-clad leg over the other. "What newspaper are you with again?"

"I'm a stringer for *The Washington Post*," Moira said. These credentials had been presented to her by Jalal Essai. She didn't know where he had obtained them and she didn't care. All that concerned her was that they would hold up under scrutiny. He assured her that they would, and so far he'd been right.

She had arrived in Bogotá less than twenty-four hours ago and had obtained immediate permission to interview Corellos. She was mildly surprised that no one seemed to care one way or the other.

"It's fortunate that you came now. In a week or so I'll be out of here." Corellos stared at the glowing tip of the cigar. "This has been something of a vacation for me." He waved a hand. "I have everything I could want—food, cigars, bitches to fuck, anything and every-thing—and I don't have to lift a finger to get them."

"Charming," Moira said.

Corellos eyed her. He was a handsome man, in a rough, hard-muscled way. And with his dark, smoldering eyes and intense masculine presence, he was certainly charismatic. "You have to understand something about Colombia, Señorita Trevor. The country isn't in the hands of the government, no, no, no. In Colombia power is split between FARC, the Revolutionary Armed Forces of Colombia, and the drug lords. Left-wing guer-rillas and right-wing capitalists, something like that." His laugh was as raucous and as joyful as a macaw's cry. He seemed completely relaxed, as if he were at home, instead of in Bogotá's most notorious prison. "FARC controls forty percent of the country, we control the other sixty."

Moira was skeptical. "That seems something of an ex-aggeration, Señor Corellos. Should I take everything you tell me with a grain of salt?"

Corellos reached behind him and placed a Taurus PT92 semi-automatic pistol on the table between them.

Moira felt sucker-punched.

"It's fully loaded, you can check it if you want." He seemed to be enjoying her shocked reaction. "Or you can take it—as a souvenir. Not to worry, there's plenty more where that came from."

He laughed again. Then he pushed the Taurus to one side. "Listen, señorita, like most gringos I think you're a bit out of your league here. Just last month we had a war in here—the FARC guerrillas against the, uh, businessmen. It was a full-scale conflict, complete with AK-47s, fragmentation grenades, dynamite, you name it.

The guards, such as they are, backed away. The army surrounded the prison but wouldn't venture inside because we're better armed than they are." He winked at her. "I'll bet the justice minister didn't tell you about that."

"No, he didn't."

"I'm not surprised. It was a bloody fucking mess in here, let me tell you."

Moira was fascinated. "How did it end?"

"I stepped in. FARC listens to me. *Escúchame,* I'm not against them—certainly not what they stand for. The government is a dirty joke, they've got that part right, at least. They know I'll stand with them, that I'll rally my people to support them—so long as they leave us alone. Me, I don't give a fuck about politics—right-wing, left-wing, fascist, socialist, I leave the semantics to the people who have nothing better to do with their stinking lives. Me, I'm too busy making money, that's *my* life. Everyone else can rot in hell."

He tapped the ash off his cigar into a brass ashtray. "I respect FARC. I have to, I'm a pragmatist. They own most of Bogotá, we don't. And they're the ones with their own prison release program. An example: Two weeks ago, in La Picota, the other prison here, the fucking FARC blew out an entire wall, freeing ninety-eight of their comrades. To a gringo such a thing sounds preposterous, impossible, am I right? But that's life in Colombia." He chuckled. "Say what you will about FARC, they've got balls. I respect that."

"In fact, Señor Corellos, unless I've misunderstood you, that's the *only* thing you respect." Without another word, Moira reached for the Taurus, broke it down, and put it back together, all the while staring unblinkingly into Corellos's eyes.

When she put the pistol back down on the table, Corellos said, "Why do you want to speak with me, señorita? Why did you really come? It isn't to write a story for a newspaper, is it?"

"I need your help," she said. "I'm looking for a certain laptop computer Gustavo Moreno had. Just before he died, it disappeared."

Corellos spread his hands. "Why come to me?"

"You were Moreno's supplier."

"So?"

"The man who stole the laptop—one of Moreno's men working for someone else, someone unknown—was found dead on the outskirts of Amatitán, on the estancia owned by your cousin Narsico."

"That pussy, taking a gringo name! I want nothing to do with him, he's dead to me."

Moira considered a moment. "It seems to me that implicating him in the murder of this man might be a good way to get back at him."

Corellos snorted. "What, and leave it to the Mexican police to figure it out and arrest him? Please! When it comes to solving crimes they're complete idiots, all they know how to do is take bribes and siestas. Plus, Berengária would be suspect, too. No, if I wanted Narsico dead you would have found *him* in Amatitán."

"So who's running Moreno's business, who are you selling to now?"

Corellos blew cigar smoke, his eyes half lidded.

"I'm not interested in putting anyone in jail," she said. "In fact, it would be fruitless, wouldn't it? I'm just interested in finding the laptop, and there's a trail I have to follow."

Corellos stubbed out his cigar. When he made a gesture someone—significantly, not a guard—came in with a bottle of tequila and two shot glasses, which he placed between Corellos and Moira. "I'm ordering food. What would you like?"

"Whatever you're having."

He nodded, spoke to the young man, who nodded and slipped unobtrusively out. He leaned forward and poured tequila. When they had both drained their glasses, he said, "You have to understand the depth of my hatred for Narsico."

She shrugged. "I'm a gringa, we don't take such things so seriously. What I do know is that you haven't had him killed."

He waved away her words. "This is what I mean by *understanding*. Killing's too good for a shithead like him."

She was beginning to get a glimmer of where this conversation was going. "So you have something else planned."

That macaw laugh again. "It's already done. Whoever said that revenge is a dish best served cold had no Colombian blood running through him. Why wait when opportunity stares you in the face?"

The young man returned with a tray laden with food—an array of small dishes, from rice and beans to fried chilies and smoked seafood. He set the tray down, and Corellos waved him away. Immediately Corellos picked out a plate of shrimp in a fiery red sauce and ate them, head and all. As he sucked the sauce off his fingertips, he continued. "Do you know the best way to get to a man, señorita? It's through his woman."

Now she understood. "You seduced Berengária."

"Yes, I cuckolded him, I shamed him, but that's not all I did. Narsico wanted desperately to outrun his family, so I made sure that he couldn't." Corellos's eyes sparkled. "I set Berengária Moreno up as her brother's successor."

And you did it damn well, Moira thought. Essai said there was no hint of her involvement. "Do you think she had the mole inside her brother's operation?"

"If she wanted a list of Gustavo's clients she only had to ask him, which she didn't, at least while he was alive."

"Then who would?"

He looked at her skeptically. "Oh, I don't know, a thousand people, maybe more. You want me to write you a list?"

Moira ignored his sarcasm. "What about you?"

He laughed. "What? Are you kidding? Gustavo was making me a fortune by doing all the heavy lifting. Why would I fuck with that?"

Did Corellos know that Moreno's client list was on the laptop, or had he assumed it? Moira wondered. Essai didn't look like the kind of man who was after a Colombian drug lord's business; he had the aspect of someone who'd been ripped off and wanted his property back. She leaned forward, elbows on the table. "*Escúchame, hombre.* Someone made off with that laptop. If it wasn't Berengária then it has to be someone else who wants Gustavo's business, and it's just a matter of time before he acts."

Corellos took up a plate of fried chilies and popped them one after another into his mouth. His expressive lips were slick with grease. He didn't appear interested in wiping them off.

"I don't know anything about this," Corellos said coldly.

Moira believed him. If he had known, he would already have done something about it. She rose. "Maybe Berengária does."

His eyes narrowed. "The fuck she does. Whatever she knows, I know."

"You're a long way from Jalisco."

Corellos laughed unpleasantly. "You don't know me very well, do you, *chica*."

"I want that laptop, *hombre*."

"That's the spirit!" He made a sound deep in his throat astonishingly like a tiger purring. "The hour's growing late, *chica*. Why don't you stay the night? I guarantee my accommodations are better than any this city has to offer you."

She smiled. "I think not. Thank you for your hospitality—and your honesty."

Corellos grinned. "Anything for a beautiful señorita." He lifted a warning finger. "*Cuidad, chica*. I don't envy you. Berengária's a fucking piranha. Give her the slightest opening and she'll eat you up, bones and all."

When Peter Marks arrived at Noah Perlis's flat, he found it crawling with CI agents, two of whom he knew. One, Jesse McDowell, he knew very well. He and McDowell had worked together on two field assignments before Marks was promoted upstairs into management.

When McDowell saw Marks, he beckoned to him and, taking him aside, said in a hushed tone of voice, "What the hell are you doing here, Peter?"

"I'm on assignment."

"Well, so are we, so you better get the hell out of here before one of Danziger's gung-ho newbies gets curious about you."

"Can't do that, Jesse." Peter craned his neck, peering over McDowell's shoulder. "I'm looking for Jason Bourne."

"Good bleeding luck with that, laddie." McDowell shot him a sardonic look. "How many roses should I send to the funeral?"

"Listen, Jesse, I just flew in from DC, I'm tired, hungry, cranky, and in no fucking mood to play games with you or any of Danziger's little tin soldiers." He made to take a step around McDowell. "D'you think I'm afraid of any of them, or of Danziger?"

McDowell raised his hands, palms outward. "Okay, okay. You've made your point, laddie." He took Marks by the elbow. "I'll fill you in on everything, but not here. Unlike you, Danziger still owns my ass." He steered Marks out the door and into the hallway. "Let's go down to the pub and lift a few. When I get a pint or two in me, I'll screw me courage to the wall."

The Slaughtered Lamb was just the sort of London pub that had been written about for centuries. It was low, dark, ripe with the scents of fermented beer and very old cigarette smoke, some of which still seemed to hang in the air in a boozy mist.

McDowell chose a table against one wood-paneled wall, ordered them pints of the room-temperature brew and, for Marks, a plate of bangers and mash. When the food came, Marks took one whiff of the meat and his stomach turned. He had the waiter take the plate away, and settled for a couple of cheese rolls.

"This investigation's part of Justice's ongoing case against Black River," McDowell said.

"I thought that case had been wrapped up."

"So did everyone else." McDowell drained his pint and ordered another. "But it appears that someone very high up is gunning for Oliver Liss."

"Liss left Black River before any of the shit hit the fan."

McDowell took possession of the new pint. "Suspicion has been thrown his way. Point being that he may have gotten out, but it still is likely that he was one of the architects of Black River's dirty dealings. Our job is to confirm that conjecture with hard evidence, and since Noah Perlis was Liss's personal lapdog, we're tossing his place."

"Needle in a haystack," Marks said.

"Mebbe so." McDowell gulped down his beer. "But one thing we did find there was a photo of this bloke Diego Hererra. You heard he was knifed to death last night in a posh West End casino by the name of the Vesper Club?"

"I hadn't heard," Marks said. "What's it to me?"

"Everything, laddie. The man who was seen knifing Diego Hererra was with Jason Bourne. They left the club together just minutes after the murder."

Soraya drove due south as, she intuited, Arkadin— going by the name Frank N. Stein—had. Twilight was falling gently as a leaf as she pulled into Nogales. She was still in Arizona. Just across the border was the sister town, Nogales, in the Mexican state of Sonora.

She parked and strolled through the dusty central square. Finding an open-air café, she sat and ordered a plate of tamales and a Corona. Her Spanish was a good deal better than her French or her German, which meant that it was very good, indeed. And here her dark skin, Egyptian blood, and prominent nose were easily mistaken for Aztec. She sat back and allowed herself to breathe while she watched the comings and goings of people on errands, shopping, strolling hand in hand. There were many old people, sitting on benches, playing cards or chatting. Vehicles passed—old, dented cars and dusty, rusting trucks loaded with produce. Nogales's business was agriculture, shipments from its sister town continuously coming across the border for packaging and transshipping all across the United States.

She had finished her last tamale and was on her second Corona when she saw an old black Chevy, dusty and hulking, but the plates didn't match and she went back to her beer. She declined dessert but ordered coffee.

The waiter was setting the tiny cup in front of her when, over his shoulder, she saw another black Chevy. She stood up as he walked away. The plate matched the one on the car Arkadin had rented, but the driver was an eighteen-year-old punk. He parked near the café and got out. His hair was crested, his arms covered in tattoos of snakes and plumed birds. Soraya recognized the quetzal, the sacred bird of the Aztecs and Maya. Downing her espresso in one shot, she left some bills on the table and walked over to the punk.

"Where did you get that car, *compadre*?" she asked him.

He looked her up and down with a sneer. His eyes on her breasts, he said, "What business is it of yours?"

"I'm not a cop, if that's what you're worried about."

"Why should I be worried?"

"Because that Chevy is a rental car from Tucson—you and I both know that."

The punk continued his sneer. He looked like he practiced it in front of a mirror every morning.

"Do you like them?"

The punk started. "What?"

"My breasts."

He laughed uneasily and looked away.

"Listen," she said, "I'm not interested in you or the car. Tell me about the man who rented it."

He spat sideways and said nothing.

"Don't be stupid," she said. "You're already in enough trouble. I can make it go away."

The punk sighed. "I really don't know. I found the car out in the desert. It was abandoned."

"How did you start it up—did you hot-wire it?"

"Nah, I didn't have to, the key was in the ignition."

Now, that was interesting. It probably meant that Arkadin wasn't coming back for it, which meant that he was no longer in Nogales. Soraya thought for a moment. "If I wanted to cross the border, how would I do it?"

"The border station's just a couple miles south—"

"I don't want to go that way."

The punk squinted, eyeing her as if for the first time. "I'm hungry," he said. "How about buying me a meal?"

"Okay," she said, "but don't expect anything else."

When he laughed, the brittle shell of his forced bravado cracked open. His face was transformed into that of a simple kid who looked at the world through sad eyes.

She took him back to the café, where he ordered *burritos de machaca* and a huge plate of cowboy beans larded with *chiles pasados.* His name was Álvaro Obregón. He was from Chihuahua. His family had migrated north in search of work and had ended up here. Through the intervention of his mother's brother, his parents worked at a maquiladora packaging fruit and vegetables. According to him, his sister was a slut and his brothers goofed off all day instead of working. He himself was employed by a rancher. He'd come into town to pick up an order of supplies the rancher had phoned in.

"At first, I was excited about coming here," he said. "I'd read up about American Nogales and discovered that a lot of really cool people were born here, like Charlie Mingus. His music sounds like shit to me, but you know, he's famous and all. And then there's Roger Smith. Imagine banging Ann-Margret, huh! But the coolest is Movita Castaneda. I bet you never heard of her."

When Soraya said she hadn't, he grinned. "She was in *Flying Down to Rio* and *Mutiny on the Bounty,* but I only saw her in *Tower of Terror.*" He mopped up the last of his beans. "Anyway, she married Marlon Brando. Now, there was one cool actor, until he blew up like a blimp, anyway."

He wiped his mouth with the back of his hand and smacked his lips. "It didn't take long for the shine to wear off. I mean, just look around you. What a fucking dump!"

"You seem to have a good job," Soraya pointed out.

"Yeah, you try it. It sucks."

"It's steady work."

"A rat makes more money than I do." He gave a wry, lopsided smile. "But that doesn't mean I starve to death."

"Which brings us back to my original question. I want to get into Mexico."

"Why? The place is a fucking shithole."

Soraya smiled. "Who do I see?"

Álvaro Obregón made a show of having to think about it, but Soraya suspected he already knew. He looked out over the square. The lights had come on, people were on their way to dinner or heading home after some last-minute shopping. The air smelled of refried beans and other sharp, acidic scents of *norteño* cooking. Finally, he said, "Well, there are a couple of local *polleros* across the border." These were people whom you paid to guide you across the border without having to bother with customs and Immigration. "But really, there's only one to use, and you're in luck, early this morning he brought a family of migrants across from Mexico. He's here now and I can make the introductions. He's known as Contreras, though I know for a fact that's not his real name. I've dealt with him personally."

On that score Soraya had no doubt. "I'd like you to set up the meet with your *compadre* Contreras."

"It'll cost you. A hundred American dollars."

"Highway robbery. Fifty."

"Seventy-five."

"Sixty. That's my last offer."

Álvaro Obregón put his hand on the table palm-up,

and Soraya laid a twenty and a ten onto it. The bills disappeared so fast they might never have existed.

"The rest when you deliver," she said.

"Wait here," Álvaro Obregón said.

"Save time and call him, why don't you?"

Álvaro Obregón shook his head. "No cell contact, ever. Rules of the game." He rose and, seemingly in no particular hurry, sauntered off at the leisurely pace endemic to Nogales.

For just over an hour Soraya sat alone, soaking up the spangle of the night and the lilt of songs of a local banda, playing a form of brass-heavy music from Sinaloa. A couple of men asked her to dance; politely but firmly she turned them down.

Then, just as the banda segued into its second cumbia, she saw Álvaro Obregón emerge out of the shadows. He was accompanied by a man, presumably Contreras, the *pollero,* whom she judged to be in his early to midforties with a face like a map that had been folded and refolded too many times. Contreras was tall and rangy with slightly bowed legs, like a lifetime cowboy. And like a cowboy he wore a wide-brimmed hat, stovepipe jeans, and a western shirt with piping and pearl snaps.

The man and the boy sat down without a word. Up close Contreras had the sun-bleached eyes of a man used to sagebrush, dust, and the scorching desert. His skin resembled overtanned leather.

"Boy tells me you want to go south." Contreras spoke to her in English.

"That's right." Soraya had seen eyes like his before in professional gamblers. They seemed to bore into your skull.

"When?"

A man of few words, that was all right with her. "The sooner the better."

Contreras lifted his head to the moon, as if he were a coyote about to howl at it. "Just a sliver," he said. "Tonight'll be better than tomorrow, tomorrow'll be better than the next. After that..." He shrugged, as if to say the door would close.

"What's your fee?" she asked.

He gazed at her again in a neutral way. "Can't bargain with me like you did with the boy."

"All right."

"Fifteen hundred, half up front."

"A quarter, the rest when you've brought me safely across."

Contreras's mouth gave a little twitch. "You were right, boy, she is some kinda bitch."

Soraya wasn't offended; she knew it was meant as a compliment. That's how these people spoke, she wasn't going to change it and she wasn't about to try.

Contreras shrugged then and began to stand up. "I told you."

"Tell you what," Soraya said, "I'll meet your terms if you take a look at a photo for me."

Contreras studied her for a moment, then eased back into the chair. He held out his hand, just as Álvaro Obregón had. The boy learned quickly.

Soraya scrolled through the photos on her cell until she found the surveillance shot of Arkadin. She laid the phone in the *pollero*'s palm. "Have you seen him? You might have taken him south maybe nine or ten days ago." That's what she surmised from Álvaro Obregón's tale of the black Chevy abandoned in the desert: Arkadin had found a way into Mexico that bypassed official scrutiny.

Contreras did not look down at the photo, but kept his colorless eyes on her. "I don't bargain," he repeated. "Are you asking me for a favor?"

Soraya hesitated a moment, then nodded. "I suppose I am."

"Don't do favors." He glanced down at the photo. "My fee is now two thousand."

Soraya sat back and crossed her arms over her chest. "Now you're taking advantage of me."

"Decide," Contreras said. "A minute more and we'll call it an even three thousand."

Soraya exhaled. "Okay, okay."

"Let's see the color."

He meant he wanted to see the money, all of it, to make sure she'd be able to pay. When she had unrolled the hundred-dollar bills to his satisfaction, he nodded.

"Took him across ten days ago."

"Did he say where he was going?"

Contreras snorted. "Didn't say a fucking thing, not even when he handed me the money. That was fine by me."

Soraya played her last card. "Where do you *think* he was going?"

Contreras lifted his head a moment, as if sniffing something on the wind. "Man like him, not into the desert, that's for sure. I could see he hated the heat. And he sure as hell wasn't going to work at one of the maquiladoras in Sonora. This was a boss, his own man." His gaze lowered and he squinted at her. "Like you."

"So where does that leave us?"

"The coast, lady boss. Sure as we're sitting here he was going to the coast."

Bourne was asleep when the call from Chrissie came in. The sound of his cell woke him instantly, and he pressed a thumb against his eye as he answered the call.

"Adam."

Instantly alerted by the tension in that one word, he said, "What's happened?"

"There's . . . there's someone here who wants to speak with you. Oh, Adam!"

"Chrissie, Chrissie . . ."

An unfamiliar male voice took over: "Stone, Bourne, whatever you're calling yourself. You'd better get over here. The woman and her daughter are in very deep shit."

Bourne gripped the phone more tightly. "Who are you?"

"My name is Coven. I need to see you, right now."

"Where are you?"

"I'm going to give you directions. Listen carefully, I won't repeat them." Coven rattled off a complicated list of highways, roads, turns, and mileage. "I expect you here in ninety minutes."

Bourne glanced at Moreno, who was gesturing at him. "I don't know whether I can make it by—"

"You'll make it," Coven assured him. "If you don't, the little girl gets hurt. For every fifteen minutes you're late, she gets hurt worse. Do I make myself clear?"

"Perfectly," Bourne said.

"Good. The clock starts ticking *now*."

14

FREDERICK WILLARD SPENT eight straight hours connected to the Internet, trying and failing to find out who owned the Monition Club, what the organization did, where it got its money, and who its members were. During that time he took three breaks, two to use the bathroom and one to wolf down some very bad Chinese food he'd ordered online and had delivered. All around him workmen were renovating the new Treadstone offices, installing electronic equipment and specially designed soundproofed doors, and painting walls that the day before had been stripped of wallpaper.

Willard had the patience of a tortoise, but at last even he gave up. He spent the next forty minutes down on the street, walking around the block, clearing his head of paint fumes and plaster dust while he thought the situation through.

At the end of that time he returned to his office, printed out his résumé, and then went home to shower, shave, and dress in a suit and tie. He made sure his shoes were highly polished. Then, the résumé folded and tucked in his breast pocket, he drove to the Monition Club and parked in a nearby municipal underground lot.

There was a certain spring in his gait as he went up the stone steps and into the imposing lobby. The same woman manned the high desk in the center, and he went up to her and asked for the director of public relations.

"We have no director of public relations," she said with an unsmiling face. "How may I help you?"

"I wish to see the person in charge of hiring personnel," Willard said.

The woman looked at him dubiously for a moment, then she said, "We aren't hiring."

Willard put some honey into his voice and smiled. "Nevertheless, I would very much appreciate you telling whoever's in charge that I would like to see him—or her."

"You'd need to have a résumé with you."

Willard produced it.

Eyeing it, the receptionist smiled and said, "Your name?"

"Frederick Willard."

"One moment, Mr. Willard." She dialed an internal extension and murmured into the microphone of her wireless headset. When she had disconnected she looked up at him and said, "Please have a seat, Mr. Willard. Someone will be out shortly."

Willard thanked her, then walked back to the same bench where he and Peter Marks had waited for Oliver

Liss. The receptionist went back to answering the phone and directing calls. Willard thought this system oddly antiquated. It appeared as if the personnel who worked at the Monition Club did not have direct phone lines.

This interested him, and he began to study the woman more closely. Though she was young and at first blush looked like the standard-issue receptionist, he was getting the sense that she was something altogether different. For one thing, she seemed to make the decision of whether or not he was going to get past her. For another, it looked as if she was vetting each call.

After thirty minutes or so a slim young man appeared through a door set flush with one of the wall panels. He was dressed in a charcoal-gray conservatively cut suit. His tie had what appeared to be a gold bar embroidered in its center. He went directly over to the receptionist and, bending forward slightly, spoke to her in a voice so low that even within the confines of the hushed lobby Willard could not hear what he said or what the receptionist replied.

Then he turned and, with a noncommittal smile on his face, approached Willard.

"Mr. Willard, please follow me."

Without waiting for a reply, he turned on his heel. Willard went across the lobby. As he passed the receptionist's desk, he saw her watching him.

The young man took him through the door and down a dimly lit, wood-paneled corridor. It was carpeted and decorated with paintings of medieval hunting scenes. They passed doors on either side. All of them were closed, and Willard could hear nothing at all inside. Either the offices were empty, which he doubted, or the doors were soundproofed—yet another anomaly for a workplace. At least, one that wasn't part of the clandestine services.

At length, the young man stopped in front of a door on the left, knocked once, then opened the door inward.

"Mr. Frederick Willard," the young man announced in a curiously formal manner as he stepped across the threshold.

Following him, Willard found himself not in an office but in a library, and a surprisingly large one, at that. Bookshelves lined three of the walls from floor to ceiling. The fourth wall was an immense picture window that looked out on a small but beautifully landscaped cloister garden with a central fountain in the Moorish style. It looked like something out of the sixteenth century.

In front of this window was a large refectory table of a thick, dark hardwood, polished to a high gloss. Seven high-backed wooden chairs were arranged at regular intervals around the table. In one sat a man with rounded shoulders, thick hair pushed back from his wide forehead in silver wings, and skin the color of honey. A large, very thick book was open in front of him, which he was studying with great concentration. Then he looked up, and Willard was confronted by a pair of piercing blue eyes, a large, hawk-like nose, and a hard smile.

"Come in, Mr. Willard," he said, that hard smile fixed in place. "We've been expecting you."

They use pleasure craft—very expensive yachts," Contreras said.

"To go up and down the coast," Soraya said.

"That's the safest way to transport goods up from central Mexico, where they're received from the Colombian cartels."

The desert sky was huge, so chock-full of stars that in certain places the night seemed hazed an icy blue. The barest crescent of a moon hung low in the sky, giving off precious little illumination. Contreras checked the dial of his watch; it seemed he had the schedule of the patrolling *migras* down to a science.

They were crouched in the deep shadow thrown by a clump of sagebrush and a giant saguaro cactus. When they spoke it was in the barest of whispers. She followed the *pollero*'s lead so that, like his, her voice sounded no different than the dry desert wind.

"Your man is into drugs, count on it," Contreras said. "Why else does a man like him want to sneak into Mexico?"

It was colder here than she had expected, and she shivered a little.

"Unless someone was meeting him, he would have gone straight to Nogales, stolen a car, and then headed due west to the coast."

Soraya was about to reply when he put a forefinger to his lips. She listened, and a moment later she heard what had alerted him: the soft crunch of boot soles across the ground not far from them. When a spotlight was switched on Contreras didn't even twitch, which meant he had been expecting it. The light swung in an arc, not at the area where they were hidden, but ahead of them, where the invisible border stretched, desolate and windblown. She heard a grunt, then the light was switched off and the sound of the boot soles faded away.

She was about to shift position when Contreras grabbed her and held her still. Even in the starry darkness she could feel his eyes glaring at her. She held her breath. A moment later the beam of blinding light re-ignited, sweeping a larger portion of the desert ahead. Then three shots exploded into the night, sending up tiny dust devils where the bullets impacted the earth.

She heard a brief gurgle, which might have been a laugh. The light was extinguished. Then all was stillness again, and the lonesome soughing of the wind reasserted itself.

Now we go, Contreras mouthed to her.

She nodded, following him on cramped legs as they skirted the clump of sagebrush and, circling to the right, dashed across the flat ground from the United States into Mexico. There was nothing at all to mark their transition from one country to another.

In the distance she heard the howl of a coyote, but couldn't tell from what side of the border it came. A jackrabbit, springing out of their way, startled her. She found that her heart was racing, and there was an odd sort of singing in her ears, as if her blood were rushing too quickly through her veins and arteries.

Contreras led her forward at a steady pace, never stopping, never at a loss for direction. His confidence was absolute, and she felt secure within the circumference of it. It was an odd and slightly unsettling feeling, one that made her think of Amun, of Cairo, and of their time in the Egyptian desert. Could it have been just weeks ago? It seemed like such a long time since she'd seen him, and their text messages were becoming fewer and shorter as time went on.

The night was now starless, as profoundly dark as the bottom of the ocean, as if even hours from now there would be no dawn, no sun rising in the distant eastern sky. A sudden crack of thunder came to her, but it sounded far away, streaking through the sky of another country.

They walked for a long time, through a flat, monotonous landscape that seemed scarcely alive. At last, Soraya saw the glow of lights, and shortly thereafter Contreras led her into Nogales, Sonora.

"This is as far as I go," the *pollero* said. He was looking not toward the lights, but out into the blackness of the eastern outskirts of town.

Soraya handed him the balance of his fee, and he pocketed it without counting it.

"The Ochoa has clean rooms, and the management doesn't ask questions." Then he spat casually between his dusty cowboy boots. "I hope you find what you're looking for," he said.

She nodded, watching him head east toward an unknown destination. When the night had swallowed him up, she turned and walked until the dust turned to packed earth and then to streets and sidewalks. She found the Ochoa without difficulty. There was some kind of all-night festival going on. The central square was lit up; at one end a mariachi band played something fast and cacophonous, at the other booths were set up selling freshly made tacos and quesadillas. In between, crowds drifted or danced or staggered, drunk, yelling friendly curses at the musicians or anyone who would listen. Here and there a fight broke out, blood chants rose up. A horse whinnied and, snorting, stamped its hooves.

The lobby of the Ochoa was all but deserted. The night clerk, a small man with a wiry body and the face of a prairie dog, was watching a Mexican telenovela on a small portable TV with bad reception. He sat rapt in his airless cubicle, seeming not to notice. He scarcely glanced at Soraya, handing her a key when she paid the one-night price of the room, posted on a rate card above his head. He did not ask for her passport or any other form of identification. She could have been a mass murderer for all he cared.

Her room was on the second floor and, since she'd asked for quiet, in the back. There was, however, no air-conditioning. She opened the window wide and looked out. The room overlooked a dingy alleyway and a blank brick wall, the rear of another building, possibly a restaurant, judging by the long row of garbage cans lined up on one side of a doorway, closed off by only a screen door. A bare fluorescent bulb threw a sickly blue light over the garbage cans. The shadows were as purple as bruises. As she watched, a man in a heavily stained apron pushed open the screen and sat on one of the garbage can lids. He rolled a joint, stuck it in his mouth, and lit up. As he drew in the smoke, his eyes closed. She heard some noises. At one end of the alley a couple was having sex up against the wall. The cook, lost in his pot-induced reverie, ignored them. Maybe he didn't even hear them.

She turned away from the window and checked out the room. As Contreras had told her, it was clean and neat, even the bathroom, thank God. Disrobing, she turned on the shower, waited for the water to turn hot, then stepped in, luxuriating in the heat, the grime and sweat sluicing off her. Slowly, her muscles lost their tension and she began to relax. All at once a wave of tiredness swept over her and she realized that she was exhausted. Stepping out of the shower, she gave her body a vigorous toweling off. The thin, rough terry turned her skin red beneath its dusky hue.

The shower had left the room stifling. With the towel held against her, she crossed to the window to catch the benefits of whatever fitful breeze was blowing. That's when she saw the two men leaning against the wall of the restaurant. In the illumination cast by the fluorescent bulb she saw that one of them was checking something on his PDA. She ducked back behind the faded curtain an instant before the second man glanced up at her window. She could see his face, dark and closed as a fist. He said something to his companion, which made him look up at her window as well.

The Ochoa was no longer safe. She backed up, put on her dirty clothes, and went to the door. When she pulled it open, two men rushed in. One held her hands behind her back while the other put a cloth over her mouth and nose. She tried to hold her breath, tried to work herself free of the iron grip holding her fast. She could make no headway. This silent, futile fight went on for some minutes, her thrashing only depleting her lungs' store of oxygen. Then, despite her willpower, her autonomic system took control and she took a breath, then another. A terrible smell invaded her, she tried to cry out. Tears came to her eyes, rolled down her cheeks. She tried to take a gulp of fresh air. Then the blackness rushed in and her body collapsed into her captors' arms.

* * *

Arkadin saw the dorsal fin cutting through the water. Judging by its size, the shark was a large one, ten or twelve feet long. It was coming straight at the stern of the cigarette. Not surprising, considering the amount of blood in the water.

Arkadin had worked on Stepan for three hours and the man was a bloody wreck, curled on his side in a fetal position, weeping uncontrollably, blood from a thousand cuts dripping in pink rivulets as it mingled with the seawater on the deck.

Pavel had witnessed this interrogation—the bloodletting and, eventually, Stepan's screams of innocence—and then it had been his turn. He had expected Arkadin to use his gutting knife on him, as he had on Stepan, but a key part of interrogation was surprise, the terror of the unexpected.

Arkadin had tied Pavel's feet to the winch and had lowered him headfirst over the stern of the boat. He lengthened the time underwater with each plunge, so that by the end of the sixth or seventh Pavel was certain he was going to drown. Then Arkadin had cut him, slashing him under each eye. As the blood ran, he plunged Pavel back underwater. This had continued for perhaps forty minutes. Then the shark showed up. Pavel must have seen the shark. When El Heraldo hauled him up he looked mortally terrified.

Taking advantage of the weakness, Arkadin punched Pavel three times in rapid succession as hard as he could, breaking two or three of Pavel's ribs. Pavel began to gasp, his breathing became painfully difficult. Responding to his boss's signal, El Heraldo lowered Pavel back into the water. The shark nosed in, curious and interested.

Pavel began a panicked thrashing in the water. The thrashing only made the shark more interested. Sharks had poor eyesight, relying on scent and motion. This one scented fresh blood, and the thrashing led it to believe that its prey was injured. Putting on speed, it headed directly for the injured creature.

Arkadin saw the sudden acceleration of the dorsal fin and lifted his arm, a signal to El Heraldo, who cranked the winch. Just before his head and shoulders cleared the water, Pavel's body shuddered and swung wildly as the shark struck. When El Heraldo had Pavel dangling in the air, he gave a strangled cry and, drawing his handgun, leaned over the stern of the cigarette and pumped the magazine empty, firing shot after shot into the creature's immense bulk.

As the water churned wildly, turning black with the shark's blood, Arkadin crossed to the winch, swung it, and lowered a screaming, weeping Pavel to the deck. Arkadin let El Heraldo have his fun. Ever since his younger brother had lost a leg to a tiger shark three years ago, El Heraldo got a murderous look in his eye whenever he saw a dorsal fin. El Heraldo had revealed this grisly piece of family history one night when he was very drunk and very sad.

Arkadin turned his attention to Pavel. What the repeated near drownings had started, the shark had finished. Pavel was in very bad shape. The shark had taken a chunk of his left shoulder and cheek. He was bleeding profusely, it was the least of his problems. He'd been traumatized by the shark attack. His eyes were wide and staring, darting from place to place but not focusing. His teeth were chattering uncontrollably, and there was the stink of excrement coming off him.

Ignoring all that, Arkadin squatted down beside his captain and, putting a hand on his head, said, "Pavel Mikhailovich, my very good friend, we have a serious problem to resolve. And only you can resolve it. Either Stepan or you has been passing information to someone outside our organization. Stepan swears it's not him, which, I'm afraid, leaves you as the guilty party."

Pavel, weeping and howling in pain and terror, was unresponsive, until Arkadin bounced the back of his head off the deck.

"Pull yourself together, Pavel Mikhailovich! Focus! Your life hangs in the balance." When Pavel's gaze alighted on him and stayed there, Arkadin smiled and stroked his hair. "I know you're in pain, my friend, and good God, you're bleeding like a stuck pig! But that will all be over soon. El Heraldo will patch you up in no time, he's a master, believe me.

"Look, Pavel Mikhailovich, here's the deal. Tell me who you're working for, what you've passed on, tell me everything and we'll patch you up. You'll be as good as new. What's more, I'll let it be known that Stepan was the mole. Your employer will relax, you'll continue as before, passing on information, except you'll be passing on only the information I feed you. How does this sound? Agreed?"

Pavel moaned and nodded, clearly not trusting himself yet to speak.

"Good." Arkadin looked up at El Heraldo. "Have you finished with your fun?"

"The sonovabitch's dead." El Heraldo spat in the water with some satisfaction. "And now its friends have come to feast on it."

Arkadin looked back down to Pavel and thought, *It's the same with this sonovabitch.*

The man with the piercing blue eyes gestured. "Please sit down, Mr. Willard, would you like something to drink?"

"I could do with a whiskey," Willard said.

The young man whom Willard had followed vanished, only to reappear moments later with a tray on which sat an old-fashioned glass with whiskey, a tumbler of water, and another of ice.

Someone else seemed to be walking on Willard's legs, pulling out a chair, and sitting down at the refectory table. The young man set the three glasses in front of Willard, then went out the library door and closed it silently behind him.

"I don't understand how you could be expecting me," Willard said. Then he remembered his eight hours of scouring the Internet in search of information on the Monition Club. "My computer's ISP number is protected."

"Nothing is protected." The man took hold of the book and, turning it around, pushed it over to Willard. "Tell me what you make of this."

Willard looked down at an illustration of a series of letters and odd symbols. He recognized the Latin letters, but the others were unknown to him. Then a little thrill rippled down his spine. Unless he was mistaken, this series was the same as the engraving in the photos Oliver Liss had showed him and Peter Marks.

He looked up into those electric-blue eyes and said: "I don't know what to make of it."

"Tell me, Mr. Willard, are you a student of history?"

"I like to think so."

"Then you know about King Solomon."

Willard shrugged. "More than most, I imagine."

The man across from him sat back and laced his fingers over his lean stomach. "Solomon's life and times are steeped in myth and legend. As in the Bible, it's often difficult, if not impossible, to discern truth from fiction. Why? Because his disciples had a vested interest in obscuring the truth. By far the most outrageous stories arose concerning the hoard of Solomon's gold. Vast amounts that supposedly staggered the imagination. Historians and archaeologists now routinely ignore these stories as distorted or patently false. For one thing, where did all this gold come from? Solomon's legendary mines? Even if the king had harnessed ten thousand slaves, he could not have amassed such a legendary hoard in his brief lifetime. So now it's taken for gospel that there was no such thing as King Solomon's gold."

He leaned forward and tapped the book illustration with his crooked forefinger. "This string of letters and symbols tells a different story. It is a clue—but, oh, more than a clue, much more. It is a key telling those who would listen that King Solomon's gold does, indeed, exist."

Willard gave an involuntary chuckle.

"Has something struck you as amusing?"

"Forgive me, but I find this melodramatic gibberish hard to take seriously."

"Well, you're free to leave whenever you want. Now, if you wish."

As the man was turning the open book back toward himself, Willard reached out and stopped him.

"I'd really rather not." Willard cleared his throat. "You were speaking of truth versus fiction." He paused only a moment. "Perhaps it would help if you told me your name."

"Benjamin El-Arian. I'm one of a handful of resident scholars the Monition Club employs to deal with matters of ancient history and how it impacts the present."

"Again, you'll forgive me, but I don't for a moment believe that I was suddenly and out of the blue granted an interview with a simple scholar after trolling through the Internet for eight hours trying to find source material on the Monition Club. No, Mr. El-Arian, though you may well be a scholar, that can hardly be all you are."

El-Arian contemplated him for some time. "It seems to me, Mr. Willard, that you're far too thoughtful and perceptive to find anything I say amusing." He took the book and turned the page. "And please let us not forget that it was you who came here, seeking knowledge, presumably." His eyes lit up in what might have been an instant of merriment. "Or were you thinking of seeking employment in order to infiltrate us as you did with the NSA?"

"I'm surprised you're aware of that, it was hardly common knowledge."

"Mr. Willard," El-Arian said, "there isn't anything about you we don't know. Including your role in Treadstone."

Ah, at last we come to the crux of the matter, Willard thought. He waited, his expression perfectly neutral, but watching Benjamin El-Arian as if El-Arian were a spider sitting in the center of his web.

"I know Treadstone is something of a hot-button

issue with you," El-Arian said, "so I'll tell you what I know. Please don't hesitate to correct me if I have any facts wrong. Treadstone was started by Alexander Conklin, inside Central Intelligence. His brainchild gave birth to only two graduates: Leonid Danilovich Arkadin and Jason Bourne. Now you have resurrected Treadstone, under the aegis of Oliver Liss, but almost immediately Liss is dictating to you even more than CI did to your predecessor." He paused to give Willard time to correct him or make objections. When his guest remained silent, he nodded. "All this is prologue, however." He tapped the open book again. "Since Liss has given you orders to find the gold ring with this engraving, it might interest you to know that he is not operating as an independent entity."

Willard tensed. "So who am I actually working for?"

El-Arian's smile held a sardonic edge. "Well, like all things in the matter, it's complicated. The man who has been providing his funding and intel is Jalal Essai."

"Never heard of him."

"Nor should you have. Jalal Essai does not move in your circles. In fact, like me, Essai makes it his business to remain unknown to people like you. He's a member of the Monition Club—or, rather, he was. You see, for some years this particular ring was presumed lost. It's the only one of its kind, for reasons that will become clear to you momentarily."

El-Arian rose and, crossing to a section of the bookcases, pressed a hidden stud. The section swung outward, revealing a tea service consisting of a chased brass pot, a plate with an array of tiny powdered cakes, and six glasses, each narrow as a shot glass but perhaps three times its height. He loaded them onto a tray and brought them back to the table.

In a ceremonial manner, he poured tea for them both, then gestured toward the plate of cakes for Willard to help himself. He settled himself, sipping and savoring his drink, which, Willard discovered, was sweet mint tea, a Moroccan staple.

"Back to the matter at hand." El-Arian took a sweet and popped it in his mouth. "What the ring's engraving told us was this: King Solomon's gold is fact, not fiction. The engraving contains specific Ugaritic symbols. Solomon employed a platoon of seers. These seers, or some of them at any rate, were versed in alchemy. They had discovered that intoning certain Ugaritic words and phrases in conjunction with scientific procedures they developed could turn lead into gold."

Willard sat stunned for a moment. He didn't know whether to laugh or cry. "Lead into gold?" he said finally. "Literally?"

"Literally." El-Arian popped another sweet into his mouth. "This is the answer to the seemingly unsolvable mystery I proposed before, namely, how Solomon amassed such a hoard of gold in his short lifetime."

Willard shifted in his seat. "Is that what you people do here? Chase fairy tales?"

El-Arian produced one of his enigmatic smiles. "As I said, you're free to leave anytime you wish. And yet you won't."

Out of sheer spite, Willard got to his feet. "How do you know that?"

"Simply because, even if you aren't yet convinced, the idea is too compelling."

Willard produced his own enigmatic smile. "Even if it is a fairy tale."

El-Arian pushed his chair back and crossed to the part of the bookcases where he had gotten the tea and cakes. Reaching into the shadows, he pulled something out, brought it back, and placed it on the table in front of Willard.

Willard held El-Arian's eyes for a moment, then dropped his gaze. He picked up a gold coin. It appeared ancient. On it was imprinted a pentagram star, along with the inscription GRAM, MA, TUM, TL, TRA in the spaces between the points. In the center of the star was a symbol so worn away as to be incomprehensible.

"That pentagrammic star is the symbol of King Solomon, though various sources depict it as a six-pointed star, a cross engraved with Hebrew letters, even a Celtic knot. But it was the pentagrammic star that was engraved on the ring he always wore, which was said to have magic properties. Among them, it allowed him to trap demons and speak to animals."

Willard laughed. "You don't believe such claptrap."

"Certainly not," El-Arian said. "On the other hand, that gold coin is without doubt part of Solomon's hoard."

"I don't see how you could be certain," Willard said. "No expert exists who could verify such a thing."

El-Arian's curious smile returned. "For one thing we have verified its age. But more importantly we discovered something else," he said. "Turn the coin over please."

To Willard's surprise and bewilderment, the obverse of the coin was totally different.

"You see, this side isn't made of gold," El-Arian said. "It's made of lead, the original metal before it was transformed into gold."

15

MOIRA SET OUT from Guadalajara early in the morning, driving into the heart of blue agave country in the Mexican state of Jalisco. The sky was huge, with just a few brushstrokes of cloud floating in the vivid blue. The sun was searing, and the morning grew hot very quickly. Toward noon she was obliged to roll up the windows and turn on the air conditioner. She lost cell service several times, and without her GPS she had some difficulty finding Amatitán.

She used the time to put her interview with Roberto Corellos into its proper perspective. Why did he tell her that he'd chosen Berengária to keep her brother's business going? Why on earth would he trust a woman to handle his livelihood? Moira had met many men like Corellos, and none of them was enlightened when it came to females. Screwing, cooking, having babies, that was the extent of their expectations of women.

She mulled these questions over for hours until at last she caught sight of Amatitán. Corellos had a burning need for revenge. In a hot-tempered man of his blood, revenge was a matter of honor. Cuckolding his cousin wouldn't be enough for him. It made sense that Corellos would want to ensnare Narsico in the kind of life his cousin had tried so desperately to put behind him. *That* was revenge.

If Berengária was, indeed, heir to the drug business, then it followed a man must be running the show behind the scenes. Who? Corellos wasn't going to tell her, and there was nothing she had to barter with except her body, which she was not about to use. But Berengária was another story. Piranha she might be, but Moira had had dealings with piranhas before. What had aroused her suspicions most was that Corellos hadn't been concerned that whoever had stolen the laptop now had access to Gustavo's client list. The only reason for this was that Corellos was already in business with him.

The endless fields of blue agave passed by on either side. Workers toiled in the fields, sweating and grunting with their efforts. The Skydel estancia was just ahead.

If, as she now believed, Essai's laptop—the computer stolen from Gustavo Moreno—contained the drug lord's client list, then there must be something else on it of great importance to her employer, and she was willing to bet that it wasn't simply his family history, as he'd claimed. Then why had Essai lied to her? What was he hiding?

* * *

Oliver Liss has lied to you from the first day he met you," Benjamin El-Arian said.

"I expect everyone to lie to me," Willard said. "It's a necessary evil of the life I lead."

The two men were walking in the Moorish cloister outside the Monition Club library. Here they were sheltered from the wind. The sun, high in the sky, spilled its warmth onto their shoulders.

"So you're at peace with it."

"Of course not." Willard inhaled deeply. There was something planted in the cloister, an herb or spice, whose scent he found pleasant and familiar. "My life is a war. I sift through the lies, I've trained myself to see past them. Then I act accordingly."

"You already know that Oliver Liss has no intention of allowing you to run Treadstone as you see fit."

"Of course, but I needed someone to get Treadstone off flatline. His agenda and mine were never going to coincide. However, it was Liss or no one."

"Now there's someone else," El-Arian said. "Liss is owned by Jalal Essai. As I told you. Essai was a member of the Monition Club. Currently he's on his own."

"What would make him do that?" Willard asked.

"The same thing that kept you from walking out of the library."

"King Solomon's gold?"

El-Arian nodded. "Once he discovered that the Solomon ring wasn't lost, he decided he wanted the gold for himself."

Willard stopped and turned toward El-Arian. "Just how much gold are we talking about here?"

"It's difficult to know with any degree of precision,

but if I had to guess I'd put the amount somewhere between fifty and a hundred billion dollars."

Willard gave a low whistle. "That's enough incentive for an army to go rogue." Then he scratched the side of his head. "What I can't work out is why you're telling me all this."

"Bourne has the Solomon ring," El-Arian said. "And Treadstone's other graduate, Leonid Arkadin, is in possession of a certain laptop. Some years ago, Bourne was sent by Alex Conklin to steal the laptop from Jalal Essai. This he did, but for some reason unknown to us he never delivered it to his boss. For years we have searched for it, in vain. It seemed as if it had vanished completely. Then one of our moles sent us information through an agent of ours, Marlon Etana, that Arkadin was in possession of the stolen laptop. How did he obtain it? A Colombian drug lord by the name of Gustavo Moreno was killed in a raid a month or so ago, but the laptop containing his detailed client list was not found in his compound. Somehow Arkadin had it spirited away, and now he's used it to muscle his way into Moreno's business."

"This is the same laptop that was stolen from Jalal Essai?"

"It is."

"How in God's name did it end up with Gustavo Moreno?"

El-Arian shrugged. "A mystery we have yet to solve."

Willard mulled this over for a moment. "In any event, you can't be interested in a list of drug distributors," he said. "What's so special about this particular laptop?"

"The hard drive contains a hidden file that provides a key to the location of King Solomon's gold."

Willard appeared startled. "Are you telling me that Arkadin knows where the gold is?"

El-Arian shook his head. "I doubt Arkadin knows of the hidden file's existence. As I said, he stole it to get Moreno's client list. But even if he did know of the file, he wouldn't be able to access it. It's protected."

"Nothing is protected," Willard said, "as you yourself told me."

"Except for this file. No decryption program, no computer on earth can unlock it. There is only one way to read the file. The laptop has been fitted with a special slot. Fit the Solomon ring into the slot, an internal reader scans the engraving on the inside, and the file opens."

"So Essai had the laptop," Willard said. "What about the ring?"

"Jalal Essai had them both."

"I don't see how that makes sense. Why wouldn't he have gone after Solomon's gold himself?"

"Because even if he had opened the file, he wouldn't have been able to act on it." El-Arian, moving from sunlight to shadow, seemed to change in size as well as presence, as if there were two of him moving slightly out of sync with each other. "There is a section of the instructions missing from the file."

"And Essai doesn't have it."

"No, he doesn't."

"Who does?" Willard asked.

"It resides in a special room inside a house in Tineghir, a town in the High Atlas Mountains of Morocco."

Willard shook his head. "I know it's easy to ask after the fact, but why was Essai entrusted with the ring and the laptop?"

"His family is the oldest, the most religiously strict. It was felt that he was the best choice."

There was a small silence as both men presumably contemplated the misjudgment that had been made.

"What I still don't understand is why all this is happening now. At one point, you must have had both the ring and the laptop. Why didn't you get the gold then?"

"We would have, of course," El-Arian said, "but we were unable to do so. We lacked that section of the instructions. After decades of searching, the full set was discovered by chance after an earthquake in Iran uncovered an archaeological treasure trove of information, much of it spirited out of the great Library at Alexandria before the first fire. One scroll contained information on King Solomon's court."

"And this came to light after the ring disappeared and the laptop was stolen."

"That's right." El-Arian spread his hands. "So now you see how your agenda and ours coincide. You want to bring Bourne and Arkadin together to learn once and for all who is the ultimate warrior. We want the Solomon ring and the laptop."

"Forgive me, but I don't see the relationship."

"We have tried, unsuccessfully, to get the laptop from Arkadin. I've lost every man I've sent to kill him, and I'm tired of sending people I know to a certain death. Similarly, I know that CI has been trying for years to kill Bourne, also without success. No, the only way for us to obtain what we want is to bring the two men together."

"Bourne likely has the Solomon ring with him, but will Arkadin have the laptop?"

"He doesn't let it out of his sight lately."

They began walking again, around and around the central fountain, where a robin was drinking while nervously watching them. Willard could relate to the bird's nervousness.

"If I didn't believe Oliver Liss," Willard said, "why should I believe you?"

"I don't expect you to believe me," El-Arian said. "But to prove my sincerity, this is what I propose: You help me get Bourne and Arkadin together—something you want, anyway—and I'll take Oliver Liss off your back."

"How are you going to do that? Liss is a man with a great deal of power."

"Believe me, Mr. Willard, Oliver Liss doesn't know the meaning of power." Benjamin El-Arian turned. His eyes caught the sunlight and seemed to spark like an engine starting up. "He will be removed from your life."

Willard shook his head. "I'm afraid promises aren't good enough. I'll be wanting half down, the remainder when I've brought Bourne and Arkadin together."

El-Arian spread his hands. "We're talking about a man, not money."

"That's your problem to solve," Willard said. "I'll start the ball rolling when—but only when—your actions back up your words."

"Well, then." El-Arian smiled. "I'll just have to arrange a change of scenery for Mr. Liss."

The Skydel hacienda sprawled at the center of the immense estancia. It was built in the Spanish colonial style with its white stucco walls, carved wooden shutters, wrought-iron grillwork, and curved terra-cotta roof tiles. A woman in a maid's uniform opened the door to Moira's knock and, when she introduced herself, led her across a terrazzo-floored foyer, through a large, cool living room, out onto a flagstone patio that overlooked a clay tennis court, gardens, and a swimming pool where a woman—presumably Berengária Moreno—was doing laps. Beyond this vista stretched the ubiquitous blue agave fields.

The heady scent of Old World roses came to Moira as she was led toward a man sitting at a glass-and-wrought-iron table, laden with food on Mexican fired-clay plates, and pitchers of red and white sangria stuffed with slices of fresh fruit.

The man rose at her approach, smiling broadly. He wore a terry-cloth short-sleeved top and surfer's swimming trunks, revealing a lean, hairy body.

"Barbara!" he called over his shoulder. "Our guest is here!"

Then he held out his hand and gripped Moira's. "Good afternoon, Señorita Trevor. Narsico Skydel. It's a pleasure to meet you."

"The pleasure's all mine," Moira said.

"Please." He gestured. "Make yourself at home."

"Thank you." Moira chose a chair near him.

"White or red?"

"White, please."

He poured two glasses of white sangria, handed her one, then sat. "You must be hungry after your long trip." He indicated the food. "Please help yourself."

By the time she had loaded a plate Berengária Moreno—known here as Barbara Skydel—had finished her laps and, toweling off, was coming up the stone pathway to the patio. She was a tall, slim woman, her water-slicked hair pulled back from her handsome face in a ponytail. Moira imagined her with Roberto Corellos, cuckolding her husband. Barbara reached the patio and, barefoot, walked over. Her handshake was cool, firm, and business-like.

"Narsico's publicist said you're writing a piece about tequila, is that right?" Her voice was deep for a woman, and vibrant, as if at an early age she'd been taught to sing.

"It is." Moira took a sip of her sangria.

Launching into his opening pitch, Narsico informed her that tequila was made from the *piña*, the heart of the agave plant.

Barbara interrupted him. "What sort of a piece are you writing?" She sat on the opposite side of the table from the two of them, which Moira thought a telling choice. The natural thing would be to sit next to your husband.

"It's sociological, really. The origins of tequila, what it has meant to the Mexicans, that sort of thing."

"That sort of thing," Barbara echoed. "Well, to begin with tequila isn't a *Mexican* drink at all."

"But the Mexicans had to know about the agave plant."

"Of course." Barbara Skydel took a plate and filled it with food from different serving platters. "For centuries the *piña* had been cooked and sold as candy. Then the Spaniards invaded. It was the Spanish Franciscans who settled in this fertile valley and founded the town of Santiago de Tequila in 1530. It was the Franciscans who conceived of fermenting the *piña*'s sugars into a potent liquor."

"So," Moira said, "the agave was yet another aspect of Mexican culture appropriated and changed by the conquistadores."

"Well, it's worse than that, really." Barbara licked her fingertips, reminding Moira of Roberto Corellos. "The conquistadores merely killed the Mexicans. It was the Franciscans who traveled with them, systematically dismantling the Mexican way of life and replacing it with the particularly cruel Spanish version of Catholicism. Ethnically speaking, it was the Spanish church that destroyed Mexican culture." She smiled with her teeth. "The conquistadores were merely soldiers, they were after Mexican gold. The Franciscans were the soldiers of God, they wanted the Mexican soul."

As Barbara poured herself a goblet of blood-red sangria, Narsico cleared his throat. "As you can see, my wife has become a fierce advocate of the Mexican way of life."

He seemed embarrassed by this discussion, as if his wife was guilty of bad manners. Moira wondered how long Barbara's convictions had been a bone of contention between them. Did he disagree with her, or did he think her outspokenness on this issue was bad PR for his company, which was, after all, wholly dependent on consumers?

"You didn't always hold that conviction, Señora Skydel?"

"Growing up in Colombia, I knew only the struggle of my people against our dictator-generals and fascist armies."

Narsico sighed theatrically. "Mexico has changed her."

Moira did not miss the hint of bitterness in his voice. She studied Barbara as she ate, an elemental act that often revealed more about people than they realized. Barbara ate quickly and aggressively, as if there were a need to defend her food, and Moira wondered what her upbringing had been like. As the only female child she would have been served last, with her mother. Also, she was wholly concentrated on her food, and Moira imagined it was a sensual experience for her. Moira liked the way she ate, she found it endearing, and she thought again of Corellos's description of her as a piranha.

At that moment Narsico's cell phone buzzed, and taking it up, he rose and excused himself. Moira noticed that Barbara ignored him as he walked back inside the hacienda.

"As you can already see," Barbara said, "there are a number of ways to tell this story." She had a very direct way of speaking, and of looking at you when she spoke. "I'd like to influence the way you tell it."

"You already have."

Barbara nodded. She was one of those fortunate women with excellent bone structure, lucid skin, and a tight, athletic body, all of which naturally defied the passing of time. It was impossible to guess her precise age. Judging by her manner, Moira supposed she might have reached forty, though she looked a good five or six years younger.

"Where are you from?"

"Actually, I just came from Bogotá," Moira said. She knew she was taking a chance, but she didn't have the time to draw this out, and she felt the need to take advantage of Narsico's absence. "I saw Roberto Corellos,

Narsico's cousin." She watched the other woman's face carefully. "And, coincidentally or not, an old friend of yours."

Something dark and cold passed across Berengária Moreno's face. "I don't know what you mean, Corellos and I never saw eye-to-eye," she said coldly.

"How about mouth-to-mouth?"

For a long, uncomfortable moment Barbara sat perfectly still. When she opened her mouth again she no longer looked handsome, or even appealing, and Moira knew precisely what Corellos had meant. *Here comes the piranha,* she thought.

In a low voice filled with menace Barbara said, "I could have you thrown out on your ass, beaten senseless, or even—" She bit back her words.

"Or what?" Moira said, egging her on. "Have me killed? Well, we know your husband wouldn't have the balls to do it."

Unexpectedly, Barbara Skydel exploded into laughter. "Oh, *Jesus mio,* can you imagine?" But almost immediately she sobered up. "Roberto had no business telling you about what happened."

"You'll have to take that up with him."

Moira noticed Barbara glance back at the house where Narsico, still on his cell, paced up and down behind one of the French doors.

Barbara stood. "Why don't we go for a walk?"

After hesitating for a moment, Moira drank off the last of her sangria and, rising, followed Barbara down past the tennis court, toward the gardens. When they were far away from the hacienda, in among a dusty stand of dwarf pine trees, Barbara turned to her and said, "You interest me. Who are you, because you sure as hell aren't a reporter."

Moira mentally braced herself for the worst. "What makes you say that?"

Barbara leaned in toward her in the menacing manner of certain men. "Roberto never would have told a reporter about us. He wouldn't have told you a goddamn thing."

"What can I say?" Moira shrugged. "He liked me."

Barbara snorted. "Roberto doesn't like anyone, and he only loves himself." She cocked her head, and abruptly her manner changed from menacing to seductive. Backing Moira against the trunk of a tree, she put her hand up, twining a wisp of Moira's hair around her forefinger. "So then you fucked him, or at least gave him a blow job."

"He didn't touch me."

The back of Barbara's hand stroked Moira's cheek. Was Barbara jealous, trying to seduce her, or just screwing with her mind?

"Somehow you got to him. How did you do it?"

Moira smiled. "I graduated top of my class in charm school."

Barbara's long fingers were like feathers against her cheek and ear. "What did Roberto see in you? He may be a brute and a swine, but one of his great strengths is sizing up people virtually from the moment he meets them. So I'm left wondering why you've come here." She pressed her lips against Moira's cheek. "It isn't to interview my husband, I think we've established that much."

Moira felt she needed to shock Barbara in order to gain the upper hand. "I've come to investigate the murder of the man found on your property several weeks ago."

Barbara stepped back. "You're police? The *American* police are interested in the murder?"

"I'm not police," Moira said. "I'm federal."

All the breath seemed to go out of Barbara. "Christ," she said. "That's how you got to Roberto."

Moira said, "Berengária, I want you to take me to the place where the body was found. I want you to take me there now."

Bourne drove Ottavio Moreno's gray Opel, following precisely the directions Coven had given him. Beside him, Ottavio was readying all the purchases Bourne had made. There was silence between them, just the thrumming of the tires on the road, the hiss of oncoming traffic working its way through the closed windows.

"Twenty minutes," Bourne said finally.

"We'll be ready," Ottavio replied without lifting his head from his work. "Don't worry."

Bourne wasn't worried, it wasn't in his nature, or if it had once been, his Treadstone training had long since burned it out of him. He was thinking of Coven, the man with what was without doubt a CI field ops code name. He well knew that CI trained and directed a cadre of field operatives who specialized in wet work. He needed to know everything he could about Coven before their encounter, and there was only one person who could help him.

Taking out his cell, he punched in a number he hadn't used in some time. When the familiar voice answered, he said, "Peter, it's Jason Bourne."

* * *

Peter Marks was on his way to see Chief Inspector Lloyd-Philips, who was waiting for him at the Vesper Club, when the call came in. He fairly vibrated when he heard Bourne's voice.

"Where the hell are you?" Marks, in the back of one of those huge London cabs, found himself shouting.

"I need your help," Bourne said. "What do you know about Coven?"

"The CI field op?"

"You didn't say *our field op*. Have you left CI, Peter?"

"Actually, I quit not so long ago." Marks had to will his heart rate back down to acceptable levels. He needed to find out where Bourne was and get to him. "Danziger has created a toxic atmosphere that I wouldn't tolerate. He's slowly getting rid of anyone loyal to the Old Man." He coughed as a sudden chill went through him, and he shivered briefly. "You know he canned Soraya."

"I didn't."

"Jason, I want you to know... I'm damn glad you're alive."

"Peter, about Coven."

"Right, Coven. He's as dangerous—and as success-ful—as they get." Marks thought for a moment. "Hard, remorseless, a real shit."

"Would he harm a child?"

"What?"

"You heard me," Bourne said.

"Jesus, I don't think so. He's a devoted family man, if you can believe it." Marks took a breath. "Jason, what the hell is going on?"

"I don't have time now—"

"Listen, I was sent to London to find out what the hell happened at the Vesper Club."

"Peter, the incident at the Vesper Club happened last night. If you really are in London—"

"I am. I'm on my way to the Vesper Club now."

"You were already on the plane when I was at the club, so cut the bullshit, Peter. Who are you working for now?"

"Willard."

"You're Treadstone."

"That's right. We're working for the same—"

"I don't work for Treadstone, or Willard. In fact," Bourne went on, "when I see Willard again, I'm going to wring his neck. He sold me out. Why did he do that, Peter?"

"I don't know."

"Good-bye, Peter."

"Wait! Don't hang up, I need to see you."

There was a brief pause. Marks found that his hand was sweating so badly, the phone almost slipped from his grip. "Jason, please. This is important."

"Aren't you going to ask me why I was with the man who knifed Diego Hererra?"

"You can tell me, if you want. But frankly, I don't care. I know you must've had a good reason."

"Good man. Willard is training you well."

"You're right, of course, Willard's a perfect shit. He'll do anything to resurrect Treadstone."

"Why?"

Marks hesitated. He'd never liked hitching his star to Willard's dream, but at the time he felt he'd had no choice. And of course, Willard had played him perfectly, working on his desire to get revenge against Danziger and his puppet master, Bud Halliday. When Willard had promised him that he'd find a way to take Halliday down, and Danziger with him, he was in. But Willard had made a mistake when he'd asked Marks to betray Bourne. Willard, having no loyalty except to the idea of Treadstone, couldn't conceive of the idea of personal loyalty, let alone have an inkling of its power.

He took a deep breath and said, "Willard wants to get you and Arkadin together so he can determine once and for all which of Treadstone's training protocols is superior. If Arkadin kills you, then he'll go back to the original protocols, make some minor adjustments, and start training recruits."

"And if I kill Arkadin?"

"Then, Jason, he says he'll have to study you to find out how your amnesia has changed you, so he can alter the Treadstone training program accordingly."

"A monkey in a cage."

"I'm afraid so, yes."

"And you're meant to take me back to Washington?"

"No. It's not that simple. But if you'll meet me, I'll explain everything."

"Maybe, Peter. If I think I can trust you."

"Jason, you can. You absolutely can." Marks believed this fervently, with every fiber of his being. "When can we—?"

"Not now. Right now, what I need from you is everything you know about Coven—specifically his methodology, tendencies, and what, if it comes to it, he's capable of."

* * *

Bourne listened to Peter Marks, filing away everything he said. Then he told him he'd be in touch and disconnected. For a time, he concentrated on the traffic piling up, allowing his subconscious to work on the problem at hand—that is, how to neutralize Coven without jeopardizing Chrissie and Scarlett.

Then he saw a sign for George Street and immediately recalled his afternoon in Oxford. And yet his thoughts were not of Chrissie and Professor Giles. As if it were yesterday, he recalled his visit to the Centre for the Study of Ancient Documents at the Old Boys' School in Oxford's George Street. He'd gone in the guise of David Webb, visiting professor of linguistics, but inside, the Bourne identity had asserted itself. He knew, but he didn't know *how* he knew, that in this moment in time he'd still had in his possession the laptop he had stolen from Jalal Essai. He had taken time out from his classes at Oxford to enter the Centre for the Study of Ancient Documents. What had he done there, what was he researching? He couldn't remember. But he did know that whatever he'd discovered there had led him to keep the laptop. What had he done with it? It was on the cusp of his memory, like the burning edge of the sun in eclipse. He almost had it, almost.

And then the turnoff Coven had described was coming up on the right, and he had to step away from the cusp, let it go, because it was time to confront Coven.

16

WE'LL HAVE TO walk from here." Barbara climbed out of the jeep. Despite the lingering heat, she had changed into jeans, cowboy boots, and a plaid shirt, the sleeves rolled up to her elbows.

Moira followed her. They had driven for perhaps a mile, due west of the hacienda but still well within the boundaries of the immense estancia. In the distance rose dusty blue hills, and the sweet, almost fermented scent of the blue agave thickened the air. The sun wallowed just above the horizon. The ground, storing the heat of the day, was baking. To the west, the sky was white and glaring.

"*Ai*, Narsico said this would all blow over, but I knew different."

"Why is that?" Moira said.

"That's the way things always happen."

"What things?" Moira pressed.

"You get fucked by the smallest things."

"Murder is a small thing?"

Barbara lifted her chin in a gesture of contempt. "You think I give a rat's ass about someone I don't even know?"

"What became of the police investigation?" she asked as they walked through the arid scrubland.

"The usual." Barbara squinted into the sun. "An inspector from Tequila asked some questions, but there was no identification on the man, and no one claimed the body. He spent several weeks interviewing us and everyone on our staff. He made a complete nuisance of himself. He kept saying that there was a reason the victim was found on our estancia. We became prime suspects, but he and his kind are so inept that finally he was forced to give up spewing innuendos and speculation. Then, complete silence. So far as I knew, the case was closed."

"That's the Mexican perspective," Moira said. "For us, the murder has taken on larger implications."

The concern Moira had heard before crept back into Barbara's voice. "Like what?"

"For one thing, we know that the victim worked for your late brother in his compound outside Mexico City, so a link has been established between you and the victim."

"He worked for Gustavo? I had no idea. I had nothing to do with Gustavo's business dealings."

"Really? The fact that you've been sleeping with his supplier makes that difficult to believe."

"And for another?"

Moira deliberately kept silent. It appeared that they

were approaching the crime scene, or at least the spot where the body had been dumped, because Barbara slowed and began to look around.

"This is it." Barbara pointed to a spot a few feet ahead of them. "That's where the body was found."

In this arid climate, footprints from several weeks ago were still visible, but they were inextricably overlaid with the boot prints of the police. Moira picked her way slowly around the periphery, scrutinizing the ground.

"The earth hasn't been dug up, or even disturbed very much. It doesn't look like the crime scene was scoured."

"It wasn't. They dragged us out here while they were here," Barbara said.

Moira began her investigation in earnest. Snapping on a pair of latex gloves, she pawed through the dirt, dust, and scrub. By whatever mysterious means, Jalal Essai had obtained copies of the forensic photos of the victim, which showed him lying on his left side. His wrists were tied behind his back and his legs were bent at an angle, his head bent forward. From this, it could be deduced that he had been kneeling at the moment of his demise. Essai had tried to get the autopsy report, as well, but it had been lost by either the coroner's office or the police, both of which seemed incompetent.

"Another thing," she said, wanting to continue to heighten Barbara's tension, "we know the victim left the compound less than thirty minutes before the raid during which your brother was killed." She raised her gaze to peer into Barbara's eyes. "Which means that he had advance warning of the raid."

"Why are you looking at me?" Barbara said. "I told you I had nothing to do with Gustavo's business."

"Are you going to keep saying that until I believe you?"

Barbara folded her arms over her chest. "Damn you to hell, I had nothing to do with this man's death."

Moira was looking for a spent shell casing. The one curious thing about the photos was that it was clear the victim had been shot with a small-caliber handgun. One shot to the base of the skull. The lack of powder or flash burns on either the victim's skin or his clothes indicated that the killer hadn't shot at particularly close range, which you would certainly want to do if you meant to kill a man with one shot from a small-caliber weapon.

Forty minutes of sifting topsoil through her fingers produced nothing. By this time she had made one complete circuit of the crime scene at a calculated distance from where the body was found. Of course, it was possible that the victim had been killed elsewhere and dumped here, but she didn't think so. If, as she suspected, the killer's motivation was not only to silence the victim but also to implicate the Skydels, he would want the killing to occur on their property.

At a wider radius from the kill spot, more scrub grew, and Moira, once again down on her knees, began to excavate around the base of these gray-green plants. The sun was lowering, passing through a stray band of striated cloud. The landscape turned blue-gray in the false twilight. Moira sat back on her hams, waiting for more light. When the sun began to emerge, the crime scene was pierced with brilliant shards of red-gold, scattering across the ground at an acute angle. Their shadows stretched out behind them, attenuated giants.

Out of the corner of her eye Moira saw a bright

flash, instantaneous, like the wink of a diamond facet, and then it was gone. She turned her head and quickly picked her way to the spot where she had seen the flash. Now there was nothing. Still, she drove her fingers into the ground, pushing them forward, turning over the dusty earth.

And there it was, suddenly, in the palm of her hand, as the granules of dirt fell away. Carefully, she plucked it up between thumb and forefinger and moved it into the sunlight. The flash came again, and she read the markings on the case, her heart beating hard and fast.

Barbara took a step closer. "What have you found?" Her voice was a little breathless.

Moira rose to her feet. "Has it ever occurred to you that the victim was deliberately shot on your estancia?"

"What? Why?"

"As I said, the victim worked for your brother, Gustavo. However, he was someone else's creature. This someone tipped the victim to the raid, and the victim escaped. Why was he tipped off, only to be killed within hours of his escape?"

Barbara, mute, shook her head.

"When he left Gustavo's compound he took with him your brother's laptop, which contained all of Gustavo's drug contacts."

Barbara licked her lips. "The person who controlled him killed him?"

"Yes."

"Shot him to death on my estancia."

"Yes. To try to implicate you," Moira said. "What saved you was luck in the form of the incompetence of the local police."

"But why would this person want to implicate me in the murder?"

"I'm speculating here," Moira said, "but I'd say he wanted to get you out of the picture."

Again, Barbara shook her head, mutely.

"Consider: The person who has Gustavo's laptop holds your brother's business in his hands. His plan was to muscle his way in and get rid of anyone who stood in his way."

Barbara's eyes were wide and staring. "I don't believe you."

"That's where this shell casing comes in." Moira held up the item in question. "The forensic photos showed that the victim was shot to death with one bullet to the base of the skull. The oddity was that the killer used a small-caliber handgun, even though he wasn't standing right behind the victim. I figured that he had to be using special ammunition, and I was right."

She placed the spent casing in Barbara's hand. Barbara held it up and looked at the markings in the last of the fading light.

"I can't read the writing."

"That's because it's Russian Cyrillic. The manufacturer is Tula. This casing is from a very special bullet, a hollow-core that's filled with cyanide. Not surprisingly, it's illegal, and only available in Russia. It's not even sold over the Internet."

Barbara looked at her. "The killer is Russian."

"The man who muscled his way into Gustavo's business." She nodded. "That's right, I know you're only fronting your brother's business. I know you and Roberto have a new partner."

That did it. Barbara's face fell. "Goddammit, I told Roberto that Leonid was out to get him, but he just laughed at me."

"Leonid?" Moira's heart gave a thump in her chest. "Is Leonid Arkadin your partner?"

"Roberto said, *'What do you know, you're a woman, women know what they're told to know, nothing more.'* "

Moira grabbed her arm in order to focus her. "Barbara, is Leonid Arkadin your partner?"

Barbara looked away. She bit her lip.

"Is it loyalty or fear that's keeping your mouth shut?"

Moira could just make out one curve of Barbara's thin smile. "I'm loyal to no one. In this business it doesn't pay. That's another thing my husband doesn't understand."

"Then you're scared of Arkadin."

Barbara's head swung around, and there was a violent look in her eyes. "The fucker muscled his way in. He strong-armed Roberto, for Christ's sake, said he had Gustavo's client list. Roberto said those were his people. Arkadin said that was in the past. He said that Gustavo was dead, he had the list, and the clients were his, as well. He said the best solution was to share the profits equally, that if Roberto didn't agree he'd contact them without Roberto's permission or help and supply them from other sources.

"Roberto tried three times to kill Arkadin. All the attempts failed. Then Arkadin told him, *'Fuck you, Gustavo's clients are mine now, go find yourself some other pigeons to feed.'* I thought Roberto was going to have a coronary. I calmed him down."

"Your husband must've liked that," Moira said drily.

"My husband's a pussy, as you can see for yourself," Barbara said. "But he's devoted to me and he serves his purpose." She lifted her arms to encompass the whole of the estancia. "Besides, his business would be in the toilet without me."

The sun had slid behind the mountains in the west. It was growing dark very quickly now, as if an immense blanket had been thrown across the sky.

"Let's get back to the jeep," Moira said as she took the shell casing from Barbara.

On the way back to the hacienda, Barbara said, "You know Arkadin, I gather."

Moira knew as much as Bourne had told her. "Well enough to know that his next step will be to take over Corellos's business completely. That's how Arkadin operates." It was how he'd appropriated Nikolai Yevsen's arms distribution in Khartoum. He'd find some way to suborn a La Modelo guard or a FARC inmate or maybe one of Corellos's many women inside prison, pay them enough to assuage their fear of the drug lord. One day soon, Moira thought, Corellos would wind up dead in his luxurious cell.

"Arkadin is already pissed at Roberto and me," Barbara said as she guided the jeep over the unpaved road. "The latest shipment has been delayed. The boat had to pull in for repairs because its engine overheated. If you know anything about Mexico, you know that those repairs weren't going to happen in a matter of hours, or even overnight. The boat will be ready by tomorrow evening, but I know that's not going to satisfy him." Her hands were gripping the wheel so tightly, her knuckles had turned white as bone.

"I understand, Berengária, honestly I do."

"Why do you disrespect me? I've been Barbara for years."

"I respect your real name. You should embrace it, not reject it."

When Berengária did not reply, Moira continued. "Arkadin has his rules, and they're inflexible. Both you and Roberto will forfeit something for the delay."

Berengária stared straight ahead. "I know."

"And listen, *mami*, if this shipment should fail to reach its destination, someone else will be paying you a visit, someone not nearly as kind and understanding as I am. You can be sure that's how Arkadin wants it and how it's going to be."

Berengária thought for a long time. The sun had already slipped behind the purple mountains. The sky seemed scrubbed of clouds. In the east darkness was gathering. They seemed to drive for a long time, as if Berengária was driving in circles, as if she was reluctant to return to the hacienda. At length, she braked and put the jeep in neutral. Then she turned to Moira.

"What if," she said with a particular ferocity, "that's not how I want it to be?"

Moira experienced the joy of the wheel turning, of Berengária finally being in her sights. She returned her fierceness with a grin. "There I think I can help you."

Berengária stared at her with an intensity that to an-other woman might have been disturbing. But Moira understood what it was she wanted, what their quid pro quo would be. She admired this woman, and pitied her as well. Difficult enough to be a strong woman in a man's world, but to maintain your strength in the Latino world was a task worthy of an Amazon. And yet, above and beyond her personal feelings was the knowledge that Berengária was her target. What she needed from Berengária she would get. Now she knew how to get it.

Leaning over very slowly, she took Berengária's head in her hands and pressed her lips to hers.

Berengária's eyes opened wide for just a split instant before they fluttered closed. Her lips softening, then opening, she gave herself over to the kiss.

Moira felt the moment of her capitulation with both a sense of triumph and compassion. Then she felt Berengária's hand on the nape of her neck, the pressure of passion unleashed, and she sighed into Berengária's sweet mouth.

My name is Lloyd-Philips, Chief Inspector Lloyd-Philips."

Peter Marks introduced himself and shook the proffered hand, which was pale, limp, and nicotine-stained. Lloyd-Philips, in a cheap suit, frayed at the cuffs, sported a gingery mustache and thinning hair that might once have been the same color, but now seemed dusted with ash.

The chief inspector tried to smile, but couldn't quite make it. Maybe those muscles had atrophied, Marks thought wryly. He showed Lloyd-Philips his bogus credentials, which claimed he worked for a private firm under the auspices of the DoD and, therefore, had the power of the Pentagon behind him.

They were standing in the deserted lobby of the Vesper Club, which had been cordoned off by the police as a crime scene.

Marks said: "One of the alleged perpetrators might be a person of interest to my superiors. That being the case, I'd appreciate a look-see at the relevant CCTV tape from last night."

Lloyd-Philips shrugged his thin shoulders. "Why not? We're already printing up flyers with the photos of the two men's faces to distribute to the metropolitan police and personnel at all train stations, airports, and shipping terminals."

The chief inspector led him through the casino proper, down a corridor, and into the back rooms, one of which was hot and smelled of electronics. A technician sat in front of a complex board filled with dials, sliders, and a computer keyboard. Just above were two lines of monitors, each showing a different part of the casino. From what Marks could see, no nook or cranny had been ignored, even the lavatories.

Lloyd-Philips bent over the technician, murmured something, to which the man nodded and started punching keys. The chief inspector reminded Marks of a character out of any one of a hundred British spy novels. His vaguely dyspeptic expression of long-suffering boredom marked him as a career bureaucrat with one eye closed and the other on his approaching pension.

"Here we go," the technician intoned.

One of the monitors went black, then an image appeared. Marks saw the bar in the high-rollers' room. Then Bourne and another man he recognized as the now deceased Diego Hererra moved into the frame and stayed there. They were speaking, but they were partly turned away from the camera, and it was impossible to make out what they were saying.

"Diego Hererra entered the Vesper Club at approximately nine thirty-five last night," Lloyd-Philips said in his slightly bored donnish voice. "With him was this man." He pointed to Bourne. "Adam Stone."

The video continued. Another man—presumably the killer—came into the picture. It was when he began to approach Bourne and Diego Hererra that things got interesting.

Marks leaned forward tensely. Bourne had moved in front of Hererra, as if to block the killer's advance. But something curious happened as they spoke to each other. Bourne's attitude changed. It was almost as if he knew the killer, but judging by his initial expression that couldn't be true. Yet Bourne allowed him to come over to the bar, to stand next to Hererra. And then Diego slumped over. Bourne grabbed the killer by the lapels, as he should have done in the first place. But then the second strange thing happened. Bourne didn't beat the crap out of the killer. Marks was frankly astonished to see the two of them take on the three bouncers who appeared from the casino's main rooms.

"And there you have it," Chief Inspector Lloyd-Philips said. "The perpetrator used some kind of high-frequency sound weapon to render everyone unconscious."

"Have you identified the killer?" Marks asked.

"Not yet. He doesn't appear on any of our electronic nets."

"This club is members-only. The manager must know who he is."

Lloyd-Philips looked distinctly annoyed. "According to the club's records, the suspect's name is Vincenzo

Mancuso, but though there are actually three men with that name in England, none of them matches the man on the tape. Nevertheless, we dispatched inspectors to interview the three Vincenzo Mancusos, only one of whom resides in the London environs. All have alibis that check out."

"Forensics?" Marks asked.

The chief inspector looked ready to bite Marks's head off. "No suspicious fingerprints were found, and there was no sign of the murder weapon. On my orders the men fanned out within a mile radius of the club, pawing through dustbins, peering down storm drains, and the like. They even dredged the river, though no one had a hope of finding the knife. All searches have so far proved fruitless."

"And what of the other man—Adam Stone?"

"Vanished off the face of the earth."

Which means the investigation is at a standstill, Marks thought. *This is a high-profile murder investigation. No wonder he's edgy.*

"Adam Stone is the person of interest to my superiors." Marks drew the chief inspector away from the technician. "They—and I—would consider it a personal favor if you suppressed Stone's photo from the flyers."

Lloyd-Philips smiled, not a pretty sight. His teeth were as nicotine-stained as his fingertips.

"I've made a career of not giving personal favors. That's how I keep my nose clean and my pension intact."

"Nevertheless, in this instance my superiors at DoD would be grateful if you made an exception."

"Listen, laddo, I brought you in here as a courtesy." The chief inspector's eyes were suddenly as flinty as his voice. "I don't care if your superiors are five-bloody-star generals, London's my bailiwick. *My* superiors—Her Majesty's Government—don't appreciate you lot coming over here and leaning on us like we're a bunch of colonial yobs. An' I don't like it one ickle bit, either." He lifted a warning finger. "A word in your shell-like: Naff off before I get really hacked and decide to detain you as a material witness."

"Thanks for your hospitality, Chief Inspector," Marks said drily. "Before I go, I'd like a copy of the photos of Stone and the un-ID'd man."

"Anything to get you out of my bloody hair." Lloyd-Philips tapped the tech on the shoulder, the tech asked for the number of Marks's cell, then pressed a button; a moment later a digital still from the security tape of the two men side by side appeared on Marks's phone.

"All right, then." The chief inspector turned to Marks. "Don't make me regret what I've done. Stay well away from me and my case and you'll get on well."

Back out on the street, the sun was struggling to be seen through masses of streaming cloud. The city roared all around Marks. He checked the photo on his PDA. Then he punched in Willard's private line and got right to his voice mail. Willard's phone was off, which, calculating the hour back in Washington, Marks thought odd. He left a detailed message, asking Willard to run the photo of the man who had knifed Diego Hererra through the Treadstone data banks, which had been amassed from those of the usual alphabet soup of CI, NSA, FBI, DoD, plus some others to which Willard had gained access.

From a detective-inspector outside the club to whom

he showed his ID, Marks obtained Diego Hererra's home address. Forty minutes later he arrived just as a silver Bentley limousine turned the corner and pulled up outside Hererra's house. The liveried driver emerged, walked smartly around the gleaming grille to open the rear door. A tall, distinguished man who looked like an older version of Diego emerged. With a somber expression and a heavy tread the man climbed the steps to Diego's front door and inserted a key in the door.

Before he could disappear inside, Marks strode up and said, "Mr. Hererra, I'm Peter Marks." When the older man turned around to peer at him, Marks added, "I'm terribly sorry for your loss."

The elder Hererra paused for a moment. He was a handsome man, with a leonine shock of white hair, worn long over his collar in the current Catalan style, but he appeared ashen beneath his deep outdoorsman's tan. "Did you know my son, Señor Marks?"

"I'm afraid I didn't have that pleasure, sir."

Hererra nodded somewhat absently. "It seemed Diego had very few male friends." His mouth twitched in a parody of a smile. "His preference was for women."

Marks took a step forward and held his creds up for the other to see. "Sir, I know this is a difficult time, and I apologize in advance if I'm intruding, but I need to talk to you."

Hererra continued to look through Marks as if he hadn't heard a word he'd said. Then he seemed to focus. "Do you know something about his death?"

"This isn't a conversation for the street, is it, Señor Hererra."

"No, of course not." Hererra's head twitched. "Please

forgive my lack of manners, Señor Marks." Then he gestured. He had very large, square hands, the capable hands of a skilled laborer. "Come inside and we'll talk."

Marks went up the steps, across the threshold, and into the late Diego Hererra's house. He heard the older man coming in after him, the door close behind him, and then there was a knife blade across his throat, and Diego Hererra's father was close behind him, holding him in an astonishingly powerful grip.

"Now, you sonovabitch," Hererra said, "you'll tell me everything you know about my son's murder, or by Christ's tears I'll slit your throat from ear to ear."

17

BUD HALLIDAY SAT in a semicircular banquette at the White Knights Lounge, a bar in an out-of-the-way area of suburban Maryland where he often came to unwind. He nursed a bourbon-and-water while he tried to clear his mind of the clutter that had built up over the long day.

His parents were Mainline Philadelphians who could trace their respective families back to Alexander Hamilton and John Adams, respectively. They had been childhood sweethearts who, with the predictability of their ilk, were divorced. His mother, a society doyenne, now lived in Newport, Rhode Island. His father, plagued with emphysema from years of inveterate smoking, rattled around the family mansion, trailed by oxygen tanks and a pair of full-time Haitian nurses. Halliday saw neither of them. He'd turned his back on the hermetically sealed golden glow of their society world when, to their horror and mortification, he had gleefully enlisted in the marines at the age of eighteen. While at boot camp he had imagined his mother fainting at the news, which gave him a great measure of satisfaction. As for his father, he'd probably chewed off the end of his cigar, blamed his wife for his disappointment, and gone off to the insurance company he owned, and which he ran with ruthless and appalling success.

Finding that he'd finished his bourbon, Halliday flagged down the waiter and ordered another.

The twins arrived at the same time as his drink, and he ordered them chocolate martinis. They sat down on either side of him. One was dressed in green, the other in blue. The one in green was a redhead, the other blond. Today, at least. They were like that, Michelle and Mandy. They liked to play off their eerie echoes of each other, but at the same time asserting their differences. They were tall, almost six feet, with figures as lush and luscious as their lips. They could have been models, or possibly even actresses, given the expert way they played roles, but were neither vain nor empty-headed. Michelle was a theoretical mathematician, and Mandy was a microbiologist at the CDC. Michelle, who could have had her pick of chairs at any of the top universities in the country, instead worked for DARPA—the Defense Advanced Research Projects Agency—cooking up new cryptographic algorithms that could foil even the fastest computer, even used in tandem. Her latest used heuristic techniques, meaning it learned from every attempt to break it, as if it were a self-educating entity, changing on the fly. It required a physical key to unlock it.

Never had two more fertile minds been wrapped in such delectable and erotic packages, Halliday thought as the waiter set their chocolate martinis in front of them. They all raised their glasses in a silent toast to another night together. When they were off duty, the girls loved sex, chocolate, and sex, in that order. But they weren't off duty yet.

"What's your assessment of the ring?" Halliday asked Michelle.

"It would help," she said, "if you had given me the real thing instead of a set of photos."

"Given that I didn't, what's your best guess?"

Michelle took a sip of her drink as if needing time to set her thoughts in order or to figure out how to express them to Halliday, a mental midget compared with her and her twin.

"It seems likely to me that the ring is a physical key."

Halliday got interested in a hurry. He was keeping a sharp lookout. "Meaning?"

"Just what I said. It may be the algorithm I'm working on, but the odd inscription on the inside of the ring appears to me to be like the ridges of a key." Responding to Halliday's quizzical look, she changed tack. Taking out a felt-tip pen, she drew on Halliday's napkin.

"Here we have a common key to a lock. It has ridges cut into it that are unique to it. Most common locks have twelve pins inside the lock cylinder, six upper and six lower. When the key is inserted in the cylinder, the ridges raise the upper pins above the shear line, allowing the shaft inside the cylinder to turn and the lock to open.

"So now consider each ideogram of the engraving inside the ring as a notch. Slip the ring into the right lock and presto, Open Sesame."

"Is this possible?" he asked.

"Anything's possible, Bud. You know that."

Halliday stared at her drawing, suddenly galvanized. Her theory took a big leap of faith to believe, but the woman was a stone-cold genius. He couldn't afford to dismiss any theory she put forward no matter how loopy it might sound on first blush.

"What's in store for us tonight?" Mandy asked, clearly bored with this topic.

"I'm hungry." Michelle pocketed her pen. "I haven't eaten a thing all day, except for a Snickers I found in my drawer, and that was so stale the chocolate had turned white."

"Finish your drink," Halliday said.

She feigned a pout. "You know how I get when I drink on an empty stomach."

Halliday chuckled. "So I've been told."

"Well, it's true and then some," Mandy said. And in another voice entirely, deeper, with plenty of vibrato, a singer's voice: "Dat li'l girl, she get freak-eee!"

"Whereas dis one," Michelle said in precisely the same voice, "she already got her freak on!"

Both of them threw their heads back and laughed for precisely the same amount of time. Halliday, watching them, turning his head from side to side, felt a throbbing in his forehead, as if he were observing a tennis match from too close.

"Ah, there you are!" Mandy said as their foursome was about to be completed.

"We thought you might not be coming," Michelle said.

Halliday palmed his diagram-covered napkin and hid it in his lap. Both the girls noticed but said nothing, simply smiling into the face of the newcomer.

"There is no power on earth." Jalal Essai slid into the banquette and kissed Mandy in the place on her neck she liked best. "That could possibly have kept me away."

Peter Marks stood very still. The man behind him smelled of tobacco and anger. The knife he held to Marks's throat was razor-sharp, and Marks, who certainly had enough experience in these matters, had no doubt that Hererra would slit his throat.

"Señor Hererra, there's no need for these melodramatics," he said. "I'll gladly share with you everything I know. Let's just keep calm and not lose our heads here."

"I'm perfectly calm," Hererra said grimly.

"All right." Marks tried to swallow. His throat had dried up. "I'll admit up front that what I know isn't very much."

"It's got to be more than that bastard Lloyd-Shithead was willing to share. He told me to concentrate on making arrangements to bring my son back to Spain, which he said wouldn't be possible until the medical examiner was through with him."

Now Marks understood why Hererra was in a fury. "I agree, the chief inspector is something of a dick." He swallowed. "But he's of no consequence now. I want to know why Diego was murdered almost as much as you do. Believe me, I'm determined to find out." This was true. Marks would never find Bourne without discovering what had happened last night in the Vesper Club, and why Bourne would leave with the murderer as if they were friends. Something wasn't adding up.

He felt Hererra breathing behind him. It was deep and even, which to Marks was very frightening indeed, because it meant that despite his grief this man was in full possession of all his faculties. This spoke of a powerful personality; it would be suicidal to fuck with him.

"In fact," Marks continued, "I can show you a photo of the man who murdered your son."

The knife blade trembled a moment in Hererra's huge fist, then it was withdrawn, and Marks stepped away. He turned to face the older man.

"Please, Señor Hererra, I understand the depth of your sorrow."

"Do you have a son, Señor Marks?"

"I don't, sir. I'm not married."

"Then you can't know."

"I lost a sister when I was twelve. She was only ten. I was so angry I wanted to destroy everything in sight."

Hererra contemplated him for a moment, then said, "So you know."

He took Marks into the living room. Marks sat down on a sofa, but Hererra remained standing, looking at the photos of his son and, presumably, his many girlfriends that lined the mantel. For a long time, the two men remained like that, Hererra silent, Marks unwilling to disturb the older man's grief.

At length, Hererra turned and, crossing to where Marks sat, said, "I'll see that photo now."

Marks dug out his PDA, scrolled to the media section, and brought up the photo he'd gotten from Lloyd-Philips's IT tech.

"He's on the left," Marks said, pointing to the as-yet-unidentified man.

Hererra took the PDA and stared down at the screen for so long that Marks thought he had turned to stone.

"And the other man?"

Marks shrugged. "An innocent bystander."

"Tell me about him, he looks familiar to me."

"Lloyd-Shithead told me his name is Adam Stone."

"Is that so." Something slithered across Hererra's face.

Marks impatiently pointed again. "Señor, this is important. Do you know the man on the left?"

Hererra thrust the PDA back into Marks's hand, then went to the bar setup and poured himself a brandy. He drank half straight off, then, in an effort to compose himself, set the glass carefully down. "Christ almighty," he murmured under his breath.

Marks rose and came over to where he was standing. "Señor, I can help you if you'll let me."

Hererra looked over at him. "How? How can you help me?"

"I'm good at finding people."

"You can find my son's murderer?"

"With some help, yes, I believe I can."

Hererra appeared to consider this for some time. Then, as if making up his mind, he gave a little nod. "The man on the left is Ottavio Moreno."

"You know him?"

"Oh, yes, señor, I know him very well. Since he was a little boy. I used to hold him in my arms when I was in Morocco." Hererra picked up his brandy and drained the glass. His blue eyes looked bleak, but Marks caught the storm of anger far back in the shadows beneath the intelligent brow.

"Are you telling me that Ottavio is the half brother of Gustavo Moreno, the late Colombian drug lord?"

"I'm telling you that he's my godson." The anger boiled forward into the set of his jaw, the slight tremor of his hand. "That's why I know he couldn't have killed Diego."

Moira and Berengária Moreno lay entwined in each other's arms. The plush owner's cabin smelled of musk, marine oil, and the sea. Beneath them, the yacht rocked gently as if wanting to lull them to sleep. They knew, each in her own way, that sleep was out of the question. The yacht was due to leave the dock in less than twenty minutes. Slowly, they rose, their bodies love-bruised, their senses on overload, as if they had slipped out of time and place. Wordlessly, they dressed, and minutes later emerged from belowdecks. The velvet sky arched over them with what seemed like protective arms.

After she had a brief talk with the captain, Berengária nodded to Moira. "They've completed all the tests. The engine is in perfect running order. There should be no more delays."

"Let's hope not."

Starlight spangled the water. Berengária had flown them in Narsico's single-engine Lancair IV-P to Lic. Gustavo Díaz Ordaz International Airport on the Pacific coast. From there it was a short drive to the surfer's paradise of Sayulita, where they met the yacht. All told, the trip took just over ninety minutes.

Moira stood next to Berengária. The crew, busy preparing to get under way, paid them no mind. It only remained for Berengária to debark.

"You've called Arkadin?"

Berengária nodded. "I spoke to him while you were freshening up. He'll be there to meet the boat just before dawn. Of course after the delay, he's going to want to board and check the entire shipment himself. You must be ready for him before then."

"Don't worry." Moira touched her arm and produced in the other woman another little tremor. "Who is the recipient?"

Berengária slid her arm around Moira's waist. "You don't really need to know that."

When Moira said nothing, Berengária leaned against her and sighed deeply. "My God, what a fucking snake pit this has turned out to be. Fuck men. Fuck them all!"

Berengária smelled of spice and salt spray, scents Moira liked. She found it intriguing to seduce another woman. There was nothing repellent about it, it was simply part of the job, something different, a challenge for her in every sense of the word. She was a sexual creature but, apart from one pleasant but inconsequential college experiment, had always been heterosexual. There was an edge of danger to Berengária she found attractive. In fact, making love to her was far more satisfying than it had been with a number of men she had bedded. Unlike those men—and excepting Bourne—Berengária knew when to be fierce and when to be tender, she took the time to seek out the secret places that touched Moira's pleasure centers, concentrating on them until Moira convulsed over and over again.

Not surprisingly, she was unlike Roberto Corellos's dismissive description of her as a piranha. She was both tough and vulnerable, a complexity to which a man like Corellos would be deaf, dumb, and blind. She had made her way in a man's world, having run and ruthlessly expanded her husband's business, yet she had been as terrified of her brother as she was now of Corellos and Leonid Arkadin. Moira could see that Berengária had no illusions. Her power was as nothing compared with theirs. They commanded a respect among their respective troops that she could never enjoy no matter how hard she tried.

Once again, Moira felt her mixed emotions of admiration and pity, this time because the moment Moira sailed away to her rendezvous with Arkadin, Berengária would be left to an undetermined fate. Caught between the corrosive power of Corellos and the contemptible weakness of Narsico, the future would not go well for her.

Which was why she kissed her hard on the lips and held her tight, because it would be for the last time, and Berengária deserved at least that modicum of solace, no matter how fleeting.

She ran her tongue around Berengária's ear. "Who is the client?"

Berengária shivered and held her tighter. At length, she leaned back enough to engage Moira's eyes. "The client is one of Gustavo's oldest and best, which is why the delay caused such problems."

Tears glittered in her eyes, and Moira knew she understood that tonight had been both the beginning and the end for them. This curious woman had no illusions, yes. And for an instant, Moira felt the pang of loss one feels when an ocean or a continent separates two people who had once held each other.

In a final acquiescence, Berengária bowed her head. "His name is Don Fernando Hererra."

Soraya awoke with the taste of the Sonoran Desert in her mouth. Assaulted by aches and pains, she rolled over onto her back and groaned. She stared up at the four men towering over her, two on each side. They were dusky-skinned, like her, and like her they were of mixed blood. It took one to know one, she thought groggily. These men were part Arab. They looked so much alike, they could have been brothers.

"Where is he?" one of the men said.

"Where is who?" she said, trying to identify his accent.

Another of the men—one on the opposite side—squatted down in the comfortable manner of a desert Arab, his wrists on his knees.

"Ms. Moore—Soraya, if I may—you and I are looking for the same person." His voice was calm and assured, and as casual as if they were two friends finding an equitable solution to a recent squabble. "One Leonid Danilovich Arkadin."

"Who are you?" she said.

"We ask the questions," said the man who had spoken first. "You provide the answers."

She tried to get up, but discovered that she had been staked out—cords around her wrists and ankles were wrapped around tent pegs that had been driven into the ground.

As the first light of dawn leaked into the sky, tendrils of pink crawled toward her like a spider.

"My name isn't important," the man squatting beside her said. One of his eyes was brown, she noticed, the other a watery blue, almost milky, like an opal, as if it had been damaged or ravaged by disease. "Only what I want is important."

Those two sentences seemed so absurd she felt the urge to laugh. People were known by their names. Without a name there was no personal history, no profile possible, just a blank slate, which was apparently how he wanted it. She wondered how she could change that.

"If you won't talk to me voluntarily," he said, "we'll have to try another way."

He snapped his fingers, and one of the other men handed him a small bamboo cage. No-Name took it gingerly by the handle and, swinging it past Soraya's face, set it down between her breasts. Inside was a very large scorpion.

"Even if it stings me," Soraya said, "it won't kill me."

"Oh, I don't want it to kill you." No-Name unlatched the door and with a pen started to prod the scorpion out. "But if you don't tell us where Arkadin is hiding, you will begin to have seizures, your heart rate and blood pressure will rise, your vision will become blurred, need I go on?"

The scorpion was hard and shiny-black, its tail arched high over its carapace. When sunlight touched it, it seemed to glow as if with an inner power. Soraya tried not to watch it, tried to damp down the fright rising inside her. But there was an instinctual response that was difficult to control. She heard her heartbeat pounding in her ears, felt a pain beneath her sternum as the fright built. She bit her lip.

"And if you should receive multiple stings without treatment, well, who knows how badly you'll suffer?"

As delicately as a ballet dancer the creature ventured forth on its eight legs until it stood in the valley between Soraya's breasts. She fought back the urge to scream.

Oliver Liss sat on a narrow bench in the weight room of his health club. His chest and arms were shiny with sweat. A towel was draped around his neck. He was on his third set of fifteen biceps reps when the redhead walked in. She was tall, with square shoulders, an upright bearing, and an epic rack. He'd seen her here a number of times before. One hundred dollars to the manager, and now he knew her name was Abby Sumner, she was thirty-four, divorced, and childless. She was one of the endless fleet of lawyers toiling for the Justice Department. He had already speculated that her long hours had resulted in her divorce, but it was this same extended work schedule that attracted him. Less time for her to get in his way once the affair started. He had no doubt that it would start, no doubt at all. It was simply a matter of when.

Liss finished his reps, put the dumbbells back in their slots, then toweled off while he made his recon assessment. Abby had gone straight for the bench press and, having selected weights, slid under the bar. That was Liss's cue. He rose and, strolling over to the bench press, looked down at her with his actor's megawatt smile and said, "Do you need a spotter?"

Abby Sumner looked up at him with large blue eyes. Then she returned his smile.

"Thank you. I could use one; I've just gone up in weights."

"It's a little unusual to see a woman bench-pressing, unless she's in training."

Abby Sumner's smile remained in place. "I do a lot of heavy lifting at work."

Liss laughed softly. She lifted the weights off the rests and began her reps, while he held his hands a bit beneath the bar in case she faltered. "It sounds like I wouldn't want to get in your way."

"No," she said. "You wouldn't."

She appeared to be having little or no difficulty with the higher weight. Liss's difficulty lay in keeping his eyes off her breasts.

"Don't arch your back," he said.

She pulled her spine back down to the bench. "I always do that when I increase weight. Thanks."

She finished her first set of eight reps, and he helped her guide the bar back onto the rests. While she took a short breather, he said, "My name's Oliver and I'd love to take you to dinner sometime."

"That would be interesting." Abby looked up at him. "Unfortunately, I don't mix business with pleasure."

Responding to his quizzical expression, she slid out from under the bar and stood up. She really was an impressive woman, Liss thought. She glanced over to the juice bar, where a clean-cut man was drinking one of those phosphorescent-green glasses of wheatgrass juice. The man drained his glass, set it down, and began to saunter toward them.

Abby brought her gym bag up onto the bench and, reaching into it, brought out several folded sheets of paper, which she handed to Liss.

"Oliver Liss, my name is Abigail Sumner. This judicial order from the attorney general of the United States authorizes me and Jeffrey Klein"—here she indicated the wheatgrass drinker, who was now standing beside her—"to take you into custody pending an investigation into allegations made against you while you were president of Black River."

Liss gaped at her. "This is nonsense. I was investigated and absolved."

"New allegations have come to light."

"What allegations?"

She nodded at the papers she had given him. "You'll find the list enumerated in the attorney general's order."

He opened the order but couldn't seem to focus on the letters. He shoved the papers back to her. "This must be some kind of mistake. I'm not going anywhere with you."

Klein produced a pair of manacles.

"Please, Mr. Liss," Abby said, "don't make this more difficult on yourself."

Liss turned this way and that, as if contemplating escape or a last-minute reprieve from Jonathan, his guardian angel. Where was he? Why hadn't he warned Liss of this new investigation?

Colonel Boris Karpov returned to Moscow with a heart of stone. His visit with Leonid Arkadin had been sobering on many levels, not the least of which was the terrible

bind he was in. Maslov had suborned a number of apparatchiks inside FSB-2, including Melor Bukin, Karpov's
immediate superior. Like all of the intel Arkadin had provided him, the proof was both damning and irrefutable.

Karpov, in the backseat of the black FSB-2 Zil, stared
unseeingly out the window as his driver headed into the
city from Sheremetyevo Airport.

Arkadin had suggested going to President Imov with
the evidence Karpov now had in his possession. The very
fact that Arkadin suggested it made Karpov suspicious,
but even if Arkadin had his own reason for wanting him
to go to Imov, he might still do it. The stakes, however,
could not be higher, both for his career and for him, personally.

He had two choices: He could take the evidence
against Bukin to Viktor Cherkesov, the head of FSB-2.
The problem there, however, was that Bukin was
Cherkesov's creature. If the evidence against Bukin was
made public, Cherkesov would, by association, come under suspicion. Whether or not he knew of Bukin's perfidy,
he'd be finished, forced to resign in disgrace. Rather than
allow that to happen, Karpov could envision him eliminating the damning evidence against his friend—and that
would include Karpov himself.

He had to admit that Arkadin was correct. Going to
President Imov with the evidence was the safest choice,
because Imov would be only too happy to bring down
Cherkesov. In fact, he very well might be so grateful that
he'd name someone inside FSB-2 he could trust—like
Karpov—as the new head of the agency.

The more Karpov thought this through the more
sense it made. And yet lurking in the background was

the niggling voice that told him once this scenario came to pass, he would owe a great debt to Arkadin. That, he knew instinctively, was not a great position to be in. But only if Arkadin was alive.

He laughed a little as he told his driver to take a detour to the Kremlin. Sitting back, he punched in the number of the president's office.

Thirty minutes later he was admitted into the president's residence, where a pair of Red Army guards showed him into one of a number of chilly, high-ceilinged anterooms. Over his head, like a frozen giant spider's web, an ornate crystal-and-ormolu chandelier hung, giving off faceted light that struck the similarly ornate Italianate furniture, upholstered in silks and brocades.

He sat while the guards, at opposite ends of the chamber, watched him. A clock on a spotted marble mantel *tick-tocked* mournfully, chiming the half hour, then the hour. Karpov went into a form of meditation he used to pass time during the many lonely vigils he'd had to endure over the years in more foreign countries than he cared to count. Ninety minutes after his arrival a young steward sporting a sidearm appeared to fetch him. Karpov was instantly alert. He was also refreshed. The steward smiled, and Karpov followed him down so many halls and around so many corners, he had difficulty in placing himself within the immense residence.

President Imov was sitting behind a Louis XIV desk in his comfortably furnished study. A cheerful fire was burning in the hearth. Behind him the magnificent domes of Red Square could be seen rising like strange missiles toward the mottled Russian sky.

Imov was writing in a ledger with an old-fashioned fountain pen. The steward withdrew without a word, soundlessly closing the double doors behind him. After a moment Imov looked up, removed his wire-rimmed glasses, and gestured to the single armchair set in front of the desk. Karpov crossed the carpet and seated himself without a word, patiently waiting for the interview to begin.

For a time, Imov regarded him with his slate-gray eyes, which were narrow, slightly elongated. Perhaps he had some Mongol blood in him. In any case he was a warrior, having fought to elevate himself to the presidency, then fought even harder to stay there against several fierce opponents.

Imov was not a large man, but he was impressive just the same. His personality could fill a ballroom when it suited him. Otherwise, he was content to let the stature of his office suffice.

"Colonel Karpov, it strikes me as odd that you have come to see me." Imov held his fountain pen as if it were a dagger. "You belong to Viktor Cherkesov, a *silovik* who has openly defied Nikolai Patrushev, his opposite number at FSB, and by extension me." He twirled the pen deftly. "Tell me, then, is there a reason why I should listen to what you have to say, since your boss has sent you here instead of coming himself?"

"I did not come at the behest of Viktor Cherkesov. In fact, he has no idea I'm here, and I'd rather it stayed that way." Karpov placed the cell phone with the incriminating evidence against Bukin on the desk between them and withdrew his hand. "Also, I belong to no man, Cherkesov included."

Imov's gaze remained on Karpov's face. "Indeed. Since Cherkesov stole you away from Nikolai, I must say that's welcome news." He tapped the end of the pen against the desktop. "And yet I can't help but take that statement with a grain of salt."

Karpov nodded. "Perfectly understandable."

When his eyes moved to the cell phone, Imov's followed. "And what have we here, Boris Illyich?"

"Part of FSB-2 is rotten," Karpov said slowly and distinctly. "It has to be cleansed, the sooner the better."

For a moment, Imov did nothing; then he set down the fountain pen, reached out for the cell phone, and turned it on. For a long while after that, there was no sound whatsoever in the study, not even, Karpov noted, the hushed footfalls of the secretarial and support staffs that must infest the place. Possibly, the study was soundproof as well as electronic-bug-proof.

When Imov was finished, he held the cell phone precisely as he had held the fountain pen, as if it were a weapon.

"And who, Boris Illyich, do you envision purging the FSB-2 of its rot?"

"Whomever you choose."

At this response, President Imov threw his head back and laughed. Then, wiping his eyes, he reached into a drawer, opened an ornate silver-clad humidor, and withdrew two Havana cigars. Handing one to Karpov, he bit the end off his and lit it with a gold lighter that had been a gift from the president of Iran. When Karpov produced a book of matches, Imov laughed again and pushed the gold lighter across the desk.

Colonel Boris Karpov found the lighter extraordinarily heavy. He flicked on the flame and luxuriously drew the cigar smoke into his mouth.

"We should begin, Mr. President."

Imov regarded Karpov through a veil of smoke. "No time like the present, Boris Illyich." He swung around, contemplating the onion domes of Red Square. "Clean the fucking place out—permanently."

It was ironic, when you thought about it, Soraya thought. Despite having multiple eyes—she could not for the life of her remember how many—scorpions couldn't see well, depending on tiny cilia on their claws to sense movement and vibration. At the moment that meant the rise and fall of her chest.

No-Name watched the scorpion with a mixture of impatience and contempt as it sat there, unmoving. Clearly, it didn't know where it was or what it wanted to do. That's when he took his pen and jammed the end of it onto the scorpion's head. The sudden attack startled and infuriated it. The tail twitched and struck, and Soraya gave a little gasp. No-Name used the pen to prod the creature back into its cage. He swung the door closed and latched it.

"Now," No-Name said, "either we wait for the venom to take effect, or you tell us where to find Arkadin."

"Even if I knew," Soraya said, "I wouldn't tell you."

He frowned. "You're not going to change your mind."

"Go screw yourself."

He nodded, as if having anticipated her stubbornness.

"It will be instructive to see how long you last after the scorpion stings you eight or nine times."

With a languid pass of his hand, he signaled the scorpion handler, who unlatched the cage's door and was about to open it when, with a deafening report, he was blown backward in a welter of blood and bone. Soraya turned her head and saw him sprawled on the ground, his entire forehead gone. More shots were fired, and when she turned back the other men lay on the ground. No-Name was clutching his ruined right shoulder, biting his lip in pain. A pair of legs ending in dusty boots came into her field of vision.

"Who—?" Soraya looked up, but between the first symptoms of the scorpion venom and the sun in her eyes she couldn't see. Her heart seemed about to pump out of her chest, and her entire body was throbbing as if with a very high fever. "Who—?"

The male figure squatted down. With the back of his sunburned hand he swatted the cage off her chest. A moment later she felt the ropes that bound her being loosened, and she shook them off. As she squinted up, a cowboy hat was placed over her head, the wide brim shading her from the glaring sunlight.

"Contreras," she said, seeing his creased face.

"My name is Antonio." He put one arm beneath her shoulders and helped lift her up. "Call me Antonio."

Soraya began to weep.

Antonio offered her his gun, an interesting piece of custom work: a Taurus Tracker .44 Magnum, a hunter's handgun, with a wooden rifle stock affixed to it. She took the Taurus, and he stood her up. She was staring down at No-Name, who stared back, teeth bared. She felt shaky, her brain was on fire. She watched him watching her. Her forefinger curled around the trigger. She aimed the Tracker and pulled the trigger. As if jerked by invisible strings, No-Name arched up once, then lay still, his blind eyes reflecting the rising sun.

She stopped crying.

18

COVEN WENT ABOUT his work with a frightening calm. He had spent the hours after trussing up Chrissie and Scarlett familiarizing himself with the house. As for Chrissie's father, he'd bound and gagged him and stuffed him in a closet. He left them for forty minutes for a trip to a hardware store, where he bought the largest portable generator he could carry by himself. Returning to the house, he checked on his captives. Chrissie and her daughter were still securely tied to the twin beds upstairs. The father was either asleep or unconscious, Coven didn't care which. Then he had lugged the generator into the basement and with little difficulty hooked it up to the electrical system, as a backup if the lights went out. He ran a test. The thing ticked like a geriatric grandfather clock. It was severely undersize for its task. Even cutting back on the circuits he connected, he determined that he'd have a maximum of ten minutes of light before the generator conked out. Well, it would have to do.

Then he went back upstairs and stared at Chrissie and Scarlett while he smoked a cigarette. The daughter, though only a preteen, was prettier than the mother. If he were another sort of person he would avail himself of that very young, tender body, but he despised that degenerate trait in men. He was a fastidious person, a man of moral rectitude. It was how he dealt with his job, how he managed to stay sane in what he considered an insane world. His personal life was pure vanilla, as dull as a bus driver's gray existence. He had a wife—his high school sweetheart—two children, and a dog named Ralph. He had mortgage payments, a dotty mother to support, and a brother he visited fortnightly in a loony bin, though these days they didn't call it that. When he came home from a long, hard, often bloody assignment, he kissed his wife hard on the lips, then went to his children and—whether they were playing, sitting in front of the TV, or asleep in bed—bent over them and inhaled their milky-sweet scent. Then he ate a meal his wife had prepared, took her upstairs, and fucked her silly.

He lit another cigarette from the end of the butt, and stared down at mother and daughter spread-eagled side by side on the twin beds. The girl was a child, inviolate. The thought of harming her was thoroughly repellent to him. As for the mother, she didn't appeal to him, too skinny and wan looking. He'd leave her to someone else. Unless Bourne forced him to kill her.

Back downstairs, he rummaged through the larder, opened up a can of Heinz baked beans, and ate the contents cold from the backs of his two fingers. All the while he listened to the tiny sounds around him, breathed in and mentally cataloged the scents in each room. In short, he moved around the house until he'd familiarized himself with every idiosyncrasy, every nook and cranny. Now it was his territory, his high ground, his eventual place of victory.

Then he returned to the living room and switched on all the lamps. That's when he heard the gunshot. Rising, he drew his Glock from its leather holster and, pulling back the drapes, peered out the front window. He tensed as he saw Jason Bourne zigzagging at top speed toward the front door. With a squeal of rubber and a spray of gravel, a gray Opel slewed around broadside to the front of the house. The driver's door opened, and the driver fired a shot at Bourne. He missed. Then Bourne was on the front steps, and Coven went to the door, his Glock at the ready. He heard two more shots and, crouching down, swung the door open. Bourne was sprawled face-down on the steps, a stain of blood spreading over his jacket.

Coven ducked back as another shot was fired. He darted out even as he squeezed off one shot after another. The gunman ducked back inside the Opel. Coven grabbed Bourne's jacket with his free hand and hauled him over the sill. He fired off one more shot, heard the gunman put the Opel into gear and speed off. He kicked the door shut behind him.

He checked Bourne's pulse, then went to the window. Pulling aside the curtains again, he peered into the driveway but could see no sign of either the gunman or the Opel.

Turning back into the living room, he bent over

to Bourne's prone form and pressed the muzzle of the Glock to the side of Bourne's head. He was turning him over when the lights flickered, dimmed, then came on again. From the basement, he heard the grandfather-clock ticking of the backup generator. He had scarcely enough time to register that the power to the house had been cut when Bourne knocked the Glock away and struck him a powerful blow on his sternum.

The man you're looking for is in Puerto Peñasco, no doubt." Antonio handed Soraya back her cell phone. "My *compadre,* the marina's harbormaster, knows the gringo. He's taken up residence in the old Santa Teresa convent, which has been abandoned for years. He has a cigarette boat he takes out each evening just after sunset."

They were seated in a sunny cantina on Calle de Ana Gabriela Guevara in Nogales. Antonio had spent some time helping Soraya clean up, getting her ice to use in the compress she placed against the spot between her breasts where the scorpion had stung her. The reddish patch did not swell, and whatever symptoms she had felt in the desert were now mostly gone. She also had Antonio buy her half a dozen bottles of water, which she started drinking right away to fight her dehydration and more quickly move the venom out of her system.

After an hour or so, she felt better. Then she bought new clothes in a store on Plaza Kennedy, and they went to get something to eat.

"I'll drive you to Puerto Peñasco," Antonio said.

Soraya popped the last bite of her *chilaquiles* into her

mouth. "I think you have better things to do. You're no longer making money off me."

Antonio made a face. On the ride back into Nogales he had told her his real name was Antonio Jardines. He'd taken *Contreras* as his business name. "Now you offend me. Is this how you treat the man who saved your life?"

"I owe you a debt of thanks." Soraya sat back, contemplating him. "What I can't understand is why you're taking such a personal interest in me."

"How to explain?" Antonio sipped his *café de olla*. "My life is defined by the space between Nogales, Arizona, and here, in Nogales, Sonora. A fucking boring strip of desert that's been known to drive men like me to drink. My only concern is the fucking *migras* and, believe me, that's not much of anything." He spread his hands. "There's something else, too. Life here is full of neglect. In fact, you could say that life here is *defined* by neglect, the kind that rots the soul and infests all of Latin America. No one gives a shit—about anyone, or anything, except money." He finished off his *café de olla*. "Then you come along."

Soraya considered this. She took her time because she didn't want to make a mistake, although she could hardly be certain of anything here. "I don't want to drive into Puerto Peñasco," she said finally. She had been thinking about this all through the meal. Antonio finding out that Arkadin had a cigarette sealed the deal. "I want to arrive there by boat."

Antonio's eyes glittered. Then his forefinger made a bobbing motion. "This is what I'm talking about. You don't think like a woman, you think like a man. This is what I would do."

"Can your *compadre* at the marina arrange it?"

He chuckled. "You see, you do need my help."

Bourne struck a second blow. He had been shot with blanks by Ottavio Moreno and was covered in pig's blood from a plastic bag he'd punctured. Coven, who didn't react one way or another to the blows, drove the butt of the Glock down onto Bourne's forehead. Bourne grabbed his wrist and twisted hard. Then he caught one of Coven's fingers and broke it. The Glock went flying across the living room floor, fetching up beside the cold grate.

Bourne pushed Coven off and rose on one knee, but Coven kicked his leg out from under him and Bourne toppled backward. Coven was on him in an instant, driving his fist into Bourne's face, landing blow after blow. Bourne lay still. Coven rose and aimed a kick at Bourne's ribs. Without seeming to move at all, Bourne caught his foot before it could land and wrenched the ankle to the left.

Coven grunted as the anklebones snapped. He landed hard, immediately rolled over, and scrambled on elbows and knees toward where the Glock lay beside the grate.

Bourne took up a brass sculpture from a chair-side table and threw it. The sculpture slammed into the back of Coven's head, driving his chin and nose into the floor. His jaws snapped shut and blood gushed from his nose. Undeterred, he grabbed the Glock and, in one fluid motion, swung it around and squeezed off a shot. The bullet struck the table beside Bourne's head, toppling it and the lamp on it onto Bourne.

He tried to fire again, but Bourne leapt on him, wrestling him onto his back. He grabbed a fire poker and swung it down hard. Bourne rolled away and the poker bounced against the floor. Coven stabbed out with it, catching Bourne's jacket, piercing it and pinning him to the floor. He rammed the end of the poker into the wood, then rose painfully over Bourne. Taking up the ash shovel, he brought the long brass handle across Bourne's throat and, using all his weight, pressed down.

It was 123 miles from Nogales to Las Conchas, where an associate of Antonio's *compadre* had driven the boat they would pick up. She had asked for a big boat, and an ostentatious one, something to catch Arkadin's attention and keep it until he got a good look at her. In the Nogales Mall, before they had set out, she had bought the most provocative bikini she could find. When she'd modeled it for Antonio, his eyes almost popped out of his skull.

"*¡Madre de Dios, qué linda muchacha!*" he had cried.

Because of the aftereffect of the scorpion sting, she bought a diaphanous cover-up, also some beach towels, a pair of huge Dior sunglasses, a fashionable visor, and a fistful of sunscreen, which she lost no time in slathering on.

Antonio's friend was named Ramos, and he had brought exactly the right kind of boat: big and flashy. Its diesels thrummed and gurgled as she and Antonio boarded and were shown around below by Ramos. He was a small, dark, rotund man, with curling black hair, tattoos on his massive arms, and a ready smile.

"I have guns—pistols and semi-automatics—if you need them," he said helpfully. "No extra charge, except for spent rounds."

Soraya thanked him, but said weapons wouldn't be necessary.

Soon after returning above deck they got under way. Puerto Peñasco was just over five miles due north.

Over the rumble of the diesels, Ramos said, "We have a couple of hours before sunset, when Arkadin usually takes out the cigarette. I have fishing gear. I'll take you to the fifty-one-mile reef, where there's plenty of halibut, black sea bass, and red snapper. How about it?"

Soraya and Antonio fished off the reef for about an hour and a half before they packed it in and swept in toward the marina. Ramos pointed out Arkadin's cigarette as he cut the speed rounding the headland and nosed in toward the docks. There was no sign of Arkadin, but Soraya could see an older Mexican preparing the boat to get under way. The Mexican was dark-skinned, with a face fissured by hard work, salt wind, and scorching sunlight.

"You're in luck," Ramos said. "He's coming."

Soraya looked in the direction Ramos indicated and saw a powerful-looking man striding down the dock. He wore a baseball cap, black-and-green surfer's bathing trunks, a torn Dos Equis T-shirt, and a pair of rubber sandals. She slipped off her cover-up. Her dark, oiled skin gleamed sleekly.

The dock was long, jutting out into the marina, and she had time to study him. He had dark hair, cut very short, a rugged face that gave away nothing, very square shoulders, like a swimmer, but his arms and legs were more like a wrestler's, long and muscular. He looked as if he had every reason to be confident, walking with a minimum amount of effort, almost gliding, as if his feet were made of ball bearings. There was a source of energy about him, like a ring of fire, that she could not comprehend, but it made her uneasy. She thought there was something familiar about him, which made her unease almost painful. And then, with an electric jolt that frightened her to her core, she knew what it was: He moved just like Jason.

"Here we go." Ramos steered the boat in front of the cigarette and put it in idle so that they drifted in toward the slip.

Arkadin was saying something to the Mexican and laughing when Ramos's boat caught the periphery of his vision. He looked up, squinting against the oblique sunlight, and at once saw Soraya. His nostrils flared as his gaze took in her aggressive, exotic face, her body, which in the tiny bikini was as good as being naked—even better, Soraya felt, because it left the tiniest bit to his imagination. She raised one arm, as if to keep her visor on her head, but really the gesture accentuated the sensuality of her body.

And then, just like that, he turned away and said something to the Mexican that made him chuckle. Soraya was disappointed. Her fingers gripped the railing as if she wanted to throttle it.

"The gringo's a fucking *maricón*, that's all there is to it," Antonio said.

Soraya laughed. "Don't be idiotic." But his comment had lifted her out of her temporary sense of defeat. "I haven't given him enough of a challenge." Then an idea occurred to her and, turning to Antonio, she put her arms on his shoulders. Gazing into his eyes, she said, "Kiss me. Kiss me and don't stop."

Antonio looked happy to oblige. He grabbed her around the waist and planted his lips on hers. His tongue seemed to scald her as it probed between her teeth and into her mouth. Soraya arched her back, molding her body to his.

Ramos maneuvered the boat a bit too close to the cigarette's bow, causing the gringo and El Heraldo to turn. As El Heraldo ran to the bow, gesticulating and cursing him mightily, the gringo stood watching Soraya and Antonio locked in their amorous embrace. He seemed interested now.

Shouting his apologies, Ramos steered the boat back on course and eased it into its slip. A marina hand stood by to loop the mooring ropes fore and aft as Ramos cut the engines, and threw the coils to him. Then Ramos stepped off the boat and headed toward the harbormaster's office. Arkadin continued to stare at Soraya and Antonio Jardines, though he hadn't moved an inch.

"Enough," Soraya said into Antonio's mouth. *"¡Basta, hombre! ¡Basta!"*

Antonio was reluctant to let her go, and she pushed him away first with one hand, then with both. By the time she had managed to free herself, Arkadin was on the dock, heading their way.

"Mano, you're like a fucking *pulpo,"* she said loudly, only partly for Arkadin's benefit.

Antonio, relishing his role, grinned at her and wiped his lips with the back of his hand. Then Arkadin was on board and between them.

"*Maricón,* what are you doing here? Get out of my face," Antonio said.

Arkadin straight-armed him off the boat and into the water. The Mexican on the cigarette laughed uproariously.

"That wasn't a good idea," Soraya said coldly.

"He was hurting you." Arkadin said it as a clear statement of fact.

"You have no idea what he was doing." Soraya kept up her frozen exterior.

"He's a man, you're a woman," Arkadin said. "I know exactly what he was doing."

"Maybe I liked it."

Arkadin laughed. "Maybe you did. Should I help the sonovabitch back onto the dock?"

Soraya looked down at Antonio snorting water out of his nose. "I could have done that." Then she looked back at Arkadin. "Leave the sonovabitch where he is."

Arkadin laughed again and offered her his arm. "Maybe you need a change of scene."

"Maybe I do. But it won't be with you."

Then she pushed past him, climbed off the boat, and walked slowly and provocatively back up the dock.

Bourne felt his lungs burning. There were black spots in his vision. Soon enough the bar across his throat would crack his hyoid bone, and it would be all over for him. Reaching out, he grabbed Coven's fractured ankle and squeezed as hard as he could. Coven shouted in surprise and pain, the pressure came off Bourne's throat as Coven reared back, and, shoving the bar upward, Bourne rolled out from under it.

Coven, a murderous look in his eye, found the Glock and aimed it at Bourne. At that moment the ticking of the generator ceased and the house was plunged into darkness. Coven squeezed off a shot, narrowly missing Bourne, and Bourne rolled away into deepest shadow. He held still for the space of ten long breaths, then rolled again. Coven fired another shot, but this struck well wide of the mark. It was clear he had no idea where Bourne was located.

Bourne could hear Coven moving around. Now that the lights had been extinguished, Coven had lost the advantage of being on his territory. Coven would have to think of another way to reestablish his dominant position.

If Bourne were in his shoes, he'd try to get to Chrissie and Scarlett, use them as leverage to flush him out. He stayed very still, listening intently to the direction in which Coven was moving. It was from left to right. He was passing the fireplace. Where was he headed? Where was he keeping his captives?

Bourne pictured as much of the ground-floor interior as had registered after Coven had dragged him inside. He could see the fireplace, the two upholstered armchairs, the side table and lamp, the sofa, and the stairs leading up to the second story.

The creak of a step tread betrayed Coven, and without a second thought Bourne sprang from his hiding place, scooped up the lamp, and jerked its cord out of the electrical socket. He threw it hard against the wall to his left as he leapt up onto the cushion of the armchair. Coven fired two shots in the direction of the crash as Bourne launched himself over the railing of the staircase.

He slammed into Coven, hurling him against the back wall before landing atop him. Coven, shaken, nevertheless squeezed off two more shots. He missed, but the flashes burned Bourne's cheek. Coven lunged for Bourne, trying to swat him with the barrel of the Glock. Bourne kicked out, splintering one of the railing balusters. Wrenching it out of its socket, he swung it against the side of Coven's face. Coven grunted as his own blood spattered the wall and he rolled away from another blow. He lashed out with his foot, slamming the sole of his shoe into Bourne's face. Tumbling backward, Bourne fell away from him, and, bracing himself against the wall, Coven fired twice more into the confined space of the staircase.

Either of the shots would have hit Bourne had he not already vaulted over the banister. He hung there in darkness. When he heard Coven scrambling up the stairs, he flexed his arms and, rising up, rolled his body back over the banister. Taking the treads three at a time, he raced up to the second floor. He knew two things now: Coven was going for his hostages, and the Glock had run through its magazine. Coven needed time to reload and was at his most vulnerable.

But when Bourne reached the second-floor landing there was no discernible movement. He crouched and, listening, waited. More windows meant light, but it was faint and inconstant, as the overgrown tree branches outside scraped against the house. He could see four doors: four rooms, two on either side. He opened the door into the first room on the left, which was empty, put his ear against the inside wall that abutted the next room. He heard nothing. He went back to the doorway. Coven fired at him as Bourne raced across the hallway and into the first room on the right. Bourne had given him time to reload.

Wasting no time, Bourne crossed to the window, unlatched it, and, opening it wide, climbed through. He was faced with a thick tangle of oak branches into which he climbed. Moving through the oak, he made his way to the window of the second room on the right. A shadow moved in there, and he went very still. Dimly, he could make out a pair of twin beds. He thought he saw figures lying on them: Chrissie and Scarlett?

Reaching up to the branch lying more or less horizontally over his head, he swung himself back and forth to gain the required momentum, then launched himself feet-first through the window. The old glass shattered into a thousand crystalline fragments, causing Coven to instinctively cover his face with his forearm.

Landing, Bourne flew across the room, striking Coven shoulder-first. The two men slammed against the far wall and went down in a heap. Bourne punched him three times, then lunged for the Glock. But Coven was ready, and when Bourne's defense opened up, he struck a hammer blow on his burned and bleeding cheekbone, Bourne went down, and Coven raised the Glock, not at Bourne, but at Scarlett, who lay bound and spread-eagled on the nearest bed. His angle was such that he had no clear shot at Chrissie, who lay on the bed nearer the window.

Coven was breathing heavily but still managed to say, "All right, get up. You have five seconds to put your hands behind your head. Then I shoot the girl."

"Please, Jason, please. Do what he says." Chrissie's voice was high, tight with a mortal terror that bordered on hysteria. "Don't let him hurt Scarlett."

Bourne looked at Chrissie, then delivered a scissors kick that jerked Coven's extended gun arm down and away from Scarlett.

Coven cursed under his breath as he struggled to regain control of the Glock. That was his mistake. Keeping the scissors grip on Coven's arm, Bourne jackknifed his body. He head-butted Coven in his already broken and bloody nose. Coven howled in pain but still tried extricating his arm. Bourne smashed the sole of his shoe into Coven's kneecap, shattering it. Coven collapsed, and Bourne stepped on the knee. Coven's eyes watered and his jowls shook so hard, shivers went down his body.

Wrenching the Glock away from him, Bourne pressed its muzzle into Coven's right eye.

When Coven tried to make a countermove, Bourne said, "If you do that, you'll never walk out of the room. Who will take care of your wife and children then?"

Coven, his visible eye bloodshot and staring, subsided. But as Bourne removed the muzzle, he exploded upward, using his shoulder and hip. Bourne bore the attack with equanimity, allowed Coven to drive him backward, to expend whatever reserve of energy he had left, then brought the butt of the Glock down on Coven's skull, shattering the orbital bone. Coven tried to scream, but no sound emerged from his mouth. His eyes rolled up into his head as he fell at Bourne's feet.

19

BORIS KARPOV WALKED through a wind-blown Red Square, breathing deeply while he thought of how to proceed against Bukin and, by association, the very dangerous Cherkesov. President Imov had given him everything he asked for, including absolute secrecy until he could ferret out all the moles in FSB-2. The place to start was Bukin. He knew he could break Bukin. Once he did, the other moles would come to light without difficulty.

A light snow was falling, the flakes, small and dry, swirling in the wind. Lights twinkled off the golden and striped onion domes, and tourists took flash photos of one another against the ornate architecture. He took a moment to drink in the peaceful scene, all too rare in Moscow these days.

Retracing his steps, he plodded back to his limo. The

driver, seeing him returning, fired the ignition. He got out from behind the wheel and opened the rear door for his boss. A tall blonde in a ruddy fox coat and knee-high boots strode past. The driver's eyes lingered on her as Karpov ducked and climbed in. The door slammed shut behind him.

He said, "HQ," when the driver slid behind the wheel. The driver nodded wordlessly, put the limo in gear, and they drove out of the Kremlin.

It was an eleven-minute drive to FSB-2 headquarters on ulitsa Znamenka, depending on traffic—which, at this hour, wasn't as bad as it could be. Karpov was lost in thought. He was figuring out a way to get Bukin alone, to cut him off from his contacts. He decided to invite him to dinner. On the way, he would instruct his driver to divert their car to the vast construction site on ulitsa Varvarka, a dead zone for cell phone traffic, so he and Bukin could "discuss" his treachery undisturbed.

The driver stopped at a red light, but when it turned green he did not put the car in gear. Now, through his smoked-glass window, Karpov saw that a Mercedes limo had drawn up beside them. As he watched, the rear door opened and a figure emerged. It was too dark to see who it was, but a moment later the door to his car was wrenched open—odd since his driver always auto-locked all doors—and the figure, ducking its head, slid onto the seat beside him.

"Boris Illyich, always a pleasure to see you," Viktor Cherkesov said.

He had a smile like a hyena, and he smelled like one, too, Karpov observed.

Cherkesov, whose yellow eyes made him look ravenous, even bloodthirsty, leaned forward slightly to speak to the driver. "The ulitsa Varvarka, I think. The construction site." Then he sat back, his repellent smile glimmering in the semi-darkness of the limo's interior. "We don't want to be disturbed, do we, Boris Illyich."

It was not a question.

Mandy and Michelle were asleep, entwined around each other, which was how they always slept after a long erotic workout. In contrast, Bud Halliday and Jalal Essai had retired to the living room of the apartment they jointly owned under a pseudonym so well documented that the ownership could never be traced back to them.

Out of courtesy rather than choice, Halliday was sipping a glass of sweet mint tea as he sat opposite Essai.

"I've been meaning to tell you," Halliday said in his most casual voice. "Oliver Liss is in federal custody."

Essai sat up. "What? Why didn't you tell me right away?"

Halliday gestured toward the bedroom, where the twins were sound asleep.

"But . . . what happened? It seemed he was safe."

"These days, it seems, no one is safe." Halliday was searching for the humidor. "Quite without warning, the Justice Department has opened a new investigation into his associations when he was running Black River." He looked up suddenly, impaling Essai with his gaze. "Will the investigation ripple out to you?"

"I'm completely insulated," Jalal Essai said. "I made certain of this from the beginning."

"Okay then. Fuck Liss. We move on."

Jalal Essai seemed nonplussed. "You're not surprised?"

"I think Oliver Liss has been skating on thin ice for some time."

"I need him," Jalal Essai said.

"Correction: You needed him. When I said move on, I meant it."

Halliday found the leather-bound humidor and extracted a cigar. He offered it to Essai, who declined. Then he nipped off the end, stuck it in his mouth, and lit up. He rolled the cigar through the flame as he puffed away.

Essai said, "I suppose Liss had outlived his usefulness."

"That's the spirit." Halliday felt calmer now that he had the smoke inside him. Sex with Michelle always got his heart hammering to the point of pain. The woman was a fucking gymnast.

Essai helped himself to more tea. "With Liss, I was just following orders from an organization I've left behind."

"Now the two of us are in business," Halliday observed.

Essai nodded. "The business of a hundred billion in gold."

Halliday frowned as he stared at the glowing end of his cigar. "You feel no remorse at betraying the Severus Domna? After all, they're your own kind."

Essai ignored the racist remark. He'd become inured to Halliday the way one comes to ignore the ache of a cyst. "*My kind* are no different from *your kind,* inasmuch as there are those who are good, those who are bad, and those who are ugly."

Halliday guffawed so hard he almost choked on the smoke. He sat forward laughing and coughing. His eyes watered.

"I must say, Essai, for an Arab you're quite all right."

"I'm Berber—Amazigh." Essai stated this as fact, without a trace of rancor.

Halliday eyed him through the smoke. "You speak Arabic, don't you?"

"Among other languages, including Berber."

Halliday spread his hands, as if the other's answer proved his point. He and Jalal Essai had met in college, where Essai spent two years as an exchange student. In fact, it was because of Essai that Halliday became interested in what he perceived as the growing Arab threat to the Western world. Essai was Muslim, but strictly speaking an outsider in the highly splintered and religicized Arab world. Through the lens of Essai's worldview, Halliday recognized that it was only a matter of time before the Arab world's sectarian battles spilled over their boundaries and became a series of wars. For that very reason he cultivated Essai as a friend and adviser, realizing only much later, when Essai was becoming disinterested in Severus Domna's objectives, that Essai had been dispatched to the States, to his college specifically, to cultivate him as a friend and ally.

When greed got the best of Essai, when he confessed what his original motivation had been, all of Halliday's worst prejudices against Arabs were confirmed. He hated Essai, then. He'd even plotted to kill him. But in the end, he had abandoned his revenge fantasies, seduced, as Essai had been, by King Solomon's gold. Who could resist such a glittering prize? He and Essai, as Halliday came to realize in a repellent moment of understanding, had more in common than seemed possible, given their disparate backgrounds. Then again they were both soldiers of the night, inhabiting the world of shadows that existed on the edges of civilized society, protecting it from destructive elements both without and within.

"The Severus Domna is no different from any tyrant—fascist, communist, or socialist," Jalal Essai said. "It lives to accumulate power, to allow its members to influence world events for the sole purpose of amassing more power. In the face of such power, mere human politics becomes irrelevant, as does religion."

Essai sat back, crossing one leg over the other. "In the beginning Severus Domna was motivated by the desire for change, a meeting of the minds between East and West, among Islam and Christianity and Judaism. A noble goal, I admit, and for a time they succeeded, if only in small ways. But then, like all altruistic endeavors, this one fell afoul of human nature."

He suddenly sat forward, on the edge of the sofa. "And I tell you this, there is no stronger motivation in human beings than greed, even fear. Greed, like sex, makes men stupid, blind to fear, or to the need for anything else. Greed distorted the goals of Severus Domna to such an extent that they became virtually irrelevant. The members continued to pay lip service to the original mission, but by then Severus Domna was rotten to the core."

"What does that make us?" Halliday continued to puff on his cigar. "We're as greedy as the Severus Domna, perhaps more."

"But we're aware of what drives us," Jalal Essai said

with a glint in his eyes. "We're both clear-eyed and clear-headed."

Scarlett stared up at Bourne while he untied her. Her cheeks were tear-streaked. She wasn't crying now, but she was trembling uncontrollably and her teeth were chattering.

"Is Mum okay?"

"She's fine."

"Who are you?" Tears were coming, more fitfully this time. "Who was that man?"

"My name is Adam, and I'm a friend of your mum's," Bourne said. "I asked her to help me and she took me to Oxford to see Professor Giles. You remember him?"

Scarlett nodded, sniffling. "I like Professor Giles."

"He likes you, too. Very much."

His voice was soothing, and she seemed to be calming down. "You flew into the room like Batman."

"I'm not Batman."

"I know that," she said somewhat indignantly, "but you've got blood all over you and you're not hurt."

He plucked at his damp shirt. "It's not real blood. I needed to fool the man who kidnapped you and your mother."

She regarded him appraisingly. "Are you a secret agent like Aunt Tracy?"

Bourne laughed. "Aunt Tracy wasn't a secret agent."

"Yes, she was."

That indignant note in her voice warned Bourne not to treat her like a child.

"What makes you think that?"

Scarlett shrugged. "You couldn't talk to her without her holding something back. I think secrets were all she had. And she was always sad."

"Are secret agents sad?"

Scarlett nodded. "That's why they become secret agents."

There was something pure and profound in that statement, but for the moment Bourne was content to let it go. "Professor Giles and your mum helped me with a problem. Unfortunately, this man wanted something of mine."

"He must've wanted it badly."

"Yes, he did." Bourne smiled. "I'm very sorry I led you and your mother into danger, Scarlett."

"I want to see her."

Bourne lifted her into his arms. She seemed cold as ice. He carried her over to the bed by the window. Chrissie was covered in shards of glass. She was unconscious.

"Mummy!" Scarlett leapt out of Bourne's arms. "Mummy, wake up!"

Bourne, noting the edge of terror in Scarlett's voice, bent over Chrissie. Her pulse was good, her breathing even.

"She's okay, Scarlett." He pinched Chrissie's cheeks and her eyelids fluttered, then opened. She looked up into his face.

"Scarlett."

"She's right here, Chrissie."

"Coven?"

"Adam flew through the window like Batman," Scarlett said, proud of her new knowledge.

Chrissie frowned, noticing Bourne's shirt. "All that blood."

Scarlett gripped her mother's hand tightly. "It's fake, Mum."

"Everything's fine now," Bourne said. "No, don't move yet." He scooped the glass off her as best he could. "All right, unbutton your blouse." But her fingers trembled too badly for her to grip the buttons properly.

"My arms are killing me," she said softly. She turned her head and smiled into her daughter's face. "Thank God you're safe, sugarplum."

Scarlett burst into fresh tears. Chrissie looked up at Bourne as he undid her buttons, shrugged her out of the blouse so that the last of the glass shards fell harmlessly on either side of her.

Then he lifted her up. When he'd swung her away from the bed, he put her down. As they stepped over Coven's lifeless body, Chrissie shuddered. They stopped in the room she had been using to get sweaters for her and Scarlett, who, in a kind of delayed reaction, was leaking tears as she knelt to put on her sweater, which was yellow with a pattern of pink bunnies eating ice-cream cones. Halfway down the stairs she began to whimper.

Chrissie put an arm around her. "It's all right, sugarplum. Everything's all right, Mum has you now," she whispered over and over.

When they reached the ground floor, she said to Bourne, "Coven tied my father up, he's here somewhere."

Bourne found him, bound and gagged, in one of the kitchen closets. He was unconscious, either from the blow that caused the bruised swelling on his left temple or from the lack of oxygen. Bourne laid him on the kitchen floor and untied him. It was dark with the power still off.

"My God, is he dead?" Chrissie said as she and Scarlett ran in.

"No. His pulse is strong." He took his finger away from the carotid and began to free him from his bonds.

Chrissie, her courage disintegrating at the sight of her father so helplessly incapacitated, began to soundlessly weep, but this caused Scarlett to sob, so she bit her lip, holding back more tears. She ran cold water in the sink, soaked a dishcloth, and filled up a glass. Crouching down beside her daughter, she placed the folded towel against Bourne's cheek, which had started to swell and discolor.

Her father was thin, in the manner of many older people. His face was time-ravaged and somewhat lopsided, so that Bourne guessed he'd had a stroke not so long ago. Bourne shook him gently, and his eyelids fluttered open, his tongue ran around his dry lips.

"Can you sit him up?" Chrissie asked. "I'll get some water into him."

Supporting her father's back, Bourne sat him up slowly and carefully.

"Dad, Dad?"

"Where is that sonovabitch who hit me?"

"He's dead," Bourne said.

"Come on, Dad, drink some water." Chrissie was observing her father closely, fearful that at any moment he would pass out again. "It'll make you feel better."

But the old man paid her no mind. Instead he was staring intently at Bourne. He licked his lips again and accepted the glass his daughter held for him. His knobby Adam's apple bobbed spastically as he drank. He choked.

"Easy, Dad. Easy."

His hand fluttered up, and she took the rim of the glass away from his mouth. Then his forefinger unfurled, pointing at Bourne.

"I know you." His voice was like sandpaper over metal.

Bourne said, "I don't think so."

"No, no. You came into the Centre when I ran it. That was years ago, of course, when the Centre was in Old Boys' School in George Street. But I'll never forget it because I had to call an ex-colleague by the name of Basil Bayswater, a first-class wanker if ever there was one. He made a killing in the market and retired to Whitney. Spent all his time playing an ancient form of chess or something. Disgraceful waste of time.

"But you." His forefinger touched Bourne's chest. "I never forget a face. I'll be goddamned. You're Professor Webb. That's it! David Webb!"

20

PETER MARKS RECEIVED the call from Bourne, brief and succinct, and with mixed feelings agreed to come to the address Bourne gave him. In a way, he was surprised that Bourne had called him back. On the other hand, Bourne didn't sound like himself, which caused Marks to wonder what sort of situation he was heading into. His relationship with Bourne was all one-way: through Soraya. He knew something of her history with Bourne, and he'd always wondered whether she had allowed her personal feelings to color her opinion of him.

The official CI line was, and had been for some time, that Bourne's amnesia had made him unpredictable, and therefore dangerous. He was a rogue agent, loyal to no one and nothing, least of all CI. Though CI had been forced to use him in the past, it was always through deception or coercion, because there seemed no other way to control him. And not even those methods had proved to be a sure thing. Though Marks was personally aware of Bourne's recent work bringing down Black River and stopping an incipient war with Iran, he knew next to nothing about the man. He was a complete enigma. It was futile to predict his responses in any given situation. And then there was the fact that many people who had tried to get close to him had died sudden and violent deaths. Happily, Soraya wasn't one of them, but Marks worried that it might be just a matter of time.

"Bad news?" Don Fernando Hererra said.

"Just more of the same," Marks said. "I've a meeting to go to."

They were seated in the living room of Diego Hererra's home, surrounded by photos of him. Marks wondered whether being here was painful or comforting for the father.

"Señor Hererra, before I go, is there anything more you can tell me about your godson? Do you know why he was at the Vesper Club last night, or why he might have stabbed Diego? What sort of relationship did they have?"

"None, to answer your last question first."

Hererra took out a cigarette and lit up but didn't seem interested in smoking it. His eyes roved the room, as if afraid to alight on any one thing for long. Marks suspected that he was nervous. About what?

Hererra contemplated Marks for some moments. The ash from his unsmoked cigarette toppled soundlessly to the carpet, where it lay between his feet. "Diego did not know of Ottavio's existence, at least so far as his relationship to me was concerned."

"Then why would Ottavio kill Diego?"

"He wouldn't, therefore I refuse to believe that he did."

Hererra told his driver to take Marks to the nearest rental-car office. He insisted that he and Marks exchange phone numbers. Those words of disbelief resounded in Marks's head as he punched the address Bourne had given him into the GPS program on his PDA.

"I want to stay abreast of your investigation," Hererra said. "You promised me that you would find my son's killer. You should know that I take all promises made to me extremely seriously."

Marks saw no reason to doubt him.

Fifteen minutes after he drove out of the rental-car lot, his PDA buzzed and he read a text message from Soraya. Within minutes Willard called him.

"Progress."

"I've made contact," Marks said, meaning Bourne.

"You know where he is?" A slight quickening of Willard's voice.

"Not yet," Marks lied. "But I will soon."

"Good, I'm in time."

"Time for what?" Marks asked.

"The mission has changed somewhat. I need you to facilitate a meeting between Bourne and Arkadin."

Marks searched for hidden meaning in Willard's voice. Something back home had changed. He hated being out of the loop and felt at an immediate disadvantage. "What about the ring?"

"Are you listening to me?" Willard snapped. "Just do as you're ordered."

Now Marks was certain that he was being denied access to a major development. He felt the old anger against the machinations of his superiors rising up in his throat like bile.

"Has Soraya Moore made contact?" Willard continued.

"Yes. I just received the rearranged text message from her."

"Contact her," Willard said. "Coordinate your efforts. You need to get the two men to the following place." He gave Marks an address. "How you do it is up to you, but I do have some information Arkadin should find interesting." He told Marks what El-Arian had told him about the missing piece of information without which the file on the laptop's hard drive was useless. "You have seventy-two hours."

"Seventy-two—?" But he was talking to dead air. The conversation was over.

At the next intersection, Marks checked the GPS map on his PDA to make sure that he hadn't missed a turn while talking with Willard. The morning had started out sunny, but clouds had rolled in, turning everything to shades of gray. Now a light drizzle blurred the edges of even the sharpest angles on buildings and signs.

The light turned green and, as he left the intersection behind, he noticed a white Ford moving into his lane right behind him. He knew a tail when he saw one. He'd seen the white Ford before, several vehicles behind him, though now and again he'd lost sight of it behind a large produce truck. The Ford was occupied by only the driver, who wore dark glasses. Stepping on the accelerator, he sent his rental car lurching forward as he ground the gearshift up from first to third more quickly than the transmission could easily handle. There was a moment between second and third when the car hesitated, and he was afraid he'd stripped the gears. Then it leapt forward so fast he almost slammed into the rear end of the truck in front of him. He swerved to the right-hand lane, accelerating further as the white Ford slid in behind him.

He was in a section of London dense with traffic, boutiques, and larger stores. A sign for an underground garage came up so fast he had to swerve into its entrance at the last possible instant. He scraped the front left fender on the concrete wall, then corrected and hurtled down the ramp into the neon-lit concrete cavern.

He pulled into a parking spot that was so tight, he had to roll down the window to slide out. By that time, he heard the squeal of tires and figured the white Ford was still hot on his trail. He saw the open stairwell next to the elevator, ducked into it just as a white car flashed by. The stairwell smelled of grease and urine. As he rushed up the stairs two and three at a time, he heard a car door slam and the fast slap of shoe soles against concrete, and then someone was running up the stairs behind him.

As he was about to whip around a corner, he came upon a homeless man, so drunk he had passed out. Bending over, Marks held his breath as he dragged the drunk up the stairs, placing him across the tread just around the corner. Retreating into shadow on the stairs above, Marks waited, breathing deeply and easily.

The sounds of pounding footsteps came closer, and Marks tensed himself into a half crouch. His tail raced around the corner and, as Marks had planned, didn't see the drunk until it was too late. As he stumbled, pitching forward, Marks leapt down the stairs, driving his

knee into the top of the man's head. The tail lurched
backward, stumbling again over the drunk and sprawling
onto his back.

Marks saw him pulling a Browning M1900 from beneath his jacket. Marks kicked it upward just before he
fired a shot. The noise held and echoed so deafeningly
in the confined space, the drunk opened his eyes and sat
bolt upright. The man with the Browning grabbed the
drunk by the collar and pressed the gun's muzzle into the
side of his head.

"You'll come with me now." He had a heavy accent,
Middle Eastern perhaps. "Or I shoot his brains out." He
jerked the drunk so hard, spittle flew from his slack lips.

"Oi, yer wanker!" the drunk shouted, completely
confused. "Piss off!"

The gunman, as contemptuous as he was incensed,
slammed the side of the drunk's head with the barrel of
the Browning. Marks launched himself across the gap.
The heel of his hand made contact with the gunman's
chin, shoved it hard upward, exposing his neck. While
he wrestled with the gun hand, he drove his fist into the
gunman's throat. The cartilage gave way and the gunman
collapsed, gasping without getting oxygen into his system. His eyes were wide and rolling. He could only make
animal gruntings, but soon enough even that ceased.

The drunk whirled with astonishing agility and kicked
the gunman in the crotch. " 'Ow 'bout that now, yer
bleedin' pisspot!" Then, muttering to himself, he stumbled down the stairs without a backward glance.

Quickly now Marks went through the gunman's
pockets, but all he found was keys to the white Ford
and a wad of money. No passport, no identification of

any kind. He had dark skin, black curling hair, and a full beard. *One thing for sure,* Marks thought, *he's not CI. So who was he working for and why the hell was he following me?* He wondered who could know he was here except for Willard and Oliver Liss.

Then he heard the whistle raised by foot police and knew he had to get out of there. Once more, he studied the dead man, wishing there was some identifier, like a tattoo or . . .

That's when he saw the gold ring on the third finger of his right hand and, stooping, worked it off. He hoped there might be a commemorative engraving on the inside.

There wasn't. There was something far more interesting.

Soraya saw Leonid Arkadin again in the lone marina restaurant. Or, rather, he must have been searching for her, because engrossed in her fiery shrimp and yellow rice she didn't see him enter. Her waiter brought her a drink—a tequini, he said—from the man at the bar. Soraya glanced up, and of course it was Arkadin. She looked into his eyes as she picked up the martini glass. She smiled. That was all the encouragement he needed.

"You're persistent, I'll give you that," she said when he'd sauntered over.

"If I were your lover, I wouldn't let you eat dinner alone."

"My ex pool boy? I sent him packing."

He laughed and gestured to the booth in which she sat. "May I?"

"I'd prefer you didn't."

He sat down anyway and put his drink on the table,

as if marking out his territory. "If you let me order, I'll pay for your dinner."

"I don't need you to pay for my dinner," she said flatly.

"Need has nothing to do with it." He lifted his hand and the waiter glided over. "I'll have steak, bloody, and an order of tomatillos." The waiter nodded and left.

Arkadin smiled, and Soraya was astonished at how genuine it seemed. There was a deep warmth to it that frightened her.

"My name is Leonardo," he said.

She snorted. "Don't be ridiculous. No one in Puerto Peñasco is named Leonardo."

He seemed crestfallen, like a little boy caught with his hand in the cookie jar, and now she was beginning to make sense of his approach to women. She could see how magnetic he was, how compelling an impression he made, exuding the security of a powerful man with a softer core of vulnerability. What woman could resist that? She laughed silently to herself and felt better, as if at last she was standing on solid ground, in a place where she could confidently move forward with her assignment.

"You're right, of course," Arkadin said. "It's actually Leonard, just plain Leonard."

"Penny." She held out a hand, which he held briefly. "What are you doing in Puerto Peñasco, Leonard?"

"Fishing, sport racing."

"In your cigarette."

"Yes."

Soraya finished up her shrimp just as his steak and tomatillos arrived. The steak, bloody as ordered, was smothered in chilies. Arkadin dug in. *He must have a cast-iron stomach,* she thought.

"And you?" he said around bites.

"I came for the weather." She pushed the tequini away from her.

"You don't like it?"

"I don't drink alcohol."

"Alcoholic?"

She laughed. "Muslim. I'm Egyptian."

"I apologize for sending you an inappropriate gift."

"No need." She waved away his words. "You couldn't have known." Then she smiled. "But you're sweet."

"Ha! Sweet is one thing I'm not."

"No?" She cocked her head. "What are you, then?"

He wiped the blood off his lips and sat back for a moment. "Well, to tell you the truth I'm something of a hard-ass. My partners thought so, especially when I bought them out. So did my wife, for that matter."

"She's also in the past?"

He nodded as he dug into his food again. "Nearly a year now."

"Children?"

"Are you kidding?"

Arkadin certainly had a gift for spinning yarns, she thought appreciatively. "I'm not much of a nurturer, either," she said, somewhat truthfully. "I'm entirely focused on my business."

He asked her what that might be without looking up from his steak.

"Import-export," she said. "To and from North Africa."

His head came up slowly, but very deliberately. She

felt her heart beating against her rib cage. It was, she thought, like coaxing a shark onto the hook. She didn't want to make the slightest mistake now, and felt a little thrill pass through her. She was very close to the precipice, to the moment when her fictional self would fuse with her real self. This moment was why she chose to do what she did. It was why she hadn't walked away from Peter when he'd recruited her for the assignment, why she had set aside the demeaning aspect of what she was expected to do. None of that mattered. What mattered was standing a hairbreadth from the precipice. This precise moment was what she lived for, *and Peter had known this long before she did*.

Arkadin wiped his mouth again. "North Africa. Interesting. My former partners did a fair amount of business in North Africa. I didn't like their methods—or, to be honest, the people they were dealing with. That was one of the reasons I decided to buy them out."

He was quick on his feet, Soraya thought, improvising like crazy. She was liking this conversation more and more.

"What line are you in?" she asked.

"Computers, peripherals, computer services, that sort of thing."

Right, she thought, amused. She put a thoughtful expression on her face. "Well, I could connect you with some reliable people, if you like."

"Maybe you and I could do business."

Bite! she thought with some elation. *Time to reel in the shark, but very slowly and very carefully.*

"Hm. I don't know, I'm already near capacity."

"Then you need to expand."

"Sure. With what capital?"

"I have capital."

She eyed him warily. "I don't think so. We know nothing about each other."

He set his knife and fork down, and smiled. "Then let's make getting to know each other our first order of business." He lifted a finger. "In fact, I have something to show you that just might entice you into doing business with me."

"And what might that be?"

"Ah-ah-ah, it's a surprise."

Calling the waiter over, he ordered two espressos without asking her if she wanted one. As it happened, she did. She wanted her senses to be on full alert because she had no doubt that at some point tonight she would have to fend off his amorous advances in a way that would lead him on, not turn him off.

They chatted amiably while drinking the espressos, finding their way toward feeling comfortable with each other. Soraya, seeing how relaxed he was, allowed herself to relax, as well, at least as far as she was able. Beneath, however, she felt the tension of steel cables singing through her body. This was a man of enormous charm, as well as charisma. She could see how so many women were magnetically drawn into his orbit. But at the same time the part of her that had pulled back, observing at an objective distance, recognized the show he was putting on, and that she was not seeing the real Arkadin. After a time, she wondered whether anyone had. He had so successfully walled himself off from other human beings that she suspected he was no longer accessible even to himself. And at that moment, he seemed to her a lost little boy, long exiled, who could no longer find his way home.

"Well," he said as he set down his empty cup, "shall we move on?" He threw some bills onto the table and, without waiting for a reply, slid out of the booth. He held out his hand and, after a moment's deliberate hesitation, she took it, allowing him to swing her out of her seat.

The night was mild, without a breath of a breeze, heavy as velvet drapes. The sky was moonless, but the stars blazed in the blackness. They strolled away from the water, and then north, paralleling the beach. To their right, the light-smear of Puerto Peñasco seemed part of a painting, a world apart.

Streetlights gave way to starlit darkness and then, abruptly, the lights of a large stone structure that looked vaguely religious in nature. She saw the cross set into the stone above the wood-and-iron door.

"It used to be a convent." Arkadin unlocked the door and stood aside for her to enter. "My home away from home."

The interior was sparsely furnished, but aromatic with incense and candle wax. She saw a desk, several armchairs, a refectory table and eight chairs, a pew-like sofa festooned with ill-matched pillows. All of it was heavy, dark wood. None of it looked comfortable.

As they walked through the living room, Arkadin lit thick cream-colored candles in iron stands of varying heights. The effect in the convent's immense stone interior was increasingly medieval, and she smiled to herself, suspecting that he was setting the scene for romance or, in this case, seduction.

He opened a bottle of red wine and poured it into

an oversize Mexican goblet, then he filled another with guara juice. Handing her the juice, he said, "Come. This way."

He led her farther into the gloom, pausing to light candles along the way. The far wall was almost all brick fireplace, as enormous as any in an English baronial hall. She could smell the old ash and creosote coating the fire-brick after decades of use and, judging by what she saw, years of neglect.

Now Arkadin lit a particularly large candle and, hold-ing it high as one would a torch, walked toward the shadows of the fireplace. The impenetrable darkness be-gan to give grudging way to the inconstant illumination of the flame.

As the shadows retreated, a shape took form in the fireplace, a chair. And on the chair sat a figure. The figure was bound to the chair by its ankles. Its arms, presum-ably bound at the wrists, were behind it.

As Arkadin brought the candle still closer, the light from the flame rose up from the figure's ankles to legs, torso, finally revealing its face, bloody and swollen so badly that one eye had closed.

"How do you like your surprise?" Arkadin said.

The goblet of juice shattered on the floor tiles as it slipped from Soraya's grip.

The man bound to the chair was Antonio.

It was like a chess match, Bourne staring at the old man, trying to place him as the director of the Centre for the Study of Ancient Documents when he had been in Oxford as David Webb, the old man staring at him more certain with every passing second of Bourne's identity.

Chrissie was staring at them both, as if trying to figure out which would checkmate the other. "Adam, is my
father right? Is your name really David Webb?"

Bourne saw a way out—the only way—but he didn't
like it. "Yes," he said, "and no."

"Either way, your name isn't Adam Stone." Chrissie's
voice held a metallic edge. "Which means you lied to
Trace. She knew you as Adam Stone, and that's how I
know you."

Bourne turned to look at her. "*Adam Stone* is as
much my name as *David Webb* used to be. I've been
known by different names at different times. But they're
only names."

"Damn you!" Chrissie got up, turned her back, and
stalked into the kitchen.

"She's pretty angry," Scarlett said, watching him with
her eleven-year-old face, beautiful yet not fully formed.

"Are you angry?" Bourne asked.

"You're not a professor?"

"In fact, I am," Bourne said. "A professor of linguistics."

"Then I think it's cool. D'you have a whole bunch of
secret identities?"

Bourne laughed. He liked this child. "When the need
arises."

"Bat-Signal!" She cocked her head, and in the
straightforward manner of children, said, "Why did you
lie to Mum and Aunt Tracy?"

Bourne was about to say something about Tracy, but
just in time reminded himself that as far as Scarlett was
concerned her aunt was still alive. "I was in one of my

secret identities when I met your aunt. Then Tracy told your mum about me. It was the best way I could get her to listen to me quickly."

"If you're not Professor David Webb who the hell are you?" Chrissie's father said, visibly gathering himself.

"I was Webb when I knew you," Bourne said. "I didn't come to Oxford, to you, under false pretenses."

"What are you doing here with my daughter and granddaughter?"

"It's a long story," Bourne said.

A spark of cunning came into the old man's face. "I'll bet it has something to do with my older daughter."

"In a way."

The old man clenched a fist. "That damn engraving."

A little chill traveled down Bourne's spine. "What engraving?"

The old man peered at him curiously. "Do you not remember? I'm Dr. Bishop Atherton. You brought me a drawing of a phrase you said was an engraving."

And then Bourne remembered. He remembered everything.

Book Three

Book Three

21

ANTONIO SLUMPED IN the furious darkness of the convent's hearth, a darkness so thick and black it seemed to obliterate not just light, but life itself.

Soraya took several steps toward him, peering into the gloom.

"He's not your pool boy," Arkadin said. "That's clear enough."

She said nothing, knowing that he had begun to bait her in order to gain information. This, in itself, was a hopeful sign, indicating that Antonio hadn't talked, despite the beating he'd received.

Deciding that outrage was her best course, she turned on Arkadin. "What the hell do you think you're doing?"

When Arkadin smiled it was like a wolf appearing through pine trees. "I like to know who my prospective partners are." His smile lengthened, like knives being unsheathed. "Especially ones that fall into my lap so conveniently."

"Partners?" She laughed harshly. "You must be fucking dreaming, my Russian friend. I wouldn't partner with you for—"

He grabbed her then, pressing his lips against hers, but she was ready for him. She folded herself against him and slammed her knee into his groin. His hands on her trembled for a moment, but he did not let her go. His lupine grin never faltered, but there were tears glittering in the corners of his eyes.

"You won't get me," she said softly but icily, "either way."

"Yes, I will," he said, just as icily, "because you came here to get me."

Soraya had nothing to say to this, but she was hoping he was making a stab in the dark, because otherwise she was blown all to hell. "Let Antonio go."

"Give me a reason."

"We'll talk."

He massaged his groin gently. "We already talked."

She bared her teeth. "We'll try another form of communication."

He put a hand on her breast. "Like this?"

"Untie him." Soraya tried not to grit her teeth. "Let him go."

Arkadin appeared to consider her request. "I think not," he said after several moments of tense silence. "He means something to you, which makes him valuable as leverage." Reaching into his pocket, he produced a switchblade. It *snikked* open and, pushing her away, he advanced on Antonio. "What should I cut off first, do you think? Ear? Finger? Or something even lower down?"

"If you cut anything off..."

He turned to her. "Yes?"

"If you cut anything off you'll never be able to sleep while I'm lying beside you."

He leered at her. "I don't sleep."

She had begun to despair for Antonio's life when her cell rang. Without waiting for Arkadin to give her permission, she answered it.

"Soraya." It was Peter Marks.

"Yes."

"What's happened?" Intuitive as ever, he'd picked up on the tension in her voice.

She stared into Arkadin's eyes. "Everything's hunky-dory."

"Arkadin?"

"You bet."

"Excellent, you've made contact."

"More than."

"There's a problem, I get it. Well, you'll have to find your way out of it and fast, because our mission's become urgent."

"What the hell is going on?"

"You need to get Arkadin to the following address within seventy-two hours." Then he recited the address Willard had given him.

"That's an impossible order to fill."

"Obviously, but it's got to be done. He and Bourne have to meet, and that's where Bourne will be."

A pinpoint of light appeared in the darkness ahead of her. *Yes,* she thought, *it just might work.* "Okay," she said to Peter, "I'll put a rush on it."

"And make sure he takes his laptop with him."

Soraya let out a breath. "How d'you propose I do that?"

"Hey, that's why you get the big bucks."

He rang off before she could tell him to go to hell. With a grunt of disgust, she pocketed her cell.

"Business problems?" Arkadin said in a mocking tone.

"Nothing that can't be solved."

"I like your can-do attitude." Mocking her still, he brandished the switchblade. "Are you going to solve *this* problem?"

Soraya put a thoughtful expression on her face. "Possibly." Walking past him, she went into the hearth, where Antonio watched her with the one eye that wasn't swollen shut. She was shocked to find him grinning at her.

"Don't mind me," he said in a hoarse voice, "I'm having fun."

Without Arkadin being able to see, she put her forefinger to her lips, then pressed it to his. It came away bloody. She turned back to Arkadin. "It all depends on you."

"I don't think so. The ball's in your court."

"Here's how this will work." She emerged back into the flickering candlelight. "You let Antonio go and I'll tell you how to find Jason Bourne."

He burst out laughing. "You're bluffing."

"When it comes to someone's life," she said, "I never bluff."

"Still, what does an importer-exporter know about Jason Bourne?"

"Simple enough." Soraya had already worked out her

answer. "From time to time, he uses my company as a cover." This was a plausible enough story to give him reason to believe her.

"And why does an importer-exporter think I care where Jason Bourne is?"

She cocked her head. "Do you?" This was no time to back down or show weakness.

"And what if you're not what you say you are?"

"What if you're not what you say *you* are?"

He waggled a forefinger at her. "No, I don't think you're an importer-exporter."

"All the more intriguing then."

He nodded. "I confess I like mysteries, especially when they bring me closer to Bourne."

"Why do you hate him so?"

"He's responsible for the death of someone I loved."

"Oh, come on," she said. "You never loved anyone."

He took a step toward her, but whether it was a threat or simply to get closer to her was difficult to tell.

"You use people, and when you're finished with them, you crumple them up like a used Kleenex and throw them in the garbage."

"And what of Bourne? He's exactly like me."

"No," she said, "he's not like you at all."

His smile broadened, and for the first time it was without even a hint of menace or irony. "Ah, finally I have a useful bit of knowledge about you."

She almost spit in his face, but she realized that would make him even happier, because it would indicate just how close he'd come to the bone.

All at once something seemed to change in him. He reached out and ran his fingertips along the line of her jaw. Then, indicating Antonio with the tip of the switch-blade, "Go ahead, untie the stubborn fucker."

As she entered the hearth one last time and knelt to free Antonio, he added, "I don't need him anymore. I have you."

This is how it happened." Chrissie was standing in the kitchen, facing the window over the sink. There was nothing to see, except the grayness of dawn creeping through the treetops like gauze. She had said nothing when Bourne walked into the room, but she started when she felt him beside her.

"How what happened?" Bourne said into the silence.

"How I came to lie to you." Chrissie turned on the hot water and, placing her hands in the stream, began to wash them as if she were Lady Macbeth. "One day," she said, "a year or so after Scarlett was born, I looked in the mirror and said to myself, *You have a body that's been abandoned*. Perhaps a man can't understand. I had abandoned my body to motherhood, which means I had abandoned myself."

Her hands moved in the water, washing, washing. "From that moment, I began to hate myself, and then, by extension, my life, which included Scarlett. Of course, that was something I couldn't tolerate. I fought against it and immediately fell into a dreadful depression. My work began to suffer, so obviously that the department chair suggested and then gently but firmly insisted I take a sabbatical. Finally, I agreed, I mean I hadn't a choice, had I? But when I locked my office door behind me, when I drove out of Oxford, drowsing like Avalon in the mist, I knew something drastic had to be done. I knew it was no coincidence that I had locked myself away in a place that never changed. Like my father, I was safe in Oxford, where everything is pre-planned, pre-ordained, even; where there's no possibility of even the slightest deviation. That's why he reacted to Trace's life choices the way he did. They terrified him, so he lashed out at her. It wasn't until that day, leaving Oxford behind, that I understood that family dynamic and how it had affected me. It occurred to me that I might have chosen my safe life for him, not for myself."

She turned off the water and dried her hands on a dish towel. The backs were red and raw looking. "I need to get my family out of here."

"As soon as a friend shows up we'll leave," Bourne said.

"Scarlett."

"She's with your father."

She looked back, almost wistfully, through the doorway into the living room. "Scarlett, at least, loves my parents." She sighed. "Let's go outside. I'm finding it difficult to breathe in here."

Through the kitchen door they emerged into the dewy morning. The air was chill, and when they spoke little puffs of steam emerged from their mouths. The bases of the trees were still black, as if the roots were holding on to the dead of night. Chrissie shivered and wrapped her arms around herself.

"What happened?" Bourne said.

"Nothing that made sense, it was simply blind luck that I met Holly."

Bourne was startled. "Holly Marie Moreau?"

She nodded. "She was looking for Trace and found me instead."

Everything in this puzzle seems to return to Holly, he thought. "And you became friends?"

"More than friends, and less," she said. "I know that doesn't make much sense." She shrugged. "I went to work for her."

Bourne frowned. He felt like a miner inching along a tunnel without lights, but nevertheless knowing by instinct which way to turn. "What was she doing?"

Chrissie gave a little embarrassed laugh. "She was what she euphemistically called a stocker. Now and again she traveled to Mexico for two or three weeks at a time. At a client's request, she'd stock a *narcorrancho*. *Narcorranchos* are shell estates owned by the Mexican drug lords out in the desert somewhere, usually in the north, in Sonora, but sometimes in a more southerly state like Sinaloa. Apart from a caretaker and maybe a guard or two, no one lives in them full-time.

"Anyway, she took me to Mexico City, to the after-hours clubs, the brothels, where she chose from a list she kept updated weekly, like a calendar or a day planner. We took the girls to whichever *narcorrancho* was owned by the current client. There were only a handful of Mexicans there when we arrived, some peons, and heavily armed soldiers who sneered at us even while they drooled over the girls. My job was to spruce up the interior and settle the girls in their various bedrooms. The peons did the heavy lifting.

"Gradually, the cars would come—Lincoln Town Cars, Chevy Suburbans, Mercedeses, all with blacked-out windows, wallowing under their armor plating. The security forces would set up a strict perimeter as if we were in an army bivouac during wartime. Then the provisioners would arrive with fresh meat, fruit, cases of beer, crates of tequila, and, of course, mountains of cocaine. The barbecuing of beef and the spit-roasting of whole pigs and lambs would begin. Salsa and disco music blared louder and louder. The roasters stank of sweat and beer so you couldn't let them near you. Then the bosses arrived with their bodyguards and it was like the Day of the Dead, a festival beyond all festivals."

Bourne's mind was racing at a pace that dizzied even him. "One of Holly's clients was Gustavo Moreno, wasn't it?"

"Gustavo Moreno was her best client," Chrissie said.

Yes, Bourne thought, *it had to be. Another missing piece of the puzzle.*

"He spent more than any of the others. He loved to party all night long. The later it got, the louder and wilder the partying."

"You were a long way from Oxford, Professor."

She nodded. "A long way from civilization, too. But then so was Holly. She lived a double life. She said she'd had plenty of practice growing up in Morocco because her family was very strict, very religious, devout, even. A woman had few rights, a girl even fewer. Apparently her father broke away from the rest of the family—which was led by his brother, Holly's uncle. According to Holly, they had a terrible falling-out. He took her and her mother away to Bali, a place that was the opposite of their village in the High Atlas Mountains. She told no one else about her secret life in Mexico."

Untrue, he thought. *She told me, or I found out, some-*

how. Which must be how the laptop ended up in Gustavo Moreno's hands. I must have given it to him. But why? In this puzzle, he thought, *there's always another blank to fill in, another question to answer.*

Chrissie turned to him. "I take it you knew Holly."

When he didn't reply, she said, "You must be shocked by what I've just told you."

"I'm sorry you lied to me."

"We lied to each other." Chrissie couldn't keep an edge of bitterness out of her voice.

"I have too much experience in lying." He had a feeling that he'd asked Holly to take him to Mexico on one of her trips. Or had he coerced her into it?

"Why did you quit?" he said.

"You could say that I had an epiphany in the Sonoran Desert. It's not surprising we hooked up. She and I were both running away from our former lives, from who we were. Or, rather, we had lost our way in our lives, we no longer knew who we were or who we wanted to be. We were intent on rejecting who we were *expected* to be." She stared down at her reddened hands as if she didn't recognize them. "I had thought that the life I'd left—the cloistered sanctuary of Oxford—wasn't real. But after a time I realized that it was Holly's life that wasn't real."

The sky had lightened further. Birds called from the treetops, and a slight wind brought the smell of damp earth, of living things.

"One night, very late, I wandered into a spare room, or that's what I thought. And there was Holly on top of Gustavo Moreno, grinding away. I watched for a moment, as if they were two strangers acting in a porno.

Then I thought, *Fuck, that's Holly.* You could say that I woke up." She shook her head. "But I don't think Holly ever did."

Bourne didn't think so, either. Sad, but true. Holly had been many things to many people, none of them the same. Those multiple identities had allowed her to burrow deeper into herself, to hide from everyone, when it was her uncle he was certain she feared most.

At that moment Scarlett poked her head out and said, "Hey, you two, we have visitors."

Inside, both Ottavio Moreno and Peter Marks stood in the living room, eyeing each other warily.

"What the hell is this?" Bourne said.

"Here is Ottavio Moreno, the man who knifed Diego Hererra," Marks said to Bourne. "And you're protecting him?"

"It's a long story, Peter," Bourne said. "I'll explain it in the car on the way to—"

Marks turned to Moreno. "You're the brother of Gustavo Moreno, the Colombian drug lord."

"I am," Ottavio Moreno said.

"And the godson of Don Fernando Hererra, the father of the man you knifed to death."

When Moreno said nothing, Marks continued. "I've just come from Don Fernando. He's heartsick, as you can imagine. Or maybe you can't. In any event, he doesn't think you murdered his son. The police, on the other hand, are certain you did." Without waiting for a reply, he whirled on Bourne. "How the hell could you let this happen?"

Then Ottavio Moreno made a tactical mistake. "I think you'd better calm down," he said. He should have kept his mouth shut, but possibly he'd been stung by Marks's words as well as his tone.

"Don't tell me what to do," Marks said heatedly.

Bourne had half a mind to let the two men come to blows, if only to relieve the built-up tension of the last couple of hours, but there was Chrissie and her family to think of, so he stepped in between the two. Gripping Marks at the elbow, he steered him out the front door, where they could talk without being overheard. Before he could say a word, though, Moreno came storming out.

He headed straight for Marks, but before he was halfway there a shot from the trees stopped him in his tracks. Even as he staggered backward, even as the second shot took part of his skull off, Bourne had flung himself behind Moreno's Opel. As Marks followed him, another shot cracked through the stillness of early morning.

Marks stumbled and fell.

Boris Karpov accompanied Viktor Cherkesov into the construction site on ulitsa Varvarka. They passed through a gap in the chain-link fence and descended via a ramp into the dead zone. Cherkesov kept them going until they were deep in the heart of the morass of rusting steel girders and cracked concrete blocks; evil-looking weeds sprouted everywhere like tufts of hair on a giant's back.

Cherkesov stopped them as they approached the bashed-in side of a derelict truck, which had been stripped of tires, electronics, and engine. It was canted over to one side like a ship on its way to the bottom of the sea. The truck was green, but someone had artistically covered it with obscene graffiti in silver spray paint.

Cherkesov's mouth twitched in an imitation of a smile as he turned away from contemplating the graffiti.

"Now, Boris Illyich, please be kind enough to tell me the gist of your impromptu meeting with President Imov."

Karpov, seeing no other recourse, obliged him. Cherkesov did not interrupt him once, but listened thoughtfully as Karpov outlined what he had learned about Bukin and those moles under his command. When he was finished, Cherkesov nodded. He produced a Tokarev TT pistol but didn't aim it at Karpov, at least not exactly.

"Now, Boris Illyich, the question for me is what to do next. First, what shall I do with you? Shall I shoot you and leave you to rot here?" He seemed to spend some time contemplating this option. "Well, to be honest, that would do me no good. By going directly to Imov you have made yourself invulnerable. If you are killed or disappear Imov will initiate a full-scale investigation, which will sooner rather than later wind up at my doorstep. As you can imagine, this would inconvenience me greatly."

"I think it would do more than inconvenience you, Viktor Delyagovich," Karpov said without inflection. "It would be the beginning of your end and the triumph of Nikolai Patrushev, your bitterest enemy."

"These days, I have bigger fish to fry than Nikolai Patrushev." Cherkesov said this softly, contemplatively, as if he had forgotten that Karpov was there at all. Then, all at once, he snapped out of it, his eyes refocusing on the colonel. "So killing you is out, which is fortunate, Boris Illyich, because I like you. More to the point, I admire your tenacity as well as your intelligence. Which is why I won't even bother to bribe you." He grunted, a sort of laugh gone bad. "You might be the last honest man in Russian intelligence." He waved the Tokarev. "So where does that leave us?"

"Stalemate," Karpov offered.

"No, no, no. Stalemate is good for no one, especially you and me, especially at this moment in time. You gave Imov the evidence against Bukin, Imov gave you an assignment. We both have no choice but for you to carry it out."

"That would be suicide for you," Karpov pointed out.

"Only if I stay on as head of FSB-2," Cherkesov said.

Karpov shook his head. "I don't understand."

Cherkesov had a miniature two-way radio to his ear. "Come down now," he said to whoever was on the other end of the line.

There was a smirk on his face that Karpov had never seen before. He took a step toward the colonel and, in a moment, gestured. "Look who's coming, Boris Illyich."

Karpov turned and saw Melor Bukin picking his way through the rubble.

"Now," Cherkesov said, slapping the Tokarev into Karpov's hand, "do your duty."

Karpov held the Tokarev behind his back as Melor Bukin approached them. He wondered what Cherkesov had told him, because Bukin was totally relaxed and unsuspecting. His eyes opened wide when Karpov brought out the Tokarev and aimed it at him.

"Viktor Delyagovich, what is the meaning of this?" he said.

Karpov shot him in the right knee, and he went down like a smokestack being demolished.

"What are you doing?" he cried as he clutched his ruined knee. "Are you mad?"

Karpov advanced on him. "I know about your treachery and so does President Imov. Who are the other moles inside FSB-2?"

Bukin stared up at him wide-eyed. "What, what? Moles? I don't know what you're talking about."

Karpov calmly and deliberately blew his left kneecap to smithereens. Bukin screamed and writhed on the ground like a worm.

"Answer me!" Karpov commanded.

Bukin's eyes were bloodshot. He was pale and trembling in shock and agony. "Boris Illyich, doesn't our history mean anything? I'm your mentor, I was instrumental in bringing you into FSB-2."

Karpov loomed over him. "All the more reason that I be the one to clean your dirty house."

"But, but, but," Bukin sputtered, "I was just following orders." He pointed at Cherkesov. "*His* orders."

"How easily he lies," Cherkesov said.

"No, Boris Illyich, it's the truth, I swear."

Karpov squatted by Bukin's side. "I know how we can solve this problem."

"I need a fucking hospital," Bukin moaned. "I'm bleeding to death."

"Tell me the names of the moles," Karpov said. "Then I'll take care of you."

Bukin's bloodshot eyes darted between him and Cherkesov.

"Forget him," Karpov said. "I'm the one standing between you and bleeding out here in this cesspit."

Bukin swallowed heavily, then gave up the names of three men inside FSB-2.

"Thank you," Karpov said. He stood up and shot Bukin between the eyes.

Then he turned to Cherkesov and said, "What's to stop me from killing you or taking you in?"

"You may be incorruptible, Boris Illyich, but you know which side of the bread is buttered, or will be." Cherkesov took out a cigarette and lit up. He did not once look at his fallen lieutenant. "I can clear the way for you to become head of the FSB-2."

"So can President Imov."

"True enough." Cherkesov nodded. "But Imov can't guarantee that one of the other commanders won't drop polonium into your tea or slip a stiletto between your ribs one night."

Karpov knew very well that Cherkesov still had the power to identify and sweep away any of his potential enemies inside FSB-2. He was the only one who could clear Karpov's path.

"Let me get this straight," he said. "You're proposing that I take your job?"

"Yes."

"And what of you? Imov will want your head."

"Of course he will, but he'll have to find me first."

"You'll go into hiding, become a fugitive?" Karpov shook his head. "I don't see that future for you."

"Neither do I, Boris Illyich. I am going to the seat of a higher power."

"Higher than the FSB?"

"Higher than the Kremlin."

Karpov frowned. "And what would that be?"

Cherkesov's eyes glittered. "Tell me, Boris Illyich, have you ever heard of Severus Domna?"

22

MARKS GRABBED HIS left thigh, grimacing in pain. The unseen sniper continued to pepper the area. Bourne darted out, took hold of Marks, and dragged him to safety.

"Keep your head down, Peter."

"Tell that to your pal Moreno," Marks said. "My fucking head *is* down."

"You're welcome." Bourne inspected the wound, determining that the bullet hadn't severed an artery. Then he ripped a sleeve off Marks's shirt and used it as a tourniquet, tying it around his thigh above the wound.

"I'm not going to forget this," Marks said.

"No, only I do that," Bourne said with such a sardonic edge that Marks had to laugh, albeit drily.

Bourne edged around the front of the Opel. He breathed easily and deeply as he scanned the thick line of trees. He'd been up in one of them not so very long ago, and he used his eidetic memory, honed by his Treadstone training, to reconstruct the best possible places for a sniper to secrete himself. By the way both Ottavio Moreno and Marks fell he had a clear idea of where the shooter must be. He put himself in the sniper's head: Where would he put himself that both had a clear view of the front door and was deeply sheltered?

He heard Chrissie calling, and from the level of anxiety in her voice realized that she must have been shouting to him for some time. Crawling back to the other end of the Opel, he called, "I'm okay. Stay inside until I come get you."

Scuttling back to the taillights, he sprinted out of cover, hurling himself into the tree line. A volley of shots smacked into the Opel's front end. From the beginning of the attack, he'd counted the shots. After the last flurry, he'd calculated that the sniper needed time to reload. A couple of seconds was all he needed to reach the protection of the trees. Now he went hunting.

In among the pines and oaks, perpetual shadows clung to the thick jigsaw of branches. Here and there, light filtered through in tiny diamonds, winking and glittering as the wind stirred the woods. Bourne, in a semi-crouch, picked his way through the underbrush, taking care not to crunch down on twigs or pinecones. He made no sound. Every five or six paces he stopped, watching and listening as a fox or a stoat will, alert for both prey and enemies.

He caught sight of a small flash of black-and-brown, blurred, winking out almost before it had a chance to register. He headed toward it. Briefly he considered taking to the trees, but was concerned that dislodged debris would give away his position. At some point he changed direction, veering away, circling to come upon the sniper from the side. As he continued, he repeatedly checked behind and above him for any sign of the sniper.

The glint of metal up ahead pushed him onward at a more rapid pace. Peering out from behind the bole of an oak, he could see the right shoulder and hip of the sniper. He knelt behind a dense patch of underbrush, then scuttled around behind him. A narrow gap between two pines afforded him an excellent view of the front door and driveway. Bourne caught a glimpse of Ottavio Moreno on the ground in a pool of blood. Marks was hidden behind the flank of Moreno's Opel. Bourne supposed the sniper was waiting for someone to move. He seemed bent on shooting to death everyone who ventured outside the house. Was he NSA, CI, or a soldier of Severus Domna? Only one way to find out.

Bourne approached slowly and cautiously, but at the last moment the sniper must have sensed him because he drove the wooden stock of his Dragunov SVD back into Bourne's midsection. Then he whirled, swinging the barrel of the Dragunov against Bourne's shoulder. He was a slim, flat-faced man with small black eyes and a pushed-in nose.

He battered Bourne to his knees and then, with another blow of the Dragunov, onto his back. He pressed the rifle's muzzle against Bourne's heart.

"Don't move, don't say a word," he said. "Just hand over the ring."

"What ring?"

The sniper swung the muzzle of the Dragunov into

Bourne's jaw, drawing blood. But at the same instant Bourne smashed the sole of his shoe into the man's knee. It bent inward, the bones cracked, and the sniper gasped. Bourne was rolling away even as the sniper squeezed off a shot. The bullet plowed into the ground where Bourne had been lying, splitting an old, rotting board full of long carpenter's nails.

From one knee, the sniper began to wield the Dragunov like a club, swinging it back and forth to keep Bourne at bay while he caught his breath. Finally, with a concerted effort, he staggered to his feet. That was when Bourne lowered his shoulder and drove it into him. They went down. At once, the sniper tried to maneuver Bourne onto the nails sticking wickedly out of the board. Bourne twisted away, and now the two of them struggled for possession of the Dragunov. Until Bourne lifted an elbow, jamming it into the sniper's Adam's apple. He began to choke and Bourne drove a fist into the side of his head. The sniper's body went limp.

Bourne checked his hands but found no ring. Then he went through his pockets. His name was Farid Lever, according to his French passport, but that told Bourne nothing. The passport could be real or a fake, he had no time to scrutinize it. Lever, or whoever the hell he was, had on him five thousand British pounds, two thousand euros, and a set of car keys.

Emptying the Dragunov's magazine, he flung the rifle into the woods then slapped the sniper back into consciousness.

"Who are you?" Bourne said. "Who do you work for?"

The black eyes looked up at him impassively. Reaching down, Bourne squeezed the sniper's ruined knee. His eyes opened wide and he gasped, but not another sound came out of his mouth. It soon would, Bourne vowed. This was a man who had shot two people, one of them dead. Prying open the sniper's mouth, he shoved his fist in. The man gagged, arching up. He tried to twist away, to move his head from side to side, but Bourne kept a firm grip on him. As his hands came up, Bourne slapped them down and pressed harder, pushing his fist in deeper.

The sniper's eyes began to water, he coughed and gagged again. Then his gorge rose up uncontrollably and he tried to vomit, but there was nowhere for it to go. He began to asphyxiate. Terror flooded his face, and he nodded as vigorously as he was able.

The moment Bourne extracted his fist, the sniper rolled over on his side and vomited, his eyes tearing, his nose running. His body shook all over. Bourne took him by the shoulders and turned him onto his back. His face was a mess; he looked like a kid who'd gotten the worst of a street fight.

"Now," Bourne said. "Who are you and who do you work for?"

"Fa...Fa...Farid Lever." Understandably, he was having trouble speaking.

Bourne held up the French passport. "One more lie and this gets stuffed down your throat, and I promise you I won't pull it out."

The sniper swallowed, wincing at the sour taste in his mouth. "Farid Kazmi. I belong to Jalal Essai."

Bourne took a shot in the dimness. "Severus Domna?"

"He was." Kazmi had to stop either to regain his

breath or to get more saliva in his mouth. "I need water. Do you have any water?"

"Those two men you shot needed water, too. One of them is dead, the other isn't, but neither is getting any," Bourne said. "Continue. Jalal Essai..."

"Jalal was a member of Severus Domna. He has broken away from them."

"That's a very dangerous course. He must have a damn good reason."

"The ring."

"Why?"

Kazmi's tongue came out, trying to moisten his dry lips. "It belongs to him. For years he thought it was lost, but now he knows that his brother stole it from him years ago. You have it."

So Jalal Essai is Holly's dreaded uncle, Bourne thought. The puzzle was at last taking shape. Holly the hedonist on one side, and her uncle Jalal the religious extremist on the other. What if Holly's father had left Morocco to protect her from his brother, who would surely have clamped down on Holly's natural tendencies, stifled her, killed her, in a manner of speaking? And then, after his death, who had stood between Holly and her uncle? But in a blinding flash of memory he knew: It was him. Holly had somehow recruited him to protect her from Jalal Essai. He had done that, but the curious relationship among Holly, Tracy, Perlis, and Diego Hererra—a relationship she had failed to tell him about—had undone her. Perlis had found out about the ring from her and had killed her to get it.

"I was to get the ring at all costs," Kazmi said, bringing Bourne back into the present.

"No matter how many lives it took."

Kazmi nodded, wincing with pain. "No matter how many." Something lurked in those black eyes. "Jalal will get it, too."

"What makes you say that?"

A look of serenity bloomed on Kazmi's face and Bourne lunged for his mouth. But it was too late. His molars had ground open a fake tooth, and the cyanide inside was already shutting down his systems.

Bourne sat back on his haunches. When Kazmi had breathed his last, he rose and headed back toward the house.

Peter Marks lay on the ground, keeping as still as possible. Moving only caused a further loss of blood. Though well trained, he had never before been wounded in the field, or anywhere else, had never even experienced an accident like falling off a ladder or missing a stair tread. He lay as if dead, hearing his breath sawing in and out of his mouth, feeling the blood pulsing in his leg as if it had developed a second heart, but a heart that was malevolent, black as night, a heart that was close to death, or in whose chambers death had inveigled itself like a thief.

Marks felt his life was about to be stolen from him prematurely, as it had been from his sister. How close he felt to her at this moment, as if at the last instant he had snatched her from the doomed plane, holding her close while they soared through the clouds. This abrupt awareness of the tenuousness of his own life did not frighten him so much as change his perspective. He lay, helpless and bleeding, and watched an ant struggle with a freshly fallen leaf, a new leaf, a luminous green, until moments ago bursting with life. The leaf was clearly too big for the ant, but the insect was undeterred, tugging and pulling, dragging the recalcitrant leaf over pebbles and roots, the huge impediments of its world. Marks loved that ant. It refused to give up no matter how difficult its life had become. It persevered. It abided. This, too, Marks resolved to do. He resolved to look out for himself and for the people he cared about—Soraya, for instance—in a way that he could not have imagined, let alone foreseen, before he had been shot.

And so he lay for some time, hearing nothing but the occasional soughing of the wind through the woods. Which was why, when he heard Chrissie's voice calling, he said, "This is Peter Marks. I've been hit in the leg. Moreno's dead, and Adam went after the sniper."

"I'm coming out to get you."

"Stay where you are," he shouted back. Dragging himself forward, he struggled to sit with his back against the Opel. "The area isn't secure."

But a moment later she appeared at his side, crouched down behind the safety of the car's bullet-ridden flank.

"Stupid move," he said.

"You're welcome."

It was the second time someone had said that to him today and he didn't like it. In fact, he didn't like much of anything in his life at the moment, and he became momentarily disoriented, wondering how in the world he had allowed himself to get into this sorry state. He loved no one and so far as he knew no one loved him, not currently, anyway. He supposed his parents had loved him in their gruff overriding way, and surely his sister had. But who else? His latest girlfriend had lasted six months, just about par for the course, before she got fed up with his long hours and inattention, and walked out. Friends? A few. But like Soraya, he used them or they used him. He felt suddenly sick to his stomach and shuddered.

"You're going into shock," Chrissie said, understanding him better than he could imagine. "We'd better get you into the house and warmed up."

She helped him to stand, balanced on his good leg. He put his arm around her, and she helped him toward the house. He moved shakily and, stumbling over a rock or a root, almost sent them both tumbling over.

Christ on a crutch, he thought wildly, *I'm full of self-pity today,* and was even more thoroughly disgusted with himself than he had been a moment ago.

Her father, who had emerged from the house, rushed to Marks's other side and helped her with her burden. The old man kicked the door shut when they were inside.

Bourne came upon the woman almost without warning. She was half buried in crisp, dead leaves. Her face was turned away from him, eyes closed. Her long hair was streaked with blood, but from the way she lay, it was impossible to tell whether she was dead or alive. A neighbor out walking, it had been her bad luck to stumble upon Kazmi. Beneath the fall of leaves, he could make out bits and pieces of her red-and-black-checked flannel shirt, jeans, and hiking boots. Leaves appeared to have been kicked over her with considerable haste.

He needed to return to Peter Marks and to the people in the house, but he couldn't bypass the woman until he found out whether she was alive and, if so, how badly she was injured. Creeping closer, he put a hand out to find the pulse in her carotid artery.

Her eyes snapped open, her hand rose up, clutching a hunting knife by its handle. The point stabbed out toward his chest and, as he moved, sliced through his shirt and across the skin covering his breastbone. She sat up, coming after him. Leaves fell away from her like freshly turned earth from an animated corpse. Bourne grasped her wrist, redirecting the knife away from him, but she had a second knife in her other hand. Struggling with her, he saw it very late, and took the point on the bone of his shoulder.

She was well trained and surprisingly strong. She scissored her legs, catching his right ankle, taking him off balance. He fell backward and she was on him. He had control of one wrist, but the knife blade scythed in to slit his throat. Using the carpenter's nail like a push dagger, he slapped his hand against the side of her neck, puncturing her carotid artery.

A fountain of blood arced out, pulsing with each slackening beat of her heart. The woman toppled over into the leaves that had covered her. She looked up at him with Kazmi's enigmatic smile, that smile that made him believe that Jalal Essai wasn't finished with him, that had put him on alert, that had caused him to keep the carpenter's nail hidden in his left hand. Were Kazmi and the woman working together? Had she been his backup? It seemed so to him, a diabolical scheme that made of Jalal Essai a formidable enemy with whom he had a difficult and shadowed past, a man who doubtless nursed a blood grudge against him.

* * *

As Chrissie and her father sat Marks down in a chair, they heard rifle shots. Chrissie gave a little gasp and ran to the door, pulling it open against her father's shouted warning. Still in the shadows of the doorway, she peered out past the driveway and the Opel to the woods beyond, but she could see nothing, even though she strained with every ounce of her strength to penetrate the foliage, to spot a sign that Bourne was still alive. What if he was wounded and needed help?

She had already made up her mind to go after him, as she imagined Tracy would have done in the same circumstances, when she saw him emerging through the branches. Before she could take a step, someone flashed past her, down the steps.

"Scarlett!"

Scarlett raced down the driveway, skirted the dead man, passing around the trunk of the car, and flung herself into Bourne's arms.

"This is real blood, your blood," she said a bit out of breath, "but I can help you."

Bourne was about to brush her gently away, but her obvious concern changed his mind. She genuinely wanted to help, and he couldn't take that away from her. He knelt down beside her so that she could check his cuts and bruises.

"I'll get bandages from Granddad's kit." But she made no move to leave him, digging in the dirt with her fingers as children will when they're embarrassed or at a loss for words. Then she put her face up to his. "Are you all right?"

He smiled. "Imagine tripping over a rock."

"Just scratches and bruises?"

"That's all."

"That's good then. I—" She held something up for him to see. "I found this just now. Does it belong to Mr. Marks? This is where he was lying."

Bourne took it and rubbed the dirt off. It was a Severus Domna ring. Where had it come from?

"I'll ask Mr. Marks when we get inside." He pocketed the ring.

At that moment Chrissie came up, out of breath not only from the all-out sprint but also from the terror of having her daughter exposed to more danger.

"Scarlett," she said.

Bourne saw that she was prepared to scold her daughter until she glimpsed her examining Bourne's superficial wounds with absolute concentration and she, like Bourne, shut her mouth to allow this mini-drama to play out.

"If you let me put bandages on your cuts," Scarlett said, "you'll be fine."

"Then let's go inside, Dr. Lincoln."

Scarlett giggled. Bourne stood up, and the three of them returned in silence to the house, where Bourne went directly to where they had sat Marks. Chrissie's father was tending him with materials from an astonishingly well-stocked first-aid kit. Marks's eyes were closed, his head back. Bourne guessed the professor had administered a sedative.

"The first-aid kit's from the trunk of Dad's car," Chrissie said as Scarlett rummaged around for bandages and Mercurochrome. "He's been a hunter all his life."

Bourne sat cross-legged on the rug while Scarlett ministered to him.

"The wound's a clean one," Professor Atherton said of his own patient. "Bullet went clear through, so the chance of infection is low, especially now that I've cleaned it out." He took the Mercurochrome from Scarlett, applied it to two squares of sterile gauze, placed the gauze over the entrance and exit wounds, then expertly wrapped the whole in surgical tape. "Seen much worse in my day," he said. "The only problem now is to make sure he rests and gets some fluids in him as soon as possible. He's lost a lot of blood, though not nearly as much as if he didn't have the tourniquet on."

Finished, he looked up from his patient to see Bourne. "You sure look like crap, whatever-the-hell-your-name-is."

"Professor, I need to ask you a question."

The old man snorted. "Is that all you do, son, ask questions?" He put a hand on the arm of Marks's chair and levered himself up to a standing position. "Well, you can ask me anything you like, doesn't mean I'll answer you."

Bourne stood as well. "Did Tracy have a brother?"

"What?"

Chrissie frowned. "Adam, I already told you that Tracy was my only—"

Bourne held up his hand. "I'm not asking your father whether you and your sister had a brother. I'm asking if *Tracy* had a brother."

A malevolent expression gathered on Professor Atherton's face. "Bugger'n'blast, son, in days gone by I'd've boxed your ears for saying something so bloody-minded."

"You didn't answer the question. Did Tracy have a brother?"

The professor's expression darkened further. "You mean a half brother."

Chrissie took a step toward the two men, who were now faced off like street fighters about to settle a grudge. "Adam, why are you—?"

"Don't get all gutted up over nothing." Her father waved away her protest. And then to Bourne: "You're asking me if I had sexual relations with another woman and something came of it?"

"That's right."

"Never did," Professor Atherton said. "I loved the girls' mother and I've been faithful to her for longer than I care to remember." He shook his head. "I think you've made rather a hash of this."

Bourne was unfazed. "Tracy worked for a dangerous man. I had to ask myself why because it seemed doubtful that she would work for him willingly. Then Chrissie provided a partial answer. Tracy told this man she had a brother who was in trouble."

At once Professor Atherton's demeanor altered radically. All color drained out of his face; he might have fallen if Chrissie hadn't stepped to his side to support him. With some difficulty she got him to sit down in the chair opposite Marks.

"Dad?" She knelt beside him, his clammy hand in hers. "What is this? Is there a brother I don't know about?"

The old man kept shaking his head. "I had no idea she knew," he mumbled as if to himself. "How the bloody hell did she find out?"

"So it's true." Chrissie shot Bourne a glance, then redirected her attention to her father. "Why didn't you and Mum tell us?"

Professor Atherton sighed deeply, then passed a hand across his sweating brow. He looked at his daughter blankly, as if he didn't recognize her, or he was expecting to see someone else.

"I don't want to talk about it."

"But you must." She seemed to rise up, stiffening her spine, and she leaned in toward him as if to lend her words more weight. "You have no choice now, Dad. You have to tell me about him."

Her father remained silent, impassive now, as if free of a fever that had gripped him.

"What's his name?" she implored. "Can't you tell me that much?"

Her father's eyes would not meet hers. "He had no name."

Chrissie sat back, as if he had slapped her across the face. "I don't understand."

"And why would you?" Professor Atherton said. "Your brother was born dead."

23

JALAL ESSAI WAS a marked man and he knew it. As he sat on a bridge chair he'd opened up in his darkened bedroom, he considered these factors: Breaking with Severus Domna had not been an easy decision—or rather, while the decision had been easy, the actual implementation had been difficult. But then it was always difficult, Essai thought, deliberately putting oneself in harm's way. He had not acted on his decision until he had worked out the methods of implementation, drawing up a list in his mind of all the possible paths he could take, then eliminating them one by one until he reached the one with the fewest objections, the most acceptable level of risk, and the best odds of success. This methodical approach was how he arrived at every decision: The process was the most logical. Also, it had the added benefit of calming his mind, not unlike his prayers to Allah, or contemplating a Zen koan. The empty mind fills itself with possibilities unavailable to others.

So he sat, absolutely still, within the darkness of his apartment, the blackness of his bedroom where all the blinds were drawn against nighttime's streetlights and the passing headlights of the occasional car or truck. Night, and the threat of night. Night was to him what a cup of espresso was to others, a calm and satisfying state of reflection. He could navigate his way through darkness, even nightmares, because Allah had blessed with the light of the true believer.

It was 3 AM. He knew what was coming, which was why he had chosen not to run. A runner makes an excellent target as he leaves his own territory. He stumbles—and he dies. Essai did not intend to stumble. Instead he had prepared his bedroom for the inevitable, and he was willing—content even—to remain in place until the enemy showed his face.

He heard the sound first. A tiny scratching, as if of mice, from the living room, in the direction of the front door. The sound very quickly ceased, but he knew the enemy must have picked the lock on his door, because someone was in the apartment. Still, he did not move. There was no reason to move. He cast his gaze on the bed, where a lump under the covers revealed to his enemy's eyes the presence of a sleeping body.

The quality of the darkness changed, deepening, becoming thicker, dense with the pulse of another human being. Essai's focus narrowed even more. His enemy, now in the kill zone, bent over the bed.

Essai felt the motion as a stirring of the air as his enemy drew out a dagger and plunged it into the figure sleeping in the bed. At once the plastic skin punctured, spraying the would-be killer with a geyser of battery acid with which Essai had filled the inflatable sex toy.

His enemy reacted in predictable fashion by falling backward, limbs pinwheeling. On the floor he tried and failed to wipe the acid off his face, neck, and chest. This action only served to smear the acid over more of his face, neck, and chest. He gasped, but because the acid was eating his lips and tongue he could not get out any words or even a scream. A nightmare scenario for him, Essai thought, as he rose from the chair at last.

Kneeling over the enemy—the man Severus Domna had sent to kill him for his disloyalty—he smiled the smile of the just, the righteous in Allah's beneficent eyes, and putting a forefinger against his lips he whispered, "Shhhhh," so low that only he and his enemy could hear.

Then he took up the assassin's dagger and picked his way to the doorway into the hall. Pressing himself against the wall, he waited, emptying his mind of expectation. Into this divine emptiness came the most probable route the second man would take. He knew there was a second man, just as he knew his assassin would not use a pistol to kill him, because these were the two major methods of operation Severus Domna employed: stealth and backup. Methods he himself had used in going after Jason Bourne and the ring.

A diagonal shadow falling across the width of the hall bore out his thesis. Now he knew where the second assassin was, or rather had been, because he was on the move. His compatriot had had enough time to effect the kill, and now he was closing the gap between them to determine if anything was amiss.

Something certainly was amiss, a fact confirmed to him as the dagger, thrown with great accuracy by Essai, penetrated his chest between two ribs and pierced his heart. He fell heavily, like a wildebeest taken down by a lion. Essai approached him, knelt, and determined there was no pulse, no life left. Then he returned to his bedroom, where the first assassin was writhing on the floor with ever-more-uncoordinated movements.

Snapping on a lamp, he studied the man's face. He did not recognize him, but then he didn't expect to. Severus Domna would not have sent anyone he could identify on sight. Squatting down beside the man, he said, "My friend, I pity you. I pity you because I have chosen not to end your life and therefore your suffering. Instead, I will leave you as you are."

Pulling out a cell phone burner, he dialed a local number.

"Yes?" Benjamin El-Arian said.

"Delivery for you to pick up," Essai said.

"You must be mistaken. I didn't order anything."

Essai put the cell to the assassin's mouth, and he made sounds like a cow in distress.

"Who is this?"

Something had changed in El-Arian's voice, a febrile element that Essai, the cell to his ear again, was able to catch.

"I estimate you have thirty minutes before your assassin dies. His life is in your hands."

Essai closed the cell and, standing, ground it to bits beneath his heel.

Then he addressed the assassin for the last time: "You will tell Benjamin El-Arian what happened here, and then he will deal with you as he sees fit. Tell him that the same fate awaits anyone he sends after me. That's all you need to do now. His time—and yours—is over."

Moira, standing on the starboard side of the yacht, watched the exchange of infrared signals through the night glasses the captain had handed her moments before. She could see the cigarette boat lying to as the yacht came up on it. Moving her field of vision slightly, she saw two figures in the cigarette besides the signaler. A man and a woman. The man was almost certainly Arkadin, but who was the woman and why would he have someone else on board? Berengária had told her Arkadin came out to meet her boats with just a mate, an old Mexican named El Heraldo.

The captain continued to keep the yacht's engines idling as it slid through the black waves on its own momentum. Now Moira could make out Arkadin's face, and beside him was—Soraya Moore!

She almost dropped the night glasses overboard. *What the hell?* she thought. For every plan there was a wrench that could jam up the works. Here was hers.

The quiet lapping of the water was all she heard as the cigarette came up alongside the yacht. A crewman tossed down a rope ladder; another manned the winch. Meanwhile two other crewmen were busy hauling up the cargo from belowdecks. Berengária had explained the routine in detail. A crate was loaded into the net to be winched down to the cigarette so Arkadin could inspect the contents.

As this was happening, Moira leaned over the rail,

peering down at the people in the cigarette. Soraya saw her first, her mouth forming an O of silent surprise.

What the hell? she mouthed up to Moira, who had to laugh. They'd both had the same reaction on seeing each other.

Then Arkadin caught sight of her. Frowning, he climbed the ladder. The moment he swung aboard the yacht he drew out a Glock 9mm and aimed it at her midsection.

"Who the hell are you?" he said. "And what are you doing on board my boat?"

"It's not your boat, it belongs to Berengária," Moira said in Spanish.

Arkadin's eyes narrowed. "And do you belong to Berengária also?"

"I belong to no one," Moira said, "but I am looking out for Berengária's interests." She had thought about the possible answers to his questions during the entire trip up the coast of Mexico. What it boiled down to was this: Arkadin was a man first, a homicidal criminal second.

"Just like a woman to send a woman," Arkadin said, as disdainful as Roberto Corellos.

"Berengária is convinced you no longer trust her."

"This is true."

"Perhaps she no longer trusts you."

Arkadin gave her a dark look but said nothing.

"This is a poor state of affairs," Moira acknowledged. "And no way to run a business."

"And how does the woman who does not own you suggest we proceed?"

"For a start, you might lower the Glock," Moira observed.

By this time Soraya had made her way up the ladder and now appeared, swinging her legs over the yacht's brass railing. She seemed to size up the situation immediately, looking from Moira to Arkadin and back again.

"Fuck you," Arkadin said. "And fuck Berengária for sending you."

"If she had sent a man, the chances are good the two of you would have killed each other."

"I would have killed him, certainly," Arkadin said.

"So sending a man would not have been the smart thing to do."

Arkadin snorted. "Fuck, we're not in the kitchen." He shook his head in disbelief. "You're not even armed."

"Therefore, you won't shoot me," Moira said. "Therefore, you will be willing to listen when I talk, when I negotiate, when I propose a way to go forward without suspicion on either side."

Arkadin watched her as a hawk watches a sparrow. Perhaps he no longer considered her a threat, or possibly what she said had gotten through to him. In any event, he lowered the Glock and tucked it away at the small of his back.

Moira looked pointedly at Soraya. "But I won't talk or negotiate or propose anything with someone unfamiliar. Berengária told me about you and your boatman, El Heraldo, but now I see this woman here. I don't like surprises."

"That makes two of us." Arkadin jerked his head in Soraya's direction. "A new partner, on probation. She doesn't work out, I put a hole in the back of her head."

"Just like that."

Arkadin walked to where Soraya stood and, cocking his thumb and forefinger as if they were a gun, he pressed its muzzle to the base of her skull. "Boom!" Then he turned and, smiling in the most charming manner, said, "So speak your mind."

"There are too many partners," Moira said bluntly.

This gave Arkadin pause. "For myself," he said at length, "I don't care for partners in the least." He shrugged. "Unfortunately, they're a part of doing business. But if Berengária wants out..."

"We were thinking more of Corellos."

"She's his lover."

"This is business," Moira said. "What she did with Corellos was to keep the peace between them." Now she shrugged. "What better weapon does she have?"

Arkadin seemed to look at her in a new light. "Corellos is very powerful."

"Corellos is in prison."

"I doubt for much longer."

"Which is why," Moira said, "we hit him now."

"Hit him?"

"Kill, terminate, murder, call it what you like."

Arkadin paused a moment, then burst out laughing. "Where in the world did Berengária find you?"

Moira, glancing at Soraya, took a not-so-wild guess, thinking: *Pretty much the same place you found your new partner.*

Why would she do that?" Professor Atherton had his head in his hands. "Why would Tracy tell anyone that she had a brother?"

"Especially when that put her in Arkadin's debt," Chrissie added.

"She did more than mention her brother," Bourne said. "She concocted an elaborate lie about him being alive and in debt over his head. It's as if she wanted Arkadin to have something on her."

Chrissie shook her head. "But that doesn't make sense."

It did, Bourne thought, if she had been sent to get close to Arkadin. To report on his deals and his whereabouts, for example. He was not, however, about to speculate with these people.

"That question can wait," he said. "After the shots in the woods, we need to get out of here." He turned to Professor Atherton. "I can carry Marks, can you maneuver on your own?"

The old man nodded curtly.

Chrissie gestured. "I'll help you, Dad."

"See to your daughter," he said gruffly. "I can take care of myself."

Chrissie packed up the first-aid kit. She carried it out the front door, holding Scarlett's hand. Bourne picked Marks up, sliding him up onto his shoulder.

"Let's go," he said, herding the professor outside.

Chrissie took him around to his car, which was parked out back. Bourne packed Marks into the rental, which was miraculously unscathed. Chrissie pulled her father's car around, and Scarlett clambered in.

Bourne approached her.

"What happens now?" she asked.

"You go back to your life."

"My life." Her laugh was uneasy. "My life—and my family's life—will never be the same."

"Maybe that's a good thing."

She nodded.

"In any case, I'm sorry."

"Don't be." She smiled wanly. "For a moment, I was Tracy, and now I know that I never wanted to be like her, I just thought I did." She put a hand on his arm, briefly. "It was good she met you. You made her happy."

"For a night or two."

"More than many get in a lifetime." Her hand dropped away. "Trace chose her life, it didn't choose her."

Bourne nodded. Turning away, he peered into her car. When he tapped on the glass, Scarlett opened the window. He placed something in her hand and closed her fingers around it.

"This is just between us," Bourne said. "Don't look at it until you're home and alone."

She nodded solemnly.

"Let's go," Chrissie said, not looking at Bourne.

Scarlett raised her window. She said something Bourne couldn't hear. He put his hand flat against the window. On the other side, Scarlett pressed her hand over his.

Marks had left the key in the ignition and now Bourne started it up.

A combination of the noise and vibration as Bourne came out of the driveway and turned onto the road woke Marks from his stupor.

"Where the hell am I?" he mumbled thickly.

"On your way to London."

Marks nodded in the manner of a drunk who is struggling to reacquaint himself with how the world works. "Fuck, my leg hurts."

"You were shot, you lost some blood, but you'll be fine."

"Right." Then something in his face changed and a shudder passed through him as if the memories of recent events had resurfaced. He turned to Bourne. "Listen, I'm sorry. I've acted like a shit."

Bourne said nothing as he continued to drive.

"I was sent out to find you."

"I figured that out."

Marks rubbed his eyes with his knuckles in an effort to clear his head of the last cobwebs. "I work for Treadstone now."

Bourne pulled the car over to the side of the road. "Since when has Treadstone re-formed?"

"Since Willard found a backer."

"And who might that be?"

"Oliver Liss."

Bourne had to laugh. "Poor Willard. Out of the frying pan."

"That's it exactly." Marks's tone was mournful. "The whole thing's a total fuckup."

"And you're part of the fuckup."

Marks sighed. "Actually, I'm hoping to be part of the solution."

"Really? And how would that work?"

"Liss wants something you have—a ring."

Everyone wants the Dominion ring, Bourne thought, but he remained silent.

"I was supposed to get it from you."

"I'd be curious to know how you were going to do that."

"To be honest, I don't have a clue," Marks said, "and I'm no longer interested in that."

Bourne was silent.

Marks nodded. "You have a right to be skeptical. But I'm telling you the truth. Willard called just before I arrived at the house. He told me the mission had changed, that I was now to get you to Tineghir."

"In southeast Morocco."

"Ouarzazate, to be precise. Apparently, Arkadin is being brought there, too."

Bourne was silent for so long Marks felt compelled to say, "What are you thinking?"

"That Oliver Liss is no longer calling the shots at Treadstone."

"What makes you say that?"

"Liss would no more order you to get me to Ouarzazate than he would open a vein." He looked at Marks. "No, Peter, something's changed radically."

"I felt that myself, but what?" Marks took out his PDA and went on a number of government news sites. "Jesus," he said at last, "Liss was taken into custody by the Department of Justice pending an investigation into his role in illegal Black River dealings." He looked up. "But he was cleared of those charges weeks ago."

"I told you something's radically changed," Bourne said. "Willard is taking orders from another source."

"It has to be someone very high up the food chain to get the investigation reopened."

Bourne nodded. "And now you're as much in the dark as I am. It looks like your boss sold you down the river without even a second's thought."

"Frankly, this comes as no surprise." Marks rubbed his leg. His pain-filled exhale was a whistle of protest.

"There's a doctor in London who'll be discreet about the gunshot wound." Bourne put the car in gear and, checking for traffic, pulled out onto the road. "Just so you know, Diego led me into a trap. There were enemies waiting for me at the club."

"Did Moreno have to kill him?"

"We'll never know now," Bourne said. "But Ottavio saved my life back there. He didn't deserve to be shot down like a dog."

"Which brings me to who the hell was firing at us."

Bourne told him about Severus Domna and Jalal Essai without going into detail about Holly.

"I was attacked in London. I pulled an odd gold ring off the forefinger of my assailant's right hand." He fished around in his pockets. "Shit, I seem to have lost it."

"Scarlett found it. I gave it to her as a souvenir," Bourne said. "Every member of Severus Domna carries one."

"So this is all about an old Treadstone mission." Marks seemed to consider the implications for a moment. "Do you know why Alex Conklin wanted the laptop?"

"No idea," Bourne said, though he thought he did know now. Was there anyone besides Soraya and Moira he could trust? Though he knew Soraya and Peter were good friends he still didn't know whether he could trust Marks.

Marks shifted uncomfortably. "There's something I need to tell you. I'm afraid I roped Soraya into joining Treadstone."

Bourne knew that Typhon could not run successfully without her, so he assumed that Danziger was systematically dismantling the old CI and remaking it in the image of Bud Halliday's beloved NSA. Not that it was any of his concern. He hated and distrusted all espionage agencies. But he knew the good work that Typhon had accomplished under its original director, and later under Soraya. "What is Willard having her do?"

"You won't like this."

"Don't let that stop you."

"Her mission is to get close to Leonid Arkadin and the laptop."

"The same laptop that Conklin had me steal from Jalal Essai?"

"That's right."

Bourne wanted to laugh, but then Marks would ask questions he wasn't prepared to answer. Instead he said, "Was it your idea for Soraya to get close to Arkadin?"

"No, it was Willard's."

"Took him some time to come up with it?"

"He told me about it the day after I recruited her."

"So chances are he had the assignment in mind for her when he asked you to recruit her."

Marks shrugged, as if he couldn't see how it mattered.

But it mattered very much to Bourne, who saw in Willard's thinking a pattern. All the air went out of him. What if Soraya wasn't the first female Treadstone had recruited to keep an eye on its first graduate? What if Tracy had been working for Treadstone? Everything fit. The only reason Tracy would lie, deliberately putting herself in Arkadin's power, was so that he would hire her and keep her close, allowing her to pass on intel about both his whereabouts and his business ventures. A brilliant plan, which had worked until Tracy had been killed in Khartoum. Then Arkadin had vanished again. Willard needed a way to regain contact, so he had resorted to a tried-and-true Treadstone tactic. Arkadin used women like dish towels. They would be the last people he would suspect of keeping tabs on him.

"Soraya found him, I take it."

"She's with him now in Sonora and knows what to do," Marks said. "Do you think she can get him to Tineghir?"

"No," Bourne said. "But I can."

"How?"

Bourne smiled, remembering the entry in Noah Perlis's notebook. "I'll need to text her the information. She'll know what to do with it."

They were in the outskirts of London now. Bourne got off the motorway at the next exit and pulled over in a side street. Marks handed him his PDA and recited Soraya's number. Bourne punched it in, then pressed the SMS button, composed the text, and sent it.

After returning Marks's PDA, he resumed driving. "I don't know how it's happened," he said, "but Severus Domna is running Willard and Treadstone."

"What makes you say that?"

"Jalal Essai is Amazigh. He comes from the High Atlas Mountains."

"Ouarzazate."

"So is Willard taking orders from Essai or Severus Domna?"

"For the moment it doesn't matter," Bourne said,

"but my money's on Severus Domna. I doubt Essai has the clout to get Justice to take Liss into custody."

"Because Essai has broken away from Severus Domna, right?"

Bourne nodded. "Which makes the situation that much more interesting." He made a left turn, then a right. They were now on a street of neat, white Georgian row houses. A Skye terrier, industriously sniffing at steps, led his master along the pavement. The doctor was three houses down. "It's not often my enemies are at each other's throats."

"I take it you're going to Tineghir, despite the danger. That couldn't have been an easy decision."

"You have your own tough decision to make," Bourne said. "If you want to stay in this business, Peter, you'll have to return to DC to take care of Willard. Otherwise, one way or another, he'll wind up destroying you and Soraya."

24

FREDERICK WILLARD KNEW about the White Knights Lounge. He'd known about it for some time, ever since he had started compiling his own private dossier on Secretary of Defense Halliday. Bud Halliday possessed the kind of arrogance that all too often brings men of his lofty status down into the dust with the rest of the peons who painfully labor over their lives. These men—like Halliday—have become so inured to their power, they believe themselves above the law.

Willard had witnessed Bud Halliday's meetings with the Middle Eastern gentleman whom Willard had subsequently identified as Jalal Essai. This was information he'd had when he met with Benjamin El-Arian. He didn't know whether El-Arian was aware of the liaison, but in any event he wasn't about to tell him. Some information was meant to be shared only with the right person.

And that person appeared now, right on time, flanked by his bodyguards like a Roman emperor.

M. Errol Danziger came over to where Willard sat and slid into the ancient banquette. Its stained and ripped Naugahyde skin spoke of decades' worth of benders.

"This is a real shithole," Danziger said. He looked like he wished he'd worn a full-body condom. "You've slid down in the world since you left us."

They were sitting in an anonymously named rheumatic bar-and-grill off one of the expressways that linked Washington with Virginia. Only pub-crawlers of a certain age and liver toxicity found it inviting; everyone else ignored it as the eyesore it was. The place stank of sour beer and months-old frying oil. It was impossible to say what colors its walls were painted. An old nondigital juke played Willie Nelson and John Mellencamp, but no one was dancing or, by the looks of them, listening. Someone at the end of the bar groaned.

Willard rubbed his hands together. "What can I get you?"

"Out of here," Danziger said, trying not to breathe too deeply. "The sooner the better."

"No one we know or who'd recognize us would come within a country mile of this cesspit," Willard said. "Can you think of a better place for us to meet?"

Danziger made a disagreeable face. "Get on with it, man."

"You've got a problem," Willard said without further preamble.

"I've got a lot of problems, but they're none of your business."

"Don't be so hasty."

"Listen, you're out of CI, which means you're no-body. I agreed to this meet out of—I don't know what—acknowledgment of your past services. But now I see it was a waste of time."

Willard, unruffled, would not be taken off topic. "This particular problem concerns your boss."

Danziger sat back as if trying to get as far away from Willard as the banquette would allow.

Willard spread his hands. "Care to listen? If not, you're free to leave."

"Go ahead."

"Bud Halliday has, shall we say, an off-the-reservation relationship with a man named Jalal Essai."

Danziger bristled. "Are you trying to blackmail—?"

"Relax. Their relationship is strictly business."

"What's that to me?"

"Everything," Willard said. "Essai is poison for him, and for you. He's a member of a group known as Severus Domna."

"Never heard of it."

"Very few people have. But it was someone in Severus Domna who got Justice to take another look at Oliver Liss and incarcerate him while it's investigating."

A drunk began to wail, trying to duet with Connie Francis. One of Danziger's gorillas went over to him and shut him up.

Danziger frowned. "Are you saying the US government takes orders from—what?—can I assume from this one name that Severus Domna is a Muslim organization?"

"Severus Domna has members in virtually every country around the globe."

"Christian *and* Muslim?"

"And, presumably, Jewish, Hindu, Jain, Buddhist, whatever other religion you'd care to name."

Danziger snorted. "Preposterous! It's absurd to think of men from different religions agreeing on a day of the week to meet, let alone working together in a global organization. And for what?"

"All I know is that its objectives are not our objectives."

Danziger reacted as if Willard had insulted him. "*Our* objectives? You're a *civilian* now." He made the word sound ugly and demeaning.

"The head of Treadstone can hardly be classified as a civilian," Willard said.

"Treadstone, huh? Better to call it *Headstone*." He laughed raucously. "You and Headstone are nothing to me. This meeting is terminated."

As he began to slide out of the banquette, Willard played his ace. "Working with a foreign group is treason, which is punishable by execution. Imagine the ignominy, if you live that long."

"What the hell does that mean?"

"Imagine you in a world without Bud Halliday."

Danziger paused. For the first time since he walked in, he seemed unsure of himself.

"Tell me this," Willard continued, "why would I waste our time on nonsense, Director? What would I have to gain?"

Danziger subsided back onto the banquette. "What do you have to gain by telling me this fairy tale?"

"If you thought it was a fairy tale, I would be talking to myself."

"Frankly, I don't know what to think," Danziger said. "For the moment, however, I'm willing to listen."

"That's all I ask," Willard said. But, of course, it wasn't. He wanted much more from Danziger, and now he knew he was going to get it.

On the way back to the office, Karpov had his driver pull over. Out of sight of everyone, he vomited into a clump of tall grass. It wasn't that he'd never killed anyone before. On the contrary, he'd shot a great many miscreants. What made his stomach rebel was the situation he was in, which felt like the underbelly of a rotting fish or the bottom of a sewer. There must be some way out of the coffin he found himself in. Unfortunately, he was caught between President Imov and Viktor Cherkesov. Imov was a problem all rising *siloviks* had to deal with, but now he was beholden to Cherkesov and he was certain that sooner or later Cherkesov would ask him for a favor that would curl his toes. Looking into the future, he could see those favors multiplying, taking a toll until they shredded him completely. Clever, clever Cherkesov! In giving him what he wanted, Cherkesov had found the one way around his, Karpov's, incorruptibility. There was nothing to do but what good Russian soldiers had done for centuries: Put one foot in front of the other and move forward through the mounting muck.

He told himself this was all in a good cause—getting rid of Maslov and the Kazanskaya was surely worth any inconvenience to him. But that was like saying *I was only following orders,* and depressed him further.

He returned to the backseat of his car, brooding and murderous. Five minutes later his driver missed a turn.

"Stop the car," Karpov ordered.

"Here?"

"Right here."

His driver stared at him in the rearview mirror. "But the traffic—"

"Just do as you're told!"

The driver stopped the car. Karpov got out, opened the driver's door, and, reaching in, hauled the man out from behind the wheel. Unmindful of the honking horns and squealing brakes of the vehicles forced to detour around them, he bounced the driver's head off the side of the car. The driver slid to his knees, and Karpov drove a knee into his chin. Teeth came flying out of the driver's mouth. Karpov kicked him several times as he lay on the pavement, then he slid behind the wheel, slammed the door shut, and took off.

I should have been an American, he thought as he wiped his lips over and over with the back of his hand. But he was a patriot, he loved Russia. It was a pity Russia didn't love him back. Russia was a pitiless mistress, heartless and cruel. *I should have been an American.* Inventing a melody, he sang this phrase to himself as if it were a lullaby, and in fact it made him feel marginally better. He concentrated on bringing down Maslov and how he would reorganize FSB-2 when Imov named him director.

His first order of business, however, was dealing with the three moles inside FSB-2. Armed with the names Bukin had vomited up, he parked the car in front of the nineteenth-century building housing FSB-2 and trotted up the steps. He knew the directorates that the moles worked in. On the way up in the elevator, he took out his pistol.

He ordered the first mole out of his office. When the mole balked, Karpov brandished the pistol in his face. *Siloviks* all over the floor emerged from their dens, their secretaries and assistants picked their heads up from their mind-numbing paperwork to follow this unfolding drama. A crowd formed, which was all the better, as far as Karpov was concerned. With the first mole in tow, he went into the second mole's office. He was on the phone, turned away from the door. As he was swinging back, Karpov shot him in the head. The first mole flinched as the victim flew backward, his arms wide, the phone flying, and slammed into the plate-glass window. The victim fell to the floor, leaving behind an interesting abstract pattern of blood and bits of brain and bone on the glass. As stunned *siloviks* crowded into the doorway, Karpov snapped photos with his cell phone.

Pushing his way through the agitated throng, he frog-marched the now shivering first mole to his next stop, a floor up. By the time they appeared, news had spread and a crowd of *siloviks* greeted them in silent astonishment.

As Karpov was dragging his charge toward the office of the third mole, Colonel Lemtov shouldered his way to the front of the group.

"Colonel Karpov," he shouted, "what is the meaning of this outrage?"

"Get out of my way, Colonel. I won't tell you twice."

"Who are you to—"

"I'm an emissary of President Imov," Karpov said.

"Call his office, if you like. Better yet, call Cherkesov himself."

Then he used the mole to shove Colonel Lemtov aside. Dakaev, the third mole, was not in his office. Karpov was about to contact security when a terrified secretary informed him that her boss was chairing a meeting. She pointed out the conference room, and Karpov took his prisoner in there.

Twelve men sat around a rectangular table. Dakaev was at the head of the table. Being a directorate chief, he would be more valuable alive than dead. Karpov shoved the first mole against the table. Everyone but Dakaev pushed back their chairs as far as they could. For his part, Dakaev sat as he had when Karpov barged in, hands clasped in front of him on the tabletop. Unlike Colonel Lemtov, he didn't express outrage or appear confused. In fact, Karpov saw, he knew perfectly well what was happening.

That would have to change. Karpov dragged the first mole along the table, scattering papers, pens, and glasses of water, until the man fetched up in front of Dakaev. Then, staring into Dakaev's eyes, Karpov pressed the muzzle of his pistol into the back of the first mole's head.

"Please," the prisoner said, urinating down his leg.

Karpov squeezed the trigger. The first mole's head slammed against the table, bounced up, and settled into a pool of his own blood. A Pollock-like pattern spattered across Dakaev's suit, shirt, tie, and freshly shaven face.

Karpov gestured with the pistol. "Get up."

Dakaev stood. "Are you going to shoot me, too?"

"Eventually, perhaps." Karpov grabbed him by his tie. "That will be entirely up to you."

"I understand," Dakaev said. "I want immunity."

"Immunity? I'll give you immunity." Karpov slammed the barrel of the pistol against the side of his head.

Dakaev reeled sideways, bouncing off a terrified *silovik* paralyzed in his chair. Karpov bent over Dakaev, who lay huddled half against the wall.

"You'll tell me everything you know about your work and your contacts—names, places, dates, every fucking thing, no matter how minute—then I'll decide what to do with you."

He hauled Dakaev to his feet. "The rest of you, get back to whatever the hell you were doing."

Out on the floor he encountered absolute silence. Everyone stood like wooden soldiers, unmoving, afraid even to take a breath. Colonel Lemtov would not meet his eyes as he took the bleeding Dakaev over to the bank of elevators.

They went down, past the basement, into the bowels of the building where the holding cells had been hewn out of the naked rock. It was cold and damp. The guards wore greatcoats and fur hats with fur earflaps, as if it were the dead of winter. When anyone spoke, his breath formed clouds in front of his face.

Karpov took Dakaev to the last cell on the left. It contained a metal chair bolted to the raw concrete floor, an industrial-size stainless-steel sink, a toilet made of the same material, and a board projecting from one wall on which was a thin mattress. There was a large drain situated beneath the chair.

"Tools of the trade," Karpov said as he pushed Dakaev into the chair. "I admit to being a little rusty, but I'm sure that won't make a difference to you."

"All this melodrama is unnecessary," Dakaev said. "I have no allegiance, I'll tell you whatever you want to know."

"Of that I have no doubt." Karpov began to run the water in the sink. "On the other hand, a self-confessed man of no allegiance can hardly be trusted to tell the truth willingly."

"But I—"

Karpov shoved the muzzle of the pistol into his mouth. "Listen to me, my agnostic friend. A man without allegiance to something or someone isn't worth the beating heart inside him. Before I hear your confession, I will have to teach you the value of allegiance. When you leave here—unless you do so feet-first—you will be a loyal member of FSB-2. Never again will people like Dimitri Maslov be able to tempt you. You will be incorruptible."

Karpov kicked his prisoner out of the chair onto his hands and knees. Grabbing him by his collar, he bent him over the sink, which was now filled with ice-cold water.

"Now we begin," he said. And shoved Dakaev's head under the water.

Soraya watched Arkadin dancing with Moira, presumably to make her jealous. They were in one of Puerto Peñasco's all-night cantinas, filled with shift workers coming and going from the nearby maquiladoras. A sad ranchera was bawling from a jukebox, luridly lit up like someone's bad idea of the UFO in *Close Encounters of the Third Kind*.

Soraya, nursing a black coffee, watched Arkadin's hips moving as if they were filled with mercury. The man could dance! Then she pulled out her PDA and studied the texts from Peter Marks. The last one contained instructions on how to lure Arkadin to Tineghir. How did Peter come up with this intel?

She had hidden her shock at seeing Moira behind her professional facade. The moment she had climbed aboard the yacht she'd felt the floor fall out from under her. The game had changed so radically that she had to play catch-up, and fast. Which was why she had hung on each word of the conversation between Moira and Arkadin not only for content but also for tonal nuance, any clue as to why Moira was actually here. What did she want from Arkadin? Surely the deal Moira was making with him was as bogus as her own.

Outside, the night was very dark, without moonlight. Because of the cloud cover, only a wan halo of stars toward the crown of the sky was visible. Inside, the cantina stank of beer and body odor. The room was raucous with a desperation tinged by hopelessness and despair. She felt surrounded by people for whom tomorrow didn't exist.

She wished that she and Moira could talk to each other, if only for the briefest moment, but under Arkadin's eye that was impossible. Even going to the ladies' room at the same time would doubtless arouse his suspicion. She didn't know Moira's cell number, so texting her was out. There remained only a verbal conversation laced with coded messages. If they were on parallel paths, or even by chance the same one, it was essential they not get in each other's way.

Arkadin and Moira were dripping sweat when they

returned to the table. Arkadin ordered beers for them, and another coffee for Soraya. Whatever might happen tomorrow, he was clearly enjoying being with the two women tonight.

"Moira," Soraya said, "do you know anything about the Middle East, or is your expertise strictly in the Americas?"

"Mexico, Colombia, Bolivia, and to some extent Brazil are my territories."

"And you work alone?"

"I have a company, but right now I'm on special assignment to Berengária Moreno." Moira gestured with her chin. "And you?"

"My own company, though there's a conglomerate that's looking for a hostile takeover."

"Multinational?"

"Strictly American."

Moira nodded. "Import-export, you said?"

Soraya stirred some sugar into her coffee. "That's right."

"You might be able to use my, ah, expertise against hostile bidders."

"Thank you, but no." Soraya sipped her coffee, then put the cup back in its saucer. "I have my own, ah, enforcers."

"What do you call a thought in a woman's head?" Arkadin leaned forward, looking from one to the other. "A tourist!" He laughed so hard he almost choked on his beer. Then, noting their somber expressions, "Shit, lighten up, ladies, we're here to have fun, not talk business."

Moira looked at him for a moment. "What do you

get when you cross a Russian with a Vietnamese? A car thief that can't drive."

Soraya laughed. "*Now* we're having fun."

Arkadin smiled. "Have any more?"

"Let's see." Moira drummed her fingers on the table. "How about this? Two Russians and a Mexican are in a car. Who's driving? The police."

Arkadin laughed and shook his finger at Moira. "Where do you pick up these jokes?"

"In prison," Moira said. "Roberto Corellos loves making Russians the butt of jokes."

"Time to switch to tequila," Arkadin said, signaling the waiter. "Bring a bottle," he said to the young woman who came over. "Something fine. A reposado or añejo."

Instead of another ranchera, the jukebox began to play "Twenty-four Hours from Tulsa." Gene Pitney's high twang rang out over the laughter and shouts of the drunken patrons. But morning was coming, and with it a change in the clientele. As the night owls slowly staggered out, the night-shift people from the maquiladora drifted in, heads aching, tails dragging. There were fewer of them, as well, most of them stumbling home to fall into bed without taking off their clothes.

Before the tequila got to the table, Arkadin had grabbed Moira's hand and was swinging her onto the dance floor, which for the first time all night was larger than a postage stamp. He held her close while they swayed to the Burt Bacharach melody.

"You're something of a smart-ass," he said, smiling like a shark.

"It didn't come easy," she said.

He laughed. "I can only imagine."

"Don't bother."

Arkadin swung her around. "You're wasting your time in South America. You should come to work for me."

"Before I set up Corellos's murder?"

"Let that be your last assignment." He stuck his nose into the side of her neck and inhaled deeply. "How are you going to do it?"

"I thought you said no business."

"Just this one bit, then it's all fun. I swear."

"Corellos is addicted to women. I have a connection to his supplier. When is a man more vulnerable than after sex? I'll find someone who's good with a knife."

Arkadin pulled her hips harder into him. "I like it. Set it up right away."

"I want a bonus."

He nuzzled her neck, licked her sweat. "I'll give you anything you want."

"Then I'm yours."

Karpov's cell phone rang while he was in the process of reprogramming Dimitri Maslov's mole. Dakaev was drowning, or more precisely, he believed he was drowning, which was, after all, the point. But ten minutes later, when Dakaev was back in his stainless-steel chair and Karpov was pouring tea into a glass, his cell rang again. This time he answered it. A familiar voice was on the other end of the line.

"Jason!" Karpov cried. "How excellent to hear your voice."

"Are you busy?"

Karpov glanced over at Dakaev, slumped over, his

chin on his chest. He looked barely human, which was also the point. You couldn't build something new without tearing down what had been there before.

"Busy? Yes. But never too busy for you. What can I do for you?"

"I assume you know Dimitri Maslov's lieutenant, Vylacheslav Oserov."

"You assume correctly."

"Do you think you can find a way to get him somewhere?"

"If you mean somewhere like hell, yes I can."

Bourne laughed in his ear. "I was thinking of something a little less terminal. A place, let us say, in Morocco."

Karpov took a sip of tea, which was in desperate need of sugar. "May I ask why you need Oserov in Morocco?"

"He's bait, Boris. I intend to catch Arkadin."

Karpov thought of his sojourn in Sonora, his deal with Arkadin, and added him to the list of President Imov and Viktor Cherkesov. He had promised Arkadin his chance at Oserov, but fuck that. *I'm too old and too bloody-minded to owe so many dangerous people so much,* he thought. *One less is a step toward none.*

Then he looked over at Dakaev, the conduit to Dimitri Maslov and, therefore, Vylacheslav Oserov. After what he had just been through, he had no doubt that the prisoner would jump at the chance to do what Karpov asked of him.

"Tell me in detail what you need done." Listening, Karpov smiled contentedly. When Bourne was finished, he chuckled deeply. "Jason, my friend, what I wouldn't give to be you!"

* * *

Just after sunrise they were all sweaty enough to want to go into the water. At the convent, Arkadin gave Moira and Soraya oversize T-shirts. He was in surfer trunks that came down to his knees. His upper body and limbs were a museum of tattoos that, if interpreted correctly, traced his career in the *grupperovka*.

The three of them waded through the surf, pulled and pushed by the waves rushing onto the golden sand. The sky was still pink, paling out to the color of butter. Gulls dipped and swooped over their heads and tiny fish nibbled at their feet and ankles. The water came up and slapped them in the face, making them laugh like children. The unalloyed joy of being let free in the ocean.

Out beyond the surf line, Moira thought it odd that Arkadin kept diving for seashells rather than stare at her breasts through the wet T-shirt, especially after the way he'd been dancing with her at the cantina. She had found out little enough information about Soraya's mission from the coded conversation Soraya had started and Arkadin had nipped off with his misogynistic joke.

While Arkadin was still trolling for shells, she set off after Soraya to see if the two of them could speak briefly. Diving through an incoming wave, she began to swim out to where Soraya was drifting on her back, but something caught her left ankle, jerking her back.

Jackknifing her body, she looked behind her. Arkadin had hold of her. She pushed back at him, palms against his chest, but he only drew her more closely to him. She rose up, breaking the surface, and found herself face-to-face with him.

"What do you think you're doing?" She scrubbed the sheeting water off her face. "I can't stand properly."

He let her go immediately. "I've had enough and I'm hungry."

Moira turned and shouted to Soraya, who plunged down from her float and paddled over.

"We're going to breakfast," Moira said.

The two women waded out of the surf with Arkadin just behind them. They had reached the high-tide line, hillocks of dry sand ahead, when Arkadin bent over. Using the scythe-like edge of the seashell, he severed the tendons at the back of Moira's left knee.

25

THE VILLAGE OF Whitney, Oxfordshire, lay twelve miles west of Oxford, on the Windrush River. All that was missing were Hobbits and Orcs. Bourne drove out from London in a rental car. The afternoon was cool and dry with peeks of sun now and again through the rolling clouds. He hadn't lied to Peter Marks; he had every intention of going to Tineghir. But first there was something he needed to do.

Basil Bayswater lived in a thatch-roofed cottage straight out of a Tolkien novel. It had quirky round windows and flower shoots springing up in neat beds lining a white gravel walkway that led up to the front door. This door was thick and wooden, with a roaring brass lion's-head knocker in its center. Bourne used it.

Several moments later a man quite a bit younger than he had expected opened the door.

"Yes? How may I help you?" He had long hair brushed straight back off his wide forehead, dark, watchful eyes, and a strong chin.

"I'm looking for Basil Bayswater," Bourne said.

"You're looking at him."

"I don't think so," Bourne said.

"Ah, you must mean Professor Basil Bayswater. I'm afraid my father passed away three years ago."

Moira screamed as blood bloomed in the water like a stranded jellyfish. Arkadin caught her as she canted over.

"My God," Soraya cried, "what've you done?"

Moira continued to scream, bent double, clutching her left leg.

Arkadin, ignoring Soraya for the moment, bared his teeth at Moira. "Did you think I didn't recognize you?"

Something icy congealed in the pit of Moira's stomach.

"What do you mean?"

"I saw you in Bali. You were with Bourne."

In her mind's eye she saw the flight through the village of Tenganan, and then Bourne being shot by a sniper hidden in the forest.

Her eyes opened wide.

"Yeah, that was me." He laughed, throwing the bloody seashell up in the air and catching it as if it were a ball. "You were with Bourne. You're his lover. And now fate has brought you to me."

Soraya was both outraged and terrified. "What the hell is happening here?"

"We're about to find out." Arkadin turned to her.

"This is Jason Bourne's lover, but perhaps the two of you know each other."

With a force of will, Soraya kept her panic down. "I don't know what you're talking about."

"Okay, I'll spell it out for you. I never bought your story, but I wasn't going to send you away until I found out what you really wanted. I strongly suspect Willard sent you. He tried this trick on me once before with a woman named Tracy Atherton. He sent her to keep an eye on me, to report back on all my business dealings. And it worked. She was dead by the time I figured it out. But you I fingered from the get-go, because Willard is a creature of habits, especially ones that have worked for him."

"Let her go," Soraya said, more agitated with each passing moment.

"I might do that," Arkadin said. "I might even let her live. But that's entirely up to you."

Soraya walked over and took Moira away from him. Gently and slowly, she lowered her to the ground. Then she slid her wet shirt over her head and, winding it around Moira's left thigh, pulled it as tight as she could and tied it. By that time Moira had passed out, from either the shock or the pain, or both.

"It's you I want," Arkadin continued. "You're the one talking about Khartoum, you're the one who wants to get me there. You tell me who you are and what you know and I'll consider lightening Moira's punishment."

"We need to get her to the nearest hospital," Soraya said. "This wound has to be cleaned out and disinfected as soon as possible."

"Again"—Arkadin spread his hands—"up to you."

Soraya looked down at the back of Moira's knee. *Dear God*, she wondered, *will she ever walk normally again?* She knew the longer they waited to get Moira into the hands of a competent surgeon, the worse off she'd be. She'd seen tendons severed like this. They weren't easy to repair, and who knew how badly the nerves were affected?

She let out a long breath. "What do you want to know?"

"For starters, who are you?"

"Soraya Moore."

"*The* Soraya Moore, director of Typhon?"

"Not anymore." She stroked Moira's damp hair. "Willard has resurrected Treadstone."

"No wonder he wants to keep an eye on me.
What else?"

"Plenty," Soraya said. "I'll tell you on the way to hospital."

Arkadin loomed over her. "You'll tell me now."

"You might as well kill us both right here."

Arkadin cursed her, but in the end he acceded to her demand. Hefting Moira in his arms, he carried her back to the convent. While he slid her into the backseat, Soraya went to get a shirt. She was rooting through Arkadin's desk when he found her.

"Fuck, no," he said and, grabbing her wrist, dragged her outside.

Half throwing her into the passenger's seat of the car, he said, "I will kill you as soon as look at you." Then he went around the front of the car, slid behind the wheel, and fired the ignition.

"You're right." Soraya kept Moira's leg elevated as

they sped through the outskirts of Puerto Peñasco. "Willard wanted me to get close to you, to report on your whereabouts and your business dealings."

"And? I sense there's something more."

"There is," she said. She knew she had to sell this part perfectly. She no longer believed absolutely in her ability to outsmart him, but this much she needed to do. "Willard has become interested in a man I'm sure you know, because he works for Maslov: Vylacheslav Oserov."

Arkadin's knuckles turned white on the steering wheel, but his voice betrayed nothing of what he must be feeling. "Why would Willard be interested in Oserov?"

"I have no idea," Soraya said. This much, at least, was true. "But I do know that yesterday a Treadstone agent ID'd Oserov in Marrakech. He tracked Oserov out into the Atlas Mountains, to a village called Tineghir."

They arrived at Santa Fe General, on Morua Avenue, but Arkadin made no move to get out of the car.

"What was Oserov doing in Tineghir?"

"Looking for a ring."

Arkadin shook his head. "Speak plainly."

"This particular ring somehow unlocks a hidden file on a laptop hard drive." She looked at him. "I know, I don't understand it, either." All of this information had been in the last text message she had received from Peter. She opened the rear door. "Can we get Moira into the ER, please?"

Arkadin got out of the car and slammed the door she had just opened. "I want more."

"I've told you all I know."

He stared into her face. "You see what happens to people who fuck with me."

"I'm not fucking with you," Soraya said. "I've betrayed a trust, what more do you want from me?"

"Everything," he said. "I want everything."

They rushed Moira into the emergency room. While the personnel were hooking her up and taking her vitals, Soraya asked for the name of the best neurosurgeon in Sonora. She spoke idiomatic Spanish; furthermore, she looked Latina. These attributes opened doors for her. When she got the surgeon's private number, she called him herself. His PA said he was unavailable until Soraya threatened to find the PA and wring his neck. The surgeon came on the line shortly thereafter. Soraya described Moira's injury and told him where they were. He said considering a cash bonus of two thousand American dollars was involved, he'd be over immediately.

"Let's go," Arkadin said the moment she disconnected.

"I'm not leaving Moira."

"We have further business to discuss."

"Then we can discuss it here."

"Back at the convent."

"I'm not going to fuck you," she said.

"Thank God, fucking you would be like fucking a scorpion."

The irony of his comment made her laugh despite her worry and despair. She went to look for coffee, and he followed her.

Bourne drove to Oxford as fast as he dared without attracting the attention of the police. The city was precisely as he had left it both times he had been there.

The quiet streets, the quaint stores, the lifelong denizens going about their chores, the tearooms, the bookstores, all like a miniature created by an obsessive eighteenth-century academic. Driving its streets was like visiting the inside of a snow globe.

Bourne parked near where Chrissie had left her Range Rover when they had come together, and he trotted up the steps of the Centre for the Study of Ancient Documents. Professor Liam Giles was also right where he had been when they had last been there, bent over his desk in his voluminous office. He looked up as Bourne entered, blinking owlishly, as if he didn't recognize him. Bourne saw that it wasn't Giles after all, but another man of Giles's approximate build and age.

"Where's Professor Giles?"

"On leave," the man said.

"I'm looking for him."

"So I gather. May I ask why?"

"Where is he?"

The man blinked his owlish blink. "Away."

Bourne had looked up Giles's official bio on the way over, which was available on the Oxford University Web site.

"It's about his daughter."

The man behind Giles's desk blinked. "Is she ill?"

"I'm not at liberty to say. Where can I find Professor Giles?"

"I don't think—"

"It's urgent," Bourne said. "A matter of life or death."

"Are you being deliberately melodramatic, sir?"

Bourne showed the man the EMS credentials he'd lifted after the crash. "I'm quite serious."

"Dear me." The man gestured. "He's in the loo, at the moment. Battling the eel pie he ingested last night, I shouldn't wonder."

The neurosurgeon was young, dark as an Indian, with the long, delicate fingers of a classical pianist. He had very delicate features, so he wasn't, in fact, an Indian. But he was a hard-nosed businessman who would not proceed until Soraya had pressed a roll of bills into his hand. Then he rushed away from them, consulting with the ER doctors who had done the workup on Moira while he strode toward the OR.

Soraya drank her shitty coffee without tasting it, but ten minutes later, while she paced the hallway uselessly, it began to burn a hole in her stomach, so when Arkadin suggested they get something to eat she agreed. They found a restaurant not far away from the hospital. Soraya checked to make sure it wasn't colonized by insects before she sat down. They ordered their food, then sat and waited, sitting across from each other but looking elsewhere, or at least Soraya was.

"I saw you without your top," Arkadin said, "and I liked what I saw."

Soraya snapped into focus. "Fuck you."

"She was an enemy," he said, referring to Moira. "What law is she protected by?"

Soraya stared out the window at a street as unfamiliar to her as the dark side of the moon.

The food came and Arkadin began to eat. Soraya watched a couple of young women with too much makeup and too little clothing on their way to work.

Latinas showing off their bodies with such casualness still astonished her. Their culture was so far from hers. And yet she felt right in tune with the aura of sorrow here. Hopelessness she could understand. It had been the cultural lot of her gender from time immemorial, and was the major reason she had chosen the clandestine services where, despite the usual gender bias, she was able to assert herself in ways that made her feel good about herself. Now, for the first time, she saw those girls in their too-tight tops and too-short skirts in a different light. Those clothes were a way—perhaps their only way—to assert themselves in a culture that continually demeaned and devalued them.

"If Moira dies, or if she can't walk—"

"Spare me the toothless threats," he said, mopping up the last of his huevos rancheros.

That was Arkadin's business, she thought. No matter what he might think to the contrary, he was in the business of demeaning and devaluing women. That was the subtext in everything he said and did. He had no heart, no remorse, no guilt, no soul—nothing, in short, that defined and distinguished a human being. *If he isn't a human being,* she thought with a kind of irrational terror, *what is he?*

The men's loo was five doors down from Professor Giles's office. Giles was clearly being sick behind the closed door of one of the stalls. A sour stench had pervaded the room, and Bourne strode over to the window and shoved it open as far as it would go. A sticky breeze slowly stirred the stench as a witch will her bubbling pot.

Bourne waited until the noises had subsided. "Professor Giles."

For some time, there was no answer. Then the stall door was wrenched open and Professor Giles, looking distinctly green around the gills, staggered out past Bourne. He bent over the sink, turned on the cold water, and buried his head beneath the flow.

Bourne leaned against the wall, arms crossed over his chest. When Giles picked his head up, Bourne handed him a handful of paper towels. The professor took them without comment, wiping his face and hair. It was only as he threw the wadded towels into the trash that he appeared to recognize Bourne.

At once his back stiffened and he stood up straight. "Ah, the prodigal returns," he said in his most professorial tone.

"Did you expect me?"

"Not really. On the other hand, I'm hardly surprised to find you here." He gave Bourne a wan smile. "Bad pennies continue to turn up."

"Professor, I'd like you to once again get in touch with your chess-playing colleague."

Giles frowned. "That may not be so easy. He's reclusive and he doesn't like answering questions."

I can imagine, Bourne thought. "Nevertheless, I'd like you to try."

"All right," Giles said.

"By the way, what's his name?"

Giles hesitated. "James."

"James what?"

Another hesitation. "Weatherley."

"Not Basil Bayswater?"

The professor turned away, facing the door.

"What question do you want to put to him?"

"I'd like him to describe the afterlife."

Giles, who had been headed for the door, paused, turning slowly back to Bourne. "I beg your pardon?"

"Since Basil Bayswater's son buried him three years ago," Bourne said, "I would think he'd be in a perfect position to tell me what it's like to be dead."

"I told you," Giles said, somewhat sullenly, "his name is James Weatherley."

Bourne took him by the elbow. "Professor, no one believes that, not even you." He moved Giles away from the door to the far end of the loo. "Now you'll tell me why you lied to me." When the professor remained silent, Bourne went on. "You never needed to call Bayswater for the translation of the engraving inside the ring, you already knew it."

"Yes, I suppose I did. Neither of us was truthful with the other." He shrugged. "Well, what can you expect from life? Nothing is ever what it seems."

"You're Severus Domna."

Giles's smile had gained a bit more traction. "There's no point denying it, now that you're about to hand over the ring."

At that moment, as if he'd had his ear to the door, the man who had been behind the professor's desk entered the loo. With the SIG Sauer in his hand he looked quite a bit less owlish. Immediately two more men, larger, muscular, armed with silenced pistols, came in just behind him. They fanned out, their weapons trained on Bourne.

"As you can see," Professor Giles said, "I haven't given you a choice."

26

VYLACHESLAV OSEROV WAS nursing not only his facial wounds but also a planet-size grudge against Arkadin, the man who had tormented him for years, and who was the cause of his hideous disfigurement in Bangalore. The chemical fire had eaten through layers of skin and into the flesh itself, which made recovery difficult and a return to normalcy impossible.

For days after he returned to Moscow, he had been swathed in thick bandages through which seeped not only blood but a thick yellow fluid whose stench made him gag. He had refused all painkillers and when the physician, on Maslov's orders, tried to inject him with a sedative, he broke the man's arm and very nearly his neck.

Every day, Oserov's howls of pain could be heard all over the offices, even in the toilets, where the other men congregated for a brief respite. His cries of agony were so dreadful, like an animal being dismembered, they frightened and demoralized even Maslov's hardened criminals. Maslov himself was forced to tie him to a column, like Odysseus to the mast, and tape his mouth shut in order to give him and his people some respite. By this time, Oserov had deep gouges on his temples, bloody like tribal scars, where in his agony he had dug his nails through the skin that had not been burned away.

In a way, he had become an infant. Maslov couldn't send him to a hospital or a clinic without awkward questions being asked, an FSB-2 investigation being initiated. So Maslov had tried to set him up at Oserov's apartment, which was in a dreadful condition of disrepair, having been reclaimed, like an abandoned jungle temple, by insects and rodents alike. No one could be induced to stay there with Oserov, and Oserov could not be expected to survive there on his own. The office was the only option.

Oserov could no longer look at himself. No vampire avoided mirrors more assiduously than he did. Also, he hated being seen in sunlight, any strong light, for that matter, behavior that gave rise to his new moniker among the Kazanskaya, *Die Vampyr*.

He sat now brooding in Maslov's offices, which by necessity were moved every week. In this room, which Maslov had designated his, the lights were out and the shades drawn against the daylight. One lamp across the room from where he slumped down cast a small circle of illumination across the scarred floorboards.

The fiasco in Bangalore, his failure to kill Arkadin or, at least, gain the laptop for Maslov, had scarred him in more ways than one. His physical appearance had been compromised. Worse, he had lost the confidence of his boss. Without the Kazanskaya, Oserov was nothing. Without Maslov's confidence, he was nothing within the Kazanskaya. For days now he had been racking his brains as to how to get back in Maslov's good graces, how to restore the majesty of his position as field commander.

No plan, however, had presented itself. It meant nothing to him that his mind, torn apart by the agony of his wounds, was scarcely able to put two coherent thoughts together. His only thought was of revenge against Arkadin, and to get for Maslov what he wanted most: that accursed laptop. Oserov didn't know why his boss wanted it, and he didn't care. His lot was to do or die, that's how it had been ever since he had joined the Kazanskaya and that was how it would remain.

But life was strange. For Oserov salvation came from an unexpected quarter. A call came through. So sunk in black thoughts was he that at first he refused to take it. Then his assistant told him that it had come in on a scrambled cell line, and he knew who it must be. Still, he resisted, thinking that at the moment he had neither the interest nor the patience for anything Yasha Dakaev had to report.

Oserov's assistant poked his head in the door, which he had strict orders never to do.

"What?" Oserov barked.

"He says it's urgent," his assistant told him, and quickly withdrew.

"Goddammit," Oserov muttered, and picked up the phone. "Yasha, this better be fucking good."

"It is." Dakaev's voice sounded flat and faraway, but then he was always having to find out-of-the-way nooks and crannies in the FSB-2's offices to make his calls. "I have a line on Arkadin's movements."

"At last!" Oserov sat up straight. He heart seemed to pump at full speed again.

"According to the report that just came across my desk, he's on his way to Morocco," Dakaev said. "Ouarzazate, a village in the High Atlas Mountains called Tineghir, to be precise."

"What the fuck is he going to do in Buttfuck, Morocco?"

"That I don't know," Dakaev said. "But our intel says he's on his way."

This is my chance, Oserov thought, jumping up. *If I don't take it, I might as well eat my Tokarev.* For the first time since that last night in Bangalore, he felt galvanized. His failure had paralyzed him, he had been gnawing at himself from the inside out. He'd become disoriented with shame and rage.

He called his assistant in and gave him the particulars.

"Get me the fuck out of here," he ordered. "Book me on the first flight out of Moscow that's heading in the right direction."

"Does Maslov know you're off again?"

"Does your wife know that your mistress's name is Ivana Istvanskaya?"

His assistant beat a hasty retreat.

He turned away and started formulating a plan. Now that he'd been given a second chance, he vowed he would make the most of it.

* * *

Bourne raised his hands. At the same time, he kicked Professor Giles in the small of the back. As Giles, arms flailing, stumbled toward the three gunmen, Bourne whirled, took a long stride toward the open window, and dived through it.

He hit the ground running at full speed, but soon enough, as the adjoining university building loomed up, he was required to slow his pace to match that of Oxford's denizens. Pulling off his black overcoat, he stuffed it in a trash bin. He looked for and found a knot of adults, professors most likely, walking from one building to the next, and slipped into their midst.

Moments later he saw the two Severus Domna gunmen as they raced from the Centre. They immediately split up in a military-like formation.

One of the men came toward him, but he hadn't yet seen Bourne, who eeled his way to the opposite side of the knot. The professors were debating the merits of the right-wing German philosophers and, inevitably, the effect Nietzsche had on the Nazis, Hitler in particular.

Unless he had a chance to get to Professor Giles alone, which he doubted, Bourne had no desire for another physical encounter with Severus Domna. The organization was like a Hydra: Lop off one head and two took its place.

The gunman, who had hidden his weapon beneath his overcoat, approached the knot of professors, oblivious as they were locked in their philosophical ivory tower. Bourne presented the gunman with his anonymous back. The gunman would be looking for a man in a black overcoat. Bourne was happy to take any edge he could.

The knot of professors trotted up the steps and, in elegant fashion, poured into the university building. Bourne, debating the finer points of Old German with a white-haired professor, stepped across the threshold.

The gunman reacted as he glimpsed Bourne's reflection in the glass pane of the open door. Taking the steps two at a time, he tried to shoulder his way through the knot of men who, though elderly, were certainly not passive, especially when it came to decorum and protocol. As one, they formed a living wall, pushing back at him in the manner of a phalanx of Roman soldiers advancing on the barbarian enemy. The gunman, taken aback, retreated.

The pause gave Bourne the time he needed to slip away from the professors, down the corridor with its sounds of well-shod feet and hushed conversations bouncing off the polished marble floor. A line of square windows, high up, bestowed sunlight on the crowns of the students' heads like a benediction. The wooden doors blurred by as Bourne made for the rear of the Centre. Bells sounded for the beginning of the four o'clock classes.

He raced around a corner, into the short corridor leading to the rear door. But the Severus Domna gunman pushed through it. They were alone in the back corridor. The gunman had his overcoat draped over his right arm and hand, which held the silenced pistol. He aimed it at Bourne, who was still sprinting.

Bourne went down, sliding on his backside along the marble floor as a shot whizzed by overhead. He barreled into the gunman with the soles of his shoes, knocking him over. The pistol flew out of his grip. Bourne rolled over, slammed his knee into the point of the gunman's chin. His body went slack.

Voices echoed down the corridor from just around the corner. Scrambling to his feet, Bourne scooped up the pistol, then dragged the gunman out the rear door, down the steps, and deposited him behind a thick box-wood hedge. He pocketed the pistol and continued along the university pathways at a normal pace. He passed fresh-faced students, laughing and chatting, and a dour professor, huffing as he scurried, late for his next lecture. Then Bourne was out onto St Giles' Street. In typical English fashion, the afternoon had turned gloomy. A chill wind swept across the gutters and store-fronts. Everyone was bent over, shoulders hunched, dashing like boats fleeing an oncoming storm. Bourne, blending in as he always did, hurried to his car.

Go," Moira said, when she was out of recovery and had gained full consciousness.

Soraya shook her head. "I'm not leaving you."

"The worst has already happened," Moira said quite rightly. "There's nothing left here for you to do."

"You shouldn't be alone," Soraya insisted.

"Neither should you. You're still with Arkadin."

Soraya smiled, somewhat sadly, because everything Moira said was true. "Still and all—"

"Still and all," Moira said, "someone's coming to look after me, someone who loves me."

Soraya was slightly taken aback. "Is it Jason? Is Jason coming for you?"

Moira smiled. She had already drifted off to sleep.

* * *

Soraya found Arkadin waiting for her. But first she needed to speak with the young neurosurgeon, who was, in his own way, optimistic in his prognosis.

"The main thing in instances like these where nerves and tendons are involved is how quickly the patient receives medical attention." He spoke formally, as if he were Catalan, rather than a Mexican. "In this respect, your friend is extremely fortunate." He tipped his hand over, palm down. "However, the wound was ragged rather than clean. Plus, whatever she was cut with wasn't clean. As a result, the procedure took longer, and was both more delicate and more complicated than it might otherwise have been. Again, fortunate that you called me. I don't say this out of self-aggrandizement. It's a matter of record, a fact. No one else could have managed the procedure without botching or missing something."

Soraya sighed with relief. "Then she'll be fine."

"Naturally, she'll be fine," the neurosurgeon said. "With a proper course of rehab and physical therapy."

Something dark clutched at Soraya's heart. "She'll walk naturally, won't she? I mean, without a limp."

The neurosurgeon shook his head. "In a child, the tendons are elastic enough that it might be possible. But in an adult that elasticity—or rather a good part of it—is gone. No, no, she'll have a limp. How noticeable it will be depends entirely on the outcome of her rehab. And of course, her will to adapt."

Soraya thought for a moment. "She knows all this?"

"She asked and I told her. It's better that way, believe

me. The mind needs more time to adapt than the body does."

"Can we get out of here now?" Arkadin said, after the neurosurgeon had vanished down the corridor.

Shooting him a murderous look, Soraya brushed past him, striding through the bustling lobby and out onto the street. Puerto Peñasco looked as strange as a dream, as unfamiliar as if it were located in a Bhutanese valley. She looked at the people passing by as slowly as sleepwalkers. She saw their Aztec or Mixtec or Olmec features and thought of beating hearts carved from the chests of living sacrifices. She felt as if she were covered in congealed blood. She wanted to run, but felt paralyzed, rooted to the spot as if by the hands of all the sacrificial dead buried beneath the ground.

Then she felt Arkadin close beside her and shuddered as if waking from one nightmare into another. She wondered how she could stand to be near him, to talk to him after what he'd done to Moira. If he had exhibited even an iota of remorse, she might have felt differently. But all he had said was, *"She's the enemy."* Which meant, of course, that she herself was also the enemy, that the same thing, or worse, could happen to her.

Without a word being exchanged between them, he herded her back to his car, and soon enough they set off back to the convent.

"What do you want from me now?" she asked him in a dull voice.

"The same thing you want from me," he said. "Destruction."

* * *

The moment they entered the convent, Arkadin began to pack. "While you were going through your hand-wringing, I made reservations for us."

"For us?"

"Yes," he said without missing a beat. "You and I are going to Tineghir."

"If I go anywhere with you I'll be sick to my stomach."

He paused and turned to face her. "I think you'll be useful to me when I get to Morocco, so I don't want to kill you. But I will if you give me no other choice." He went back to his methodical packing. "Unlike you, I know when to cut my losses."

It was at that moment that Soraya caught sight of the laptop, which, for her, had taken on a mythical significance. He was right, in his own way, she thought. As right as Moira had been. It was time to get past her personal abhorrence at his actions. It was time to return to acting like a professional. Time to cut her losses.

"I've always wanted to see the High Atlas Mountains," she said.

"You see?" He tucked away the laptop. "That wasn't so difficult, was it?"

Jalal Essai, sitting in an anonymous car he had boosted early this morning, watched Willard emerge from the Monition Club. As Essai observed, he did not move as if he had been defeated by the receptionist, or had waited in vain to be seen by a member of the club. Rather, he descended the stairs as Fred Astaire might, lightly and trippingly, as if to music playing in his head. This jaunty attitude disturbed Essai. It also raised the hackles on the back of his neck, which was far worse.

Essai, whose life was in constant jeopardy ever since his home had been invaded by Severus Domna, knew from being on the other side that a passive response, such as flight, would only result in his eventual death. The organization would come after him again and again, until someway, somehow, somewhere it succeeded in terminating his life. Under these extreme circumstances, there was only one way to stay alive.

Willard turned a corner and stopped, looking to flag down a taxi. Essai pulled over to the curb and rolled down the passenger's-side window.

"Need a lift?" he said.

Willard, startled, drew back as if affronted. "No, thank you," he said, and returned to scanning the traffic for an empty cab.

"Mr. Willard, please get into the car."

When Willard looked back, he saw the man holding a wicked-looking EAA 10mm Hunter Witness pistol, aimed at his face.

"Come, come," Essai said, "let's not make a scene."

Willard opened the door and slid into the passenger's seat without a word.

"How, may I ask, are you going to drive this vehicle and at the same time keep me under control?"

In answer, Essai slammed the barrel of the Hunter Witness against the side of Willard's head just above his left ear. Willard sighed as his eyes rolled up. Essai leaned the unconscious body against the window and returned the pistol to its shoulder holster. Then he put the car in gear, waited for a gap, and slid out into traffic.

He drove south through the district. At some invisible demarcation, the massive government buildings vanished, replaced by local businesses, cheap retail outlets, fast-food chains, storefront missions, and corner bars. Outside the bars, young men in hoodies loitered, exchanging small packets of dope for wads of bills. Old men sat on stoops, head in hands or leaning back against the gray stone steps, eyes half closed, heads nodding. Caucasians grew rare as hen's teeth, then disappeared altogether. This was a different Washington, one tourists never saw. Congressmen, either. Patrol cars were few and far between. When one did appear, it rolled at speed, as if its occupants couldn't wait to be elsewhere, anywhere but here.

Essai pulled the car over in front of something that passed for a hotel. Its rooms went by the hour, and when he dragged Willard inside, supporting him, the whores assumed Willard was a drunk, passed out on his feet. They showed Essai their flyblown wares. He ignored them.

He placed a doctor's black bag on the scarred counter of the attendant's foul-smelling cubbyhole and slid a twenty across. The attendant was whey-faced, slim as a twig, neither young nor old. He was watching porn on a portable TV.

"What," Essai said, "no concierge?"

The attendant laughed but didn't turn his glassy eyes from the TV screen. Without looking he unhooked a key from a pegboard and dropped it on the counter.

"I don't want to be disturbed," Essai said.

"Everyone wants the same thing."

He slid across another twenty, the attendant snapped

it up, selected a different key, and said, "Second floor in the back. You could die in there and no one would know."

Essai took the key and the black bag.

There was no elevator. Getting Willard up the stairs proved something of a chore, but Essai managed. A grime-laden window at the far end of the narrow hallway let in light that seemed both leaden and exhausted. A bare bulb burned halfway down, highlighting the constellations of obscene graffiti scrawled on the walls.

The room looked like a jail cell. The bare-bones furnishings—a bed, a dresser with a drawer missing, a rocking chair—were either gray or colorless. The window looked out on an air shaft, where it was always nighttime. The room smelled strongly of carbolic and bleach. Essai did not want to think of what had gone on there in the past.

Dumping Willard on the bed, he set down the doctor's bag, opened it, and placed a number of items in a neat line on the stained coverlet. This bag and its contents were always with him, a habit that had been ingrained in him at an early age, when he had been in training to move to America, to insinuate himself into the lives of the people Severus Domna selected. He had no idea how the group came up with Bud Halliday's name or how it suspected that he would rise so quickly into the firmament of American politics, but then he was used to Severus Domna's uncanny prescience.

Using a box cutter, he stripped off Willard's clothes, then unwrapped a Depends and fitted it around his loins. He slapped Willard's cheeks lightly enough to rouse him slowly out of his unconscious state. Before Willard was fully conscious, he elevated his head and shoulders, and tipped a bottle of castor oil down his throat. At first, Willard choked and gagged. Essai eased off, then fed the viscous liquid to him more slowly. Willard swallowed it all.

Disposing of the bottle, Essai slapped Willard hard on one cheek, then the other, sending blood rushing into his head. Willard started awake, his eyes blinking rapidly. Then he looked around.

"Where am I?" His voice was thick and furred.

When his tongue ran around his lips, Essai reached for the roll of duct tape.

"What's this taste?"

As Willard started to retch, Essai slapped a length of tape across his mouth.

"If you vomit, you'll suffocate. I advise you to clamp down on your gag reflex."

He sat on the chair, rocking slowly as Willard struggled to regain his equilibrium. When he saw his prisoner winning that battle, he said, "My name is Jalal Essai." His eyes opened wide at Willard's response. "Ah, I see you've heard of me. Good. That makes my job easier. You've just come from seeing Benjamin El-Arian. It was El-Arian, I warrant, who told you about me. He painted me as the villain, I have no doubt. Well, heroes and villains—it's all in your point of view. El-Arian would deny this, but then he's proved himself to be irresolute, like a reed blown first this way then that by shifting winds."

Essai rose, crossed to the bed, and ripped the tape off Willard's mouth.

"I know you're wondering about that taste in your mouth." He smiled. "You swallowed a bottle of castor oil." He pointed. "Hence the diaper. Not long from now some very nasty stuff is going to be coming out of you. The diaper will help contain it, or at least some of it. I'm afraid there will be too much for it to absorb, and then..." He shrugged.

"Whatever you want from me you won't get."

"Bravo! That's the spirit! But sadly for you, I've already gotten what I want. Like others El-Arian has dealt with or sent after me, you'll be dumped on his doorstep. This procedure will continue until he ceases his actions and forgets about me."

"He's not about to do that."

"Then he and I have a long road to travel." Essai wadded up the tape and threw it away. He stuffed the roll back into the black bag. "You, however, have a significantly shorter road to travel."

"I don't feel well." Willard said this in a curious voice, as if he were a querulous child talking to himself.

"No," Essai said, stepping back from the bed, "I don't suppose you do."

27

NIGHT STILL LAY along the macadam roads and concrete sidewalks the following morning when Bourne arrived at Heathrow Airport. It was drizzling and chilly, and he was happy to get out of London. His flight left at seven twenty-five and arrived in Marrakech at one fifteen, with a brief stopover in Madrid. There were no direct commercial flights.

He was sitting in the only coffee shop open at that hour, its plastic chairs and tables wan in the fluorescent lights, sipping over-roasted coffee that tasted like ashes when Don Fernando Hererra appeared, walked over, and sat down without either invitation or greeting.

"I'm sorry for your loss," Bourne said.

Don Fernando said nothing. Lost within his beautiful suit, he seemed to have aged since the last time Bourne had seen him, though only a week or so had passed. He was staring absently at a display of luggage in the window of a store across the concourse.

"How did you find me?" Bourne said.

"I suspected you were going to Marrakech." Abruptly he turned to Bourne and said, "Why did you kill my son? He was only trying to help you as I asked him to do."

"I didn't kill him, Don Fernando." It was then Bourne felt the nick of the knife point on the inside of his thigh. "Do you think that's wise?"

"I have traveled far beyond wise, young man." His eyes were pale, liquid, filled with anguish. "Now I am a father grieving for his dead son. That's all I am, that's all the life this old frame can muster."

"I would never harm Diego," Bourne said. "I think you know that."

"There is no one else but you." Don Hernando's voice, though soft, was like a cry full of pain and suffering. "Betrayal, betrayal!" He shook his head. "The only other possibility is Ottavio Moreno. He's my godson. He would never lay a hand on Diego."

Bourne sat very still, feeling a trickle of blood down his leg. He could end this at any moment, but he chose to let the situation play out because a violent end wouldn't help him. He was extremely fond of Don Hererra; he couldn't lift a finger against him. "And yet, it was Ottavio who knifed Diego," he said.

"Lies!" The old man was quivering. "What possible reason—?"

"Severus Domna."

At once Don Hererra blinked. A tic started in his right cheek. "What's that you say?"

"You've heard of Severus Domna, I take it."

The old man nodded. "I've crossed swords with a few members over the years."

This interested Bourne greatly. Now he was doubly glad he had chosen not to act. "I have something Severus Domna wants," Bourne said. "Its emissaries have followed me in London, Oxford—elsewhere here. Somehow one of them got to Diego. His assignment was to bring me to the Vesper Club, where they were waiting for me. Ottavio found out. He might have acted too hastily, but he was protecting me, I assure you."

"You and he know each other?"

"We did," Bourne said. "He died yesterday."

The old man's face grew hard. "How?"

"He was shot by a man employed by Jalal Essai."

Don Hererra's head swung around. Life was beginning to bloom on his cheeks. "Essai?"

"He wants the same thing Severus Domna wants."

"He's no longer with the group?"

"No." Slowly Bourne became aware of the knife point being withdrawn.

"My sincere apologies," the old man said.

"I know you must have been proud of Diego."

For a time, Don Hererra said nothing. Bourne waved down a waiter and ordered two coffees. When cup and saucer were set down in front of Don Hererra, the old man stirred in some sugar, then took a sip, wincing at the taste.

"I can't wait to get back to Sevilla." His eyes engaged Bourne's. "Before you go, there is something I must tell you. I used to hold Ottavio Moreno in my arms when I visited his mother. Her name is Tanirt and she lives in Tineghir." He paused; his gaze was probing, and he was once again his old canny self. "That is where you're headed, isn't it?"

Bourne nodded.

"Be very careful, señor. Tineghir is the nexus of Severus Domna. Tineghir is where it was born, where it first flourished, due mostly to Jalal Essai's family. But the Essais were split when Jalal's brother turned his back on Severus Domna, uprooted his family, and moved to Bali."

That would be Holly's father, Bourne thought.

"Benjamin El-Arian, whose family coveted the Essais' power, used the schism to gain influence. So far as I know, he has been the leader of Severus Domna for some years now."

"So it's all-out war between Essai and El-Arian."

Don Fernando nodded. "From what I've been able to glean, Severus Domna doesn't take kindly to members leaving the fold. Blood in, blood out." He finished off his coffee. "But back to Tanirt. I've known her for a long time. She is, in many respects, the female I've been closest to most of my adult life, and that includes my late wife."

"I think I should know if she's your mistress."

The old man smiled. "Tanirt is a special person, which you will discover for yourself when you speak with her." He leaned forward. "*Escúchame,* señor, she is the first person you must see when you arrive in Morocco." He scribbled a line on a scrap of paper. "Call her at this number when you arrive. She will be expecting you. Her advice will serve you well, there can be no doubt. She sees all sides of every situation."

"Am I to believe that she was Gustavo Moreno's mistress, and now she's yours?"

"When you meet her you will understand," Don Fernando said. "But this much I will say. Tanirt is no one's mistress. She is who she is. It is not for any man to have her in that way. She is . . ." He looked away for a moment. ". . . wild."

Dimitri Maslov received the news that Colonel Boris Karpov was getting a haircut and shave at the Metropole barbershop with cautious optimism. Karpov, also a cautious man, never got his hair cut at the same place twice.

Maslov summoned Oserov, but was informed that Oserov was AWOL, having left Moscow the day before. Maslov, seething, had had enough of Oserov. In fact, he'd kept him on this long only to piss off Arkadin, for whom he harbored both a father's love and a spurned parent's bitter hatred. But Oserov's humiliating failure in Bangalore had sunk him fatally. He had become all but useless to Maslov, having acquired the stink of defeat.

"Where did he go?" Maslov inquired of Oserov's assistant. They were standing in the offices, surrounded by Maslov's crew.

"Tineghir." The assistant coughed and licked his dry lips. "Morocco."

"Why did he go to Morocco?"

"He . . . he didn't tell me."

"Did you try to find out?"

"How would I do that?"

Maslov drew his custom-made Makarov and shot the assistant between the eyes. Then he turned a murderous gaze on each of his men, slowly. The ones closest to him stepped back a pace, as if struck by an invisible blow.

"Anyone who thinks he can take a piss without my order, step forward."

No one moved.

"Anyone who thinks he can disobey an order, step forward."

No one breathed.

"Yevgeny." He turned to a stocky man with a scar beneath one eye. "Arm yourself and your two best men. You're coming with me."

Then he stalked back into his office, went to the cabinet behind his desk, and began to pick through weaponry. If the debacle in Bangalore had taught him anything it was that if you want to get something difficult done, do it yourself. Times had changed. He knew it, yet he hadn't wanted to believe it. Everything was more difficult than it had been. The government had become aggressively hostile, the *siloviks* had run off the more pliable oligarchs, and good people were harder and harder to find. The easy money had been made. Now he had to claw and scratch for every dollar. He was working double the hours just to make the profit he'd earned ten years ago. It was enough to make you weep for lost youth. *The fact of the matter is,* he thought as he fitted a suppressor to the muzzle of his Makarov, *it's no fun being a criminal anymore. Now it's work, pure and simple.* He'd been reduced to the level of an apparatchik, and he hated it. This new reality was a bitter pill for him to swallow. He was exhausted from trying to keep his head above water. And then, to top it all off, Boris Karpov had become his personal bête noire.

Well armed, he slammed the cabinet doors shut. Hefting his Makarov, he discovered a newfound vigor.

After so many years behind a desk, it felt good to hit the streets, to take the law into his own hands, to shake it until it went limp and gave up. He felt ready to bite off its head.

The Metropole barbershop was situated off the vast, marble-and-ormolu lobby of the Federated Moskva Hotel, an old and venerable establishment located between the Bolshoi Theater and Red Square. The building was so ornate, it seemed at any moment on the verge of imploding from the encrustations of cornices, balustrades, carved stone panels, massive lintels, and projecting parapets.

The Metropole was set up with three old-fashioned barber's chairs, behind which were a mirrored wall and the cabinets that contained the various implements of the trade: scissors, straight razors, shaving cream machines, tall glass jars of a blue liquid disinfectant, neatly folded towels, combs, brushes, electric hair clippers, canisters of talcum powder, and bottles of bracing aftershave.

Currently all three chairs were occupied by clients over whom had been spread black nylon smocks that snapped at the neck. The two men at either end were getting their hair cut by barbers in the traditional Metropole white uniforms. The man in the middle, reclining on his chair with a hot towel wrapped around his face, was Boris Karpov. While his barber stropped a straight razor, Karpov whistled an old Russian folk melody he remembered from his childhood. In the background a dinosaur of a radio played a staticky news report, announcing the latest government initiative to combat growing unemployment. Two men, one young, one old, sat in wooden chairs on the other side of the shop, reading copies of *Pravda* while waiting their turn.

Yevgeny's men had reconnoitered the hotel lobby for ten minutes, assiduously checking for FSB-2 agents. Finding none, they signaled to their boss. Yevgeny, in a long winter overcoat similar to the ones his men wore, entered the Federated Moskva, along with a family led by an unsmiling Intourist guide. While the guide led the family to reception, he walked directly to the Metropole, assuring himself that Boris Karpov was, indeed, the man in the center chair getting his face scraped. As soon as the barber lifted the towel from Karpov's face, Yevgeny turned and signaled to his man who was standing by the revolving door. This man, in turn, signaled Maslov, who got out of the black BMW parked in front of the hotel, went across the sidewalk, and up the steps.

The moment he appeared through the revolving door, Yevgeny and his men went into action, just as had been planned. The two men stationed themselves on either side of the Metropole entrance. There was no other egress.

Yevgeny walked in and, drawing his Makarov pistol, used the barrel to signal to the two men waiting to get the hell out. He swung the muzzle of the Makarov in the general direction of the clients getting their hair cut to keep them and their barbers from moving. He nodded and Maslov entered.

"Karpov, Boris Karpov." Maslov had his Makarov at the ready. "I understand you're looking for me."

Karpov opened his eyes. His gaze rested on Maslov a moment. "Shit, this is awkward."

Maslov grinned wolfishly. "Only for you."

Karpov raised a hand from under his smock. The barber took the edge of the straight razor from his cheek and stepped back. Karpov looked from Maslov to Yevgeny to the two armed men who now appeared in the doorway.

"This doesn't look good for me, but if you'll listen I think we can work a deal."

Maslov laughed. "Listen to this, the incorruptible Colonel Karpov begging for his life."

"I'm just being pragmatic," Karpov said. "I'm soon to become the head of FSB-2, so why kill me? I'd be an excellent friend to have, don't you agree?"

"The only good friend," Maslov said, "is a dead friend."

He took aim at Karpov, but before he could squeeze the trigger, an explosion blasted him backward off his feet. A hole had appeared in Karpov's smock from the bullet he had fired. He threw off the smock at the same time as the two other clients—both FSB-2 undercover agents—fired through their smocks. Yevgeny's two men went down. Yevgeny killed one of Karpov's men before Karpov shot him three times in the chest.

Karpov, his face still covered with shaving cream, walked over to where Maslov lay on the black-and-white tile floor.

"How do you feel?" He aimed his pistol at Maslov's face. "At the end of an era?"

Without waiting for a reply, he squeezed the trigger.

Moira opened her eyes after what seemed like days or weeks of sleep, and saw Berengária Moreno's face.

Berengária smiled, but it was a smile full of concern. "How do you feel?"

"Like I've been hit by a train." Her left leg was in a full cast, suspended by a sling-and-pulley system, so the lower half was above the level of her head.

"You look beautiful, *mami*." Berengária's voice was light and breezy. She kissed Moira lightly on the mouth. "I have a private ambulance waiting downstairs to take us back to the hacienda. A full-time nurse and a physical therapist have already settled into their guest rooms."

"You didn't have to do that." It was a stupid thing to say. Luckily, Berengária had the good grace to ignore it.

"You'll have to get used to calling me Barbara."

"I know."

Then her tone changed, her voice softened, and she leaned close to Moira. "I was sure I'd never see you again."

"Which only goes to prove that there are no sure things in life."

Berengária laughed. "God knows."

"Barbara..."

"*Mami*, please, I'll be angry if you think I expect anything. I would do anything for you, including leaving you alone, if that's your wish."

Moira put her hand against Barbara's cheek. "Right now, all I want is to recover." She sighed deeply. "Barbara, I want to be able to run again."

Barbara put her hand over Moira's. "Then you'll make it so. And I'll help you, if that is your wish. If not..." She shrugged.

"Thank you."

"Get better, *mami*. That's how you'll thank me."

Moira's expression clouded over. "You know, I wasn't lying to Arkadin. Corellos has to be dealt with, and the sooner the better."

"I know." Barbara almost mouthed the words, so softly did she speak.

"It will take some thought, but the problem will give me something to concentrate on besides my leg."

"I'm tempted to say just concentrate on getting better, but I know you'll laugh in my face."

Moira's expression darkened even further. "You're in the wrong business, you know that, don't you?"

"It was my brother's life."

"I'm tempted to say that it doesn't have to be yours, but I know you'll laugh in my face."

Barbara smiled ruefully. "God knows there's no escaping family." Absently, she stroked Moira's cast. "My brother was good to me, he protected me, he looked out for me when others tried to take advantage of me." She looked into Moira's eyes. "He taught me to be tough. He taught me how to hold my head up in the world of men. Without him I don't know where I'd be."

Moira thought about this for some time. One compelling reason to stay with Barbara was so she could convince her to leave her brother's business behind, despite her perceived obligation to him. Moira hadn't been in touch with her own family for years, didn't even know whether her parents were still alive. She wondered if she cared. Her own brother was another matter entirely. She knew where he was, what he was doing, and with whom he associated. She was certain he knew nothing of her. They had severed ties in their early twenties. Unlike with her parents, she felt something for him, but it wasn't good.

She took a deep breath and exhaled the stale air of her past. "I'm healing faster than the surgeon had expected, and no one thinks more highly of his work than he does."

Barbara's eyes twinkled. "Well, you know, nothing is as we expect."

This time, both women laughed together.

Benjamin El-Arian sat behind his desk in his study. He was on the phone with Idir Syphax, the top-echelon member of Severus Domna in Tineghir. Syphax had confirmed that both Arkadin and Bourne were on their way to Morocco. El-Arian wanted to make certain that every detail he had worked out for their strategy was understood and in place. This was no time for surprises; he had no illusions concerning the nature of the two men.

"Everything is prepared inside the house?"

"Yes," Idir said in his ear. "The system has been checked and rechecked. Most recently by me, as you requested. Once they're in, they won't be able to get out."

"We built a better rat trap."

A chuckle. "That's the size of it."

Now El-Arian came to the most difficult question. "What about the woman?" He could not bring himself to utter Tanirt's name.

"We cannot touch her, of course. The men are terrified of her."

With good reason, El-Arian thought. "Leave her alone, then."

"I will pray to Allah," Idir said.

El-Arian was pleased. Pleased also that Willard had actually made good on his end of the bargain. He was about to add a comment when he heard the screech of a car taking off from outside his Georgetown brownstone. Because he was wearing a wireless headphone he was able to get up, walk across the carpet, and peer through the slats of the wooden shutters without breaking off the call.

He saw a bundle lying awkwardly on his front steps, as if it had been dropped there. The cylindrical shape was wrapped up in an old carpet. He estimated the length to be somewhere between five and a half and six feet.

While still talking into his mike, he went down the hall, opened his front door, and hauled the carpet into his foyer. He grunted; it was very heavy. The carpet was tied in three places with common twine. He went back to his desk, retrieved a folding knife from a drawer, and returned to the foyer. Squatting down, he severed the three lengths of twine and unrolled the carpet. This unleashed an unholy stench that caused him to jump back.

When he saw the body, when he recognized it, when he realized that it was still alive, he cut short the call. Staring down at Frederick Willard, he thought, *Allah preserve me, Jalal Essai has declared war on me*. Unlike the deaths of the men he had sent to terminate Essai, this was a personal statement.

Setting aside his natural revulsion, he bent over Willard. One eye would not open, and the other was so inflamed there was no white at all.

"I will pray for you, my friend," El-Arian said.

"I have no interest in Allah or in God." Willard's dry, cracked lips scarcely moved, and something terrible must have been done to his throat or vocal cords because his voice was nearly unrecognizable. It sounded like a razor cutting through flesh. "The rest is darkness. There is no one left to trust."

El-Arian asked him a question, but the answer wasn't forthcoming. Leaning forward, he touched the side of Willard's neck. There was no pulse. El-Arian said a brief prayer, if not for the infidel, then for himself.

Book Four

Book Four

28

YOU SEEM SURPRISED," Tanirt said.

Bourne was surprised. He had been expecting a woman of Don Fernando's age, possibly a decade younger. It was difficult to tell precisely, but Tanirt seemed to be in her late thirties. This was an illusion, surely. Assuming Ottavio actually was her son, she had to be at least fifty.

"I came to Morocco with no expectations," he said.

"Liar." Tanirt was dark-skinned and dark-haired, with a voluptuous figure that had lost none of its lush ripeness. She carried herself as if she were a princess or a queen, and her huge, liquid eyes seemed to take in everything at once.

She studied him for a moment. "I see you. Your name is not Adam Stone," she said with utter certainty.

"Does that matter?"

"Truth is the only thing that matters."

"My name is Bourne."

"Not the name you were born with, but the one you go by now." She nodded, as if satisfied. "Please give me your hand, Bourne."

He had called her the moment he landed in Marrakech. As Don Fernando had promised, she was expecting him. She had given him directions on where to meet her: a sweets shop in the center of a market on the southern edge of the city. He had found the market without difficulty, parked, and proceeded on foot through the labyrinth of alleys lined with stalls and shops selling everything from incised leather goods to camel feed. The sweets shop was owned by a wizened Berber who seemed to recognize Bourne on sight. Smiling, he waved him into the interior, which smelled of caramel and roasted sesame seeds. The shop was dark and full of shadows. Nevertheless, Tanirt was illuminated, as if from within.

Now he offered her his hand, palm up, and she took it. Tanirt looked up at him. She wore simple robes, belted at the waist. Nothing was exposed, and yet her sexuality, pulsing with life, seemed utterly revealed to him.

She held his hand tenderly, her forefinger lightly tracing the lines on his palm and fingers. "You are a Capricorn, born on the last day of the year."

"Yes." There was no way she could know that, and yet she did. A tingling began in Bourne's toes, percolating up through his body, warming him, drawing him to her, as if she had established an energy link between them. Slightly disturbed, he thought about walking out of the shop, but didn't.

"You have..." She stopped short and put her hand over his, as if trying to block out her sudden vision.

"What is it?" Bourne said.

She looked up at him and at that moment he felt as if he could drown in those eyes. She had not let go of his hand. On the contrary, she held it tightly between her two palms. There was a magnetism about her that was both intensely exciting and intensely disquieting. He felt forces inside him tugging him this way and that, as if in fierce opposition.

"Do you really want me to tell you?" Her voice was that of a trained contralto, deep and rich and sonorous. Even at low volume it seemed to pierce into every packed corner of the sweets shop.

"You started this," Bourne pointed out.

She smiled, but there was nothing happy in it. "Come with me."

He followed her to the rear of the shop and out a narrow door. Once again in the labyrinthine heart of the market, he looked out at a bewildering array of goods and services: live cocks and velvet-winged bats in cages, cockatoos on bamboo perches, fat fish in tanks of seawater, a butchered lamb, skinned and bloody, hanging from a hook. A brown hen waddled by, squawking as if being strangled.

"Here you see many things, many creatures, but as for people, only Amazighs, only Berbers." Tanirt pointed south, into the High Atlas. "The town of Tineghir is centered within an eighteen-and-a-half-mile oasis at an altitude of more than five thousand feet, stretching across a relatively thin wedge of lush wadi between the High Atlas range to the north and the Anti-Atlas to the south.

"It is a homogeneous place. Like the area around it, the town is inhabited by Amazighs. The Romans called us Mazices; the Greeks, Libyans. By whatever name, we are Berbers, indigenous to many parts of North Africa and the Nile Valley. The ancient Roman author Apuleius was actually Berber, as was Saint Augustine of Hippo. So was, of course, Septimius Severus, emperor of Rome. And it was a Berber, Abd ar-Rahman the First, who conquered southern Spain and established the Umayyad Caliphate in Córdoba, the heart of what he called al-Andalus, modern-day Andalusia."

She turned to him. "I tell you this so you may better understand what is to come. This is a place of history, of conquest, of great deeds and great men. It is also a place of great energy—a power spot, if you will. It is a nexus point."

She took his hand again. "Bourne, you are an enigma," she said softly. "You have a long lifeline—an unusually long lifeline. And yet . . ."

"What is it?"

"And yet you will die here today or perhaps tomorrow, but certainly within the week."

All of Marrakech appeared to be a souk, all Moroccans vendors of something or other. Everything seemed to be bought and sold from the storefronts and marketplaces that lined the jammed streets and boulevards.

Arkadin and Soraya had been observed upon their arrival, which he had expected, but no one approached them and they weren't followed from the airport into the city. This did not reassure him. On the contrary, it made him even more wary. If the Severus Domna agents at the airport hadn't followed them, it was because they had no need to. His conclusion was that the city, probably the entire Ouarzazate region, was swarming with them.

Soraya confirmed that opinion when he voiced it. "It makes no sense you being here," she said inside a taxi that smelled of stewed lentils, fried onions, and incense. "Why are you walking into such an obvious trap?"

"Because I can." Arkadin sat with his small suitcase on his lap. Inside was the laptop computer.

"I don't believe you."

"I don't give a shit what you believe."

"Another lie, otherwise I wouldn't be here with you now."

He looked at her, shaking his head. "Within ten minutes I could make you cry out, I could make you forget all your previous lovers."

"I'm charmed, truly."

"Mother Teresa, not Mata Hari." He said this with a good measure of disgust, as if her chastity had made him lose respect for her, or at least devalue her.

"Do you imagine I care what a piece of shit like you thinks of me." It was not a question.

They bounced around in the backseat for some time. Then he said, as if continuing the previous conversation, "You're here as an insurance policy. You and Bourne have a connection. At the proper time, I mean to make the most of it."

Soraya, brooding, was silent for the remainder of the ride.

* * *

In Marrakech, Arkadin took her along a warren of streets where Moroccans peered at her, licking their lips as if they were trying to measure the tenderness of her flesh. They were engulfed by the madhouse screeches of the jungle. At length, they entered a stuffy shop that stank of machine oil. A small, bald, mole-like man greeted Arkadin in the obsequious manner of an undertaker, rubbing his hands together and bowing continuously. At the rear of the shop was a small Persian carpet. Lifting this aside, he pulled on a thick metal ring, which opened a trapdoor. Switching on a small flashlight, the mole-man descended a metal spiral staircase. At the base, he flicked on a series of fluorescent coils set into a ceiling so low they were forced to stoop as they crab-walked across the polished floorboards. Unlike the shop above, dusty, packed willy-nilly with all manner of cartons, barrels, and crates, the basement was spotless. Along the walls, portable dehumidifiers hummed quietly alongside a row of air purifiers. The basement was divided into neat aisles sided by long, waist-high cabinets, each with three drawers, each one filled with every form of hand weaponry known to modern man. Every weapon was marked and tagged in meticulous fashion.

"Well, since you know my stock," the mole-man said, "I'll leave you to make your choices. Bring what you want to buy upstairs, I'll provide what ammunition you require, and we'll settle the bill."

Arkadin nodded absently. He was consumed with passing from one drawer of the arsenal to another, calculating firepower, ease of use, rapidity of fire, and the practicality of weight and size of each weapon.

When they were alone, he removed from a drawer

what looked to Soraya like a searchlight with a large battery pack underneath it. Turning to her, he shook the searchlight. The battery pack opened and locked into place. The item was a folding machine gun.

"I've never seen that before." She was fascinated despite herself.

"It's a prototype, not on the market yet. It's a Magpul FMG, takes standard nine-millimeter Glock ammo but spits it out a shitload faster than a pistol." He ran his hand down the stubby barrel. "Nice, huh?"

Soraya thought it was. She'd dearly like one for herself.

Arkadin must have recognized the avidity of her gaze. "Here."

She took it from him, examined it expertly, broke it down, then put it back together.

"Fucking ingenious." Arkadin seemed in no hurry to take back the FMG. He seemed to be watching her, but, in fact, he was seeing something else, a scene from far away.

In St. Petersburg he'd taken Tracy to her hotel room. She had not asked him to come up, but she hadn't protested when he had. Inside, she put her handbag and key down on a table, walked across the carpet and into the bathroom. She closed the door but he didn't hear the click of a lock.

The river glittered in moonlight, black and thick and full of secrets, like an ancient serpent, always half asleep. It was stuffy in the room, so he went to the window and, unlatching it, opened it. A wind, thick as the river and smelling of it, swirled about the room. He turned, looked at the bed, and imagined Tracy there, her nakedness revealed by the moonlight.

A tiny sound, like a sigh or a catch in the throat, caused him to turn around. The bathroom door, unlatched, had opened, and now another swirl of wind pushed it farther, so that a thin wedge of buttery light fell across the carpet. He entered the wedge of light, and his gaze penetrated into the bathroom. He saw Tracy's back, or rather a slice of it, pale and unblemished. Lower was the swell of her buttocks and the deep crease between. The pulse of pleasure in his groin was so extreme it bordered on pain. There was that thing about her—his hatred and his dependence—that made him weak. He despised himself, but he could not help moving toward the door and pushing it farther open.

The door, old and peeling, creaked, and Tracy peered at him over her shoulder. Her body was revealed to him in all its glory. She looked at him with a pity and loathing that brought an animal sound to his lips. Hurriedly, he pulled the door shut. When she emerged, he could not look at her. He heard her cross the room and close the window.

"Where were you brought up?" she said.

It was not a question, but a slap in the face. He could not answer her, and for that—for many things—he burned to kill her, to feel the cartilage in her throat rupture beneath the pressure of his fingers, to feel her blood running hotly in his hands. Yet he was bound to her, as she was bound to him. They were locked in hateful orbit, with no possibility of escape.

* * *

But Tracy did *escape*, he thought now, *into death*. He missed her, hated himself for missing her. She was the only woman who had refused him. Up until now, that is. As his eyes refocused on Soraya folding up the FMG, he felt a premonitory shiver run through him. For a moment, he saw her skull, and she looked like death. Then everything snapped back into focus and he could breathe again.

Unlike Tracy, her skin was burnished a golden bronze. Like Tracy, she had revealed herself to him when she stripped off the T-shirt he had loaned her to use as a tourniquet for Moira's thigh. She had heavy breasts, the nipples dark and erect. He could see them now, beneath her top, see them as clearly as if she were still half naked.

"It's because you can't have me," Soraya said as if reading his mind.

"On the contrary, I could have you right now."

"Rape me, you mean."

"Yes."

"If you were going to," she said, turning her back on him, "you would have already."

He came up behind her and said, "Don't tempt me."

She whirled around. "Your rage is toward men, not women."

He glared at her, unmoving.

"You get off on killing men and seducing women. But rape? You'd no more consider raping a woman than I would."

His mind raced back to his hometown of Nizhny Tagil, where he had briefly become a member of Stas

Kuzin's gang, rounding up girls off the streets to stock Kuzin's savage brothel. Night after night he'd heard the girls' screams and cries as they were raped and beaten. In the end, he'd killed Kuzin and half his gang.

"Rape is for animals," he said in a thick voice. "I'm not an animal."

"That's your life: the struggle to be a man, not an animal."

He looked away.

"Did Treadstone do this to you?"

He laughed. "Treadstone was the least of it. It was everything that happened before, everything I try to forget."

"Curious. For Bourne it's just the opposite. His struggle is to remember."

"He's lucky, then," Arkadin snarled.

"It's a great pity you're enemies."

"God made us enemies." Arkadin took the weapon from her. "A god named Alexander Conklin."

Do you know how to die, Bourne?" Tanirt whispered.

"You were born on Siwa's day: the last day of the month, which is both the ending and the beginning. Do you understand? You are destined to die and be born again." This was what Suparwita had told him only days ago in Bali.

"I've died once," he said, "and was reborn."

"Flesh, flesh, only flesh," she muttered. And then: "This is different."

Tanirt said this with a force he felt through every fiber of his being. He leaned toward her, the promise of her thighs and her breasts drawing him into her orbit.

He shook his head. "I don't understand."

Her hands gripped him, pulling him even closer. "There is only one way to explain." She turned and led him back into the sweets shop. In the far corner she pushed several fragrant bales out of the way, revealing a wooden staircase, full of dust and crystals of palm sugar. They ascended to an upper floor that was, or until recently had been, someone's living quarters. The owner's daughter, judging by the posters of film and rock stars on the walls. It was brighter up here, the windows bringing in blinding sunlight. But it was also as hot as a fever. Tanirt appeared unaffected.

In the center of the floor she turned to him. "Tell me, Bourne, what do you believe in?"

He did not answer.

"The hand of God, fate, destiny? Any of those things?"

"I believe in free will," he said at last, "in the ability to make one's own choices without interference, either by organizations or by fate, whatever you want to call it."

"In other words, you believe in chaos, because man doesn't control anything in this universe."

"That would mean I'm helpless. I'm not."

"So neither Law nor Chaos." She smiled. "Yours is a special path, the path between, where no one before you has gone."

"I'm not sure I'd put it that way."

"Of course you wouldn't. You're not a philosopher. How would you put it?"

"Where is this going?" he said.

"Always the soldier, the impatient soldier," Tanirt said. "Death. It's going toward the nature of your death."

"Death is the end of life," Bourne said. "What else is there to know about its nature?"

She went to one of the windows and opened it. "Tell me, please, how many of the enemy can you see?"

Bourne stood beside her, feeling her intense warmth as if she were an engine that had been running at speed for a long time. From this lofty vantage point, he could see a fair number of streets and observe their occupants.

"Somewhere between three and nine. It's difficult to be precise," he said after several minutes. "Which one will kill me?"

"None of them."

"Then it will be Arkadin."

Tanirt cocked her head. "This man Arkadin will be the herald, but he won't be the one who kills you."

Bourne turned to her. "Then who?"

"Bourne, do you know who you are?"

He had been with her long enough to know that he wasn't expected to answer.

"Something happened to you," Tanirt said. "You were one person, now you're two."

She put the flat of her hand on his chest and his heart seemed to skip a beat—or, more accurately, to race past it. He gave a little gasp.

"These two people are incompatible—in every way incompatible. Therefore, there is a war inside you, a war that will lead to your death."

"Tanirt—"

She raised the hand that had been on his chest, and he felt as if he had sunk into a bog.

"The herald—this man Arkadin—will arrive in

Tineghir with the one who will kill you. It is someone you know, perhaps very well. It is a woman."

"Moira? Is her name Moira?"

Tanirt shook her head. "An Egyptian."

Soraya!

"That . . . that doesn't seem possible."

Tanirt smiled her enigmatic smile. "This is the conundrum, Bourne. One of you can't believe it is possible. But the other one knows that it is possible."

For the first time in Bourne's memory he felt truly helpless. "What am I to do?"

Tanirt took his hand in hers. "How you react, what you do, will determine whether you live or die."

29

"HAPPY BIRTHDAY," M. Errol Danziger said when he reached Bud Halliday by phone.

"My birthday was months ago," the secretary of defense said. "What do you want?"

"I'm waiting in my car downstairs."

"I'm busy."

"Not for this."

There was something in Danziger's voice that stopped Halliday from blowing him off. Halliday called his assistant and told him to clear his calendar for the next hour. Then he grabbed his overcoat and took the stairs down. As he walked across the White House grounds, the guards and Secret Service agents nodded to him deferentially. He smiled at the ones he knew by name.

Climbing into the back of Danziger's car, he said, "This better be good."

"Trust me," Danziger said. "It's better than good."

Twenty minutes later the car pulled up at 1910 Massachusetts Avenue, SE. Danziger, who was sitting nearer the curb, stepped out and held the door open for his boss.

"Building Twenty-seven?" Halliday said as he and Danziger trotted up the steps of one of the modern brick buildings in the General Health Campus complex. "Who died?" Building 27 housed the office of the district's chief medical examiner.

Danziger laughed. "A friend of yours."

They passed through two levels of security and took the oversize stainless-steel-clad elevator down to the basement. The elevator reeked of bleach and a sickly-sweet smell Halliday was loath to identify.

They were expected. An assistant coroner, a slight, bespectacled man with a nose like a beak and a dour demeanor, nodded to them, guiding them through the cold room. He stopped three-quarters of the way down the bank of stainless-steel doors, opened one, and slid out a corpse on a tray. A sheet was pulled up over the face. At Danziger's signal, the assistant coroner peeled back the sheet.

"Mary, Mother of God," Halliday said, "is that Frederick Willard?"

"None other." Danziger looked as if he was about to break into a jig of joy.

Halliday took a step closer. He pulled out a small mirror and stuck it under Willard's nostrils. "No breath." He turned to the assistant coroner. "What the hell happened to him?"

"Difficult to say at this time," the man said. "So many things, so little time . . ."

"The gist," Halliday said shortly.

"Torture."

Halliday had to laugh. He looked at Danziger. "Damn ironic, isn't it?"

"That's how it struck me."

At that moment the secretary's PDA buzzed. He drew it out and looked at it. He was needed at the White House.

Rather than the Oval Office, the president was in the War Room three levels down below the West Wing. Vast computer screens ringed the room, in the center of which was an oval table outfitted with all the accoutrements of twelve virtual offices.

When Bud Halliday arrived, the president was chairing a meeting with Hendricks, the national security adviser, and Brey and Findlay, the respective heads of the FBI and the Department of Homeland Security. From their grim expressions it was clear there was an emergency brewing.

"Glad you could make it, Bud," the president said, waving Halliday to a chair on the opposite side of the table.

"What's happened?" Halliday said.

"Something's come up," Findlay said, "and we'd value your advice on how to proceed."

"A terrorist attack on one of our overseas bases?"

"Rather closer to home." Hendricks appeared to be taking point. Reversing a dossier in front of him, he slid it across the table to Halliday. He spread his hands. "Please."

Halliday opened the dossier and was confronted with a photo of Jalal Essai. He stayed very calm, was pleased to see that his hand was steady as it turned the onionskin pages of the file.

When he was certain he had himself perfectly under control, he raised his gaze. "Why are we looking at this man?"

"We have information linking him to the torture and murder of Frederick Willard."

"Evidence?"

"As yet, no," Findlay said.

"But we have every indication that it will be forth-coming," Hendricks said.

"Do you want me to buy the bridge, too?" Halliday said caustically.

"What's disturbing, Mr. Secretary, is that this man Essai has flown beneath our radar, even though he represents a clear and present national security threat." This from Findlay again.

Halliday tapped the dossier. "There is intel here on Essai going back years. How could we not—?"

"That's the question we need answered, Bud," the president said.

Halliday cocked his head. "Well, I mean to say, where did this intel come from?"

"Not from your farm, clearly," Brey said.

"Nor from yours," Halliday shot back. He looked from one face to another. "You're not thinking of pinning this oversight on my people."

"It wasn't an oversight," Findlay said. "At least, not an oversight on *our* part."

There was a strained silence in the room, which was

finally broken by the president. "Bud, we thought you'd be more forthcoming."

"Shit, *I* didn't," Brey said.

"When confronted by the evidence," Hendricks added.

"Evidence of what?" Halliday said. "There's nothing I have to explain or apologize for."

"You all owe me a hundred dollars apiece," Brey said with a smirk.

Halliday glared at him with naked rage.

Hendricks picked up the phone, spoke a few words into the receiver, then set it down.

"For God's sake, Bud," the president said, "you're making this damnably difficult."

"What is this?" Halliday stood up. "An inquisition?"

"Well, you haven't helped yourself." There was deep sadness in the president's voice. "Last chance."

Halliday, standing as rigid as a war veteran's statue, ground his teeth in fury.

Then the door to the War Room opened and in walked the twins, Michelle and Mandy. Their eyes were laughing. At him.

Christ, he thought. *Jesus Christ.*

"Be seated, Mr. Secretary."

The president's voice had turned so full of suppressed anger and a sense of personal betrayal, it sent a shiver down Halliday's spine. With a sinking heart, he did as he was ordered.

Ahead of him stretched the long, humiliating road to disgrace and ruin. Listening to the tapes the twins had made of his conversations with Jalal Essai in the hideaway apartment, he wondered whether he had the courage to retreat to a quiet, private place and blow his brains out.

O serov arrived in Morocco with his face swathed in bandages. In Marrakech he found a shop where they made a wax impression and, from this template, a latex mask, white as starlight, that fit over his ruined face. Its terrible, cold stoicism belied the raging torment beneath, but he was grateful for the anonymity it afforded him. He bought a heavy black-and-brown-striped hooded *thobe* to conceal his head and the top part of his face. With it on, the hood cast the rest of his face in deep shadow.

After a brief meal, which he wolfed down without tasting, he wasted no time renting a car and planning out his route. Then he set out for Tineghir.

I dir Syphax went slowly and methodically through the house in central Tineghir. He moved from shadow to shadow like a wraith or a dream, soundlessly, light as air. Idir had been born and raised in the High Atlas region of Ouarzazate. He was used to winter's cold and snow. He was known as the man who brings ice to the desert, which meant that he was special. Like Tanirt, the local Berbers were afraid of him.

Idir was slim and well muscled, with a wide mouth of large white teeth and a nose like the prow of a ship. His head and neck were swathed in the traditional blue Berber scarf. He wore robes of a blue-and-white check.

On the outside the house was identical to its neighbors. Inside, however, it was built like a fortress, the rooms a set of nesting boxes protecting, at its heart, the keep. The walls were constructed of solid concrete reinforced with steel rods; the heartwood doors had two-inch-thick metal cores, rendering them impervious to even semi-automatic fire. There were two separate electronic security systems to get through: motion detectors in the outer rooms and infrared heat detectors in the inner ones.

Idir's family had deep ties with the Etanas reaching back centuries. The Etanas had founded the Monition Club as a way for the Severus Domna to come together in various cities across the globe without attracting attention or using the group's real name. To the outside world, the Monition Club was a philanthropic organization involved in the advancement of anthropology and ancient philosophies. It was a hermetically sealed world in which the sub-rosa members of the group could move, meet, compare work, and plan initiatives.

Idir had had his own ideas about power and succession, but before he could act Benjamin El-Arian had moved into the power vacuum created when Jalal Essai's brother had decamped. Now that Jalal Essai had shown his true colors, the Essai family was dead and buried as far as Severus Domna was concerned. His defection had occurred on El-Arian's watch. Idir had already had several conversations with Marlon Etana, the organization's top-ranking member in Europe. Together, he had told Etana, they were more than a match for Benjamin El-Arian. Etana wasn't so sure, but then years in the West had made Etana cautious, timid, even, in Idir's opinion. Not desirable traits in a leader. He had plans for

Severus Domna—big plans—beyond the scope of anything El-Arian or Etana could conceive of. He had tried negotiations, reason, and, finally, appealing to the vanity and ego of the leaders. All to no avail. That left only the path of violence.

Satisfied with his final inspection, he locked up the house and walked away. But not too far. The show was about to begin, and he had reserved for himself a front-row seat.

The moment Arkadin had acted on his suspicions, the moment he had sliced through the tendons at the back of Moira's knee, the idyll of his sojourn in Sonora was shattered. He saw it for the illusion it was. Not for him the slow pace and hot sun, the slinky dancers and the sad rancheras. His life led elsewhere. From that time forward he couldn't wait to leave Mexico. He had been bitterly betrayed. Sonora had held up to him the mirror of his life, the life to which he was bound no matter how much he might long to leave it.

In Morocco he was back in his element, a shark moving through deep and dangerous waters. But for thousands of years sharks have been bred to survive dark and dangerous waters. So, too, Leonid Arkadin.

Armed and never more dangerous, he drove out of Marrakech with Soraya, a woman he found perplexingly complicated. Until he had been gulled by Tracy, he had been used to dominating women in every sense imaginable. Conveniently forgotten was his own mother, who had controlled him completely by keeping him locked in a closet where rats had eaten three of his toes before he fought back, first by ragefully biting off their heads, then by killing his mother. He despised her so thoroughly that he had expunged her from both his consciousness and his memory. What glimpses remained were scenes from a cheap and grainy film he had seen when young.

And yet it had been his mother who had led him to view women through a particular lens. He flirted relentlessly. He felt only contempt for those who succumbed to his masculine charms. These he chewed up and threw away the moment he became bored with them. On those rare occasions when he encountered resistance—Tracy, Devra, the DJ he had met in Sevastopol, and now Soraya—he reacted differently, less surely, and doubt in himself had crept in like a fog, resulting in failure. He had failed to see through Tracy's facade; he had failed to protect Devra. And with Soraya? He didn't yet know, but he could not stop thinking about what she had said about his life being a struggle to be a man, not an animal. There was a time when he would have laughed at anyone who made such an accusation, but something had changed in him. For better or for worse he had become self-aware, and this self-awareness lent him the certainty that what she said wasn't an accusation at all, but a statement of fact.

All this went through his mind as he and Soraya drove to Tineghir. It had been chilly enough in Marrakech, but here in the snowbound High Atlas an icy wind knifed through the canyons, flooding the wadi with frozen air.

"We're coming to the end of the road," he said.

Soraya did not reply; she hadn't said a word for the entire car ride.

"Have you nothing more to say?"

His tone was deliberately mocking, but she just

smiled at him and looked out the window. This abrupt change in her demeanor disturbed him, but he was unsure what to do about it. He couldn't seduce her and he couldn't browbeat her. What was left?

Then, out of the corner of his eye, he saw the tall figure—too tall to be Berber—in a black-and-brown-striped *thobe*. The hood shadowed his face, but as the car moved past, he could see that there was no disfigurement. The figure moved with Oserov's gait, but how could it be him?

"Soraya, do you see that man in the black-and-brown *thobe*?"

She nodded.

He stopped the car. "Get out here and approach him. Do whatever you have to do. I want you to find out if he's Russian, and if he is, whether his name is Oserov. Vylacheslav Germanovich Oserov."

"And?"

"I'll be sitting right here, watching. If it's Oserov, give me a signal," he said, "so I can kill him."

She gave him an enigmatic smile. "I was wondering when I'd see it again."

"What?"

"Your rage."

"You don't know what Oserov has done; you don't know what he's capable of."

"It doesn't matter." She opened the car door and climbed out. "I've seen what you're capable of."

Soraya carefully picked her way through the teeming street toward the tall man in the black-and-brown *thobe*.

The key for her, she knew, was to remain calm and to keep her wits about her. Arkadin had outmaneuvered her once; she wasn't going to get caught out like that again. There were a number of times during the drive to Tineghir when she had calculated she had a chance of escaping, but for two reasons she never made the move. The first was that she had no real confidence that she could elude Arkadin. The second, and more important, was that she had vowed to herself that she would not abandon Jason. He had saved her life more than once. No matter what malicious stories recirculated within CI about him, she knew she could count on him for anything and everything. Now that his life was in imminent danger, she would not run away and hide. More to the point, she had to do something to change Arkadin's immediate trajectory.

Approaching the man, she began to speak to him in Egyptian-inflected Arabic. At first, he ignored her. It was possible that in the street hubbub he did not hear her, or thought she was speaking to someone else. She moved around so that she stood squarely in front of him. She spoke to him again. He kept his head slightly lowered and did not respond.

"I need some help. Do you understand English?" she said.

When he shook his head, she shrugged, turned, and made to walk away. She whirled around and said in Russian, "I recognize you, Vylacheslav Germanovich." His head came up. "Aren't you a colleague of Leonid's?"

"You're a friend of Arkadin's?" His voice was thick and clotted, as if there were something in his throat he hadn't completely swallowed. "Where is he?"

"Right over there." She pointed to the car. "Sitting behind the wheel."

Everything happened at once. Soraya backpedaled, Oserov swung around in a semi-crouch. Beneath the *thobe* he had concealed an AK-47 assault rifle. In one fluid motion he raised the AK-47, aimed it, and fired at the car. People, screaming, scattered in every direction. Oserov kept firing as he advanced across the street, drawing closer and closer to the car, shuddering on its shocks as it was sprayed with bullets.

When he came abreast of the car, he stopped. He tried to open the driver's door, but it was so distorted it would not budge. Cursing, he reversed the AK-47, using the butt to knock out what was left of the window. He peered inside. It was empty.

Whirling, he leveled the AK-47 at Soraya. "Where is he? Where is Arkadin?"

Soraya saw Arkadin slither out from beneath the car, rise up, and wrap his arm around Oserov's neck. He pulled backward with such force that Oserov's feet left the ground. Oserov tried to slam the rifle's butt into Arkadin's rib cage, but Arkadin eluded each attack. Oserov whipped his head back and forth in an attempt to keep Arkadin from gaining a stranglehold. As he did so, his mask began to slip; becoming aware of this, Arkadin ripped it off, revealing the swollen, hideously disfigured face beneath.

Soraya crossed the now empty street, approaching the two antagonists with slow, deliberate steps. Oserov dropped the AK-47 and drew out a wicked-looking dirk. Soraya could see that it was out of Arkadin's line of sight, he was unaware that Oserov was about to plunge it into his side.

* * *

Arkadin, absorbed in his life-or-death struggle with his hated enemy, breathed in the stench of an open sewer and realized that it was coming from Oserov, as if the people he had murdered had clawed their way out of the ground, twining about him like deeply rooted vines. Oserov seemed to be rotting from the inside out. Arkadin pulled him tighter as Oserov continued to struggle, continued to try to find a way out of the vise he was in. But once engaged, neither of them would let go or relinquish a hold on the other, as if their epic struggle was of one person becoming two. Two people fighting for dominion, battling in the abyss of unthinking and unreasoning rage. The conflict was not only against Oserov's crimes, but against Arkadin's own inhuman past, a past he daily tried to shove out of his mind, to bury as deeply as he could. And yet, zombified, it kept rising from its grave.

"That's your life," Soraya had said, "the struggle to be a man, not an animal."

Figures in his past had conspired to break him down, to reduce him to an animal. His one chance at being something more had arrived in the guise of Tracy Atherton. Tracy had taught him many things, but in the end she had betrayed him. He had wished her dead and now she was dead. Oserov, his enemy, embodied everyone and everything that had ever conspired against him, and now he had him, now he was slowly, inexorably squeezing the life out of him.

His attention was suddenly drawn to a movement glimpsed from the corner of his eye. Soraya was sprinting the last fifteen feet that separated them. She struck

Oserov a blow on his left wrist that paralyzed his hand. Arkadin saw the dirk as it fell at Oserov's feet.

For a frozen instant he stared into Soraya's eyes. A secret, silent communication passed between them and then, in a flash, vanished, never to be spoken of or referred to aloud. Arkadin, his heart seething with a rage that had been building for years, slammed the heel of his hand against the side of Oserov's head. The head jerked hard to the right, against the wall of Arkadin's encircling arm. The vertebrae cracked, Oserov spasmed like an insane marionette. His fingernails clawed at Arkadin's forearm, drawing rivulets of blood. He bellowed like a buffalo, and for an instant his strength was so great that he almost broke away.

Then Arkadin cracked his neck again, harder this time, and whatever burst of energy was left in Oserov drained into the gutter. Oserov gave a terrible, soft cry. He tried to say something that seemed vitally important to him, but all that escaped his mouth was his tongue and a gout of blood.

Still, Arkadin would not let him go. He continued to slam the side of his head as if the neck had not already sustained multiple fractures.

"Arkadin," Soraya said softly, "he's dead."

He stared at her, the light of madness in his eyes. Her hands were on him, trying to pry Oserov away from him, but he could feel nothing. It was as if his nerve endings were locked within the last moments of the struggle, as if his will to destroy Oserov would not terminate, would not allow him to let go. And he thought: *If I keep hold of him I'll be able to kill him again and again.*

Gradually, however, the hurricane of emotion began

to ebb. He felt Soraya's hands on him. Then he heard her voice, repeating, "He's dead," and at last he unwound his arm. The corpse collapsed into a grotesque heap.

He looked down at Oserov's ruined face and felt neither triumph nor satisfaction. He felt nothing at all. Empty. There was nothing inside him, just the abyss growing darker and deeper.

Punching a code on his cell phone, he walked to the rear of the car. He unlocked the trunk and took out the laptop in its protective case.

Looking around, Soraya could see a number of men in their Berber robes. They had been watching from the shadows. The moment Oserov slid to the ground, they began to converge on the car.

"It's Severus Domna," Soraya said. "They're coming for us."

At that moment a car screeched to a halt beside them. Arkadin opened the rear door.

"Get in," he commanded, and she obeyed.

Arkadin slid in beside her and the car took off. There were three men inside, all heavily armed. Arkadin spoke to them in rapid, idiomatic Russian, and Soraya remembered their exchange in Puerto Peñasco.

"What do you want from me now?" she had asked Arkadin.

And he had answered: *"The same thing you want from me. Destruction."*

Then she heard the words *scorched earth* and knew that he had come to Tineghir prepared to wage war.

30

BOURNE ARRIVED IN Tineghir armed with the knowledge Tanirt had given him. Inevitably, he was drawn to the crowd around the bullet-riddled car. The dead man was unrecognizable. Nevertheless, because of the severely burn-scarred face he knew it must be Oserov.

There were no police around the body or, indeed, anywhere in the area. But there were plenty of Severus Domna soldiers, which in this area probably amounted to the same thing. No one had made a motion to do anything about the corpse. Flies buzzed in ever-increasing swarms, and the stench of death was beginning to spread like an airborne disease.

Bourne passed the scene by, got out of his car several blocks away, and proceeded on foot. What Tanirt had said had changed his plan, and not, he felt, for the better. But he had no choice, she had made that quite clear.

And so he looked up. The sky was the pale and abandoned color it often is at five in the morning, though it was now deep in the afternoon. Instead of heading toward the address he had been given, the Severus Domna house, he searched for a café or restaurant and, finding one, entered it. He sat down at a table facing the front and ordered a plate of couscous and whiskey berbere, which was mint tea. He waited with one leg crossed over the other, emptying his mind, thinking of Soraya and nothing else. The small glass had been placed before him, the fragrant tea poured from a height without a drop spilled when he saw the Russian glance in as he walked slowly by. It wasn't Arkadin, but it was a Russian, Bourne could tell by his features and the way he used his eyes, which was neither Berber nor Muslim. This told him a number of things, none of them helpful.

The couscous came, but he was without an appetite. Soraya entered the café first, but Arkadin wasn't far behind. He expected Soraya to have a haunted look, but she didn't, and Bourne wondered whether he had underestimated her. If so, it would be the day's first positive sign.

Soraya picked her way through the café and sat down without saying a word. For some moments Arkadin remained in the doorway, watching everything. Bourne began to eat his couscous with his right hand, which was the custom. His left hand lay in his lap.

"How are you?" he said.

"Fucked."

He gave her a thin smile. "How many men does he have with him?"

She appeared surprised. "Three."

Arkadin came toward them. On the way, he picked up a chair from an adjacent table and sat down on it.

"How's the couscous?"

"Not bad," Bourne said. He pushed the plate across the table.

Arkadin used the ends of the fingers of his right hand to taste the couscous. He nodded, licked off the oil, and wiped his fingers on the tabletop.

Arkadin hunched forward. "We've been chasing each other a long time."

Bourne took the plate back. "And now here we are."

"Cozy as three bugs in a Moroccan carpet."

Bourne took up his fork. "It wouldn't be a good idea to shoot with the gun you have aimed at me under the table."

A flicker passed across Arkadin's face. "It's not for you to decide, is it?"

"That's a matter of opinion. I have a Beretta 8000 loaded with .357 hollow-points aimed at your balls."

A black expression was erased by Arkadin's harsh laugh. It sounded to Bourne as if he had never really learned how to laugh. "Bugs in a carpet indeed," Arkadin said.

"Besides," Bourne said, "with me dead, you'll never get out of that house alive."

"I think otherwise."

Bourne buried the tines of the fork in a mound of couscous. "Listen to me, Leonid, there are other forces at work here, forces neither you nor I can handle."

"I can handle anything. And I brought allies."

"The enemy of my enemy is my friend," Bourne said, quoting an Arab proverb.

Arkadin's eyes narrowed. "What are you suggesting?"

"We are the only two graduates of Treadstone. We were trained for situations like this. But the two of us are not exactly alike. Mirror images, perhaps."

"You've got ten seconds. Get to the fucking point."

"Together we can beat Severus Domna."

Arkadin snorted. "You're out of your mind."

"Think about it. Severus Domna brought us here, it has prepared the house for us, and it believes that when we come together one of us will wind up killing the other."

"And?"

"And then everything goes according to its plan." Bourne waited a moment. "Our only chance is to do the unexpected."

"The enemy of my enemy is my friend."

Bourne nodded.

"Until he's not."

Arkadin placed the Magpul he had been holding onto the table, and Bourne set down the Beretta that Tanirt had given him.

"We're a team," Bourne said. "The three of us."

Arkadin glanced briefly at Soraya. "Spit it out then."

"First and foremost," Bourne said, "is a man named Idir Syphax."

The house crouched in the middle of the block, its flanks rubbing up against those of its neighbors. Night had fallen, swift and complete, like a hood thrown over a head. All around the valley the mountains were pitch black. A bitter wind, knifing through the town, hurried snow crystals or grains of sand across streets and down alleys. The light from the stars was hallucinatory.

Idir Syphax was crouched on a rooftop across the street from the rear of the house. Flanking him were two Severus Domna sharpshooters, their Sako TRG-22 rifles aimed and ready. Idir watched the house as if waiting for his daughter to come home, as if feeling the danger of unknown places spreading its wings, as if the house itself were his child. And, in a way, it was. He had designed the house with advice from Tanirt. *"I want to build a fortress,"* he had told her. And she had said: *"You cannot do better than to follow the plan of the Great Temple of Baal. It was the greatest fortress known to man."* After scrutinizing what she had drawn for him, he had agreed, and he himself had helped to build it. Every board, every nail, every length of rebar, every form of concrete bore the tattoo of his sweat. The house was invented not for people, but for a thing, an idea, an ideal, even; anyway, something intangible. In that sense it was a sacred place, as sacred as any mosque. It was the beginning of all things, and the end. Alpha and omega, a cosmos unto itself.

Idir understood this but others in Severus Domna did not. For Benjamin El-Arian, the house was a Venus flytrap. For Marlon Etana, it was a means to an end. In any event, for them both, the house was a dead thing, a pack animal at best. It was not holy, it was not a gateway to the divine. They did not understand that Tanirt had chosen the spot, using the ancient incantation she possessed and he coveted. He had once asked her what language she was chanting. It was Ugaritic. She said it was spoken by the alchemists of King Solomon's court, in what is now Syria. That was why she had placed the statue in the very center of the house, the space from which its holiness emanated. He'd had to have it smuggled in because any statues of this sort were strictly forbidden by sharia. And of course, neither Benjamin El-Arian nor Marlon Etana knew of its existence. They'd have had him burned alive as a heretic. But if Tanirt had taught him anything, it was that there were ancient forces—perhaps *mysteries* was a better term—that had preceded religion, any religion, even Judaism, which were all the inventions of mankind in attempts to come to terms with the terror of death. The origins of the mysteries, Tanirt had told him, were divine, which according to her had nothing to do with man's conception of God. *"Did Baal exist?"* she had asked rhetorically. *"I doubt it. But something did."*

Save for the wind, the night was still. He knew they were coming, but he didn't know from where. All attempts to follow them had ended in failure—a failure, he told himself, that was not unexpected. On the other hand, there had been attraction. Arkadin's three men had been neutralized at the sacrifice of four of his own. These Russians were fierce warriors. Not that it mattered; Arkadin would not gain entrance no matter what he tried. All houses had vulnerabilities that could serve as points of entrance—sewers, for instance, or drains, or the place where the electrical lines came in. Because this house was not designed for people there were no sewers. Because there was no heating or cooling, no refrigerators or ovens to drain electricity, all the electrical systems ran off a giant generator in a shielded room within the house. There was, literally, no way into the house that wouldn't set off the various alarms, which would in turn trip other security measures.

His son, Badis, had wanted to come, but of course Idir wouldn't hear of it. Badis still asked about Tanirt even though at eleven he was old enough to know better. Badis remembered only when Tanirt loved his father, or at least said she loved him. Now she engendered in Idir a bone-deep terror that invaded his nights, his very sleep, shattering it with unspeakable nightmares.

It had all gone wrong when he had asked her to marry him and she had denied him.

"Is it because you don't believe I love you?" he had said.

"I know you love me."

"It's because of my son. You think that because I love Badis more than anything I can't make you happy."

"It isn't your son."

"Then what?"

"If you have to ask," she had said, *"then you will never understand."*

That's when he had made his fatal mistake. He had confused her with other women. He had tried to coerce her, but the more he threatened her, the larger her stature seemed to grow, until she filled his entire living room, asphyxiating him with her presence. And, gasping, he had fled his own home.

The sounds of the bolt-action Sakos brought his mind back into focus. He peered through the darkness. Was that a shadow flitting across the rooftop of the house? His sharpshooters thought so. In the hallucinatory moonlight there was a blur, then nothing. Utter stillness. And then, out of the corner of his eye, the shadow moved again. His heart leapt. His order for them to fire was already on his lips when from behind him he heard his name being called.

He whirled to see Leonid Arkadin standing spread-legged, an odd-looking boxy weapon in his hand.

"Surprise," Arkadin said and promptly shot off two sharp bursts from the Magpul that took off the heads of the sharpshooters. They folded like marionettes.

"You do not frighten me," Idir said. His face and robes were soaked with the blood and brains of his men. "I have no fear of death."

"For yourself, perhaps."

Arkadin motioned with his head and the woman, Soraya Moore, appeared out of the shadows. Idir gasped. She herded Badis in front of her.

"Papa!" Badis made a lunge toward his father, but Soraya caught him by the material at the back of his neck and jerked him back to her. "Papa! Papa!"

A look of terrible despair crossed Idir's dark face.

"Idir," Arkadin commanded, "throw your men over the parapet."

Idir looked at him for a moment, dumbstruck. "Why?"

"So your men will know what happened up here, so they will fear the consequences of their actions."

Idir shook his head.

Arkadin strode over to Badis and stuck the blunt barrel of the Magpul into his mouth. "I pull the trigger and even his own mother won't recognize him."

Idir blanched, then glowered impotently. He bent and picked up one of the sharpshooters, but there was so much blood the corpse slipped out of his hands.

Badis stared, wide-eyed and shivering.

Gathering the corpse to him, Idir rolled it onto the parapet. When he dropped it over the edge, they heard the sound it made smacking against the street. Badis shuddered. Quickly now Idir dumped the second corpse down onto the street. Again that thick, almost viscous sound made Badis jump.

Arkadin gestured. Soraya dragged the struggling boy to the edge of the roof and pushed his head over the side.

Idir made a move toward his son, but Arkadin waggled the Magpul, shaking his head.

"So you see death has many aspects," Arkadin said, "and eventually fear comes to us all."

And so at last the knives came fully out of their sheaths. Bourne came down off the roof when he heard the two shots. And now, as he saw Arkadin push Idir Syphax along in front of him, he came to meet them. Bourne and Arkadin stared at each other as if they were opposing agents about to exchange prisoners at the edge of no-man's-land.

"Soraya?" Bourne said.

"On the rooftop with the boy," Arkadin said.

"You didn't hurt him?"

Arkadin glanced at Idir, then shot Bourne a disgusted look. "If I'd had to, I would have."

"That wasn't our deal."

"Our deal," Arkadin said tersely, "was to get this job done."

Idir fidgeted in the tense silence, his eyes darting from one man to the other. "You two need to get your priorities straight."

Arkadin struck him across the face. "Shut the fuck up."

At length, Bourne handed Arkadin the laptop in its protective case. Then he took hold of Idir and said, "You'll lead us inside. You'll be the first through every barrier, electronic or otherwise." He produced his cell phone. "I'm in constant touch with Soraya. Anything goes wrong..." He waggled the cell.

"I understand." Idir's voice was dull, but his eyes burned with hatred and rage.

He led them around to the front door, which he unlocked with a pair of keys. The moment they entered, he punched a code into a keypad set into the wall to the left of the door.

Silence.

A dog barked, unnaturally loud in the night, and in that highly charged atmosphere moonlight seemed to strike the house with the sound of sleet.

Idir coughed and turned on the lights. "Motion detectors come first, then the infrareds." He fumbled in his pocket and pulled out a small remote control. "I can turn them both off from here."

"Without the generator everything goes down," Bourne said. "Take us to it."

But when Idir started in one direction, Bourne said, "Not that way."

A look of terror crossed Idir's face. "You've been talking to Tanirt." Breathing her name, he shuddered.

"If you know the way," Arkadin said irritably, "what the fuck do we need him for?"

"He knows how to shut down the generator without it blowing the building to bits."

That sobering news shut Arkadin up for the moment. Idir reversed directions, taking them on a route that skirted the outer rooms. They came to the first motion detector, its red eye blank and dark.

They passed it, Idir going first, as usual. They reached a door and Idir unlocked it. Another corridor unfolded like a fan, turning first this way, then that. Bourne was put in mind of the chambers of the great pyramids in Giza. Another door loomed before them. This, too, Idir unlocked. Another corridor, shorter this time and perfectly straight. They passed no doors. The walls were unadorned, stuccoed a neutral color that looked like flesh. The corridor ended at a third door, this one made of steel. They went through this. Ahead could be dimly seen a spiral staircase descending into darkness.

"Turn on the lights," Arkadin ordered.

"There is no electricity down there," Idir said. "Only torches."

Arkadin lunged at him but Bourne blocked his path.

"Keep him away from me," Idir said. "He's a lunatic."

They started down the staircase, unwinding into the darkness. At the bottom Idir lit a reed torch. He handed this to Bourne and reached into a niche in the wall where a wrought-iron basket contained a clutch of torches. He lit a second one.

"Where are the alarm systems?" Bourne asked.

"Too many animals down here," Idir said.

Arkadin glanced around at the bare poured-concrete floor, which smelled of dust and dried droppings. "What kind of animals?"

Idir pushed forward. In the flickering torchlight the lower level seemed immense. There was nothing to see but flames crackling in the darkness. The smoke thickened the airless atmosphere. All at once they found themselves in a narrow passage. Within forty paces it began to curve, and they followed it around to the right. Once again the walls were doorless, completely blank. The passage kept curving. It seemed to Bourne that they were in a spiral, moving in ever-narrowing concentric circles, and he guessed they were approaching the heart of the building. An unseen weight seemed to press down on them, making breathing difficult, as if they had plunged under a deep subterranean lake.

At last, the corridor ended, opening out into a room roughly in the shape of a pentangle, inasmuch as it had five sides. There was a deep pulsing, like the thrum of a gigantic heart. It filled the room, the vibration stirring the thick air.

"There it is." Idir nodded toward what seemed like a chunky plinth in the center of the room. On it stood a black basalt statue of the ancient god Baal.

Arkadin whirled on Idir. "What kind of crap is this?"

Idir took a step toward Bourne. "The generator is under the statue."

Arkadin sneered. "All this idiotic mumbo-jumbo—"

"The missing set of instructions is hidden inside the statue."

"Ah, that's more like it." As Arkadin picked his way toward the statue, Idir moved closer to Bourne.

"It's clear enough you hate each other," he whispered. "He moves the statue and a fail-safe packet of C-Four affixed to the side of the generator is activated on a three-minute delay. Even I can't stop it, but I can lead you out of here in plenty of time. Kill this animal so he won't harm my son."

Arkadin was reaching out for the statue. Bourne

could sense Idir holding his breath; he was ready to run. Bourne saw this moment clearly: It was the point in time that both Suparwita and Tanirt had somehow foreseen. It was the moment when his rage to revenge Tracy's death could be sated. The moment when his two warring personalities would finally tear him apart from the inside out, the moment of his own death. Did he believe them? Was there no clear-cut moment in his life? Was everything infused with the unknown of the life he could not remember? He could turn away from the dangers to him, or he could master them. The choice he made now would stay with him, would change him forever. Would he betray Arkadin or Idir? And then he realized that there was no choice at all, his path lay clearly before him as if illuminated by the light of the full moon.

Idir's plea was clever, but it was irrelevant.

"Leonid, stop!" Bourne called out. "Moving the statue will set off an explosion."

Arkadin's outstretched arm froze, his fingertips inches from the statue. He turned his head. "That's what this sonovabitch told you behind my back?"

"Why did you do that?" Idir's voice was full of despair.

"Because you didn't tell me how to turn off the generator."

Arkadin's gaze shifted to Bourne. "Why is that so fucking important?"

"Because," Bourne said, "the generator controls a series of security measures that will stop us from ever leaving here."

Arkadin stalked over to Idir and backhanded the barrel of his Magpul across the Berber's face. Idir spat out a tooth along with a thick gout of blood.

"I'm done with you," he said. "I'm now going to take you apart piece by piece. You'll tell us what we want to know whether or not you want to. You aren't afraid of death, but you have already shown me your fear. When I get out of here I'm going to throw Badis off that roof myself."

"No, no!" Idir cried, scuttling around to the side of the generator housing. "Here, here," he muttered to himself. At the base of the plinth he depressed a stone, which slid out of the way. He threw a switch, and the throb of the generator ceased. "See? It's off." He stood up. "I've done what you asked. My life is nothing, but I beg you to spare my son's life."

Arkadin, grinning, set the case on top of the plinth, unlocked it, and took out the laptop. "Now," he said, as he fired up the computer, "the ring."

Idir crept closer to the plinth. He managed to tap his fingernail along the top of the computer before Arkadin delivered a heavy backhand blow that swatted him back on his heels.

As Bourne was taking out the ring, Idir said, "It won't do any good."

"Shut the fuck up," Arkadin snapped.

"Let him speak," Bourne said. "Idir, what do you mean?"

"That isn't the right laptop."

"He's a liar," Arkadin said. "Look here—" He took the ring from Bourne and inserted it. "—it has the slot for the ring."

Idir's laughter was tinged with hysteria, or with madness.

As Arkadin slid the ring through the slot again and again, he tried in vain to bring up the ghost file on the partitioned hard drive.

"You fools!" Idir could not stop laughing. "Someone has been fucking with you. I'm telling you it's the wrong laptop."

With an inarticulate cry, Arkadin swung around.

"Leonid, no!"

Bourne leapt at him, too late to keep him from firing, but he ran full-tilt into Arkadin's right shoulder. The spray of bullets went wide, but two bullets struck Idir's chest and shoulder.

Both torches were on the floor, crackling as they burned down. They were more than half finished. Bourne and Arkadin attacked each other with hands, feet, and knees. Arkadin, the Magpul in his right hand, hammered at Bourne, who was forced to raise his hands in front of his face in order to deflect the blows. Deep contusions, then ragged cuts broke out on his wrists from the force of the Magpul's heavy barrel pounding him. He brought his knee up into Arkadin's stomach, but it seemed to have little or no effect. At the next blow Bourne grabbed the barrel, but it raked down his palm, slicing it open. Arkadin turned the muzzle on Bourne, and Bourne slammed the heel of his bleeding hand into Arkadin's nose. Blood flew as Arkadin's head snapped back, the back of it banging off the floor. He squeezed off a short burst, the noise deafening in the space. Bourne struck him again, slamming his head to the right, where a blur of movement shot toward him.

A large rat, terrified by the noise, leapt blindly at

Arkadin's face. Arkadin swung at it and missed. He rolled away, grabbed one of the torches, and thrust it out wildly. The rat leapt away, scrambling across Idir's slumped body. The flames caught its tail, the rat screamed, and so did Idir, whose robes were now alight and burning with an acrid stench. Staggering to his feet, he slapped wildly at the flames with his good arm, but staggered, off balance, and fell against the plinth. His head struck the statue of Baal, knocking it off the generator housing. It shattered against the floor.

Rising, Bourne ran toward Idir, but the greedy flames had already engulfed him, making it impossible to get close. The sickening stench of roasting meat, the bright burst of flames, and then an ominous ticking counting down the three minutes of life they had left.

Arkadin swung his arm around and fired, but Bourne had moved behind Idir, and the burst of gunfire went wide. The flaming torch was fast guttering. Scooping up one of the torches, Bourne ran back into the doorway to the corridor. Under cover, he drew the Beretta. He was about to fire back when he glimpsed Arkadin on his hands and knees, scrabbling about in the rubble of the shattered statue. He picked out an SDS memory card, brushed it off, and, rising, stuck it into the appropriate slot of the laptop.

"Leonid, leave it," Bourne shouted. "The laptop is a fake."

When there was no response, Bourne called Arkadin's name again, this time more urgently. "We have just over two minutes to find our way out of here."

"So Idir would have us believe." Arkadin sounded distracted. "Why would he tell us the truth?"

"He was terrified for the life of his son."

"In the land of the blind," Arkadin shot back, "there is no incentive to tell the truth."

"Leonid, come on! Let it go! You're wasting time."

There was no response. The moment Bourne showed his face in the pentangle, Arkadin fired at him. His torch sparking and sputtering near its end, Bourne sprinted back up the corridor the way they had come. Halfway along, the torch guttered and died. He threw it aside and kept on, his eidetic memory guiding him unerringly to the base of the spiral staircase.

Now it was a matter of outrunning the clock. By his estimation, he had less than two minutes to get out of the house before the C-4 exploded. He reached the top of the staircase, but there was no light. The door was closed.

Returning to the bottom of the stairs, he grabbed another torch, lit it, and sprinted back up to the top. Twenty seconds wasted. A minute and a half remaining. At the top of the staircase, he held the torch up to the door. It had no handle on this side. Not even a lock marred its smooth surface. But there must be a way out. Leaning in, he ran his fingertips around the edge where the door met the jamb. Nothing. On all fours he probed the lintel, found a small square that gave to the pressure of his fingertip. He jumped away as the door opened. Just over a minute left to find his way through the maze of concentric circles and out the front door.

Along the curving corridor he went, fast as he could, holding the torch high. The electric lights had been extinguished when Idir had thrown the switch turning off the generator. Once he paused and thought he could hear footsteps echoing behind him, but he couldn't be certain, and he pressed on, spiraling outward, ever outward toward the skin of the house.

He went through the two open doors and was in what he was sure must be the last of the corridors. Thirty seconds to go. And then the front door was ahead of him. Reaching it, he hauled on the handle. The door wouldn't budge. He battered on it, to no avail. Cursing under his breath, he turned back, staring down the windowless, doorless corridor. *"Everything in the house is an illusion,"* Tanirt had told him. *"This is the most important advice I can give you."*

Twenty seconds.

As he passed close to the outer wall, air stirred at the side of his head. There were no vents, so where was it coming from? He ran his hand over the wall, which, he surmised, must be the outside wall of the house itself. Using his knuckles, he rapped on the wall, listening for an anomalous sound. Solid, solid. He moved farther back down the corridor.

Fifteen seconds.

And then the sound changed. Hollow. Standing back, he slammed the heel of his shoe into the wall. It went through. Again. Ten seconds. Not enough time. Thrusting the torch into the ragged hole, he set it afire. The flames ate up the paint and the board behind it. Dropping the torch, he covered his head with his arms and dived through.

Glass shattered outward, and then he was rolling in the street, picking himself up and running, running. Behind him, the night seemed to catch fire. The house ballooned outward, the shock wave of the explosion lifting him off his feet, hurling him against the wall of the building across the street.

At first he was struck deaf. He picked himself up, staggered against the wall, and shook his head. He heard screaming. Someone was screaming his name. He recognized Soraya's voice, then saw her running toward him. Badis was nowhere to be seen.

"Jason! Jason!" She ran up to him. "Are you all right?"

He nodded but, examining him, she was already shrugging off her coat. Ripping off a sleeve of her shirt, she bound his bleeding hands.

"Badis?"

"I let him go when the house blew." She looked up at him. "The father?"

Bourne shook his head.

"And Arkadin? I made a circuit of the building and didn't see him."

Bourne looked back at the fierce blaze. "He refused to leave the notebook and the ring."

Soraya finished bandaging his hands, then they both watched what was left of the house being consumed by the fire. The street was deserted. There must have been hundreds of eyes watching the scene, but none of them was visible. No Severus Domna soldier appeared. Bourne saw why. Tanirt was standing at the other end of the street, a Mona Lisa smile on her lips.

Soraya nodded. "I guess Arkadin finally got what he wanted."

Bourne thought that must, after all, be true.

31

DIDN'T I TELL YOU," Peter Marks said crossly, "that I didn't want to see anyone."

It was a rebuke, not a question. Nevertheless, Elisa, the nurse who had been looking after him ever since he'd admitted himself to Walter Reed Army Medical Center, appeared unfazed. Marks lay in bed, his wounded leg bandaged and hurting like poison. He had refused all painkillers, which was his prerogative, but much to his annoyance his stoicism hadn't endeared him to Elisa. This was a pity, Marks thought, because she was a looker as well as being whip-smart.

"I think you might want to make an exception for this one."

"Unless it's Shakira or Keira Knightley I'm not interested."

"Just because you're privileged enough to wind up

ere doesn't give you the right to act like a petulant
hild."

Marks cocked his head. "Yeah, why don't you come
over here and see what it's like from my point of view?"

"Only if you promise not to molest me," she said with
a sly smile.

Marks laughed. "Okay, so who is it?" She had a gift
of excavating him out of even his darkest mood.

She came over and plumped up his pillow before ele-
vating the top half of the bed. "I want you to sit up for
me."

"Shall I beg, too?"

"Now, that *would* be nice." Her smile deepened.
"Just make sure you don't drool on me."

"I have so few pleasures here, don't take that away
from me." He grimaced as he pushed himself farther up
the bed. "Christ, my ass is sore."

She made a show of biting her lip. "You make it so
easy for me I can't bring myself to humiliate you even
more." She came over and, taking a brush from a side table, neatened his hair.

"Who is it, for Christ's sake?" Marks said. "The fucking president?"

"Close." Elisa went to the door. "It's the defense secretary."

Good God, Marks thought. *What can Bud Halliday
want with me?*

But it was Chris Hendricks who walked through the
door. Marks fairly goggled. "Where's Halliday?"

"Good morning to you, too, Mr. Marks." Hendricks
shook his hand, pulled over a chair, and without taking
off his overcoat sat down beside the bed.

"Sorry, sir, good morning," Marks stammered. "I don't...Congratulations are in order."

"That's the spirit." Hendricks smiled. "So, how are you feeling?"

"I'll be up and about in no time," Marks said. "I'm getting the best of care."

"I have no doubt." Hendricks placed one hand over the other in his lap. "Mr. Marks, time is short so I'll cut right to the point. While you were overseas Bud Halliday tendered his resignation. Oliver Liss is incarcerated and, frankly, I don't see him getting out anytime soon. Your immediate boss, Frederick Willard, is dead."

"Dead? My God, how?"

"A topic for another day. Suffice it to say that with all this sudden upheaval, a power vacuum has formed at the top of the pyramid, or one of them, anyway." Hendricks cleared his throat. "Like nature, the clandestine services abhor a vacuum. I have been following the systematic dismantling of CI, your old bailiwick, with something of a jaundiced eye. I like what your colleague did with Typhon. In this day and age, a black-ops organization manned by Muslims focused on the extremist Muslim world seems a rather elegant solution to our most pressing ongoing problem.

"Unfortunately, Typhon belongs to CI. God alone knows how long it will take to right that ship and I don't want to waste time." He hunched forward. "Therefore, I'd like you to head up a revitalized Treadstone, which will take up Typhon's mission. You will report directly to me and to the president."

Marks frowned deeply.

"Is something the matter, Mr. Marks?"

"Everything's the matter. First off, how on earth did you hear about Treadstone? And second, if you're as enamored of Typhon as you claim, why haven't you contacted Soraya Moore, Typhon's former director?"

"Who said I haven't?"

"Did she turn you down?"

"The relevant question," Hendricks said, "is whether you're interested."

"Of course I'm interested, but I want to know about Soraya."

"Mr. Marks, I trust you're as impatient to get out of here as you are with your questions." Hendricks rose, crossed to the door, and opened it. He nodded, and in walked Soraya.

"Mr. Marks," Secretary Hendricks said, "it's my pleasure to introduce you to your co-director." As Soraya approached the bed, he added, "I'm quite certain the two of you have many matters, organizational and otherwise, to discuss, so if you'll excuse me."

Neither Marks nor Soraya paid him the least bit of attention as he stepped out of the room, closing the door softly behind him.

Well, look who the wind blew in!" Deron stepped out of his doorway as Bourne came in. As soon as Bourne was inside, Deron gave him a huge hug. "Dammit, man, you're worse than a will-o'-the-wisp, first I see you, then I don't."

"That's the idea, isn't it?"

Then he glanced down at Bourne's bandaged hands. "What the fuck?"

"I had a run-in with something that tried to eat me."

Deron laughed. "Well, you must be okay then. Come on in." He led Bourne into his house in Northeast Washington. He was a tall, slim, handsome man with skin the color of light cocoa. He had a clipped British accent. "How about a drink or, better yet, something to eat?"

"Sorry, old friend, no time. I'm flying out to London tonight."

"Well, then, I've got just the passport for you."

Bourne laughed. "Not this time. I'm here to pick up the package."

Deron turned and looked at him. "Ah, after all this time."

Bourne smiled. "I've finally found the proper home for it."

"Excellent. The homeless make me sad." Deron took Bourne through the rambling house and into his enormous studio, fumey with oil paint and turpentine. There was a canvas on a wooden easel. "Take a look at my newest child," he said before disappearing into another room.

Bourne came around and took a look at the painting. It was almost finished—enough, anyway, to take his breath away. A woman in white, carrying a parasol against a burning sun, walked in high grass, while a young boy, possibly her son, looked on longingly. The depiction of the light was simply extraordinary. Bourne stepped in, peering closely at the brushstrokes, which matched perfectly those of Claude Monet, who had painted the original *La Promenade* in 1875.

"What do you think?"

Bourne turned. Deron had returned with a hard-ded attaché case. "Magnificent. Even better than the riginal."

Deron laughed. "Good God, man, I hope not!" He anded Bourne the case. "Here you are, safe and sound."

"Thanks, Deron."

"Hey, it was a challenge. I forge paintings and, for ou, passports, visas, and the like. But a computer? To ell you the truth the composite housing was a bitch. I vasn't sure I'd gotten it quite right."

"You did a great job."

"Another satisfied customer," he said with a laugh.

They began to drift back through the house.

"How's Kiki?"

"As ever. She's back in Africa for six weeks working to nprove the locals' lot. It's lonely here without her."

"You two should get married."

"You'll be the first to know, old man." They were at he front door. He shook Bourne's hand. "Ever get up to)xford?"

"As a matter of fact, yes."

"Give the Grand Old Dame my regards."

"I will." Bourne opened the door. "Thanks for everyhing."

Deron waved away his words. "Godspeed, Jason."

Bourne, on the night flight to London, dreamed that e was back in Bali, at the top of Pura Lempuyang, peerng through the gates that framed Mount Agung. In his lream he saw Holly Marie moving slowly from right o left. As she passed in front of the sacred mountain, 3ourne began to run toward her and, as she was pushed,

he caught her before she could fall down the steep, ston
steps to her death. Holding her in his arms, he looke
down on her face. It was Tracy's face.

Tracy shuddered and he saw the jagged shard o
glass impaling her. Blood inundated her and ran over hi
hands and arms.

"What's happening, Jason? It's not my time to die."

It wasn't Tracy's voice that echoed in his dream; it wa
Scarlett's.

London greeted him with an uncharacteristically bril
liant, crisp, blue morning. Chrissie had insisted on pick
ing him up at Heathrow. She was waiting for him jus
outside of security. She smiled as he kissed her on the
cheek.

"Baggage?"

"Only what I'm carrying," Bourne said.

Linking arms with him, she said, "How very nice to
see you again so soon. Scarlett was so excited when I told
her. We'll have lunch up at Oxford and then pick her up
from school."

They walked to the car park and got into her battered
Range Rover.

"Old times," she said, laughing.

"How did Scarlett take the news about her aunt?"

Chrissie sighed as she pulled out. "About as well as
could be expected. She was a complete wreck for twenty
four hours. I couldn't go near her."

"Children are resilient."

"That, at least, is a godsend." After winding her way
out of the airport, she got on the motorway.

"Where is Tracy?"

"We buried her in a very old cemetery just outside Oxford."

"I'd like to go straight there, if you don't mind."

She gave him a quick look. "No, not at all."

The drive to Oxford was quick and silent, both Bourne and Chrissie lost in thought. In Oxford they stopped at a florist. At the cemetery, she turned in and parked the SUV. They got out and she led him through the ranks of headstones, some very old indeed, toward a spreading oak tree. A brisk wind was blowing from the east, ruffling her hair. She stood slightly back while Bourne approached Tracy's grave.

He stood for a moment, then lay the bouquet of white roses at the foot of the stone. He wanted to remember her as she had been the night before her death. He wanted to remember only their intimate moments. But for better or for worse, her death had been the most intimate of moments between them. He didn't think he'd ever forget the sensation of her blood on his hands and arms, a crimson silk scarf being drawn across them. Her eyes looking up at him. He had so wanted to hold on to the life that was draining out of her. He heard her voice whispering in his ear and his vision clouded. His eyes burned with tears that welled but would not spill over. How he wished he could feel her breathing beside him.

Then he felt Chrissie's arm around him.

Scarlett, breaking away from a gaggle of her schoolmates, ran into his arms. He picked her up and whirled her around.

"I went to Aunt Tracy's funeral," Scarlett said wit[h] a child's terrible gravity. "I wish I had known her bet ter."

Bourne hugged her tight. Then they all got into th[e] Range Rover and, at his request, drove over to Chrissie'[s] office at All Souls College, a large, square room wit[h] windows that overlooked the ancient college grounds. I[t] smelled of old books and incense.

While Bourne and Scarlett settled themselves on th[e] sofa Chrissie used to grade papers, she made tea.

"What do you have in the briefcase?" Scarlett asked.

"You'll see," Bourne told her.

Chrissie came over with the tea service on an antiqu[e] black japanned tray. Bourne waited patiently while sh[e] poured the tea, but Scarlett squirmed until her mothe[r] offered her a sweet biscuit.

"Now," Chrissie said as she pulled up a chair, "what[']s all this about?"

Bourne placed the attaché case on his lap. "I have [a] birthday present for you."

Chrissie frowned. "My birthday is almost five month[s] away."

"Consider this an early gift." He unlocked the case[,] opened the snaps, and removed a laptop computer[,] which he placed on the table beside the tea service[.] "Come sit beside me," he said.

Chrissie rose and moved onto the sofa while Bourn[e] opened the laptop and started it up. He had made sur[e] to fully charge the battery on the flight over. Scarlett sa[t] on the edge of the cushion to be closer to the screen.

The screen swelled with images as the computer fin ished booting up.

"Scarlett," Bourne said, "do you have the ring I gave you?"

"I keep it with me." Scarlett dug it out. "Do I have to give it back?"

Bourne laughed. "I gave it to you and I meant it." He held out his hand. "Just for a moment."

He took the ring and inserted it in the slot that had been built for it. This was the laptop he had stolen from Jalal Essai, Holly's uncle, at Alex Conklin's behest. He hadn't delivered it because he had discovered what it contained and determined that it was too important to find to be given over to Treadstone, or anyone in the clandestine services. Instead he had asked Deron to make a fake laptop. Accompanying Holly on one of her trips to Sonora to stock a *narcorrancho,* he had been introduced to Gustavo Moreno. Bourne had allowed the fake laptop to fall into the drug lord's hands because having it eventually come to light in Moreno's possession would keep any suspicion on Conklin's part from falling on him.

Similarly, he had switched the Solomon ring with the one Marks had taken off his London assailant. The fact that Scarlett had found Marks's ring when Marks had been shot gave him a perfect cover for the switch. He had been correct to assume the Solomon ring would be far safer in her hands than in his own.

The two pieces fit together perfectly. The mysterious inscription engraved on the inside of the ring unlocked the ghost file on the laptop's hard drive, a PDF file, a perfect replica of an ancient Hebrew text.

Chrissie hunched forward. "What is this? It looks like ... directions?"

"You recall the discussion we had with Professo
Giles."

She glanced at him. "Funny you should mention him
A squad of MI6 came and took him away yesterday."

"I'm afraid I had something to do with that," Bourne
said. "The good professor was part of the group tha
made so much trouble for us."

"Do you mean—?" Her gaze returned to the ancien
text. "Good Lord, Jason, you don't mean to tell me—!"

"According to this file," Bourne said, "King
Solomon's gold is buried in Syria."

Chrissie's excitement grew. "At Ugarit, somewher
on or around Mount Casius, where the god Baal was said
to live." She frowned as she came to the end of the text
"But where, exactly? The text is incomplete."

"True," Bourne said, thinking of the SD card Arkadi
had found in the shattered statue of Baal. "The last bit i
lost. I'm sorry about that."

"No, don't be." She turned and hugged him tightly
"My God, what a fantastic gift."

"If it's the truth, if you find King Solomon's gold."

"No, in and of itself this text is invaluable. It provide
a trove of research material that will help shed light or
what's fact and fiction about King Solomon's court. I ...
don't know how to thank you."

Bourne smiled. "Give it as a gift to the university ir
your sister's name."

"Why, I ... Of course! What a wonderful idea! Now
she'll be closer to me, and a part of Oxford, too."

He felt the memory of Tracy settling around hin
with a contented sigh. He could think of her now in al
her incarnations and not be swamped in sorrow.

He put his arm around Scarlett. "You know, your aunt had a hand in this gift."

The girl looked up at him, her eyes wide. "She did?"

Bourne nodded. "Let me tell you about it—and about how very courageous she was."

About the Authors

ROBERT LUDLUM was the author of twenty-six international bestselling novels, published in thirty-two languages and forty countries. He is perhaps best known as the creator and author of three novels featuring Jason Bourne: *The Bourne Identity*, *The Bourne Supremacy*, and *The Bourne Ultimatum*.

ERIC VAN LUSTBADER is the author of numerous bestselling novels, including *Blood Trust*, *Last Snow*, *First Daughter*, *The Testament*, *The Ninja*, and the international bestsellers featuring Jason Bourne: *The Bourne Legacy*, *The Bourne Betrayal*, *The Bourne Sanction*, and *The Bourne Deception*.

JASON BOURNE EELED his way through the mob. He was assaulted by the bone-juddering, heart-attack-inducing, soul-shattering blast of music coming from ten-foot-tall speakers set on either end of the enormous dance floor. Above the dancers' bobbing heads an aurora borealis of lights splintered, coalesced, and then shattered against the domed ceiling like an armada of comets and shooting stars.

Ahead of him, across the restless sea of bodies, the woman with the thick mane of black hair made her way around gyrating couples of all possible combinations. Bourne pressed after her; it was like trying to push your way through a soft mattress. The heat was palpable. Already the snow on the fur collar of his thick coat had melted away. His hair was slick with it. The woman darted in and out of light, like a minnow under the sun-beaten skin of a lake. She seemed to move in a shuddering jerk-step, visible first here, then there. Bourne pushed after her, over-amplified bass and drums having highjacked the feel of his own pulse.

At length, he confirmed that she was making for the ladies' room, and, having already plotted out a short-cut, he broke off his direct pursuit and plowed the new route through the melee. He arrived at the door just as she disappeared inside. Through the briefly open door the smells of weed, sex, and sweat emerged to swirl around him.

He waited for a pair of young women to stumble out in a cloud of perfume and giggles, then he slid inside. Three women with long, tangled hair and chunky, jangling jewelry huddled at the line of sinks, so engrossed in snorting coke they didn't see him. Crouched down to peer under the doors, he went quickly down the line of stalls. Only one was occupied. Drawing his Glock, he screwed the noise suppressor onto the end of the barrel. He kicked open the door and, as it slammed back against the partition, the woman with ice-blue eyes and a mane of blonde hair aimed a small silver-plated .25 at him. He put a bullet through her heart, a second in her right eye.

He was smoke by the time her forehead hit the tiles...

Bourne opened his eyes to the diamond glare of tropical sunshine. He looked out onto the deep azure of the Andaman Sea, at the sail- and motorboats bobbing at anchor just offshore. He shivered, as if he were still in his memory shard instead of on Patong beach in Phuket. Where was that disco? When had he killed that woman? And who was she? A target assigned to him by Alex Conklin before the trauma that had cast him into the Mediterranean with a severe concussion. That was all he could be certain of. Why had Treadstone targeted her? He wracked his brain, trying to gather all the details of his dream, but like smoke, they drifted through his fingers. He remembered the fur collar of his coat, his hair, wet with snow. But what else? The woman's face? That appeared and reappeared with the echo of the flickering starbursts of light. For a moment the music throbbed through him, then it winked out like the last rays of the sun.

What had triggered the memory shard?

He rose from the blanket. Turning, he saw Moira and Berengária Moreno Skydel silhouetted against the burning blue sky, the blindingly white clouds, the vertical finger hills, umber and green. Moira had invited him down to Berengária's *estancia* in Sonora, but he had wanted to get farther away from civilization, so they had met up at this resort on the west coast of Thailand, and here they had spent the last three days and nights. During that time, Moira had explained what she was doing in Sonora with the sister of the late drug czar, Gustavo Moreno. The two women had asked for his help and he had agreed. Moira said time was of the essence and, after hearing the details, he had agreed to leave for Colombia tomorrow.

Turning back, he saw a woman in a tiny orange bikini high-stepping like a cantering horse through the surf. Her thick mane of hair shone pale-blonde in the sunlight. Bourne followed her, drawn by the echo of his memory shard. He stared at her brown back, where the muscles worked between her shoulder blades. She turned slightly, then, and he saw her pull smoke into her lungs from a hand-rolled joint. For a moment, the tang of the sea breeze was sweetened by the drug. Then he saw her flinch and drop the joint into the surf, and his eyes followed hers.

Three police were coming down the beach. They wore suits, but there was no doubt as to their identity. She moved, thinking they were coming for her, but she was wrong. They were coming for Bourne.

Without hesitation, he waded into the surf. He needed to get them away from Moira and Berengária because Moira would surely try to help him and he didn't want her involved. Just before he dove into an oncoming wave, he saw one of the detectives raise his hand, as if in a salute. When he emerged onto the surface, far beyond the surf line, he saw that it had been a signal. A pair of WaveRunner FZRs were converging on him from either side. There were two men on each, the driver and the man behind him clad in scuba. These people were covering all avenues of escape.

As he made for the *Parole*, a small sailboat close to him, his mind was working overtime. From the coordination and meticulous manner in which the approach had been made he knew that the orders had not emanated with the Thai police, who were not known for either. Someone else was manipulating them, and he suspected he knew. There had always been the chance that Severus Domna would seek retribution for what he had done to the secret organization. But further speculation would have to come afterward; first, he had to get out of this trap and away to keep his promise to Moira to ensure Berengária's safety.

Within a dozen powerful strokes he'd come up on the

Parole. Hoisting himself over the side, he was about to stand up when a fusillade of bullets caused the boat to rock back and forth. He began to crawl toward the middle of the boat, grabbing a coil of nylon rope. His hands gripped either gunwale. The WaveRunners were closer when the second fusillade came, their violent wakes causing the boat to dance and shudder so violently, it was easy for him to capsize it. He dove backward over the side, arms pinwheeling, as if he'd been shot.

The pair of WaveRunners crisscrossed the area around the overturned boat, their occupants looking for the bobbing of a head. When none appeared, the two scuba divers drew down their masks and as the drivers slowed their vehicles, tumbled over the side, one hand keeping their masks in place.

Completely invisible to them, Bourne was treading water under the overturned boat, the trapped air sustaining him. But that respite was short-lived. He saw the columns of bubbles through the transparent water as the divers plunged in on either side of the boat.

Quickly, he tied off one end of the nylon rope to the starboard cleat. When the first of the divers came at him from below, he ducked down, wrapped the cord around the diver's neck, and pulled it tight. The diver let go of his speargun to counter Bourne's attack and Bourne ripped off his mask, effectively blinding him. Then he grabbed the speargun as it floated free, turned, and shot the oncoming second diver through the chest.

Blood ballooned out in a thick cloud, dispersed by the current rising from the deep. Bourne knew it wasn't wise to stay in these waters when blood was spilled. Lungs burning, he rose, breaking the surface under the overturned boat. But almost immediately he dove back down to find the first diver. The water was dark, hazy with the gouting blood. The dead diver hung in the mist, arms out to the side, fins pointing straight down into darkness. Bourne was in the midst of turning when the nylon rope looped around his neck and was pulled tight. The first diver drove his knees into the small of Bourne's back while he hauled on the rope from both sides. Bourne tried grabbing at the diver, but he swam backward out of the way. Though it was clamped shut, a thin line of bubbles trailed from the corner of Bourne's mouth. The rope was cutting hard into his windpipe, holding him below the surface.

He fought the urge to struggle, knowing that would both pull the rope tighter and exhaust him. Instead, he hung motionless for a moment like the diver not three feet away, twisting in the current, playing dead. The diver pulled him close as he drew his knife to deliver the coup de grâce across Bourne's neck.

Bourne reached back and pressed the Purge button on the regulator. Air shot out of the regulator with such force it caused the diver to loosen his mouth, and, with a thick plume of bubbles, Bourne tore the regulator free. The cord loosened around his neck. Taking advantage of the diver's surprise, Bourne freed himself. Turning, he tried to pinion the diver's arms, but his adversary drove the knife toward his chest. Bourne knocked it away, but as he did so the diver wrapped his arms around Bourne's body so he couldn't surface to get air.

Bourne pressed the diver's octopus—the secondary regulator—into his mouth and sucked air into his fiery lungs. The diver scrabbled for his regulator, but Bourne fought him off. The man's face was white and pinched. He tried again and again to position the knife so that it would cut Bourne or the octopus, to no avail. He blinked heavily several times and his eyes began to turn up as all the life drained out of him. Bourne lunged for the knife, but the diver let it go. It spiraled down into the depths.

Though Bourne was now breathing normally through the octopus, he knew that following a purge there would be very little air left in the tanks. The diver's legs were locked around him, ankles crossed. In addition, the nylon cord had become entangled with both of them, building a kind of cocoon. He was working on freeing himself when he felt the powerful ripple. A chill rolled through him, rising from the depths. A shark came into view. It was perhaps twelve feet long, silvery-black, slanting unerringly upward toward Bourne and the two dead divers. It had smelled the blood, the thrashing bodies in the water, transmitting the telltale vibrations that told it there was a dying fish, possibly more than one, for it to feast on.

Struggling, Bourne swung around, the diver in tow. Unbuckling the harness of the second diver's air tanks, he pushed them off. Immediately, the corpse sank down amid its black clouds of blood. The shark changed course, heading directly for the mortally wounded corpse. Its mouth hinged open and it took an enormous bite out of the diver. Bourne had given himself a respite, albeit a short one. Any minute now, more sharks would be drawn to join the feeding frenzy; he had to be out of the water by then.

He unsnapped the first diver's weight belt, then pulled off his tanks. Then he fitted the mask over his face. Taking one last aborted breath, he let the tanks go—they were out of air, anyway. The two of them, locked in a macabre embrace, began to rise toward the surface. As they did so, Bourne worked on the nylon cord, unwinding it from around them. But the diver's legs were still imprisoning his hips. Try as he might, he couldn't unlock them.

He broke the surface and immediately saw one of the WaveRunners bouncing over the waves directly at him. He waved. In the mask, he was hoping the driver would assume he was one of his divers. The WaveRunner slowed as it neared him. By this time, he'd managed to untangle the rope. As the WaveRunner swung around, he grabbed onto its back. When he tapped the driver on the knee, the WaveRunner took off. Bourne was still half in the water and the vehicle's speed loosened the diver's death grip. Bourne pounded on the diver's knees, heard a crack of bone, and then he was free.

He swung up onto the WaveRunner and broke the driver's neck. Before he tossed him into the water, he unhooked the speargun from his belt. The driver of the second WaveRunner had seen what was happening and was in the process of turning when Bourne drove directly at him. The driver made the wrong choice. Drawing a handgun, he squeezed off two shots, but it was impossible to aim accurately on the bucking vehicle. By that time, Bourne was close enough to make the leap. He swung the speargun, launching the WaveRunner's driver off the vehicle even while he took control of it.

Alone, now, on the sapphire water, Bourne sped away.

More Jason Bourne Adventures!
Written by Eric Van Lustbader

Robert Ludlum's *The Bourne Betrayal*

He has lost his memory, his identity, and his past. Now Jason Bourne loses his only friend when a CIA deputy director is kidnapped. Vowing to rescue him, Bourne heads to Africa—and discovers a global network of Islamic supremacist acquiring nuclear weapons. But these madmen have anticipated Jason Bourne's every move—and plan to use him to destroy America.

Robert Ludlum's *The Bourne Sanction*

After so many adrenaline-soaked years, Jason Bourne is chafing in the quiet life of a professor. Then his academic mentor asks for help investigating the murder of a former student by a Muslim extremist sect called the Black Legion. The young man died carrying information about the group's terrorist activities, including a plan to attack the United States.

Bourne's investigation of the Black Legion turns into a deadly and tangled operation—the pursuit of the leader of a murderous terrorist group with roots in the darkest days of World War II.

Robert Ludlum's *The Bourne Deception*

After Bourne is violently ambushed and nearly killed, he fakes his own death and takes on a new identity and mission—to find his assassin.

Then an American passenger airliner is shot down over Egypt by an Iranian missile, leaving the world to wonder if it was an accident or an act of aggression. A team led by Soraya Moore, a director at Central Intelligence, is assembled to investigate the attack before the global outrage escalates into more violence. When Bourne's quest intersects with Soraya's search for the perpetrators, Bourne is thrust into a race to prevent a new world war. But it may already be too late . . .